WITCH CITY

WITCH CITY

SALEM STYLES

For Mom, Nanny, Hecate & Tituba,
four magical women who inspire me everyday.

PROLOGUE

The witch walked slowly and purposefully, her umbrella making a sharp click on the ground with each step. Cold air and dead leaves blew in from the large hole in the wall-length window, it now the shape of a broken spider's web. The witch did not mind the chill. It reminded her that she was alive.

She approached the window, placing a bony, green hand on the jagged glass. The wind blew the ragged, leathery straps of her dress around her legs, but she remained still. She surveyed the industrial landscape of the city, glowing orange and green lights illuminating the night. Her frown tightened. The city had so much potential to be great, to truly be the land of freedom for the witches of the world. Instead, it was slowly dying, rotting with the corruption from one coven or another.

No matter. The witch didn't mind that the city was dying. It was, after all, time to burn it to the ground. She would build a new city from its charred bones.

The witch focused her eye, thinking of her target. Her vision moved rapidly through the busy streets, as if the witch herself was flying past the machine-like structures, past the Hecate Trivia statue, past every crooked crevice and crossroad it had to offer. The witch steadied herself, grasping the handle of her umbrella tighter. And then, there *she* was.

The Dread Queen approached the edge of her balcony, met with cheers from an unseen crowd as the witch watched. The woman wore her usual funerary black dress, and atop black heart-shaped hair, her large dagger-like crown. Her *stolen* crown. A grinning jack-o'-lantern mask concealed her true face, orange orbs staring out. The witch sneered.

A pale, pinched woman with startling green eyes stood to the right of the Dread Queen, dressed in the glittery celestial trappings of a High Priestess. She wore a large upturned crescent moon on her forehead, giving the appearance of horns. A handsome Black man with prominent angular features, his eyes gold and sharp like a hawk's, stood to the left of the Queen. He carried an ankh staff in his hand, symbolizing his role as Hierophant, a glowing sun-like orb atop his head. The witch, watching from a distance, disliked the both of them immensely, but that was nothing compared to her utter loathing for the woman that was about to speak.

"Greetings good witches of Crone's Cross, our noble Witch City, and to all those in greater Hecatesia, our most beautiful country," the pumpkin-masked Queen said in a cool, emotionless voice. "As your Queen, and leader of the Lantern Coven, I pray to the Great Goddess that you are doing well and keeping safe during this troubling and foreboding time. As we all know, Samhaintide draws ever near. The Lord of Samhain will cross into our world looking for souls to devour, so be sure to have your jack-o'-lanterns out to protect yourselves."

Hot rage bubbled through the witch's body, her hatred intensifying. As if the Dread Queen or her coven did anything substantial to protect the citizens of Witch City. As if her imperial majesty was not complicit in how many had died from this "Lord of Samhain." She was always locked up in her castle, protected from the wicked world she had helped create.

"As that is said," the Queen continued, her cold voice sharpening, "we must remain ever-vigilant. The Monster Coven is growing in numbers, and their threat to our society is ever increasing. The Wicked Witch that leads them is the worst of them all. Her attacks have been becoming more frequent and more violent; no one is safe from being a target.

"She has started fires all over the city. Many innocent witches have been grievously injured; some have even died. The Monster Coven must be stopped at all costs, before we are all burned alive."

Wicked Witch, the witch thought, clenching her fists. *You have not seen my wickedness yet, my pretty.*

Still the Dread Queen's voice tightened.

"If you see any suspicious activity, or become aware of any information regarding the Monster Coven, report it to Lantern Coven officials immediately. This is not a request. Failure to do so will result in severe punishment. Observe."

The Queen gestured downwards with a pumpkin-head scepter. The witch shifted her gaze. Three witches, their green skin contrasting with bright red blood, were tied to stakes on an elevated platform. The rage burned hot under the witch's skin. She knew those witches. They were all valuable allies. At least their secrets would die with them.

"This is what happens when you value anarchy over order," the Dread Queen said, her voice returning to her usual emotionlessness. "These three wretches had been discovered colluding with members of the Monster Coven. Remember, witches of Crone's Cross, who is really protecting you. Lanterns light the way. Merry meet, and merry part, and merry meet again."

With those words, the pyres beneath the witches' stakes burst into flames, rising higher and higher. Shuddering, the witch pulled herself out of the vision, returning to the view of the cityscape. There was no need to watch innocent witches being burned at the stake. The witch unclenched her fist from the window, warm blood running down her hand. She snapped the piece of glass in her palm and flung it out into the night. Her whole body trembled as she tried to keep her wrath contained.

The witch closed her eye, pushing her anger down. She let a small smile form on her face, letting it grow wider and wider, until a manic cackle gripped her. She opened her eye, and raised her umbrella into the air. It transformed into a broomstick made of black wood and twigs, feeling as if it was an extension of her own body.

The Dread Queen was very powerful, and capable of many things, but she lacked foresight. The witch continued to cackle, louder and wilder. Yes, the time of the Queen's great reckoning was near. A storm was brewing, and it was on its way to Crone's Cross. When it arrived, it would tear apart the Dread Queen and her Lantern Coven like a terrible twister.

The witch placed the broomstick between her legs, and flew into the city. It was time to snuff out the Lanterns' flame.

CHAPTER

One

Boston, October 10, 2022

Alicia wrote in her notebook as fast as she could. She tried to ignore the other students as they talked loudly around her. She focused on writing her newest story; an epic tale about a witch named Aradia who saved her people from oppressive witch hunters. The notebook slid beneath her pen mid-sentence, creating a long black scribble.

"Hey!" Alicia said, looking up.

Gale, her best friend, was flipping through the pages of her notebook, a mischievous grin on her face.

"Give that back," Alicia said, holding out her hand expectantly. Gale pouted.

"You never let me read your stories," Gale said.

"You can read it when it's done," Alicia said, becoming firmer. "Give it back."

"You always say that."

Alicia continued to glare, her hand still outstretched.

"Fine, but you better tell me when you're done this time," Gale said, handing the notebook back. Their teacher, Mr. Miller, entered the classroom, frazzled as always.

"Alright class," he called, "settle down. Sorry I'm a bit late."

The students went quiet, just a few murmurs here and there. Alicia closed her notebook and sighed, already bored. She couldn't care less about American history. Why should she? They only focused on the accomplishments of white men, anyway.

"Okay, class, today, which is fitting because we are getting close to Halloween, we'll be discussing the infamous Salem Witch Trials," Mr. Miller said.

Alicia sat up a little straighter in her chair. Recently she had been trying to do some research on witchcraft to flesh out her story more, to make it more real. This could actually be interesting to her after all.

"The trials happened in the year 1692," Mr. Miller said, scribbling the date up on the board. "The village of Salem had just gone through a very harsh winter, and some of the village girls started acting very strange. They would have violent fits and would scream and go into trances. The doctors at the time, having found no physical reason as to why that was the case, believed they were afflicted with witchcraft."

Before she had even realized it, Alicia's notebook was open and she was making notes. Something about this story was drawing her in, her attention fixated on every word.

"Now, they asked the girls who had done this to them, and one of the girls, little Abigail Williams, accused the enslaved woman of the house, Tituba."

Tituba. Why did that name make her pause?

"Tituba was a woman from Barbados and told stories to the girls around the fire to pass the time during the long winter nights," Mr. Miller said, writing down each name on the board. "Abigail, along with her cousin Betty and her friend Ann, accused the woman of using Voodoo, and this would be the start of the many accusations that came afterward. This would be the start of the Salem Witch Trials."

"Excuse me," Alicia said, raising a hand. Mr. Miller sighed and turned around.

"Yes, Alicia?"

"Did Tituba survive the Witch Trials?" Alicia said.

"Yes. After she confessed to witchcraft, she was put into prison, where she was held for thirteen months, and eventually released."

"What happened to her after?"

Mr. Miller sighed again.

"No one knows, Alicia. She was an enslaved woman, and unfortunately the Puritans did not keep stringent records of the lives of their slaves. If she had never been accused of witchcraft, we may have never known who she was. Now, as I was saying, this would be the start of the Salem Witch Trials . . ." Mr. Miller's voice faded.

"Why do you care so much about Tituba?" Gale whispered.

"I don't know, she just seems interesting I guess," Alicia whispered back.

"Is that what you're going to write about now, the Salem Witch Trials?"

"I dunno, maybe."

Alicia focused on the board. Mr. Miller was writing something about ergotism and fungal poisoning. Whatever that was, it did not sound as interesting as witchcraft.

"You know there's that witch shop that's kinda close. Grandma Yaya's Cottage I think it's called. We should check it out."

Alicia looked Gale in the eyes. Her friend's mischievous grin had returned.

"We can bring Lizzie and Sarah too, make it a whole witchy adventure. It could be fun."

"I don't know if that's such a good idea," Alicia said. She had passed by that witch shop before, but was never brave enough to go in.

"Come on, maybe you'll find some inspiration for your book or something."

"Gale, Alicia, quiet down now," Mr. Miller said, facing them now. Alicia wanted to shrink and disappear now that she was keenly aware of the attention on her.

"Sorry Mr. Miller," Alicia mumbled.

"Anyway," Mr. Miller said, turning back to the board, "the theory of ergotism is a popular theory, however discredited by most scholars . . ."

"Think about it," Gale whispered.

Alicia tapped her pen on the page. For the rest of class she could not stop thinking about it. Her heart leapt at the excitement of the idea of it, but unease tempered her feelings. Witchcraft was an interesting topic to her, but to actually go to a real witch shop was something else. She always had the impression that witchcraft was dangerous, forbidden, and definitely not to be participated in.

Which made her want to go even more.

CHAPTER

Two

Alicia carefully closed the door of the apartment, her mind still buzzing with thoughts of going to the witch shop. It was not like she was actually going to try to cast any spells or anything, so there should be no harm in it. But something in her remained unconvinced.

"How was school, Alleycat?"

Alicia turned around, hoping her guilty thoughts did not show on her face. Her mother, Tana, was in her "office," at her desk as usual, typing away. She was a freelance editor, often working with independently published writers. She did not look up from her work, her tired eyes darting across the screen behind reading glasses. Tana must have been at it for hours. Her dark brown hair was pulled in a tight knot, accentuating her angular features. That meant business.

"It was fine, nothing exciting," Alicia said, looking down. "Although, we did learn something kind of interesting in history class."

"Uh-huh, what was it about," Tana said, not looking up from her computer.

"Well, it was about the Salem Witch Trials," Alicia said, looking up to see her mother's reaction. "And Tituba."

Tana stopped typing and looked up.

"What did you say?"

"It was nothing, just the Salem Witch Trials," Alicia said, holding her shoulder bag straps tightly. "Do you know anything about them?"

"We have talked about this already, Alicia, we do not talk about witches in this household," Tana said, her voice agitated as she returned to her typing.

"But Mama it's just history, it's not a big deal," Alicia said, growing quieter.

"Not a big deal?" Tana said, taking off her glasses. "Alicia, witchcraft is the Devil's work. Because Tituba taught those girls black magic, they became possessed and twenty people died because of it. It's not some fairytale, witchcraft kills people."

"So you do know something about it?" Alicia said, her eyes wide and curious.

"Don't sass me young lady. We're not going to talk about it anymore, it just invites evil. I'm going to have a word with your teacher about discussing inappropriate subject matter with students."

"But Mama—"

"Alicia, no more," Tana said, returning to her typing. "And take off that hat, you're inside."

"Yes, Mama," Alicia said, pulling off her large-rimmed black hat. She opened the door of her bedroom and slunk inside, shutting the door behind her.

Alicia breathed out through her lips, attempting to release the tension. She loved her mother, but the woman wasn't always easy to talk to. Her phone buzzed in her pocket. She took it out, staring at it, fingers trembling. It was Gale.

Lizzie & Sarah are down for the witchy adventure, are you?

She should listen to her mother. Going to the witch shop would just be inviting bad things to happen. But her mother also knew more about witches than she said. Alicia was not going to find out anything from her though, and the impulse to know more gnawed at her brain. Did Tituba really teach the girls magic? There was only one way to find out. Alicia texted Gale back.

Yeah I'm down, let's go tomorrow after school.

CHAPTER

Three

October 11

Alicia opened the door to Grandma Yaya's Cottage, ringing the bell. She was greeted by a sweet, woodsy aroma that, although pleasant, did not help relax her nerves. If her mother knew what she was up to, she would have burned her at the stake. She stood almost frozen in the doorway as she took in the shop, clinging tight to the straps of her shoulder bag. The interior was small, the lights slightly dimmed. Various curiosities crowded the shelves haphazardly. Dolls, candles, hanging herbs, and books filled every corner of the shop. This was it, the real deal. A real witch shop.

"Oh my God it's so spooky in there!" Gale said loudly with a grin.

"Yeah let's look at all the witch crap," Lizzie said.

Gale, Lizzie, and Sarah pushed Alicia in, much to her annoyance, and crammed themselves in after her. The shop seemed even smaller with all of them in it, as if they were in a crowded attic. Alicia felt trapped and small, and her face grew warm with shame as she noticed a woman staring at them from behind a cash register. The wrinkles lining her earth-brown skin were scrunched in judgment, but she said nothing.

"Maybe we should go," Alicia said half-heartedly.

"Look at this!" Lizzie said, picking up a basket off the shelf. "Voodoo dolls!"

Alicia took a closer look. The dolls were sewn in different colored cloths, with labels such as LUCK, LOVE, HEALTH, and a black one labeled REVENGE. She reached for it, and just as quickly pulled back. This was the kind of evil her mother warned her about. And who did she need revenge on anyway?

"You should use these on Will, Sarah," Lizzie said, not noticing Alicia's reaction. Sarah scoffed.

"As if any of this works anyway," Sarah said, picking up a book labeled *Curses & Hexes*, "although that prick would regret dumping me after sticking enough pins in his crotch."

The other girls laughed, Alicia nervously joining in. It did not seem right to be making fun of such stuff. That's when things always went wrong in horror stories.

"But seriously does anyone actually believe in this stuff?"

"My weird aunt does, she believes crystals help cleanse her aura, and she 'talks to the angels.'"

"I wonder if they have any of those Ouija Board things so we could summon a demon."

Alicia turned away from them, ignoring their obnoxious comments. She stepped towards the cashier, her eyes down.

"I'm sorry about them, they're being so rude," Alicia said quietly. "I was wondering actually if you have any books about the Salem Witch Trials, or Tituba. We learned a little about them in school, and I just want to know a little more."

Alicia looked up, not quite meeting the cashier's eyes. A nametag labelled "Candy" was pinned to her shirt. The woman looked at Alicia with eyes squinted in curiosity, as if trying to assess the girl's motive.

"I have a few things on that, but the one I recommend the most is *The Salem Witch Book* by Mary Black. She was a descendant of an accused

Salem Witch so it's one of the more accurate books out there. Do you want me to find it for you?" Candy said.

"No, it's alright, I'll try to find it, thank you," Alicia said.

"Alright, well it should be in that section over there, under 'Witchcraft History,'" the cashier said, pointing to a bookshelf.

"Thank you," Alicia said and walked over to the bookshelf. Before she had the chance to scan the titles, Gale grabbed her arm.

"Alicia, we just came up with a crazy idea, you have to hear it," Gale said.

"Why, what is it?" Alicia said, wary.

"Okay you know how your birthday is coming up soon, right?" Gale said, grinning from ear to ear.

"Yes, we were gonna watch monster movies at your place," Alicia said, raising an eyebrow. "I was going to finally show you the *Frankenstein* movies."

"Well we were thinking we could have a spooky bonfire instead, where we could tell ghost stories and drink."

"Yeah my brother can get us some alcohol," Lizzie said. Alicia looked at the three of them, matching devilish grins on their faces. There was something almost sinister about them.

"Why do you want to do this anyway? First you wanna go here, then you want to have a bonfire and tell ghost stories? Since when have you been into all this stuff anyway?" Alicia said.

"Look, I'm doing it for you. I know you like writing about witches, even though you won't let me read anything, so I thought all of this would be fun for you. And I mean let's be honest, none of us but you would be able to come up with a good ghost story," Gale said, her expression softening. "Besides, I'm bored, and all this Salem Witch stuff inspired me."

"You do realize that twenty people were killed because of the trials, right?" Alicia said, remembering her mother's warning.

"Shut up, you know what I mean," Gale said, gently lifting a strand of Alicia's curly black hair out of the way of her face.

Alicia looked into the girl's large blue eyes. Those eyes she could never say no to, no matter how wild the idea was, drawing her in like a siren's call. Alicia's shoulders sank, their tension releasing, her body admitting Gale had won her over.

"Fine," Alicia said.

The girls cheered, and Alicia smiled along with them, though her heart wasn't in it. Her mother's warnings still laid heavy on her mind. She tried pushing them down, it wasn't as if they were actually doing witchcraft anyway. It was all just pretend. But still, doubt lingered.

"Let's head out now, this place is honestly starting to creep me out a little," Sarah said.

"You guys can head out, I still wanna look around," Alicia said.

Alicia hugged her friends goodbye, and waited until they were all out of the store before scanning the bookshelf. Her finger stopped on a black, leather-bound volume with gold writing on the spine. *The Salem Witch Book.*

It's for research, she told herself. *It's just for research.*

Alicia slowly, carefully, slid the book out of the shelf and looked at the cover. There was a classic silhouette of a witch flying across a full moon, the number 1692 below it. Alicia's heart beat loud in her ears. Yes, this is exactly what she needed; she could feel it. Her hands trembling, she brought the book to the cashier.

"I'm sorry again about all of them. They just don't get this kind of stuff," Alicia said, avoiding Candy's eyes.

"And you do?"

Alicia looked at the cashier, taken aback. Candy's mouth was drawn up to the side in a mischievous, knowing way.

"Well, I don't know, I guess I just know a little more about this stuff," Alicia said, words spilling out. "I mean I don't do any of this witch stuff, my mom would kill me, but I just find it interesting to write about."

"So you're a storyteller, eh?" Candy said, her smirk turning into a smile.

"Well I mean I guess, I want to be at least."

The cashier nodded. "Some might say storytelling is witchcraft in a way, creating something from nothing."

"Uh, yeah, sure," Alicia said, feeling uncomfortable with where this conversation was heading. She looked up at the wall behind the cashier, noticing a large hand-sewn doll sitting in a display case. It was grayish in color, dressed in a pilgrim-like dress, and had what looked like several burn spots on it. It looked sad.

"What's that?" Alicia said. Candy followed Alicia's gaze.

"Ah, that's Goody Poppet. My auntie gave it to me when I was a young girl. Said it belonged to one of the original Salem Witches. That she used it to curse the village girls," the cashier said, her voice going low. Alicia stared wide-eyed at the cashier. The woman let out a hearty laugh.

"I'm just messing. I don't know where it came from. Have had it for a long time, though. Do you want it?"

"Oh no, I couldn't take that," Alicia said. "It looks rare and expensive."

"I wouldn't charge you for it. I only suggest because you mentioned Tituba and the Salem Witch Trials, it might be useful to you. More useful to you than me at any rate, she's just been sitting here gathering dust," Candy said.

The cashier picked up the doll and presented it to Alicia. The girl examined the doll with her eyes, looking at every stitch, at every thread out of place. Something about it pulled Alicia in, as if she was meant to have it. As if it already belonged to her.

"Are you sure?" Alicia said, not looking up from the doll.

"Absolutely. I think it's time she had a new home."

Alicia gently took the doll from Candy's hands. It was rough under her fingers, but she stroked it as if it was a pet. Feelings of joy spread through her fingertips and into her body. The doll was hers; it belonged to her.

"Thank you," Alicia said.

"You're welcome. Anyway, the book will be twenty-five dollars."

"Oh, right." Alicia paid for the book and gently placed the doll and book in her bag. Realizing she had been in the store for some time, she quickly turned and headed to the door.

"Hope you come back soon!"

Alicia stopped, turning to smile at Candy.

"I think I will."

CHAPTER
Four

Salem Village, December 1691

The air was cold and damp, the fire on the hearth meager. Tituba stared out the window, absent-mindedly stirring. Salem Village was gray and cold, an unfriendly and dismal place. Winter was particularly harsh that year. How could anyone choose to live in such a brutal place? Salem. They called it the new Jerusalem. Tituba smirked at the idea. As if there was any holiness in this land. How she longed for Barbados, the country she grew up in. If she closed her eyes, she could almost bring herself back there.

The warm ocean breeze. The saturated colors. The soul-nourishing food. The sweet scent of the flowers. How the island came alive at night. A warmth grew in her chest as she thought of those nights, a smile coming to her face. She was so young and full of life then. Now she was only a shadow of what she once was. Life had been hard in Barbados, there was no denying that, but it had been more bearable there than in this soulless village. If only she could fly back there.

"Take me to Barbados," Tituba whispered.

"What is Barbados?"

Tituba opened her eyes, nearly dropping her bowl. Abigail, the Reverend's niece, stood close to her, staring at her with her large blue eyes. Abigail was always a curious girl, though a little odd. Reverend Parris took her in after her parents had been murdered in one of those "Indian Raids" as he called them. As if the white men had not raided them first. Nonetheless, a certain heaviness followed the child. For a girl of twelve she had an unusual amount of grimness to her.

"You gave me a fright, Abby," Tituba finally replied, pitching her voice light and friendly with some effort.

Abigail's voice was cold and sullen. "I am sorry, Tituba."

"Is fine, Abby. Barbados is my country. It was a beautiful place, warmer than this cold village."

"Do you wish you could go back there?" Abigail said.

"I do Abby, I do."

"What was it like?"

Tituba's gaze went past Abigail, moving onto Betty, the Reverend's daughter, and her own daughter, Violet. They sat at the table with bored expressions, sallow as usual. Tituba's eyes softened. These poor things, all they had known was the grayness of this place. They did not know what it was like to taste the fruits of life, to dance on the beaches after dark, to run around playing in the trees, to tease the monkeys and feel the life of the earth pulsing beneath their bare feet. They were expected to live their entire lives within the cold hardship of Salem Village. Tituba had never known what true freedom was like, but she had at least known what it was like to feel alive.

Tituba glanced out the window, at the snow-covered fields and barren black trees. The Reverend would not be home until later. His wife was upstairs, sleeping as usual. The poor sickly woman. Tituba suspected she was not much longer for this world. Maybe that was what moved her. Maybe it was Abigail's cold questions. But whatever the cause, Tituba felt the thread of a story tugging her.

"Violet, Betty, come by the fire, I have a story."

CHAPTER
Five

Boston, October 19, 2022

Alicia sipped her drink, gazing at the crackling campfire. Gale, Lizzie, and Sarah sat nearby, laughing about something. Alicia's eyes locked on the fire, trying to push down the anxiety fogging her brain. It was difficult to focus on their conversation. Lighting a fire at a public park late at night was bound to draw attention, and that was the last thing Alicia wanted. At least it was warm, and the scent of burning wood soothed her slightly, but not enough.

"Lighten up, Alicia. It's your birthday! You only turn seventeen once!" Gale said.

Alicia glanced up at her.

"What?" Gale asked, rolling her eyes. "Don't give me that look, you always said you wished you could do something exciting."

"Yeah but, what if the cops come? My mother will kill me," Alicia said.

"Alicia, nobody is gonna kill you. Stop being so dramatic. It's not like we're doing drugs or breaking in somewhere," Lizzie said.

"Anyway, it's your birthday, and I promised we'd tell ghost stories, so you go first," Gale said, pointing at Alicia.

"Uh, okay," Alicia said. For a moment she let herself forget about her worries and focused on bringing a story to life, creative energies bubbling up inside her. There, in her mind, she found the thread of a story, and felt herself smile as she tugged on it.

"Long ago, people used to worship a dark, evil spirit called Sam Hain. Every year, on All Hallows' Eve, they would sacrifice a person from the village to the Dark Lord so the rest of them could survive the winter. One year, the person who was chosen to be sacrificed was a cruel and evil man that everyone called Stingy Jack."

Alicia glanced around the fire at her friends' faces. Gale's was stretched into a smile, while Lizzie and Sarah shared a nervous glance. Alicia grinned and continued.

"Stingy Jack tried to run away, but they caught him, and kept him locked up until the night arrived. In his prison cell he made a desperate prayer to Sam Hain, begging him to please spare his life. 'I will do anything, please, just let me live!' And the moment Stingy Jack finished speaking, a person in dark shrouds with long, spindly fingers appeared from the shadows and slowly approached him."

Alicia paused again, taking in the captivated stares of her friends. Gale's eyes were particularly large with excitement.

"'Do you truly mean anything?'" Alicia said in a deep, raspy voice. "'Anything, I swear it!' Jack said desperately. 'Then on All Hallows' Eve, go to the nearest pumpkin patch and sacrifice a black goat to me. Then pledge to be my servant for all eternity. I shall protect you.'"

"That sounds Satanic and messed up," Sarah interrupted.

"Shut up, that's the point," Gale said.

"Anyway," Alicia said, giving Sarah the side-eye. "Sam Hain freed Stingy Jack from this prison, and hid him in his shadows until All Hallows' Eve. When the night finally came, Stingy Jack brought a black goat to a pumpkin patch at a nearby farm. He sacrificed the goat and put it in a circle of salt and iron. He then called upon Sam Hain using a spell that the Dark Lord told him to use.

'When summer has reached its end,
when winter comes to greet us again,
this is the time of Lord Sam Hain,
ruler of darkness, coldness, and pain.
Sam Hain, Dark Lord, take my sacrifice,
I pray that it is enough to suffice!'

And then Sam Hain appeared in the circle in a gust of wind. He reached a bony, long hand out at Jack, and—"

The fire crackled loudly, several sparks shooting out at once. The girls leapt back, startled. Alicia's spine stiffened. A chill raked its way down her body as if it had claw-like fingers. Something in the atmosphere had changed. A tense unease permeated around the fire, as if something was lurking under the ground beneath their feet.

"I'm getting cold," Lizzie said, rubbing at her shoulders, but all the girls knew it wasn't the weather.

"Yeah maybe we should go," Sarah said. "Someone might see us. I feel like someone is watching us."

Alicia scoffed, suddenly annoyed. "But we haven't gotten to the good part of the story yet. Because when Sam Hain discovers Jack has trapped him in the circle, he—"

"Yeah, I'm not feeling this anymore," Gale said, and looked to the other girls. "Come on, let's go."

Gale, Lizzie, and Sarah got up. Alicia glared at the fire, sulking. All of this was Gale's idea in the first place. And now, when Alicia was getting into it, they all wanted to leave. It wasn't fair.

"Come on, Alicia. It's time to go," Gale said, reaching out a hand to help Alicia up. Alicia huffed in annoyance, ignored the offered hand, and stood up. Sometimes she wished she had other friends. She always tagged along with Gale and the others, and of course the one night it was supposed to be about her, she was once again following Gale's lead. As she got ready to douse the fire, her gaze lingered on the flames. They faded from yellow-orange to an eerie green. Alicia took a few steps back. Her friends looked over, their eyes reflecting the emerald flames.

"What are you doing?" Sarah said, her voice going high and tight.

"I'm not doing anything," Alicia said.

"Seriously, Alicia, enough. It's not even Halloween yet," Gale snapped.

And suddenly the green flames rose higher. Alicia stared, frozen on the spot. A face of a ghoulish jack-o'-lantern formed in the fire, leering at the girls. Alicia's friends screamed as the girl stood transfixed.

"FINISH WHAT YOU BEGAN!" a booming voice spoke from the flames.

"What?" Alicia asked, her voice small.

"IT BEGINS AND ENDS WITH SACRIFICE!"

A clawed hand reached out from the fire, reaching for Alicia. The girl felt sweat running down her face, her eyes wide with terror. The flames snuffed out, pitching the girls into darkness. They blinked, eyes adjusting to the thin light from the moon. A coldness rolled in, biting Alicia's skin.

"What kind of Voodoo witchcraft was that?" Sarah said, her voice short. The girls had crowded together, clutching at each other in fear.

"I don't know," Alicia said, staring at the snuffed-out fire.

"She summoned Sam Hain with that spell! She summoned the Lord of Death!" Lizzie shrieked.

Alicia turned to the girls, their faces ghostly in the moonlight. Their eyes were widened with fear, their mouths tightened in revulsion.

"No, I made that up. There is no Sam Hain!" Alicia said.

"You said that there had to be a sacrifice. You . . . you were going to sacrifice us to him!" Gale said, her eyes wide with hurt and betrayal.

"No! No, it wasn't like that at all! I don't know why that happened!" Alicia said, taking a step towards them.

"Get away you psychotic witch!" Lizzie said, and the group of three stumbled backwards as one.

"What the hell is wrong with you?" Gale asked. The girls ran off, and Alicia could only watch as they left.

"It was only a story!" she called after them. But the longer she stood there, glancing around the darkened park, the more even she didn't believe the words.

CHAPTER

Six

October 25

Alicia lied awake, staring at the ceiling fan as it whirred. For the past week she had been having nightmares about that face in the fire. Gale, Sarah, and Lizzie avoided her at school, despite her desperate attempts to explain to them that what happened was not her fault. But she was not even sure if it wasn't. Alicia hadn't even bothered to write more of her Aradia story, afraid of what her storytelling could conjure next. It was not lost on her that a demonic pumpkin face appeared right after she was telling her own twisted version of the legend of the jack-o'-lantern.

Alicia sat up and turned on her bedside lamp. She almost let out a cry, stifling it with her palm. Lying next to it was the doll that Candy had given her. She was almost sure she had put it away in her drawer. If her mother saw something like that she would burn her at the stake. Maybe she was tired and had just forgotten about it.

The girl opened the drawer to put the doll away when she noticed *The Salem Witch Book* sitting inside. She hadn't even thought about it since before her birthday. Alicia gently picked it up, feeling the worn leather under her fingers. It gave her a pleasant thrill that all old books did, the promise of hidden knowledge lying within its pages. She remembered something from her history class, about Tituba and her storytelling. It was after Tituba began telling stories that the strangeness began to happen, at least according to Mr. Miller. Alicia's heart leapt as a thought entered her mind.

What if what happened to her is what's happening to me?

Alicia excitedly flipped through the pages, the hope of finding some answers pushing her forward. The more she read, the more a strange feeling of familiarity grew. Tituba was from Barbados, possibly of Yoruba or Arawak descent. Alicia did not know too much about her own family history, only that she had some distant relatives in Barbados. Tituba's storytelling saved her life when she was accused of witchcraft, but it also shaped the events of what was to come. Alicia flipped to an illustration of Tituba. She froze, her eyes glued to the page. The illustration was old and rough, but there was no denying how uncanny it was. With her round face and soft, wide-set features, her full lips and large hooded eyes, her curly black hair and etched-in dark skin, Tituba was the mirror image of Alicia, if a bit older. She looked below the illustration to see the date.

Artist unknown, "Tituba of Salem," circa 1690-1700.

Alicia set the book down. Whoever made that illustration was alive when Tituba was, which meant that this was likely an accurate portrait of her. Was it possible that she was descended from Tituba? It would explain the strangeness of her birthday, and it was technically possible. No one knew what happened to Tituba after the Salem Witch Trials, but she did have a daughter named Violet. But if she was descended from Tituba, did that make her a witch? Alicia placed her fingers on her temples, a headache forming. Being a witch would be a very bad thing in real life. But how was she to know for sure?

An idea formed in her mind. A wicked, sinful idea, but the only one she had. The only way to know for sure would be to ask Tituba herself. And there was only one night she knew of that the dead could return to the world of the living.

Halloween.

CHAPTER

Seven

October 31

Alicia and her mother sat at their small kitchen table, scooping out pumpkin guts, the sweet, ripe aroma filling the air. There were not many Halloween traditions her mother approved of, but Tana allowed this one. Alicia's hands trembled slightly as she scooped out the insides of her pumpkin. This year she just wanted to get it over with.

"Now, you know how I usually feel about Halloween parties, but seeing as this is your last year of high school, are you sure there isn't anyone you'd rather spend time with than your old mother?" Tana said, scooping out a particularly large chunk of pumpkin guts.

"No, Gale's having a party, but I wasn't invited," Alicia said, digging a little harder into her pumpkin. Tana stopped scooping and looked at her daughter with tenderness.

"You don't need her lot anyway. I don't know why she stopped being your friend, but she doesn't deserve you," Tana said, and resumed scooping. "That girl needs her ass straightened out is all I'm saying."

Alicia smiled at her mother. She wondered if she should tell her about what really happened on her birthday.

"Mama, I . . ."

"Yes, Alleycat?"

Alicia paused, and her gut turned with nerves, twisting her hope into cowardice.

"I'm glad I'm spending tonight with you," she said instead.

"Me too," Tana said, drawing a face on the pumpkin with a smile as wide as her own. "I've been so busy recently with all the work coming my way. It's been a while since we've had some quality time. Won't be long now until you're done with school, and then off into the world."

Alicia scooped one last pile of guts out, flinging it into a bowl, and picked up a marker to draw a face on her pumpkin. Her mother was right. This was her last year at high school. Soon she would be out there, far away from all of this. Alicia would miss her mother, especially in moments like these, but she would mostly be grateful for the freedom.

"Yeah, it's wild," Alicia said.

"Any thoughts on where you want to go yet?" Tana said, starting to carve. The knife flashed in her hand, sawing into the pumpkin in a way that made Alicia squirm.

"No, but I wanna do creative writing for sure."

"Ah," Tana said. "It's been a while since I've heard you talk about writing. Are you working on anything now?"

Alicia's hand stopped. Telling her mother that she was writing a story about a witch would not go over well.

"Uh, sort of. I'm kinda writing something about a girl who is fighting to protect her people from an evil regime," Alicia said, very carefully choosing her words.

"Evil regime? Sounds like it will be interesting. You'll have to let me read it when you're done," Tana grinned at her daughter, pulling a chunk out of her pumpkin.

"Yeah, for sure," Alicia said, focusing on drawing a face. When she felt satisfied with it, she picked up a knife and began to carve. After some work with the knife, Alicia's jack-o'-lantern had a face full of jagged teeth and pointy edges. It was the face she had seen in the fire, the face that had haunted her dreams since. When it was all finished, she leaned back to take a good look. Yes, it was a spitting likeness. She turned the pumpkin, facing it to her mother.

"What do you think?"

Tana looked up from her pumpkin.

"Wow, that's gruesome! Wanna see mine?" Tana said, turning her pumpkin around. It was a skull-face, with edges that turned into the shape of flames. Alicia was impressed, her mother always seemed to outdo her every year.

"Let's put them outside," Tana said.

They took their jack-o'-lanterns out onto their small balcony that overlooked the glittering city. Tana got two candles and lit them, placing one in her pumpkin, and giving the other to Alicia. Alicia placed the candle in her jack-o'-lantern and grinned. The jack-o'-lanterns looked all the more ghoulish when lit.

"These should scare off any ghosts that are out tonight," Tana said, some seriousness coming into her voice. Alicia looked out into the city, the coolness of the night air caressing her face. As her thoughts turned to what happened on her birthday, she frowned. She hoped her mother was right.

Alicia put on her black leather jacket, her favorite wide-brimmed black hat over her braided hair, and a black t-shirt and jeans. Black was her power color, and she needed to feel as powerful as she could. On her desk she placed Goody Poppet, *The Salem Witch Book* opened to the page with the illustration of Tituba, a piece of paper with a spell she wrote, and a few candles. Alicia left an offering of honey and pumpkin seeds for her, hoping she would like them.

Alicia was alert, aware of every sound, her body shivering. What if her mother woke up? What then? Was doing this spell really worth the risk? What if she accidentally made something horrible happen? It had happened to her before, and she was not even trying to cast a spell then. But she would never figure out what happened if she didn't do something about it. Alicia told herself she just had to go for it; she was not hurting anyone. It was just a little spell to connect with Tituba.

Alicia focused on what she wanted and took a deep breath in. She opened her window, letting a cool breeze in. The haunting sound of a train echoed in her ears, as a few stray leaves blew in through the window. She stared at the moon. It was a glowing, waning crescent, like a tilted Cheshire Cat smile. It reminded her of her favorite story, the one that had inspired her to write in the first place.

"Take me to Wonderland," Alicia whispered to the moon, smiling a bit.

The girl closed her eyes and visualized a glowing, protective circle around her. She imagined Tituba watching over her, protecting her. Alicia felt safe, with warmth in her heart. She opened her eyes, lit the candles, and picked up the paper. Then she chanted.

"On this dark and witching hour,
I call upon the ancient powers.
On this All Hallow's Eve,
I call upon the powers that be.
The veil tonight is most thin,
in my circle, I invite Tituba in.
Please, by the light of candle fire,
I ask that light is brought to my desire.
By the powers of three times three,
this spell is bound, so mote it—"
"Alicia!"

Alicia froze. Slowly, as guilt and shame welled up inside her, she looked back. Standing in the doorway of her bedroom was Tana, her face contorted with a mixture of fear and anger. Her dark eyes were wide, one hand on her hip, nails practically digging into her side.

"Alicia, Alicia how could you?" Tana said, rushing forward to snuff out the candles with her own hands.

"Mama, I'm sorry, I—"

"It's all this Tituba nonsense, isn't it? I was worried when you mentioned her name, but I hoped you would just forget about it. And what, you're a witch now?" Tana asked, her voice rising with every word, finally breaking on the word "witch."

"I don't know!" Alicia cried out, lurching forward. Her mother took a step back, hands held up, and Alicia felt the distance like a cold dagger in her chest. "Mama, on my birthday something weird happened. As I was telling a ghost story to my friends, a scary face appeared in the bonfire, telling me to finish what I began, that it begins and ends with sacrifice! I'm just trying to figure out what it means!"

Tana stared, her eyes wide and unblinking. She took another step back, stumbling into the doorframe.

"I was always trying to protect you," Tana said, tears streaming down her face, "but it looks like I failed. Witchcraft got your father, and now it looks as if it's gotten you!"

Alicia was taken aback, as if something had suddenly slammed into her.

"Got my father? What are you talking about?"

"He went on and on talking about Tituba for almost a month, saying how he needed to find out if she really was his ancestor, then he started to say scary things about her being a witch, and how he might be one too, and then he disappeared."

"Tituba is my ancestor?" Alicia said, her teary eyes going wide. That would mean her suspicions were true, and would explain what happened on her birthday.

"I don't know. But I do know that witchcraft always leads down a dark path! I might have married a witch, but I won't raise one!"

"Mama, no, I'm sorry, I was just trying to—"

"I will not hear any excuses! I will not have a witch in my home!" Tana shouted.

Alicia's throat closed, her eyes wet and puffy. She never thought her mother would actually be this cruel. She expected anger, but not like this. First Gale had abandoned her, and now her own mother. The girl was not sure how much more her heart could take.

"But Mama, please!"

"Pack your things and leave!" Tana said.

"Mom!"

"Now!" Tana screamed, and with that turned and stomped out of the room. Alicia put a hand to her damp cheeks, stifling a sob. The crying would not stop. Her mother, her own mother, was kicking her out. All because she was trying to cast a spell. Her insides twisted, a sickly feeling growing in her stomach. Her mother was right, there was something wrong with her. Witchcraft was an abomination. She was an abomination.

How could you have been so foolish?

The heartbreak and tears clouding everything, Alicia only stuck a couple things into her shoulder bag: Goody Poppet and *The Salem Witch Book*. She threw her bag over her shoulders and stumbled out of her room. Alicia walked past her mother, who stepped back as if she had a contagious disease. She looked at her mother one more time for some sign of mercy, sympathy, anything. There was only fear and disgust. Tana slunk into her room and slammed the door behind her.

Suddenly anger surged through Alicia, hot and insistent. She ran to the balcony and kicked her mother's pumpkin off of it, watching it fall and land on the sidewalk with a splat, the candle flickering out into darkness. She was about to do the same to her own pumpkin, but her tears caught up with her, her anger fading. Instead, she settled for reaching down and blowing out the still flickering candle. Her mother said it brought bad luck to a house to blow out a jack-o'-lantern, that it let the spirits in. Well, Tana was going to have to face them all on her own now.

Alicia ran to the front door, blundering through her tears and the furniture, knocking over anything that was in her way. She swung the door open and ran down the hall to the fire escape, not bothering to wait for an elevator. Her breathing grew harsh and labored, her chest heaving, and her legs were burning, but she did not stop until she reached the ground floor. She took only a few seconds to catch her breath. If she waited too much longer, the reality of what had happened would sink in, and then she'd have to give in to it. She continued moving until she was out the front door and out onto the streets of the city.

CHAPTER
Eight

Alicia's face was hot from shame. Her mother was the only one that loved her, or at least Alicia had thought as much. Now she had no one and was wandering through the Boston streets, cold and alone.

How could you have been so stupid, to think you could get away with it?

The cool wind grew sharper, and crispness in the air cut against Alicia's cheeks. There was laughing and yelling around her, drunk and joyous young adults in costumes stumbling around. How happy and careless they seemed. Alicia envied them. Their lives as they knew it had not been destroyed. Gale and her friends were having a party that night. Alicia bitterly wondered how that was going.

Witch, her mind reminded her. *That's what you are. A wicked girl.*

Alicia nearly passed Grandma Yaya's Cottage, but stopped and looked at the darkened windows. For a moment she stood staring forlornly. Then as if flipped by a switch, Alicia pounded her fists on the windows, screaming. All the hurt and fear bubbled up as rage, white-hot and all-consuming, directed at this one shop. If she had not gone into that witch shop, she would not be in this mess now.

Alicia hammered on the window until her hands were sore. She closed her eyes and rested her head on the window, and the tears flowed again. It was not fair. Where was she supposed to go now? Alicia went still and listened as a train went by, the ghostly sound echoing through the night. That was what she needed, a train, to take her somewhere, anywhere, a place that she could perhaps feel safe.

Salem.

That was it. That was where she was going to go. If she was an abominable witch anyway then she might as well embrace it. She was going to go to Salem, the Witch City, where she could be someone else, maybe someone new. She checked her jacket pocket. She still had her CharlieCard tucked in her wallet, which luckily she hadn't forgotten about. It would be her ticket to Witch City.

Alicia continued forward, her boots clicking on the cobblestone sidewalk. The girl shivered in her leather jacket, holding it close to her body. Passing some barren trees, Alicia nearly missed the glowing light. BOWDOIN STATION. Despite her desperate situation, she may have found a possible way out. She ran off the sidewalk, through the open door of the station, and down the concrete steps. The lights in the station, although bright, flickered. Alicia found a map on a tiled wall. She looked it over. Where to find Salem . . .

Her eyes stopped at the end of the Blue Line. Wonderland Station.

Take me to Wonderland.

Something inside told her that was the station she needed. She would take the train to Wonderland, and from there she would take a bus to Salem. And when she arrived at the Witch City, well, she would figure that part out later. There was only going forward now.

Alicia stared out the windows of the empty train, watching the lights and brick walls speed by, clutching her bag to her chest. The excitement of going to Salem was wearing off. Loss and loneliness settled back into her, as if a cyclone had destroyed everything she knew.

And it's all your fault Alicia.

She held the bag tighter, new tears rolling down her cheeks.

So stupid, so stupid.

BEACHMONT STATION

Only two more stops until Wonderland. Where had the time gone?

REVERE BEACH STATION

One more stop until Wonderland. A sudden horror dawned on her. She left her notebooks back in Boston. All of her hard work, all of her creative energy. Her Aradia story. It was all gone. Her mother would surely burn them when she found them.

Oh God, what have I done?

This was all a mistake. Buying the book, casting the spell, taking the train, everything. What was she possibly thinking? Maybe she could go home and apologize to her mother, maybe Tana would forgive her. Alicia would be going back to the grayness of her life, pretending to be normal, but at least she would be safe. And she would have her story back. Who knew what lay ahead with her life in Salem? She had never been there. And although it was over three hundred years ago, Tituba had not exactly fared well there. Maybe she should go back.

WONDERLAND STATION

The train came to a grinding stop, the smell of burnt rubber filling the car, jolting Alicia in her seat. The doors of the train opened, and with a deep breath, she headed out of the nearest door and slung her bag over her shoulder. Alicia stood on the platform for a moment. It was empty. No late partygoers, not even creepy strangers. She would have thought that Halloween night of all nights would be busy for a subway station, but it was like nobody had been there in years. Did Wonderland Station close early on Halloween? Alicia looked back at the train, but it was already gone. For better or for worse, she was in Wonderland now.

The lights of the station were on, but dimly, occasionally flickering. They illuminated a large, wrought iron fence that went all the way up to the ceiling of the station like a twisted spider-web. There was a design of a castle on the fence with the word WONDERLAND engraved into it. She was certainly in the right place, but something was very wrong. Beyond the flickering lights of the station was only darkness, as if Wonderland Station existed in a void.

Alicia stepped forward tentatively. Wind whistled through the iron fixtures, and it echoed with a creaking, metallic sound. As she approached, the wind picked up, as did the noise, ringing higher and higher until it almost sounded like the gate was screaming. Alicia hurried across the platform and up a staircase. She passed several windows, catching her own scared rushing reflection in the dark glass. In the corner of her eye, she thought she saw someone standing behind her. She turned around. No one. Where on earth was everyone? Alicia drew her leather jacket close, cautiously going forward, looking for the exit.

Alicia reached another staircase, this one going down. The staircase got darker with each step until she could barely see. Eventually, there were no more steps. Alicia felt with her feet, probing forward in the darkness, but found only flat pavement. Finally, after walking forward as her eyes adjusted, Alicia saw a glass door, a faint glow behind it. Her heart beat hard and fast as she reached out and opened the door. She walked through.

Dim, fluorescent lighting revealed a few bus-posts next to a wide pavement road. Large concrete columns stood behind them, connecting to the station. The bus stops had a cold, lonely feeling to them, the air making her shudder. They were empty. Alicia cautiously walked forward. Had the last bus left? She looked at the bus schedule on each post, then checked her dying phone for the time. With growing despair, she realized that no more buses were coming, at least not tonight. She was entirely alone.

Alicia sat on a bench, gazing into space, trying not to think. Everything was happening all at once and it was just too much. She placed her face in her hands.

"Mama, I'm so sorry. I just wanted to find Tituba. I . . . I didn't want any of this! I just wanna go home," Alicia murmured into her hands, already wet from her tears.

"Are you alright?"

Alicia quickly looked up, startled to hear another voice. A woman dressed in shimmering black stood near her. She was tall and had a very beautiful and angular face with prominent, hollow cheekbones, skin glowing like the moon. Long white hair cascaded down from a black helmet that was spiked like a crown. Her eyes were white, giving her a ghostly look, emphasized by a glowing green lantern. Alicia was at first startled, but then remembered it was Halloween, and this woman was wearing a very impressive costume.

"I'm fine," Alicia said, wiping her eyes.

"Are you sure? You seem a little bit, if you do not mind me saying, worn down. As if the world has eaten you up. Do you need any help?"

Alicia wanted to protest, to dismiss the strange woman and to just be left alone. But she was just too exhausted to push her away.

"It's been a really long night," Alicia said, swallowing more tears. "I was trying to get to the Witch City, but now it looks like I'm stuck here."

"I'm headed to the Witch City myself. I could take you there if you want me to," the woman said. "It's just down Witchburn Road."

Alicia looked up at the woman.

"Are you sure?"

"It's your choice."

Alicia did not know if she should trust this woman. Hitch a ride with a stranger who just so happened to be going where she needed to be? It seemed like madness. But it was also madness to go on her own to Salem late at night. She might as well go all the way.

"Sure. Thanks," Alicia said. The woman smiled gently and nodded.

"Follow me, I'm parked just outside the station."

Alicia stood up as the woman turned and walked slowly, lantern held high, green light swinging along the sidewalk as they walked. A triple moon symbol decorated the back of the woman's jacket. The center moon had an elaborate design of a six-pointed starburst encased in a circle, a three-pronged labyrinth-like design surrounding it. Patches with the words PHOSPHOROS, ENODIA, and SOTEIRA surrounded the moon. The air grew colder and metallic to the taste as they walked, awakening Alicia to her senses.

"Is it usually this dead on Halloween night here? I would've thought there would be people partying or something," Alicia said nervously.

"Hard to say," the woman said deliberately and slowly. "You know, there is something truly enchanting about this night. Spirits can pass through the veil between this world and the next. It is when the nights get longer and we can feel the approach of winter. It is a time to honor the dead, though it is also a night of great revelry. And sacrifice."

Alicia stared, uneasy. Any moment now she was expecting to be jumped and knocked out by this woman's hidden gang. Either that or she was about to be sacrificed by some real witchcraft cult. But still, she followed her onwards.

They left the station, streetlights breaking the black sheet of night. Parked on the side of a crossroads was a large black motorcycle with celestial designs painted on it. It had a sidecar with a large black dog sitting inside, its head tilted in curiosity. Next to the motorcycle was a street-post with a sign: WITCHBURN RD. Alicia had been expecting a car, and her stomach twisted at the idea of being on the back of a motorcycle. Her mother had always said they were dangerous.

The woman turned and faced Alicia, as if she could hear her hesitation. Her white eyes seemed more intense than before, almost as if they were glowing. "Are you sure you want me to take you to the Witch City?"

"Well, it's either that or wait almost six hours until the next bus comes. And I don't know you or anything, but I just really need to get there," Alicia said.

I've also lost everything tonight, I have nothing left to lose, Alicia thought.

"Why do you need to get there so badly?" the woman asked.

Alicia tried to think of all the different ways she could answer this. But only one thought stuck. "I . . . I need to find answers. About my family. About myself."

The woman nodded, as if understanding more than she led on.

"Very well. You can call me Trivia."

"I'm . . ." Alicia paused. This was her chance to become someone new. To leave her old life behind and become who she really wanted to be. She would no longer be Alicia.

"Aradia. My name is Aradia."

CHAPTER
Nine

Salem Village, December 1691

A group of girls sat around Tituba. Words and whispers spread through Salem Village as quick as lightning. These girls wanted to hear the stories of Barbados, a land that sounded so colorful and magical compared to the grayness of New England life. Tituba was reluctant at first with all these village girls in the house, she knew the wrath of the Reverend Samuel Parris, but eventually gave into the desire to tell a good story. And, for the briefest of moments, Tituba could escape to Barbados too, and relive its warmth and vitality.

"Barbados is a very beautiful place, there are flowers more red than blood, the water is more blue than sky, and there are bright yellow birds that sing like angels," Tituba said, smiling as she remembered her home.

"Yellow birds?" Betty said.

Tituba nodded. "Yes, and monkeys, and—"

"What is a monkey?" Abigail said.

"A monkey looks like a hairy little man with a tail," Tituba said, smothering a laugh when the girls traded amazed glances. "But he is no man, he is a strange funny creature that likes to play tricks."

"Can a monkey speak?" a girl named Ann Putnam said.

"No, but he makes strange noises, like this," Tituba said, and imitated a monkey. Most of the girls laughed, but Tituba noticed that Abigail did not. The young girl's eyes were squinted, as if scrutinizing what the woman was saying.

"What troubles you, Abby?" Tituba said.

Abigail frowned even deeper. "I wish I could go to Barbados, and see it all myself. Salem is such a horrible place. I want to leave."

Some of the other girls nodded and made sounds of agreement.

"I wish I could leave too," an older girl named Mary Warren said. "John Proctor always thrashes me so dreadfully; I want to go to a place where I can be free."

Tituba's gaze moved to the girl. She was a pale, forlorn-looking girl with dark bangs that nearly covered her eyes, even with a bonnet. Mary was nearly twenty, and was the indentured servant of John Proctor, an outspoken man that lived just outside the village. Tituba empathized with her, knowing all too well what that felt like. At least Mary would be able to leave her master eventually. Tituba had no such freedom.

"It would be very nice if we could fly there, and leave this cold place behind," Tituba said.

"Is that possible?" Betty said, curiously.

"I have heard witches can do it, that they can fly over many lands," Abigail said, her voice hushed. The other girls gave astonished gasps.

"What do you know of witches, Abby?" Tituba asked sternly.

Abigail shrugged. "Only what uncle says. They are wicked and make pacts with the Devil."

Something in the girl's eyes told Tituba that she knew more about witches than she said. This sudden turn in the conversation to witches made Tituba uncomfortable, if a little disturbed. From her experience talk of witches always led to bad things. It was only a few years ago that a woman named Goodwife Glover had been hanged in Boston for witchcraft. Back in Barbados, she had heard talk of witches being burned in Europe.

Tituba pressed her lips together, as she wished the girls would. "Best not to speak of witches, Abby."

"I think Sarah Good is a witch, I hath heard her mumble and curse, and she looks like a frightful hag," Ann Putnam said. The other girls laughed. Sarah Good was a beggar woman in the village known for being disagreeable. She always had her little daughter, Dorothy, with her. Tituba did not like her much, but she did feel sympathy for her, and especially for her little girl.

"Now, that is enough of witches! Sarah Good is a sad creature, but there is no need to call her a witch," Tituba said, standing up. "If you must speak of witches, do it elsewhere. I will not have it here."

CHAPTER

Ten

As they rode further along, each streetlamp progressively took on an emerald hue, the warm white-yellow glow slowly twisting to an eerie green, illuminating the silhouettes of claw-like trees. Surely Aradia was headed in the right direction if even the road had begun to look witchy. She clutched on tight to Trivia's jacket, the leather cold in her hands. The further they went, the more the trees and lights became a blur, the speed awakening Aradia's spirit, her heart beating with rapid excitement. Trivia's dog sat happily in the sidecar, its tongue hanging out as its ears blew backwards.

They slowed down, passing by a signpost. There was a witch on a broomstick painted on the sign, and around it were the words:

ENTERING

Est.   1692

THE WITCH CITY

Aradia's heart beat even faster. This was it; she was finally arriving in Salem. Anticipation flooded her body, making her legs restless, as if she could run a marathon. She did not know what life was going to be like now, but at least she was finally arriving at her new home. Everything was about to change.

A massive cityscape rose up ahead. It was lit with bright green lights, giving it an emerald glow. Riding into the city they passed large industrial buildings, glittering with green and orange lights and jack-o'-lanterns. Old fashioned iron streetlights glowing with jack-o'-lantern faces appeared on every block. Broomsticks were parked next to buildings, they even passed under a few arches that were heavily decorated with them. In an empty lot a large glowing cauldron bubbled on with a few people gathered around it. A strong scent of pumpkin spice and autumn leaves permeated the air, filling Aradia's nose with nostalgic delight. It was everything Aradia hoped a Witch City would be. There were some faint city noises, and the occasional screech of cat, however it was mostly quiet. Perhaps, even in Salem, the Halloween parties really were all finished by this time.

Trivia pulled over at an intersection next to a large iron gate.

"This is as far as I can take you. Will you be alright on your own?" Trivia asked, glancing back at Aradia.

"I'll figure something out. Thank you," Aradia said, getting off the motorcycle. It took a few seconds to get her bearings, her legs wobbling.

"Good luck with Tituba. I hope you find her," Trivia said.

"Thank you," Aradia said, pausing. "Wait, how——"

The motorcycle's engine revved, and Trivia disappeared off into the night. Had she mentioned Tituba to Trivia? Aradia could not recall. Trivia had dropped her off in a quieter part of the city, with only a few, dingy dark buildings nearby, the street dimly lit by green streetlights. It was too dark and foggy to properly make out what was behind the iron gate other than some trees. She held one hand on one of the cool, hard bars of it, staring out. She had no friends, no family members there. All she had now was the city.

Small orbs of green light materialized in the dark. Aradia looked up and squinted, curious as to what they were. This could not possibly be a sign from Tituba, could it?

"Hello?" she asked cautiously, her voice barely above a whisper.

The orbs seemed to get smaller, as if they were floating away. Without thinking, Aradia pushed on the gates, and to her surprise they opened, a loud screech echoing through the dark. With some hesitation, she walked forward into the fog, feeling the crunch of dried grass and dead leaves under her boots. It became increasingly harder to see the orbs in fog, but Aradia continued forward.

Feeling a little foolish, she called out, "Tituba, is that you?"

A sudden chill ran down her spine, and she stopped. Faintly, she heard a moaning sound, as if something was in pain. She took a few more steps forward. The moaning got louder. She froze. The orbs disappeared into the fog.

"Wait!" Aradia said.

She stumbled forward. The fog grew thicker until Aradia could barely see her own hands. She turned around, desperately hoping to see some glimpse of the gate, but there was only gray cloudiness. Carefully, she walked back in the direction she came from.

And suddenly something materialized out of the fog. Aradia saw the glowing eye sockets and the green, peeling flesh of a head. It was skeletal and rotted into little more than a skull, its jaws open in a silent scream. Aradia felt herself scream and broke into a run. The effort strained her lungs, as if blood was filling them up, but she pushed on, needing to escape whatever that thing was. She tripped a few times on hard objects that stuck from the ground, slowing her down. Still she ran on.

A cold hand with sharp nails grazed the back of Aradia's leg, startling another scream from her, even as her lungs burned for air. She kicked backward and continued to run as the moaning sounds grew louder. The fog slowly dissipated. The moonlight illuminated a hill ahead of her, a large, crooked tree reaching up from its center, gravestones surrounding it.

Aradia ran up the hill, but halfway up she had to pause, bending over with hands on her knees to gasp for air. When she dared a look behind here, there was nothing, no one, just fog.

Still not convinced that she was safe, Aradia ran until she reached the top of the hill. Sweat rolled down her forehead despite the chilly air. She peered around the tree, at the seemingly endless sea of gravestones beyond the hill, green city lights in the far distance.

Aradia gasped for air, wheeling around to look for a way out even though her legs still burned and air wouldn't catch in her lungs. She stumbled down the hill, one step at a time, wincing as her thighs fought to give in. But she wasn't alone on the hill. A large group of green, skeletal creatures with glowing eye-sockets slowly trudged towards the hill—towards *her*. Gasping, she turned again and ran to the other side. Twisted to stare at the creatures, Aradia didn't see the exposed root but she felt it, her foot catching as her ankle twisted. She pitched forward, a small scream escaping. She rolled down the hill, violently bumping into a few headstones on the way down. The girl landed hard on scattered, dead leaves with a loud crunch. Pain shot through her body as she crawled forward, trying to pull herself up. She grabbed the side of a gravestone, crawling up it as her support. As she fought to find her balance, Aradia looked back.

The creatures were very close now, floating down the hill after her. Without thinking, Aradia lurched forward away from them, but pain shot up her ankle, and she slid back down against the gravestone. The creatures were now close enough to reach for her with their rotting, bony hands. Her heart hammered and she gasped for air, the smell of rot filling her nostrils. She squeezed her eyes shut in fear.

A bright light forced its way through her lids. When she cracked an eye open, she saw the creatures hissing and backing away, turning into a black, shadowy mist. Aradia put her hand on her chest, trying to breathe normally again. The light shifted from behind her, and she heard footsteps crunch on dead leaves. What was coming now? Aradia tried pulling herself upwards, but her ankle was in too much pain to go up too far. A dark figure, holding a glowing jack-o'-lantern by a handle, came into view, its face feathered and beaked like a raven's. Aradia screamed again. The raven-faced figure took a step back from Aradia.

"Easy, calm down, would yah?" a young voice said. The raven face lifted upwards like a mask, revealing the face of a teenage girl with shocking lime green skin, long straight black and purple hair contrasting against it. The green girl stared at her with judgment, her eyes a sharp violet and framed with thick black eyeliner.

"What are you doing out here without a mask or lantern?" the green girl demanded. Aradia simply stared, her heart beating faster. The girl pursed her lips, which were painted a midnight black. "You're not from around here, are you?"

Aradia shook her head, too stunned to speak.

"Where do you come from?"

"Boston," Aradia said, glad to have found her voice, her cheeks flushing. "But I took the train to Wonderland Station and then I—"

"Wait, did you say Wonderland Station?" the girl said, kneeling down to meet her.

"Yeah?" Aradia said, raising an eyebrow.

The green girl smiled, excitement lighting her eyes. "Are you from the Old Country?"

"What?"

"Wonderland Station. It's the gateway to the Old Country, right? I've heard so much about it."

"What are you talking about?"

"Every witch that has arrived from Wonderland Station is from the Old Country!" the green girl said, smiling even wider.

"But I'm not a—"

But before Aradia could say "witch," a faint moaning echoed from the darkness.

"Hecate's hags, they're back. I think I should get you outta here. It's not safe tonight," the green girl said, standing up and offering her hand.

Aradia tentatively reached up to it, trying to stand up. The pain in her ankle shot through her, and she cried out.

"What's the matter? What's wrong?"

"My ankle, I twisted it, when I was running from those things."

"Ghouls. They roam everywhere on Samhain Night, especially in graveyards like this. Here, maybe I can help, but we gotta be quick. Sit back down and hold out your leg," the green girl said, gently putting Aradia down.

Aradia held her leg out in nervous anticipation. Was this girl really a witch? Could she actually heal her? The girl placed the lantern on the ground then knelt down beside her. The witch closed her eyes and held her palms open a few inches above Aradia's ankle.

"*Hecate, Hecate, Hecate, power flow through me. I heal this girl from her pain, rid her of any ache or strain. May she be healed so she can walk free, as I do will it, so shall it be*," the green girl chanted.

Aradia's ankle glowed green as a pleasant warmth radiated through her leg. In a few seconds, the glow faded, and Aradia cautiously moved her ankle. The spell worked. The pain was gone. Astounded, she stared at the girl. Aradia had just been saved by a real witch. The witch smiled, picked up her lantern, and stood. The girl wore a purple and black kilt, a studded black leather jacket, fingerless gloves, and knee-high, black leather boots. Aradia slowly straightened up, still in awe.

"How did you do that?" Aradia said. The witch shrugged her shoulders.

"It's a spell I learned in school. It can only heal minor injuries though, so let's go," the witch said, turning.

"Wait, where are you taking me?"

"To somewhere safe. Did you see those creatures? I've known people who have disappeared on this night, and it's no mystery why. You're the first witch from the Old Country I've met and I'd rather you not die."

Another moan came from the darkness. Aradia looked back, seeing those eerie green orbs again, the fear making her hair stand on end.

"We really have to go," the young witch said and held out her open hand. "Selene!"

A black broomstick flew out from the darkness towards the witch, and she caught it in her open hand, startling Aradia. The witch lowered her raven mask back down onto her face and attached the jack-o'-lantern onto the end of the stick. She swung her leg over the broomstick and sat on it, feet planted on the ground. She looked at Aradia expectantly.

"Or does being devoured by ghouls sound like fun to you?"

Aradia's chest tightened. Could she trust her? She tentatively sat on the broomstick behind the witch and held onto the young witch's waist, her leather jacket cold to the touch.

"By the way, I'm Wanda," the witch said, lifting the broom upwards. "I love your hat."

Aradia smiled, her cheeks warming again. She held onto her hat as they flew into the night sky.

CHAPTER

Eleven

old rushes of wind blew against them, making Aradia's eyes water. She held tightly onto Wanda, her heart beating quickly, the rush exhilarating. Beneath them the ground dipped away and Aradia's stomach lurched. She closed her eyes and buried her face in the witch's back, the excitement almost too much for her.

After a while, she felt the broom stop accelerating. As they slowed to a gentler speed, Aradia loosened her grip on the witch slightly and opened her eyes. She gasped as she looked at the city below them. Green and orange lights covered the landscape like interconnected spider-webs. Bright green smoke swirled into the air and curled around in spirals coming up from twisted smokestacks. Large, industrial buildings reached high into the sky like tree branches, while shorter and squatter buildings glowed, shaped like jack-o'-lanterns. They passed over the center of the city, beneath them a large statue of three women, each holding a glowing torch.

Bordering the city to the south was a great, dark forest, with no end in sight. To the east was a large, dark body of water, broken up by a small island with its own concentrated city, an ominous dark castle in the center of it. A bridge connected the mainland part of the city with the island. Gargantuan mountains stood at the northern part of the city, bordering it from the rest of the world. The only road out of the city was to the west: Witchburn Road. Turning to the skies, Aradia flinched, holding tighter to Wanda, making the witch laugh. Large bats flew about, and a few witches flew on broomsticks. It all seemed fantastical and familiar at the same time to Aradia, like she had entered the world she was always writing about.

They flew past the moon. It was full and greenish in color, with two crescent moons flanking it. Aradia did a double take, but no matter how hard she stared, the three moons stared back, the two arcs like Cheshire grins. Was all this just a fantasy she created in her head? If it was, she was starting to hope that she would not wake up. She did not want to leave, not yet.

The wind suddenly blew fiercer, and the broom swayed violently. Aradia squeaked and held tighter as they began to descend. They nearly crashed into a branch-like post sticking out from a building, but dodged below it before it could scrape them. Maybe getting on a broomstick with a witch she just met hadn't been the best idea. But then Aradia couldn't think anymore as they dipped down even further, careening through the city.

"Hold on!" Wanda cried, or something like it, Aradia couldn't be sure over the screaming wind in her ears. The buildings surged closer and closer, and Aradia felt another scream bubbling up. The witch attempted to circle the broomstick backwards, but a sudden breeze slammed them into a sail of a tall windmill-like structure, which flung them backwards.

Screaming, feeling as if her stomach had dropped out of her, Aradia held tight to Wanda as the broom spun around. Flying over the water, ready to plummet at any second, they skidded on top of a cathedral on the edge of the island, until Aradia and Wanda were flung forward off the broom, sliding down the roof, screaming as they went.

The witch reached for the broom, but it was broken in several places, and it rolled off the roof onto the ground. The girls slid right off the edge of the roof, heading straight for the ground. Aradia closed her eyes, putting her arms out, trying to brace herself from impact, unable to scream any longer. A force froze her in the air, and slowly lowered her. She opened her eyes as her feet touched the ground, the witch floating down next to her.

"Did you do that?" Aradia asked, catching her breath.

"It was I. You have a lot of explaining to do," a severe voice said from behind them. Aradia and the witch girl tensed and slowly turned around. A ghostly pale woman dressed in flowing black robes and a triple moon headpiece stood facing them. Holding Wanda's broken broomstick in her hands, she stared at them with bright green eyes squinted in contempt, her sharp nose lifted in disapproval. When her gaze fell upon Aradia, she raised her eyebrows in suspicion.

"What is your name?" she asked. Aradia paused.

"Well?"

"Aradia. My name is Aradia."

"Aradia?" The woman scoffed. "How blasphemous, to take the name of the Holy Strega. Where are you from? There is something off, I can sense it."

"I'm from Boston. The Old Country," Aradia, said quietly, intimidated by the witch's presence. The witch's bright green eyes widened in shock, her mouth falling slightly open.

"How in the name of the Goddess did you get to this city?"

"I took a train," Aradia said, holding tightly to her shoulder bag. It sounded so silly, but it was the truth.

"And what were you doing with her?" the woman snapped, her gaze turning to Wanda.

"I found her at Old Burying Point, and I was trying to get her to safety. It is after all Samhain Night," the young witch said defiantly.

The older woman scowled. "Well, it seems as if you have been doing a simply fine job of that, crashing into the Temple of Hecate. You should not even be out tonight. What in the Goddess's name were you thinking?"

"I dunno," Wanda shrugged, her eyes on her toes. "I just never met an Old Country witch before, and she—"

"There is good reason for it. The Queen of Lanterns must hear about this at once," the woman said, dropping the young witch's broom. The wood rattled to the ground as the woman held out a claw, beckoning to them.

"No!" The young witch grabbed Aradia's arm.

Purple smoke formed around them, completely covering their view. Aradia felt slightly lightheaded, confused as to what was happening. She faintly heard the woman's frustrated cry, and then nothing. In a few seconds the smoke cleared, and they were standing on the roof of a building, tall, crumbling smokestacks around them. It overlooked the city, the cityscape like a giant factory dotted with lights. There was a neon green sign in the distance that caught Aradia's attention.

Aradia stared at it for a second, then looked over to the witch. "Why did you—"

The girl shuddered. "That was Katherine Brew, the High Priestess of the Lantern Coven."

Aradia had a lot of questions, but she started with, "What's the Lantern Coven?"

"The Lantern Coven," Wanda said, lifting up her raven mask, "is the most powerful group of witches in the city. They are headed by Gourdina, the Queen of Lanterns."

Aradia glanced at the witch, whose green skin had gone a pale, sickly color. She was frightened. "What's so bad about the Queen of Lanterns?"

"Well, I don't know if there is anything bad about the Queen of Lanterns at all, that's just the thing. I mean, some people call her the Dread Queen and I know she can definitely be scary, but, but I don't know. I just don't want to risk anything bad happening to you," Wanda said.

"Why not?"

"Because! You're from the Old Country, and that makes you special, and I don't want to lose you yet," the witch said. She frowned, crossing her arms. "I know I'm not the smartest witch but when I trust my witch's intuition, I'm always right."

Aradia felt a smile coming to her lips, but she suppressed it. *She could abandon you.* The voice in her head sounded smug, but Aradia ignored it.

"Thanks."

"Whatever. Anyway, what was your name again?"

"Aradia," she said, still trying to convince herself.

"Aradia?" Wanda said, her eyes wide. "Wait, no, it can't be."

"What do you mean?"

"You arrive from the Old Country, on a Samhain Night, and your name is Aradia."

"Yes?"

"I never believed in any of it before, but if you're here, if you're really here . . ."

"What are you talking about?" Aradia asked, her shoulders tensing.

"You're Aradia the Holy Strega! You've come to save Witch City!"

Aradia opened her mouth and then closed it.

"The Holy Strega?" Aradia said, choosing her words carefully, not wanting to betray that she had no idea what Wanda was talking about.

"Well duh. You're the first witch! There's a whole book about you. According to the Gospel of the Witches, the Moon Goddess, Hecate-Luna-Diana, sent her daughter to teach people how to be witches. Then she disappeared for a really long time, but then reappeared during the Burning Times to teach witches to protect themselves against Witch Hunters. But she was captured and burned at the stake. But before that she said she'd return when witches needed her most. And here you are," Wanda stared at her, violet eyes wide. Then she flung out her arms, barking out a laugh. "I can't hexing believe it."

"I'm not—" How was she supposed to know that the name she chose for her character, a name she thought she had made up, was the name of a witch-savior? But that did not mean she was the Aradia herself. Descended from a Salem Witch possibly, daughter of a Triple Moon Goddess she was not.

"What?" Wanda's violet eyes were wide and hopeful, a grin spread wide on her electric green face. Aradia did not have it in her to let her down. Besides, Aradia had wanted to become someone else. To leave her old life completely behind. Maybe she *could* be the Holy Strega if she believed it hard enough.

"I'm not the same person I was before. When I was burned alive, I was reincarnated into a new life," Aradia said, trying to convince herself. "Yes, and when the time was ready, the Goddess came to me and sent me here."

"That is so hexing cool," Wanda said. "Well, Aradia, welcome to Crone's Cross. I don't know what's going to happen now. I can only smoke-travel short distances, so it's a good thing that the temple wasn't far. And we're out alone on Samhain Night. Gods I have never been in as deep grave-dirt as this."

Wanda paced around anxiously. Aradia was fidgety herself. *She* had never been in as deep grave-dirt as this before.

"And why is Samhain Night so dangerous here?"

"Well, it's because the veil between worlds is thin. The Lord of Samhain himself, a creepy Old God, crosses into our world to feast on souls, and with him brings a bunch of nasty evil creeps that haunt the city."

Lord of Samhain. Like the one in her ghost story, although Wanda pronounced it "Sowen." Was it really his face she saw in the fire? Had she actually summoned an evil entity, and was that why all this had started? Aradia's stomach churned. She must have inherited Tituba's supernatural storytelling abilities. And things didn't turn out so well for Tituba.

"Is that what attacked me?" Aradia finally asked.

"What?"

"Is that what attacked me? The Lord of Samhain's minions?"

"Yeah. He brings all sorts of nasties. There's a few ways to protect yourself from them though. Jack-o'-lanterns frighten them away, costumes and masks confuse them into leaving you alone, and if all else fails leaving them offerings of food might appease them, especially if its sweet. It's good to be prepared. You never know who is going to show up at your doorstep."

Aradia looked back out at the neon orange and green lights of the city. So her mother had been right about jack-o'-lanterns. And the other Halloween traditions she was never allowed to partake in, they were also protection against evil spirits. Aradia always figured there was more to Halloween than she was taught, but she never expected it to be so real. And dangerous.

"I know, he probably would hate me for getting him out on Samhain Night, but I think he's the only one close enough to help. I'll witchboard him."

Wanda took out a small Ouija board and a planchette-shaped ring from her leather jacket. The witch moved the planchette around the board, pointing to different letters. She would then pause, and then the planchette would seem to move her finger on its own as if it was responding. Aradia stared in wonder, chills running down her spine. Ouija boards were definitely considered to be evil tools of witchcraft by her mother.

"He?" Aradia repeated. "Who?"

"My friend Erzeben. We've been friends forever," Wanda said without looking up, moving the planchette around more rapidly. "He can be a bit of a pain in the hearse sometimes, but his heart's in the right place. I think so at least."

Wanda moved the planchette around faster, her teeth bared in frustration. Then finally a satisfied smirk appeared on her face.

"Alright," Wanda said, putting the board and planchette back in her pocket, "Erzeben is going to be here tomorrow. It's too late to head home now. He's not happy about it, but he can deal with it. The number of times I've helped him with his issues . . . This is our usual spot."

"Won't anyone find us? Like the Lord of Samhain or the Queen?"

"Hopefully not. This factory has been abandoned for years. Nobody ever comes here. I don't have my lantern anymore, but I told Erz to get us three lanterns and an extra mask for you. In the meantime, we wait, and try to figure out what to do with you," Wanda said.

Aradia looked over to the witch. Her green face was illuminated by the lights of the city, glowing just as bright. Now that Aradia actually had the chance to take a proper look at her, she noticed how beautiful the green girl was. She had soft, smooth features, making Aradia want to reach out and touch her face. Her violet eyes were large and determined, inviting the girl to adventure. Her black-painted lips were a mischievous smirk, almost taunting Aradia with some hidden secret. Aradia looked down, suddenly self-conscious. She had always thought girls were pretty, but had never noticed one like this before. What did *that* mean? Aradia pushed these feelings down. There was too much going on already.

"Oh and we should probably watch out for Monster Coven over the next few nights," Wanda said, interrupting Aradia's thoughts.

"Monster Coven? That's their name?" Aradia asked. "Am I in some Halloween land or something?"

"No," Wanda said, her brows knitting together, "that's just what they're called. They're a coven of Wicked Witches. They've been known to kidnap rich witches and burn buildings and cause riots and stuff. They're led by a psychotic witch everyone calls Grim Old Mombi, the Wicked Witch of Westwitch."

"And what about you? Are you part of a coven?" Aradia asked, both intrigued and wary.

"Eh, sort of. Nothing formal or organized. There's three of us. We call ourselves the Bad Witches. Erzeben's part of it."

"Bad Witches? Why Bad Witches?" Aradia asked with a small laugh.

"Well, it's not like we're actually bad or anything. We mostly just get together and have a little fun, a kind of let's just hex the rules and do what we want, maybe get into a little bit of trouble here and there. Regular witch life isn't as exciting in Witch City as you'd might think," Wanda said.

What a thought, that being a witch could be boring. Witches were always exciting to write about, even if witches were dangerous and forbidden. Before her birthday, Aradia never went against the rules, never been a bad girl, or a bad witch either. Maybe it was time she started.

"Sounds like fun," Aradia said. Wanda smirked, and Aradia's heart fluttered in response.

"It is, but we do have two rules."

"Yeah? And what are those?"

"Bad Witches wear black, and Bad Witches have your back."

CHAPTER

Twelve

Salem Village, January 1692

Tituba awoke with a start, covered in cold sweat. She had been having terrible dreams of girls screaming and bodies hanging from trees for weeks. And fire, so much fire, as if the whole village had gone up in flames. She looked to her husband, John, who was sleeping as peacefully as he always did. The lucky bastard. Tituba had not one night of restful sleep since they were taken to Salem Village all those years ago. There was something evil in this place, something she had sensed right from the beginning, but she had a feeling that it was about to get much worse.

Tituba got up from the uncomfortable straw bed and dressed in her warmest garments. She picked up a basket of leftover foods she had tucked away in her cramped quarters, and left the house into the winter's darkness. She moved quickly with her head down, grateful for the night cloaking her from view. A hush enveloped her, with only a pale sliver of moonlight to guide her. It did not matter. Tituba knew the path well.

The woman left the Reverend's parsonage, and passed many of the dreary, ominous buildings of the village. All good, upstanding Puritan folk would be in bed at this time. Tituba was counting on it. When she passed the Sibleys' house, she took extra precaution to be quiet. Mary Sibley was known to be a very nosy neighbor, always having an opinion about everything. One day, Tituba was sure, the woman would cause a whole lot of trouble because of it.

Finally, Tituba arrived at a crossroads at the edge of a large, black forest, where all manner of devils supposedly lurked. After turning back to make sure no one followed her, she knelt in front of the crossroads and took out the food from her basket. She placed it where the roads met and looked up at the moon.

"Mama, Papa, please forgive me for taking so long," she said into the night, her voice weak. "I know this food isn't much, but I don't have much. I been doing everything I can to survive. But I am worried. Worried for Violet, my precious flower. This is a cold, mean place, and I worry that she is already becoming gray like everything here. I wish she could be free—I wish we could all be free—but I am afraid we will be trapped here for always."

Tituba thought back to her dreams. She could still hear the screams in her mind. Her gaze lowered. On every tree in the forest, she saw ghostly bodies hanging from their branches, but when she blinked the trees were bare as skeletal hands. Tituba shivered, almost to the point of convulsions.

"Something bad is coming," Tituba said, trying to stop herself from shaking. "The Devil will come to the village and turn it into a city of wickedness. Good people will turn against each other and many will be sacrificed. A coven of witches will take over Salem, and will not stop until the whole town and village is up in flames."

A sickness grew in her stomach as the words came out, causing the woman to double over. Now that Tituba had spoken the words, she had little doubt that what she said would come true.

She forced out the rest of her plea: "Please protect Violet from the Devil and the witches. Please let us survive."

Tituba continued to shake, her face in her hands. And from a short distance, barely concealed between the bare limbs of wintry trees, Abigail Williams watched. The smallest smile formed on the girl's face, like a cat that had cornered a mouse.

CHAPTER
Thirteen

Crone's Cross, November 1, 2022

Aradia awoke to the smell of smoke in her nostrils, the sound of screaming girls, and the icy chill of a late winter's night. Confusion grew as she noticed her surroundings. She was not in her bedroom at home, but in a large attic. It was mostly empty, with discarded shelves covered in cobwebs, and worn-out couches covered in dust. A draft rolled in from broken windows, chilling Aradia through her jacket. She stood up from the couch, her boots crunching on dead leaves.

Aradia put a hand on her stomach as it groaned in hunger. She had not eaten since having dinner with her mother the night before, which meant that Tana really had kicked her out, and this was real. Tears returned to her eyes. Was casting a spell to connect with her ancestor really awful enough to be left out in the cold? Swallowing her hurt, Aradia remembered that at least a witch had rescued her. Where had Wanda gone? Her heart sank with sudden fear that she had been abandoned. Again.

She peered around the loft space a bit more, then picked up her bag and flung it over her shoulder to explore farther. As an after thought, she dusted off her hat and forced it onto her curly hair, as her braids had become frizzy. If only she had packed a proper comb.

"Wanda?" Aradia called, creeping forward. "Wanda are you there?"

Still her footsteps crunched on leaves, so Aradia followed the trail to a door, which was barely ajar. Aradia opened the door, and rushed up the stairs. The view from the roof took Aradia's breath away and she stopped, clutching the rail. The city looked so different in the daytime, if she could call it that. The sky was a light green, the dark buildings contrasting sharply against it. Dark clouds formed wispy shapes, looking like eerie spirits. Instead of a sun there was a large ball of green fire in the sky. With a lurch in her gut, Aradia realized why it looked so familiar: it burned just like the green bonfire at her birthday. There had to be a connection between her and this place.

Wanda sat at the edge of the roof, hunched over her witchboard, her mask hanging around her neck. Aradia sighed in relief, and headed over. Sliding one leg over the edge and then the other, Aradia joined her, staring out at the city. Wanda looked up, a grin appearing on her face. Aradia's heart fluttered again.

"Morning, Dia! How did ya sleep?" Wanda asked.

"Okay I guess," Aradia said, flushing at the nickname just as her stomach made a loud complaint. "I don't suppose you have any food with you?"

"No, sadly. I always forget to bring some when I go out for the night, but I told Erz to bring some when he gets here. He shouldn't be long."

Aradia nodded and stared out into the city. Everything seemed so peaceful up there. Like she had not just lost her mother and her whole world all at once and was now sitting with a witch while spirits haunted a mysterious city. Maybe she was the link. Maybe Aradia herself was haunted. The ghosts of her guilt and shame were coming back to her.

"At least Samhain Night is over," Aradia said, shaking herself in the hopes of dispelling the nagging fear at the base of her neck.

"Uh, no it isn't," Wanda said in a confused tone. Aradia turned her head to face the witch.

"What?"

"I don't know how it is in the Old Country, but we have seven nights of Samhain. So seven Samhain Nights. Seven nights of absolute chaos and terror."

"Why didn't you say that before?"

Wanda shrugged her shoulders. "Guess I thought everyone just knew that."

Aradia continued to stare at Wanda, not sure what to make of her. Wanda was a real witch, green face and broomstick and all. She believed Aradia was a witch. And not just any witch, but the Holy Strega, the daughter of the Moon Goddess. Aradia took off her shoulder bag and opened it, taking out her book. Maybe there was something useful in there.

"What's that?" Wanda asked, jerking her chin at the book. Aradia stuffed the book back into her bag, suddenly feeling protective.

"Actually, it's private," Aradia said.

"Oh, come on. I wanna know what your magic is like."

"Well, you see, the thing about that is—"

A large, dark shape flew up from the edge of the roof, startling Aradia. It flew over the girls and landed somewhere behind them. Aradia held her bag, and the book in it, close. The girls stood up and turned around. Standing not far from them with an expression of contempt on his face was a ghostly pale teenage boy. Dark hair almost covered his blood-red eyes, which were glaring intensely at them. His arms were crossed over a black and green striped hoodie and black jacket. When he opened his mouth in surprise, he revealed sharp fangs that almost made Aradia gape in surprise too.

"So, this is Aradia, if she even is *the* Aradia," the boy said.

"Gods, Erz, don't be rude," Wanda said, gesturing. "Aradia, Erzeben."

"Hi," Aradia said slowly. "Are you, well, a vampire?"

Erzeben rolled his eyes.

"Some witches call us that, but the correct term is empusa, named after Empusa, a daughter of Hecate, who you should know is the Goddess of *Witchcraft*," Erzeben said.

"Erz, seriously shut up. Come on let's head inside, we're too exposed here," Wanda said.

Wanda headed back into the loft, Aradia trailing behind her while Erzeben kept his distance following them. When they were all inside and Erzeben had closed the door, Wanda turned to the empusa.

"Did you bring the mask and lanterns?" Wanda asked.

"And food?" Aradia added hopefully.

"Yes," Erzeben said. He removed three jack-o'-lanterns with a handle from a black shoulder bag decorated with pins, and gave one to Wanda, then one to Aradia. He put on a bat-winged half-mask and handed a half-mask decorated with moon symbols to Aradia. Aradia slid it on, which was surprisingly comfortable and easy to see through.

"I do not see why we are helping her though," Erzeben said as he pulled out pumpkin-shaped pastries, handing them to Wanda, who passed one to Aradia. "What if she's a fluffy bunny?"

"I'm sorry, fluffy bunny?" Aradia said as she took a bite from her pastry. It tasted like cinnamon-coated pumpkin pie, which was usually too sweet for her, but at the moment she did not care.

"Cowen, those without magic. How can we trust her? I don't know about you, but my parents always told me not to trust strangers, especially if they are strange witches from the Old Country. Like, what would your mom say?" Erzeben asked.

"She would be proud of me for not judging people, unlike you," Wanda bit back, wiping crumbs off her face and crossing her arms. "I can't believe how selfish you're being right now. I trust her enough. I mean, even Aradia's name was a secret among witches, so how else could she know it?"

"But why take the chance? With the Lantern ban on anything Old Country, we are putting ourselves at risk. All found cowen must be brought to the authorities. It's the law—you know that, Wanda."

"What ban?" Aradia said, finishing off her pastry.

Erzeben looked at her in surprise, like he had forgotten she was there. His face darkened. Wanda flashed Aradia a tight smile. "It's this stupid rule that if anyone claims to be from the Old Country they must be brought to the Lantern Coven. They view the Old Country as a threat or something, I dunno."

"For good reason!" Erzeben exploded. "They anger the spirits, especially the Lord of Samhain. It upsets the natural balance of things. Remember a few years back when a couple of witches were thought to be hiding a bunny in their basement? How they disappeared shortly after? It was on a Samhain Night."

Erzeben shook his head and started pacing across the room, his feet crunching on the leaves. "Goddess, it's like sometimes you do not have a brain, Wanda."

"Well you know what—"

"Enough, okay!" Aradia cut in, holding her hands up in defeat. "I'm not asking anyone to save me here. If you want to help me, great, but I'll make it on my own if I have to."

She did her best to look strong, even though her throat threatened to close with every word.

"I don't know what Erz is gonna do, but I'm going to look after you, make sure you don't get killed. You got that?" Wanda said, gently grabbing Aradia's hand. Aradia looked down at the warm touch, and as her heart hammered, she yanked it away.

"Why are you doing this? Why are you helping me?" Aradia asked. "You don't know for sure that I'm Aradia. I could be lying to you."

"Because I, I . . ." Wanda said. She sighed. "I would just like to have you here in one piece, alright? And if Erz is going to be a stick in the blood—"

"Hey," Erzeben said with a shrug, "I am just trying to be logical here."

"Whatever. We don't need your help, Erz, I just thought it might be nice if you did, but if you wanna be a heartless witch and don't want to, then we'll go on without you," Wanda said, walking back to the door. "Come on, Dia, let's go."

"Wait!" Erzeben said. "Where are you planning on going?"

Aradia looked at Wanda. Where could the witch possibly take her?

"We're going to find our way home. It's too far for me to smoke-travel, so we're probably going to have to take the train."

"What happened to Selene? Your broomstick?" Erzeben asked.

"It, uh, had a little accident," Wanda said, and she bit her lips like an unpleasant realization was just dawning on her. "My dad's gonna be super hexed about that."

"Are you sure it is such a good idea to bring someone from the Old Country to your dad's place?" Erzeben said.

"Stop being such a wart, Erz. Dad will be upset, but he'll understand," Wanda said as if trying to convince herself. "I mean, who could turn down the Holy Strega?"

"Still, I am not sure—" Erzeben said.

"Look, do you want to come with us or not?" Wanda interrupted, giving him a look. "I mean you can go back home now, no one's gonna stop you, but do you really want to spend Samhain alone in your mansion with Mummy and Daddy's servants? Like, aren't your parents away with their vampire cult or something?"

Erzeben seemed to draw himself up, trying to look very impressive. "It is *not* a cult, it is the Coven of the Dragon, the largest organization of empusae in Crone's Cross. They always meet the week of Samhain; it was how I was able to get out of the house in the first place."

"Whatever," Wanda said. "Are you coming or not? Bad Witches wear black, and Bad Witches—"

"Have your back. Yeah, yeah I know. I will come, but because you are my best friend, not for that," Erzeben said, shooting a side glance at Aradia.

Aradia glared and was about to say something back to him, but she stopped herself. Erzeben was not Gale, and this was not high school. He was a vampire, or empusa as he called himself, which made him dangerous.

"Good boy," Wanda asked, smiling impishly. The young witch swung open the door and boldly stepped outside. Aradia hurriedly headed out with her, not wanting to be left alone with a vampire who already hated her.

"If I die, I am haunting you both for all eternity, just to let you know," Erzeben said, following them out.

"Looking forward to it," Wanda said and put on her mask.

A shout cut through the air. "There they are!"

The teenagers turned around. Katherine Brew and two guards in black and orange uniforms flew toward them. They had been caught.

CHAPTER
Fourteen

The High Priestess and her guards approached quickly. Aradia's eyes went wide, dug her fingernails into her palms, and looked at Wanda and Erzeben. Wanda dropped her jack-o'-lantern and grabbed Aradia's and Erzeben's hands.

"You guys trust me, right?" Wanda asked.

"I'm starting to doubt that," Erzeben said. Wanda ran forward, pulling Aradia and Erzeben with her, heading straight towards the sharp edge of the roof. Aradia's eyes widened.

"Wanda, what are you doing?" she squeaked out.

Instead of answering, Wanda sped up and jumped off the edge, pulling Aradia and Erzeben with her. Aradia felt her arm pull her forward, until the terrifying moment her balance tipped and she fell, screaming as she plummeted downwards. This was it, this was how she was going to die, because she trusted some teenage witch she just met. Purple smoke formed around them as they hurtled towards concrete, clouding Aradia's vision.

The smoke cleared away quickly. They landed abruptly, Aradia's knees bending under her. They stood on some rough, dead grass, and Aradia's legs hurt from the impact, but they were alive. And then Aradia laughed as she realized what had happened. Wanda had teleported them onto the ground several streets away from the factory while in midair, Katherine and the guards flying around it in the far distance. Even as a witch, how could she possibly do that? Catching her breath, Aradia looked over to Wanda and Erzeben. Wanda looked exhausted, her breathing heavy, and Erzeben seemed too shocked for words.

Aradia took in her surroundings as she got up to her feet. The teenagers were next to a sidewalk lined with barren trees. Lampposts shaped like glowing green jack-o'-lanterns lit the streets, illuminating the industrial, concrete, and metal buildings around them. Some structures were lit with greenish light, but most were dark, although at each and every one Aradia could pick out the glowing green pinprick of a jack-o'-lantern glowing on the front door. She twisted around, craning her neck to stare up at the neon WITCH CITY sign looming above, posted at a crossroads next to a highway that snaked its way around the buildings, high above Aradia, Wanda, and Erzeben. The roads and streets were eerily empty, with only a few witches wandering about. It seemed most witches did not go out during Samhain after all.

"Wanda, you have got to warn me before you do something like that again," Erzeben said, his hand still on his stomach.

"I didn't exactly have time to. And we should really get going, before Miss Brew and her cronies come after us," Wanda said, getting up.

"Wait a second, it's because they are after Aradia, right? You do realize we're hiding a fugitive from the governing coven here? We could be locked away for that," Erzeben said.

"Oh please, as if you have had a problem with doing technically illegal stuff before. You're a Bad Witch, I think it's time you started acting like one," Wanda said.

Aradia smirked. At least someone was telling Erzeben off. But the guilt of possibly putting Wanda in danger crept into her. *You don't deserve her help anyway*, that same nasty voice in her mind told her.

Aradia cleared her throat. "If I'm going to always be a problem, maybe I should—"

"No, shut up," Wanda said without batting an eyelash. "I'm not giving you up to Katherine Shrew. Bad Witches have your back, and only a truly Wicked Witch would sacrifice someone else for their own safety. Whether we burn or fly, we do it together."

Wanda shot a glare towards Erzeben. The empusa went quiet. For a moment, an awkward silence stretched between the three of them, until they heard shouts in the air. The High Priestess and her goons were on the hunt.

"Let's go," Wanda said. Without another word, Wanda stepped off the grass and walked briskly along the sidewalk, keeping to the shadows. Aradia and Erzeben followed. They walked in silence, the few witches on the street paying no attention to them. Aradia looked at the city around her, trying to distract herself from the negative feelings that were bubbling up.

The road had been paved but clearly many years ago. They stepped over cracks like a spider's web between the dark, closely-packed buildings. There was nothing soft about this city; everything was made of sharp and crooked parts, sticking out like they wanted to trip Aradia and her new friends. Some of them reminded Aradia of a giant clockwork, with gears and pulleys protruding. Bridges and walkways connected some buildings to each other, and train-tracks and highways twisted high above them. Aradia itched to explore it all, but her eyes checked the skies for looming threats.

The road got wider, until they approached a small courtyard. In the center stood a large statue. It was of a very tall man, wearing long, flowing robes, and a wide-brimmed pilgrim hat, his face in shadow. In his left hand he was holding a lantern, in his right a broom. Aradia stared at it as they walked by, curious by it. He seemed familiar. Too familiar.

"Who is that statue of?" Aradia whispered.

"The King of Lanterns, rest in pieces," Wanda said, glancing up warily. She didn't break her stride as she continued, "He died some time ago on a Samhain Night. He was the Queen's husband. They both led the Lantern Coven together, but now she just leads by herself. And it means we're close."

"Close to what?" Aradia asked.

On the other side of the courtyard was a subway entrance, an orange sign with black lettering that read KING STATION. The doors were closed, and a notice was placed on the door. Wanda ran up to it and read it aloud.

"This station is closed due to magical difficulties. We will have it up and running as soon as possible. We apologize for the inconvenience!" Wanda said, frustration rising with every word. "Seriously? Of all times for the train to have magical difficulties! Some witches need the train! This is so hexing unfair! No wonder people disappear!"

"Well, taking this bunny back to my place would not be a good idea if you're still dumb enough to want to hide her. When my parents get back, they would hand her over to the Lantern Coven themselves, if they did not drain her first," Erzeben said, and the way his eyes trailed off Aradia had the distinct feeling he was talking about her blood. "You know what, maybe we should go to my place."

Aradia glared at him.

"Real charming, Erz," Wanda said.

"Well, I suppose we can always take her to Vivivine, she does not live far," Erzeben said.

"What good would that do? Vivivine's not even a witch," Wanda said. Not even a witch? If Vivivine, whoever and whatever she was, managed to live in Witch City without being a witch, then that gave Aradia some hope.

"No, but she is a rich socialite that is popular and has influence," Erzeben said.

"Ooo I'm Erzeben and my rich family is connected with other famous rich people," Wanda said sarcastically. "Fine, witchboard her, though I'll doubt she'll be of much help."

Erzeben smirked and took out his witchboard. Aradia watched as he moved the planchette around, her mind spinning. If Vivivine wasn't a witch, but somehow had influence, just what was she?

"Ugh, I can't get ahold of her. She's probably busy doing who knows what," Erzeben said.

"Told ya," Wanda said.

"Wait, the planchette is moving," Erzeben said, examining his witchboard. " 'Talk later. She busy now.' That's probably George, her husband. Which I guess means I will just have to witchboard her later."

Wanda groaned in annoyance. "Well, what do you witches wanna do then?"

The question took Aradia out of her gloom as she thought of the possibilities. There was so much of the city, so much of the world she wanted to explore. There were two mysteries in particular that she wanted to solve. She wanted to know what happened to Tituba, and what her connection was to Witch City, if there was one. But first she wanted to figure out how she got to the city. Aradia's thoughts turned to the woman on the motorcycle.

"Do any of you know anything about a lady named Trivia?"

Wanda grinned.

"No, but I know a place where we can find her."

CHAPTER
Fifteen

Aradia, Wanda and Erzeben moved as fast as they could through the city without catching too much attention. The city was an industrial forest made of green, black, and orange. The same symbol—a line crossed three times with crescent moons at the end and a pentacle at the bottom—appeared everywhere throughout the city.

"That's the Crone's Cross," Erzeben said when Aradia asked. "It's the symbol of the city."

Bright lights glowed in the middle of the day, and witches flew past them at high speeds. Wanda led them through the labyrinth of the streets, avoiding busier areas as much as possible, although there were not many.

"Where are you taking us?" Aradia asked as they approached a tower crowned with a large witch's hat.

"Hold on, we're almost there," Wanda said, running to the tower, motioning the other two to follow. Aradia and Erzeben trailed after her inside. They walked up a narrow staircase, illuminated by green lights hanging on the walls, their footsteps echoing metallically throughout the building. The staircase led to an open doorway, and when they reached it, breathing hard and legs exhausted, Wanda turned to Aradia and smiled.

"Trust me, it's gonna be worth it."

Aradia stepped through the doorway after the witch, and put her fingers to her chin as her mouth gaped open in wonder. They had stepped onto the brim of the witch's hat, giving an incredible view of the glowing city. Standing in the near distance was a gargantuan statue, its details clear and visible. It was of three women, each holding a glowing green torch. Aradia recognized the statue from the night before, but now she was able to see it all the more clearly. To the left was a young maiden, a crescent moon pointed up like horns rested on her forehead, her hair tied in a bun. She held a bow in her left hand, and was dressed in a short toga. The center was a matronly, regal woman, a sharp crown on long flowing hair. She held a dagger in her left hand, and was dressed in an elaborate gown, snakes coiled around her. To the right was an elderly crone, dressed in a hooded cloak, her features partially obscured. In her right hand she held a large key. The statues were beautiful and awe inspiring, as if they were goddesses themselves.

"That's the Hecate Trivia statue. It borders the two towns that make up Crone's Cross. Eastwitch, aka rich people-ville, is where we're at now. I live in Westwitch, but way on the other side. It would take us a hex of a long time to get there on foot, I'm talking days here," Wanda said.

"This city is massive," Aradia said, barely paying attention to what the witch was saying. "Are you saying that Trivia is another name for Hecate? The Goddess of Witchcraft?"

"Yup. She's kinda a big deal to lots of witches here. I didn't really know if I really believe in her, but she's called in a lot of spells and they usually work, so I dunno," Wanda said.

"How do you not know that Trivia is one of your mother's names?" Erzeben said, suspicion dripping from his words.

"Uh, I was raised by a witch named Tituba. She didn't tell me everything about my true mother. Sorry," Aradia said. Wanda smirked, looking at Erzeben. Ignoring the empusa's glare, Aradia took a few steps out, closer to the edge of the brim, drawn in by the magnificence of the statue. If Trivia was a name for Hecate, and if Trivia was the name of the woman that brought her to Witch City, could it be possible that the Goddess of Witchcraft brought her there?

"What do you want from me?" Aradia whispered.

"What was that?" Erzeben said.

"It was nothing, I—"

"ATTENTION CITIZENS OF CRONE'S CROSS!"

Aradia looked up. An orange globe materialized above the statue, and an image of a woman wearing a smiling jack-o'-lantern mask appeared in it. A large, dagger-like crown rested on hair shaped like a black heart. She was dressed in a black, Victorian dress, her shoulder-sleeves puffed.

"Who's that?" Aradia said. Before Wanda could answer her, the figure continued speaking.

"This is Gourdina, the Queen of Lanterns, speaking. I unfortunately have some distressing information to give to you all," the woman said in a calm, authoritative voice. "It has come to my attention that a Witch Hunter has been spotted in our noble city, last seen in Eastwitch. She goes by the name Aradia, as an insult to our beloved savior."

Aradia's eyes went wide. Why did the Queen think she was a Witch Hunter? There was no telling what the witches would do to her now.

"The Witch Hunter is but a teenager, but do not underestimate her," Gourdina continued, her voice as sharp as steel. "She has enlisted the help of a couple of teenaged witches to assist her in her wicked deeds. She has dark brown skin, black braided hair, and was last seen wearing all black and a lunar-themed mask. It could even be possible that she is a Monster Coven sympathizer, as she is dressed in similar attire. Approach with extreme caution if you must, although it is unadvisable to go near her. The Lantern Coven is doing its best to find her. If you encounter her, do not believe anything she says, and report her immediately to the Lantern Coven."

Aradia nervously looked back at Wanda and Erzeben. Would they believe the Queen and turn her in? Erzeben already seemed like he wanted to.

"Stay safe everyone, stay at home if you can," Gourdina said, her voice ringing out. "Remember, we are doing everything in our power to stop this threat."

The Queen of Lanterns paused, and almost seemed to be zeroing her gaze onto Aradia, making the girl feel small and suffocated.

"Lanterns light the way."

As the image of the Queen vanished, Aradia turned to Wanda and Erzeben.

"I swear, the Queen is lying. I'm not a Witch Hunter," Aradia said, holding her hands out in defense.

"Well obviously; you're the Holy Strega," Wanda said with a bored expression. "I never trust Lantern Coven propaganda."

"But what if she is a Witch Hunter?" Erzeben asked Wanda. "What if she has come here to infiltrate the city? She could be lying to you, Wanda."

"If she was a Witch Hunter she would've interrogated and killed me by now," Wanda said.

Erzeben squinted with suspicion. "Well, what does she have in her bag? She could be carrying knives and stuff in there, ready to kill us when we're no longer of use to her."

Aradia slid the bag off her shoulder and tossed it to Wanda. She had had enough of Erzeben already. "Look inside. You won't find any weapons."

Wanda shrugged and ruffled through the bag.

"There's a book called *The Salem Witch Book*, I dunno but that looks pretty witchy to me," Wanda said, glancing up at Aradia with a smile. "And hold on, what's this?"

Wanda pulled out a doll from the bag. It was Goody Poppet. Aradia's eyes went wide. She had forgotten she had taken the doll with her. Why had Candy given it to her in the first place?

"It's a poppet!" Wanda said excitedly. "See, Erz, I told you she's a witch! All she's got is witchy tools. I think it's time to give the poor girl a break. We know she's not a Witch Hunter, but the rest of the city doesn't. We need to keep her safe."

Wanda placed the doll back into Aradia's bag. Smiling, she held the bag out to Aradia. Erzeben still glared at Aradia with suspicion. Suddenly, he reached for his own bag and pulled out his witchboard, the planchette moving rapidly.

"It's Vivivine. She says we can head to her place tonight after moonrise, that 'she'll greet us with open arms,'" Erzeben said, eyes darting to the planchette's movements.

"Wonderful," Wanda said, rolling her eyes.

"If Vivivine isn't a witch, just what is she exactly?" Aradia said.

"Oh you'll see," Wanda said, her voice dripping with sarcasm. "She's 'larger than life and twice as electrifying.'"

CHAPTER

Sixteen

They wandered through the streets of the city, Wanda pointing out something every few minutes to Aradia. Aradia never tired of it: each jack-o'-lantern decoration, each witch statue, each broomstick display a new fascinating curiosity. A rebellious thrill spread up into Aradia's body with each step, breathing in the pumpkin-flavored scents. They stopped at a small Witch's Brew Café, practically a hole in the wall, to avoid detection and to have some lunch. Erzeben begrudgingly paid for their food. Aradia tried a delicious, green apple flavored potion, and a hard to swallow eye of newt soup, which at least warmed her body. After a few hours, the green sky slowly began to darken, and the trio left the downtown core to a quieter part of the city.

They arrived at an arch labelled WITCHCRAFT HEIGHTS. The buildings there were spread further apart, and not a single soul besides

Aradia and her friends were out. The roads in Witchcraft Heights were of yellow cobblestone, lined with dark, manicured hedges lined with red flowers, and full apple trees, Aradia inhaling the scent of fresh apples. Night had fallen, and their path was lit by orange lanterns hanging off posts, swinging from a whistling wind. They followed the road to a monstrously tall and wide stone tower, painted a light shade of purple. Faint music emanated from the building. It all seemed out of place on this dark and quiet night.

Aradia nervously checked that her mask held, and her hat was pulled down low as night crept in around them. She had untied her hair, so that it would not be in the noticeable braids Gourdina had mentioned. They approached the front door. It was painted a bright green, and a jack-o'-lantern with a cute face carved into it glowed on the front steps. Erzeben slammed the knocker on the door three times. They waited in silence for a few seconds, until the door swung open.

"Trick or treat!" an energetic voice called.

Standing in the doorway was an incredibly tall woman, with pale, grayish-green skin and visible stitches going down her arms, legs, neck, and face. Aradia stared in awe, looking the woman down to her black, platform heels, up to her black hair piled high on her head, lightning-bolt streaks of white going up the sides. She was beautiful and eerie, dressed in a sleeveless black dress, tied with an orange ribbon around her waist, long orange gloves that went up to her elbows, and a black lace mask that framed her large, orb-like eyes.

"Erzeben!" the tall woman said, her smile beaming and large. "So lovely to see you. It has been *such* a long time! And oh, what are your friends' names again?"

"You have met Wanda once before, and this is, uh . . ." Erzeben said, gesturing unenthusiastically at Aradia.

"Dia," Aradia interjected, blushing a bit as she used Wanda's nickname. She hoped her mask would hide it.

"So lovely to meet both of you!" the tall woman said. "My name is Vivivine, Vivivine Frankenstein, emphasis on the *steen*. Welcome to my humble home."

"Uh, Viv, are you having a party?" Wanda asked, peering around the woman's broad frame.

"Vivivine, dear. And yes, I am. I have a big one every year each Samhain Night. Did I forget to mention it?" Vivivine said. Erzeben and Wanda traded a look from behind their masks.

"I believe you did," Erzeben said finally.

"Oh. Well, silly me, you are all more than welcome to join in, the more the scarier as they say," Vivivine said, beckoning them in.

"Wait, how are we supposed to discreetly hide at your house when you have a party?" Wanda said.

"Wanda!" Erzeben said indignantly.

"Oh, don't you worry, you will be plenty safe here. There are so many people at the party that no one will notice. Hiding in plain sight is the easiest way to hide. And besides, when the clock hits the thirteenth hour, everyone cheers and goes home, for the Witching Hour will be over," Vivivine said, her grin never faltering. "Now, because Erzeben asked, and because he's the son of two good friends of mine, who sadly can never make it to my Samhain parties—they are so busy you know—I will keep you all here safe, but I simply must return to my guests. So come on in and enjoy the party."

They followed the Frankenstein woman into her house. The inside of the tower was expansive, seemingly larger on the inside. A spiral staircase stood in the center of the room, wrapping around a large fireplace and upwards around the chimney. It seemed to go endlessly skyward, no clear end to it in sight. Aradia clutched her bag strap tight, her fingers slightly trembling, as she watched the crowd. Witches danced to loud, energetic music playing from a DJ on an elevated platform, while others laughed and talked jovially as they sat at tables and stood around cauldrons. The energy of the room was high and joyous. It was almost too much.

"You okay?" Wanda yelled over the music.

"What?" Aradia asked.

"Are you alright? You look hexed out or something!" Wanda said.

"I'm—I'm fine. Just never been to a party like this before," Aradia said.

"You will have such a scream!" Vivivine said excitedly, sauntering off into the crowd.

"Don't worry about it. Just stick with us; you'll be fine!" Wanda said, gently grabbing Aradia's hand. "Trust me, it's not as scary as it looks!"

Aradia smiled nervously, trying to stay calm. Even Gale's parties were never this big, and they never had witches either. With so many witches in one place, was it really safe? If they thought she was a Witch Hunter, she would never make it out alive.

"Look, I think there's food over there!" Wanda said. "Let's get some!"

Aradia breathed in deeply, and let Wanda drag her through the crowd, Erzeben following. They made their way to a long table that had a small cauldron filled with red liquid, goblets next to it. There were plates that had varieties of snacks: pumpkin-shaped cookies, a bowl of candy corn, black and orange popcorn, slices of barmbrack bread, what looked like fried fingers, and caramel apples among other delights. Wanda immediately helped herself to the food, enjoying as much as she could. Although Aradia's stomach grumbled, she felt nervous enough that she was certain if she ate anything, she would probably be sick.

While Wanda busied herself with the food, Aradia turned to Erzeben as a distraction—and in the hopes of winning over another ally.

"Erzeben, how do you and Wanda know each other?" she asked.

Erzeben didn't even smile. "Why are you asking?"

"I was just curious," Aradia said, huffing out an awkward laugh. "Not everything has to be an interrogation, you know."

"No need to be snippy," Erzeben bit back, filling a goblet with a thick red liquid that looked like blood with a few orange slices floating in it. "Well, if you must know, Wanda and I met in school. Neither of us really had any friends at the time, so we just kind of stuck together. I was transferred from a private school because my parents were 'cutting unnecessary costs.' Everyone thought I was snobby, so they were not really nice to me—"

"I wonder why," Aradia muttered under her breath.

"Excuse me?" Erzeben said.

"Nothing," she said sweetly.

"Anyway," Erzeben said, eyeing her suspiciously, "one time Wanda and I were paired together to work on a potion in class, and we ended up spending the whole time making fun of our obnoxious classmates, and we have been together ever since."

Aradia's stomach flip-flopped when he said *together.* "So are you, well, dating?"

"What?" Erzeben stopped sipping his drink to glare at her. "You mean like courting? No. That would just be too weird on so many levels, and not in a good way. Besides, I am not into girls that way."

Aradia looked at Wanda, breathing out a sigh of relief. Even though she couldn't figure out why she felt so relieved. Wanda got her stare and smiled, making Aradia's face turn warm. The witch held out two caramel apples, presenting one to Aradia.

"You have to try these. They're so good, they're really sour and chewy, I've already had three of them," Wanda said, practically bouncing.

"I'm good, thank you," Aradia said, still not able to stomach eating anything.

"Come on, just one bite!" Wanda said, wagging the apple. Aradia was drawn in by the witch's infectious energy, unable to say no to her.

Dammit.

"Ok, fine," Aradia said, and leaned forward. She took a bite. It did had a very sour apple flavor, but also had hints of pumpkin spice, with just the right amount of caramel. Aradia's teeth sunk in, enjoying the chewiness of it.

"Well?" Wanda said, a grin on her face. Aradia nearly melted.

"You're right, it is very good," Aradia said, still chewing on the caramel.

"Told ya! You should try the popcorn, I swear the black and orange ones taste different," Wanda said, taking a bite from the other apple.

Aradia smiled, warmth in her chest, until memories of hanging out with Gale came flooding back to her, a pang of loss taking its place. Gale was always the louder, more extroverted one, but she was always there to listen to her, to include her in things. Until her birthday. She still thought it so unfair how she had immediately turned against her. Aradia had needed her and she had turned away in fear. She had to be careful to not let that happen again—which was probably why, she decided, Wanda made her so nervous.

Suddenly the front door blew open, as if by a fierce wind. A loud bang rippled through the room as everyone looked over, a wave of gasps following. Aradia could not see what had entered the tower over the crowd, but she felt herself getting more anxious. In a few seconds, the crowd stepped aside, making way for whatever was coming.

Aradia slid her way behind some of the guests and peeked through the cracks in the crowd. Two figures wearing large headpieces walked in. One was the High Priestess, her face stern, her headpiece a crescent moon. The other, wearing a headpiece of a golden sun, was a handsome man with sharp cheekbones and ebony skin, his eyes fierce and gold like a hawk's. He carried a large golden staff shaped like an ankh, which clicked loudly with every step he took. Gold and white robes trailed behind him over dried, ancient mummy linens, only his face visible. The Priestess and the man stopped, the man solemn, his golden eyes gazing around the room. Vivivine stepped forward from the crowd, smiling nervously, and made a slight bow.

"Lord Ra, Lady Katherine, what brings you to my humble little home?" Vivivine asked.

"Is there a cowan at your party? A girl from the Old Country?" Lady Katherine said.

"What? No, I do not believe so," Vivivine said.

"Are you certain?" Lord Ra said, his voice warm and deep.

"People from the Old Country do not just appear out of nowhere, your excellency," Vivivine said, her smile more strained than usual.

"Well one has," Lady Katherine said, "and she is a Witch Hunter!"

Several frightened cries echoed through the crowd. Aradia felt like the floor had gone out from under her.

"And you are absolutely certain of this?" Vivivine said. There was no trace of a smile on her broad, beautiful face now.

"Yes," Lady Katherine declared, her voice cutting through the crowd like an arrow. "I myself have encountered the Old Country girl, and have been on the hunt for her. There are some rebellious, teenage witches helping her, but for our own safety, she must be caught. She comes from Boston, a city near the Old Salem, where they hunted witches so viciously. The last of the witches left there at the end of the Burning Times, the ones that were not brutally murdered by the foul cowen. She would only come here to hunt us, to complete what her horrible ancestors had started."

Aradia's stomach turned, nausea surfacing.

"Samhain Night on its own is incredibly dangerous," Lord Ra said, scanning the room with his piercing gaze. "The Lord of Samhain has begun his Wild Hunt, and malevolent spirits, as you all know, roam the streets. Our greatest hope is to find the Witch Hunter and sacrifice her to him, so that he may spare the rest of us."

"Remember, harboring a Witch Hunter is illegal, and if anyone is discovered doing so, they will be punished with the utmost severity," Lady

Katherine added haughtily. "Do not show pity to this girl, and do not trust anything she says. She will likely burn us the first chance she gets. She goes by the name Aradia, a blasphemous insult to the Gospel of the Witches."

"If anyone finds the Old Country girl, bring her to Morrigan's Grove," Lord Ra said. "We will know what to do with her then. Merry part."

"And may the Goddess be with us all," Lady Katherine said. "Lanterns light the way."

The Hierophant brought his ankh staff down hard upon the ground so hard that it rang out with a loud crack. Glowing light came from the staff, and moved around him, entirely consuming him and the High Priestess, and in a moment they were gone. The crowd erupted into agitated shouts, growing louder and more frantic by the second.

"We need to get her out of here," Wanda said.

"What? Are you serious? If we take her anywhere, it should be to Morrigan's Grove!" Erzeben said, his voice becoming clear and sharp. "Accusing her of being a Witch Hunter is one thing, but if the Lord of Samhain wants her that is a much bigger problem!"

"We will not do that! They will sacrifice her!" Wanda said.

"There you are, children," Vivivine said, approaching them, forcing a tight smile. "I do believe it is necessary to get you out of here."

"What about your party?" Erzeben said, raising an eyebrow.

"My party can wait," Vivivine said, leaning in closer to them. "What I think is important now is to get Aradia away from a potentially angry mob."

"You still want to protect me?" Aradia asked, her head spinning. "Why?"

"Shh! Just wait here and don't act suspicious. I'm going to quickly get my husband," Vivivine said.

"What does your husband have to do with this?" Wanda said.

"Just wait a Walpurgis Night, everything will make sense. I will be back quicker than a kelpie to take you away. Okay?" Vivivine said with a smile and headed into the crowd.

"See, your mummy and daddy's friend thinks we should protect her," Wanda said, raising her eyebrows at Erzeben as if to say *I told you so.*

"But why?" Erzeben retorted. "It does not make sense to me, I mean—"

"Just shut up will you! We are not sacrificing Dia, alright?" Wanda interrupted.

"And how do you know Vivivine is not planning on doing so herself?" Erzeben asked.

"Because she could have just given her to the Lanterns. Besides, I thought you trusted her anyway," Wanda said. "Don't worry Dia, we'll get you out of here—"

"Attention! Attention everyone!" Vivivine's voice called. They looked over, and the crowd went quiet once more. Vivivine stood on the platform where the DJ was, a microphone with a pumpkin head in her hand. Standing next to her was a tall, stocky man with the same grayish-green skin as Vivivine, stitches visible on his face, his features hard and angular. He wore a black suit with orange pinstripes and an orange collared shirt, matching Vivivine.

"Thank you," Vivivine simpered at her guests. "As we can see, the Hierophant and High Priestess have given us some very shocking information. But, there is no need to panic. We do not know for sure if the girl really is a Witch Hunter, and even if she is, there is only one of her. We are not in a village being hunted by Puritans. This is *our* city that this alleged Witch Hunter is up against. There is no need to worry my friends, no need at all. Just everyone remain calm. I can understand if you all want to hurry back to your homes, but you are all more than welcome to stay for as long as you like if that will make you have a safe and spooky good time. Safety is our number one priority. Thank you."

Vivivine walked off the platform, immediately surrounded by guests bombarding her with questions until she disappeared from view. Aradia felt a tightness in her throat, like she couldn't get any air in her lungs. It was too much all at once.

"Whoa, it's gonna be okay," Wanda said to Aradia, placing a hand on her shoulder as she labored for breath.

"And how do you know that?" Erzeben said.

"Erz, come on," Wanda said, cxasperated.

A loud grunt startled Aradia. George appeared from the crowd close to the teenagers. He nodded at them, then turned and walked, snaking his way through the crowd.

"I think he wants us to follow him," Wanda said, grabbing Aradia's hand and chasing after him, Erzeben doing his best to catch up with them. A few people stared at them as they moved forward.

"Wait, where are you kids going?" an elderly witch called out, nearly grabbing Aradia's arm but they pushed past her, not stopping for anything. Most of the other witches were too involved in their own worries to notice them much.

George led them to a small, inconspicuous door at the back of the hall, away from most of the people at the party. He unlocked and opened the door, leaving it open expectantly for the three of them, but didn't say a word. Wanda headed in without a second word, pulling Aradia in with her, followed by Erzeben a moment later. George followed last and shut the door behind him. They were led into what looked like a sparse but clean garage, the only thing in it a large purple hearse. Standing next to it was Vivivine, a large pair of sunglasses on her face, her smile wide.

"How did you get here so quickly?" Aradia asked.

"Vivivine Frankenstein can find her way out of anything. It is one of my many talents," Vivivine said, beaming.

"Would you mind telling us what's going on?" Wanda asked. Vivivine let out a small sigh.

"I had a feeling that the Lantern Coven would crash my little party tonight. I'm sorry, but just because you are in a high position of power it doesn't mean I trust you with the lives of the young and innocent, especially when you have a doomsday message for us all. Children need to be protected, no matter where they come from, no matter the cost. Why, if I had my own children . . ." Vivivine broke off as if getting lost in thought. "Anyway, Samhain Night is dangerous but is not nearly as bad as people say it is. I am sure we will all be fine as long as we are careful. And besides, I promised Erzeben that I would protect all of you, and that is what I intend to do. I don't believe for a moment that this young lady is a Witch Hunter, and I have seen enough angry mobs in my lifetime to know."

"Where are you going to take us?" Aradia asked.

"My apartment on the other side of the city. Nobody but me and George know about it, so it will be a good place to hide until Samhaintide is over," Vivivine said, opening up a side door of the hearse, gesturing for them to come in.

Erzeben went forward first and climbed in. Wanda reluctantly followed. Aradia stood still, staring. So much had happened so fast and she did not know what to make of it, adrenaline still surging in her bloodstream. Vivivine held out her hand, and her smile softened.

"It is alright, I understand. This must all be very strange for you, and frightening. Especially since you are so young. How about you come sit with me instead?" Vivivine said, motioning to close the door.

"No, it's alright, thank you though," Aradia said. If she was going to get into a strange woman's car, she would prefer to be next to someone she trusted. Wanda. Vivivine nodded knowingly. Aradia took off her shoulder bag, and headed into the car. The inside had purple, cushiony seats along the sides of the hearse, completed with seatbelts. As she buckled in, Aradia heard Vivivine speaking quietly to her husband.

"I promise I will come back safely. I just, I just really need to do this. I love you so much," Vivivine said.

Aradia peaked out of the open door. Vivivine passionately embraced George, who was vacant and unresponsive. Aradia quickly looked away when Vivivine let go of her husband. The Frankenstein woman stepped into the car, and sat in the driver's seat. George shut the door behind her. Vivivine turned and smiled at the three of them.

"Are we ready to go?" They traded looks and then responded in nods. Vivivine turned to the wheel. The garage door opened and the hearse sped into the city, weaving between the few other cars on the road. Jack-o'-lanterns glowed brightly on porches, in windows and on posts hanging in the streets. It almost seemed like an ordinary Halloween night. But there was nothing ordinary about Halloween night in Witch City. There really were evil spirits, and jack-o'-lanterns really were protection from them. Witches and vampires, or empusae, were real as well, with real supernatural powers. What else was real? How much was there to the real Halloween?

"So who—or what—is the Lord of Samhain?" Aradia asked, staring out of the window to try to steady her spinning head.

There was a moment of quiet.

"Well," Vivivine said slowly, tapping her fingernails against the wheel. "Nobody really knows *what* he is exactly."

"He is a very powerful, dark entity, some say he's an ancient God of the Dead," Erzeben spoke as if reciting a story. "Others say he used to be an evil warlock that made a deal with a demon. He tricked the demon into letting him keep his soul, but when he finally died, he was not let into the

Underworld, and his vengeful spirit was forced to roam the earth forever. Whatever he is, he is the real reason we light jack-o'-lanterns on this night."

Aradia looked down. That sounded eerily similar to how her campfire story had gone. Perhaps the Lord of Samhain was really after her.

"But don't worry, the Lord of Samhain, along with all the other spooky spirits, returns back to the Underworld when the clock hits the thirteenth hour on the last night of Samhain," Vivivine said.

Aradia swallowed and stared out the windshield. In the distance, standing taller than the industrial buildings around it, a large clock tower loomed. The clock glowed orange like a pumpkin, vines like twisted arms creeping around it. The minute hand was pointed at thirteen, the hour hand was pointed just after seven.

The conversation ebbed, and soon the car filled with the gentle whirring of the engine and the faint noises of the city. Wanda eventually dozed off, her snores growing louder and louder, and Erzeben absently gazed out the window. This was really the first time since arriving in Witch City that Aradia could be alone with her thoughts.

What are you doing, have you lost your mind?

Something connected her, Tituba, and the city, but she was failing to draw any real conclusions. There had to be a reason for all of this, especially if it really was the Goddess of Witchcraft that took her there. Something told her she would find the answers she was looking for in Witch City, but she had not the faintest clue on where to find them. After Samhain was over she would go on the hunt for Tituba, this she promised herself. The girl would have to survive first. She wrote enough about monsters to know how much danger she was in.

And then Wanda shifted in her sleep, her head toppling onto Aradia's shoulder. A small, sad smile formed on Aradia's face. One thing she knew for sure is that she never had a friendship like this before, however temporary it might be. The exhaustion of the night's events weighed on her, and soon she, too, drifted off to sleep.

CHAPTER

Seventeen

Salem Village, January 1692

The girls moved forward together, their steps almost in sync. Dressed in their dark cloaks they looked like a sinister murder of crows against the whiteness of the snow. They approached the Reverend's house with purpose, Abigail in the lead. Abigail pushed open the front door, and led the march into the kitchen, where Tituba was stoking a fire. She looked upon them with apprehension, holding Violet close to her.

"I said before, I am not telling any more Barbados stories," Tituba said.

"We are not here for stories, Tituba," Ann Putnam said.

"Then what are you here for? I have chores to do, and so do you, Abby," Tituba said, pointing the poker to Abigail's direction. Abigail gave Tituba a sour look.

"Abby said you can predict the future. We want you to show us," Mercy Lewis, Ann's servant, declared.

"That is all fancy. I don't do no fortune-telling," Tituba said, turning back to the fire. The other girls looked at Abigail expectantly.

"I saw you, Tituba, casting a spell near the woods," Abigail said. Tituba whipped her gaze to the girl, her eyes wide with confusion and fear. Abigail smirked wickedly.

"Abby, I was not casting any spell. Do not say bad things like that," Tituba said, standing abruptly, dread creeping into her bones.

"But you did foretell what is to come in the future, did you not?" Abigail asked, tilting her head so her flat eyes flashed a smug warning. Tituba felt trapped. There was no explaining what had happened at the crossroads. What was certain is that the Reverend was not to know.

"What do you want, Abby?" she finally asked.

"Tell us the future. Show us what is to come," Abigail said. Tituba scrutinized the girl. The premonition of evil she had grew stronger. There was no easy way out of this. Tituba was no fortune-teller. But she remembered something that her former Mistress in Barbados had shown her years ago. It was a simple trick, a minor amusement really, but perhaps it would be enough to pacify the girls. And perhaps it would show if the Devil really was coming to Salem.

"So be it," Tituba mumbled. "Gather round the table, and be quick about it. The Reverend should be coming home well before sunset."

The girls, now with wicked glee, gathered around the kitchen table. Tituba looked to her daughter.

"Violet, go tend the Mistress, see that she is well."

Violet nodded and left the room. It was best if the girl was not involved. Tituba looked at the other girls, their gazes hungry. Yes, it definitely would be best. Tituba took a few glasses from the cupboards, filled them with water, and placed them on the table. She fetched some eggs from the cellar, and gave one to each of the girls.

"You only each get one egg; we shan't waste them," she said

"What do we do with them?" Abigail said, her voice sharp with excitement.

Tituba stared back just as sharply. "Crack the egg over the glass, and watch what shape the yoke makes. It will tell you what is to come. Your future husband perhaps, or where you shalt be, or if there will be riches in your future."

The girls took their turns cracking eggs over the glasses. Mary Warren accidentally spilled the yoke over the table. The other girls laughed.

"Can I have another one?" Mary asked.

"No, no more than one egg," Tituba said.

Mary sulked as she watched the other girls.

"Mine looks like a cross. Does that mean I shalt have a holy life?" Ann Putnam asked.

"Perhaps it means you will marry a reverend, like Abby's uncle," Mercy Lewis teased. Tituba looked over to Ann's egg. It was indeed in the shape of a cross. That troubled Tituba somewhat. A cross could have multiple connotations. Sacrifice and penance were what first came to mind. But it could also symbolize a crossroads.

"What it means is that you have many paths in your future," Tituba said, her voice heavy. "Some could lead to sacrifice, others to increase. It is up to you which path you take."

Ann Putnam seemed disappointed, but did not say anything more to it. Abigail cracked her egg, and when she looked over the glass she gave a terrible scream. Tituba rushed over to the girl's side.

"What is it, Abby?" she asked. Abigail continued to scream, and pointed to the glass. Tituba looked over. The yoke in the glass had formed into the shape of a coffin. The other girls looked over to see it as well, and they too cried out in terror. Tituba placed her hand over her own mouth, her feelings of dread returning all the stronger. If the glass did truly reveal the future, then it confirmed Tituba's biggest fear.

The Devil was coming to Salem.

CHAPTER
Eighteen

A radia woke up with a start. The dreams she had disturbed her, and they reminded her too much of when her so-called friends and her mother accused her of being a witch. She really had left everything about her old life behind. Not that she had much choice.

Aradia looked at the back of Vivivine's chair, the woman's hair towering above her headrest. The Bride of Frankenstein, or so Aradia assumed, was driving her, a witch, and essentially a vampire through a supernatural city. The girl had read *Frankenstein* before. The monster's bride was destroyed before she even was reanimated in the book. How was she even real? Did Mary Shelley base her story off true events?

Or did Mary Shelley create the monsters herself?

Aradia shivered and looked out the window to settle her nerves. The lights of the city were brighter than ever, hundreds of orange jack-o'-lantern faces spotting the cityscape. They still raced over a highway overpass, and Aradia caught a glance of many roads crisscrossing beneath it, lanterns lighting the roads.

"How far are we from your place anyway?" Wanda asked sleepily, brushing the sleep from her eyes.

"It has been a long time since I've been to this apartment, so I may have taken a wrong turn or two. But we should make it there soon, don't worry," Vivivine said, her cheerful tone never faltering.

"And you're sure of that?" Wanda pressed.

"Wanda, don't be rude," Erzeben said.

"Coming from the guy that wants to sacrifice Dia to the Lord of Samhain? Yeah, you're a model of perfect manners," Wanda bit back.

"Please, there is no need to argue," Vivivine said.

Just then Aradia felt her head whip forward and back as a violent force slammed into the side of the hearse. Her heart slammed in her chest. Was it the Lord of Samhain, or one of his undead minions? Had he found her, and was now trying to take her away? Aradia looked at Wanda, who seemed just as scared as she was.

"What the hex was that?" Wanda asked.

"I—I don't know. There aren't any other cars on the road. I'll drive faster," Vivivine said, and the hearse zoomed forward.

Aradia was slammed into the window violently as another force hit the hearse, the car sliding. Wanda clutched Aradia's hand. Aradia squeezed back just as hard. And then there came a clang from the roof. Something had landed on top of the hearse. Anxiety rushed through Aradia's body like waves, blurring everything around her.

"Hold on!" Vivivine called. The car lurched backwards, a spider-web crack appearing on the windshield. Another hit came, shoving the car back yet again and Aradia out of her seat—and the window shattered. Everyone in the hearse screamed. A large furry creature, with glowing yellow eyes, reached out gnarled hands. It grabbed hold of Vivivine who screamed and clawed at the creature, kicking out. The creature ripped her out of her seatbelt and pulled her through the smashed window.

"No!" Erzeben yelled. With no driver, the hearse spun completely out of control. Aradia, Wanda, and Erzeben were tossed around, slamming into the sides of the hearse. Aradia cried, tears streaming down her face, feeling as if she was a doll being violently shaken around. The car spun to the edge of the road. For one terrible moment Aradia felt the dip in her stomach of weightlessness, and then the freefall that pulled her upwards, yanking the scream out of her as the car went over the edge to the roads below. Aradia clutched her shoulder bag hard. They were going to die.

CHAPTER Nineteen

The hearse plummeted fast towards the ground. The air pressed in Aradia's lungs, her mind a screaming mess. At any moment they were going to make impact. Aradia braced herself for the end.

Purple smoke clouded her vision. Aradia's feet landed on solid ground, jolting her body, and the purple smoke faded away. She stood with Wanda and Erzeben at her side. They were a short distance away from the overpass and watched as the hearse fell to the ground, bursting into flames. Before anyone could catch their breath, Erzeben marched to Aradia, shoving his face up against hers.

"This is all your fault!" he yelled, and she was too shocked to even flinch. "If you had not been in the car, the Lord of Samhain wouldn't have sent those creatures to come looking for you, and Vivivine—"

"Hey! This isn't my fault, vampire!" Aradia shouted back. "I don't know what kind of creepy-ass monster that was, but it wasn't my fault!"

"Hey!" Wanda said, stepping in between them. "It was your idea to get Vivivine to drive us, remember that, Erz? And besides, whatever attacked us was not an evil spirit!"

"And how do you know?" Erzeben retorted.

"Think about it! Spirits don't have fur, ya dolt! I don't know about you, but what attacked us looked awful like a winged monkey," Wanda said. Erzeben stepped back, taking off his mask, and rubbed impatiently at his eyes. Almost like he was crying.

"I am sorry. This has all been too much," Erzeben said, his voice breaking.

"You know what, I'm scared too, this is all new to me," Aradia said. She had meant for it to sound strong, confident, but her voice was small. "My home is, or was I guess, nothing like this place. But just because I'm not from here, it doesn't mean I deserve to be treated like trash. I had enough of that in the Old Country. I don't need it here."

With that, Aradia picked up her bag and strode away.

"Where are you going?" Wanda asked.

"I'm going to try and find Wonderland Station, and see if I can find my way to the Old Salem, the other Witch City. I think this one's beyond saving," Aradia said.

"Shut up. You would die trying to find it," Wanda said. "Without us, you'd be a ghost by the end of the night."

"I'm the Holy Strega remember?" Aradia laughed hollowly. "And even if I wasn't, why go through all of this? Why protect me?"

"Because!" Wanda said, catching up. "Bad Witches have your back! Once I've decided that I'm going to look out for someone, they're my coven and that's that."

Her heart swelled. Wanda, a stranger, wanted to help her. Just like Vivivine had tried to. At that realization, she felt her hope deflate.

"I don't want to hurt you," she said, staring down at the ground. "I should really go."

Wanda grabbed Aradia's arm.

"Please," Wanda said, turning to shoot a look at Erzeben. "Erz."

Erzeben looked downwards.

"To be honest Aradia," the empusa said slowly, "you are not what I am afraid of. It's this night. Especially what happened last year with—"

"We are not talking about this right now Erz," Wanda interrupted, her eyes dark.

"Why, what happened?" Aradia said. An awkward silence stretched between them as Wanda tried to look anywhere but at Aradia.

"I lost someone, that's all I want to say about it," she finally said.

"I'm sorry," Aradia said.

Wanda flashed a thin, sad smile. "Wasn't your fault."

"No, that wasn't," Aradia said, crossing her arms. "But you both getting hurt because you're helping a 'Witch Hunter' would be. Vivivine has already been abducted, I am putting everyone in danger."

"Well, being out on Samhain Night puts us in danger no matter what, right? And—" Erzeben stopped in the middle of his speech, looking up. Aradia and Wanda followed his gaze. A group of witches flying in a straight, horizontal line were flying in their direction, carrying orange searchlights. The Lantern Coven.

"Run," Erzeben said.

The trio turned and ran to the maze of overpasses, keeping in the shadows as best they could. The orange light continued to follow them, Aradia tensing at the idea that they might have been following them. They hid under the nearest overpass, pressing tight against a pillar in the shadows. Aradia held still as best as she could, too scared to even breathe, her heartbeat pounding in her ears. Wanda knocked over a nearby hanging lantern, pitching them into complete darkness. The orange searchlights continued forward, reaching to the end of the shadows. For a few tense seconds it paused, threatening to expose them. The lights passed over the overpass, and continued forward, Aradia exhaling in relief.

"Yeah, there is no way in Tartarus that I'm letting you go out on your own," Wanda said in a loud whisper, when the searchlights were no longer in view. Aradia nodded, relenting. If she were to be captured by the Lantern Coven, there would be no chance of her survival. It would be better to stick with witches that actually knew the city than try to navigate it on her own.

"So, where do we go now?" Aradia said.

"Our best bet is to head west I think," Wanda said slowly, "and try to find some place to sleep on the way. Erz and I's old meeting place is a huge no now that the Priestess found it."

They walked out from under the overpass, and moved alongside the road, Aradia glad the roads were empty. She walked as close to Wanda as she could, not wanting to leave her side. Now that she had cooled down from the anger at Erzeben, and the stress of the accident, she realized just how much she needed Wanda. The young witch was the only one Aradia could count on.

Erzeben walked slowly next to the girls, his head downwards. Aradia wondered why he seemed so glum, then mentally chastised herself for being insensitive. Vivivine was a friend of his, or at least his family's, and she had been abducted by furry, demonic things, her fate dismal. Aradia liked Vivivine too, how kind she was and keen to protect them. She'd hate to think something bad was happening to her.

"Is there anything we can do to save Vivivine?" Aradia said after a long moment of walking in silence. "Like, what was it that attacked us?"

"Like I said, I think it was a flying monkey," Wanda said.

"A flying monkey? Those are real?" Aradia asked, not sure why she was even surprised anymore.

"Yup. The Wicked Witch of Westwitch controls them," Wanda said matter-of-factly. Aradia nearly laughed in spite of herself. A Wicked Witch controlled flying monkeys, like *The Wizard of Oz*. Another classic story proving to be real, at least partially. Did that mean there was magic in these stories?

Or was it the storytellers?

"The Wicked Witch, she's the one in charge of the Monster Coven, right?" Aradia asked.

"You got it. They're probably using tonight as an excuse to cause terror, and abducting a famous socialite like Vivivine is the perfect way to do that," Wanda said. "It's a good thing we're headed west, because that's where we'll find them."

"Wait," Erzeben said, stopping in his tracks. "Are you suggesting that we try to find the Monster Coven, spearheaded by the wickedest witch in existence, and try to rescue Vivivine from their evil clutches? Are you mad? Have you completely lost your brains?"

"Isn't Vivivine your mom's friend or something?" Wanda asked, turning to face him. "You'd just let her die at the hands of some nasty old hags? The Monster Coven is evil, and just wanna cause chaos in Witch City. Who knows what they would do to a rich famous person like Vivivine. And you're okay with that happening? I really thought you had more of a heart than that."

"No, but, but . . ." Erzeben said. "But what if she is already dead?"

"Fine, then let's try to find our way to my home, that's also west. My dad's probably worried to death about where I am anyway. One thing I know for sure though is that by the time Samhain is over, Vivivine will be long gone," Wanda said.

"You know what, fine! Let's go look for her! Everything is so melodramatic with you, you know that?" Erzeben said, raising his hands in defeat.

"I'm just saying it how it is," Wanda said.

"Is there anyone that can help us? I mean three witches against a coven, that doesn't sound like it will end well," Aradia said, then hastily added: "Even for the Holy Strega."

"Well, there is someone who might be able to help us. He knows the streets of Westwitch pretty well, even more than Wanda," Erzeben said, scratching the side of his neck.

"Debatable, but I'll allow it," Wanda said.

"Why, who is he?" Aradia asked.

"His name's Calaveran. He's a powerful brujo who's good at death magic, and also our friend. We met him last year at a party we crashed. He was the DJ," Erzeben said, his pale cheeks slightly blushing. "I think we should summon the third Bad Witch."

A loud rumbling sound came from behind them. Aradia looked back. A green light was headed in their direction, zooming along the road so fast it seemed to blur with a comet tail. Was it a car? Or was it something more sinister, like one of the Lord of Samhain's spirits? Aradia looked over at Wanda and Erzeben, who also looked unsure.

"Let's run," Wanda said.

They ran down the side of the road, Aradia's heart thundering in her ears. If there was something really bad, would they even have a chance at outrunning it? As the noise got louder it sounded familiar, like a sound that

Aradia heard many times before. It was the revving of motorcycles. She looked back. There were two of them, driving very fast, heading down the road in their direction. She whipped her head around, eyes following the glowing green bikes as they passed.

The teenagers slowed. Aradia thought that they missed them, but the bikes stopped a short distance ahead of them. She watched their riders dismount. As they walked slowly towards the teenagers, Wanda and Erzeben moved closer to Aradia.

"What are three kids doing out on a Samhain Night?" a voice called.

"What's it to you?" Wanda shot back, conjuring a fireball in her hand. "What are *you* doing out on Samhain Night?"

The figures stopped in front of them. Aradia vaguely made out that one of them was likely a woman, and that she wore a leather jacket and a snakeskin dress over leather leggings, her face concealed by a biker's helmet. The other was a tall, broad-shouldered man wearing a leather jacket and black jeans, his face also concealed by a biker's helmet, two horns protruding from it. They stood still, facing the trio, eerily blank faces tilting in curiosity.

"We take it upon ourselves to patrol Witch City on Samhain Nights, keep watch for any impending attacks from the Samhain Lord," the biker woman said.

"Does the Queen of Lanterns know about this?" Erzeben asked.

"No, and we like to keep it that way. Vigilantes are not exactly appreciated by the Lantern Coven," the male biker said.

"Vigilantes?" Wanda repeated.

"And you are not afraid of the evil spirits?" Aradia asked suspiciously. The figures let out a conspiratorial laugh.

"No, you can say we aren't," the woman said. "So, where are you little witchlings headed?"

"We're searching for a friend," Wanda said.

"Well, perhaps my companion and I could help. The safety of our city's citizens is our number one priority, especially on a Samhain Night," the male biker said.

"Why should we trust you?" Aradia asked. "Why should we trust two random bikers to take us anywhere safely?"

"Because if you don't," the woman said, pointing a two-pronged wand at Aradia and Erzeben, as the man pointed one at Wanda, "nobody is going home safely. We know who you are, and we know that you are the Witch Hunter and that the Lantern Coven wants you sacrificed to the Lord of Samhain. And we intend to deliver you as ordered."

"These are Stangs of Cain. One blast from these will bring instant death," the male biker said. "Now, I recommend that you come along with us. We don't need to make any messes, do we?"

Aradia glanced over to Wanda, hoping that she would somehow fight against their attackers. But, for the first time, the witch seemed completely vulnerable. Her brave face was lowered; her eyes glistening under her mask. If Wanda felt scared, that meant greater despair for Aradia. She was nowhere near as brave or as strong as the witch. Aradia grabbed Wanda's fireball-free hand—for strength or comfort she was not sure. Wanda turned to her, her eyes searching from her mask. And then, so subtly, she nodded and flicked her wrist. The fireball shot at the male biker, and purple smoke appeared around the three of them. Aradia heard an electrical blast, but the purple smoke already consumed them, protecting them.

The smoke cleared, and the three of them were standing next to their assailants' motorcycles. Erzeben looked over at Wanda as if she was out of her mind.

"You don't know how to ride a motorcycle!" the empusa said.

"How different can it be really from riding a broom?" Wanda asked, straddling a bike. She smirked at the other two. "You both better come on, because biker lady looks hexed."

Aradia glanced back. The male biker was on fire, and his companion was furiously looking around her, shouting in the air. As the trio stared at her, she noticed the three of them, and broke into a sprint. That was all the urging Aradia needed—she got on the motorbike and held Wanda tightly.

"There isn't room for the three of us on there," Erzeben said. "And there is no way in Tartarus that I'm driving the other one."

"Turn into a bat and follow us then; we have no time," Wanda said.

Erzeben looked annoyed, but he closed his eyes in concentration. He morphed into a large, black vampire bat, Aradia flinching. Tearing her eyes away from the boy-bat, she forced herself to ask, "Are you sure you know how to drive this?"

"Sure enough, hold on," Wanda said, and chanted something under her breath. A green light emanated throughout the entire motorcycle, and Aradia felt it surging with energy. The motorcycle rumbled as it revved up, and just as the female biker shot a red electrical blast at them, the bike took off onto the road.

A rush took over Aradia's body, her senses electrical and alive. Wanda's hair blew into Aradia's face as her own hair blew back, whipping against her cheeks. It was exhilarating. Erzeben flew next to them, doing his best to try and keep up with them. Aradia heard a couple more blasts, random streetlights exploding.

"SHE'S FOLLOWING US!" Erzeben yelled over the wind.

Aradia glanced back, gripping Wanda's waist even tighter. The biker woman was coming up close behind them on her own bike. The adrenaline in Aradia's veins increased, the rush growing even stronger. She thought she should have been scared—after all, this was an incredibly dangerous situation—and she had been in nonstop danger since arriving in Witch City. But now there was something oddly thrilling about being in the chase. Maybe it was the adrenaline, the rush, but the part of her that usually let herself be consumed by anxiety seemed to be shut off. Maybe it was her arms wrapped around Wanda, who whooped into the cold night air as the bike zoomed forward and the wind rushed, weaving their hair together.

Maybe she should write more about these things.

The motorcycle headed into a tunnel under a bridge that was lit by glowing green lanterns. How much further could they go? Aradia heard a shot and a loud crack and one of the lights when out. They drove on in the darkness, red electrical flashes shooting around them, until they finally reached the dimly lit streets. They sped on past the green and orange lights of the city, the colors blurring together. Aradia had never been more terrified and excited in her life. The road diverged into three paths ahead, and Aradia felt the bike tugging them forward.

"WHICH WAY ARE WE GOING?" Aradia shouted.

"JUST WAIT!" Wanda replied.

At the last minute, Wanda leaned hard, and the motorcycle swerved, Aradia's heart thumped in her throat as they careened down the road on the right, which led up to a highway. The biker woman missed the turn, disappearing straight down the road. Wanda let out another whoop, and

Aradia let herself relax into the other girl's back. They continued to drive fast into the night, Erzeben flying right behind them. Aradia smiled. They had lost their pursuer. At least for now.

CHAPTER

Twenty

They drove through a maze of highways. The occasional witch flew by, a streak of shadow in the sky, but the roads were mostly empty. As the minutes passed, Aradia's teeth began to chatter from the wind. The lights of the city sped past them, jack-o'-lantern grins vanishing in an instant. They drove further and further east, and Aradia felt her arms and legs cramp from holding on tight. She could only imagine how Erzeben was feeling; it looked like the empusa was struggling to keep up with them, but she did not really feel sorry for him.

"DO YOU KNOW WHERE YOU'RE GOING?" Aradia finally yelled over the wind.

"HOPEFULLY!" Wanda shouted back. Aradia did not find this very reassuring. She rested her head on Wanda's shoulder and closed her eyes.

The girl could not stop the chaos happening around her, but she could try to ignore it for a little while.

A vision of young women dancing around a bonfire flashed before her. Aradia smelled the smoke and heard the women laughing raucously. She wanted to join in, and suddenly she found herself dancing around the fire, the flames and the women blurring into each other. A warm joy rose in her body, and she did not want to stop.

The joyous laughing twisted into horrified screams and the fire whipped out in an instant. Aradia opened her eyes, jarred. The screams in her mind faded, until all she heard was the humming of the motorcycle. Had she fallen asleep? Those visions, they seemed so real. Perhaps the magic of this city was affecting her. The buildings around them seemed more familiar. They were no longer on a highway but on the main road. They drove past the factory where the High Priestess had discovered them. They were getting closer.

They reached the crossroads where the neon WITCH CITY sign stood. Wanda pulled the motorcycle over to the side of the road and got off. Aradia slowly got off, shaky from the journey, happy when her feet touched solid ground again. Erzeben landed on the seat of the motorcycle and slowly transformed back into his regular self. He looked worn out and was breathing heavily.

Wanda, slowly like she too was exhausted, conjured a fireball and looked around. There was no one around. On a brick wall behind her, the words MONSTERS NEVER DIE were spray-painted. Despite the quietness of this part of the city, Aradia had a sinking feeling that they were not alone. Wanda extinguished her fireball and sat down on a nearby bench.

"Well, I just drove for at least an hour on a motorbike, which I've never done before, and tonight has already been a long night, so I'm going to sleep," Wanda said.

"I'm pretty tired too, but are you really going to sleep on a bench in the middle of the night?" Aradia said. Wanda shrugged, and laid on the bench, closing her eyes.

"Okay then . . ." Aradia said.

"You get used to it," Erzeben said, getting off the motorcycle. "At a party we crashed last year she ended up sleeping on the ceiling."

"On the ceiling?" Aradia repeated, sure she had misheard.

"And that was not even the first time she's done that," Erzeben said. Aradia smiled in spite of herself. The young witch looked so peaceful lying on the bench, as if there were not a hundred things to worry about. She envied that. The girl could not remember the last time she actually had a peaceful sleep.

"So, what's going on with this third Bad Witch anyway? Are we still going to meet up with him, or what?" Aradia said.

"Right, let me witchboard him," Erzeben said, taking out his board, immediately moving the planchette around.

"Do we need him? I mean no offence but if Vivivine's life is in danger, should we really just be waiting to hear from him?"

"Trust me, no one wants to save Vivivine more than me, she's practically my aunt. But we're talking about the Monster Coven here, we'll need all the help we can get," Erzeben said, his voice growing softer. "He's a lot more streetwise than Wanda and me. I know Wanda thinks she's a tough witch, but he really is the real deal. And, I don't know, but I always just feel more safe I guess when he's around. If anyone can find Vivivine, it would be him."

"I see," Aradia said. There was an awkward silence. Aradia felt herself warming up a bit to Erzeben, but she still did not fully trust him. Keeping her distance, she went over to the bench and gently tried to nudge Wanda slightly over. The witch was a little heavier than Aradia thought, and she wouldn't budge. There was not much room on the bench for both of them, so Aradia settled on sitting in front of the bench, placing her bag in her lap, her shoulders against the seat. It was rather uncomfortable, and despite how exhausted she was, she could not sleep. Her thoughts were going nonstop. Her birthday, her mother, Tituba, Trivia, Vivivine. So much had happened in such a short time.

Aradia pulled out *The Salem Witch Book* from her bag, trying to calm her thoughts. Maybe if she read more of it there would be some clue as to why this was all happening to her. It was a long-shot, but she had nothing else. She looked at the index, searching for something familiar that could point her in the right direction. Her finger stopped at a word she had not been expecting.

Candy. Wasn't that the name of the cashier at the witch shop? Aradia had come far enough to know that this couldn't be a coincidence. Candy had given her that doll, Goody Poppet, for seemingly no real reason other than she thought the girl would find it useful. Aradia flipped to the page the index listed, seeing if there really was a connection.

Aradia heard something low like a growl. She looked up. Had someone said something? She slowly stood up, cautious. There did not seem to be anyone else around. From her peripheral vision she made out a dark shape lurking beneath one of the streetlights. It had long spindly fingers, reaching out. Under a tall, wide-brimmed hat, a sharp grin and triangle eyes glowed green. Did it have a jack-o'-lantern for a face? Aradia tensed up. Was that the Lord of Samhain? She gazed directly at it, but it was gone.

"Wake up! Wake up!" Erzeben's voice called. Aradia, as if broken free from a trance, shut her book and stuffed it in her bag. Wanda slowly sat up on the bench. Erzeben looked up, and Aradia and Wanda followed his gaze. Several witches were flying above the cityscape, orange searchlights illuminating the city below. A few of them were headed in their direction. Wanda immediately got to her feet.

"It's the Lanterns again! We've got to hide!" Wanda hissed.

"Where?" Aradia asked, gesturing at the wide open space around them. "Can you turn us invisible or anything?"

"No, that is university-level spell-casting," Wanda said.

"Perhaps I can do the next best thing," Erzeben said slowly.

The witches flew closer to them, their lights shining down the streets. If the Lanterns discovered them, they would have to be on the run again. Aradia hated feeling so helpless. She looked over to Erzeben. He was mumbling words under his breath, his eyes turning from blood red to black. A black smoke-like substance floated out of his mouth. A slight pang of revulsion formed in the pit of Aradia's stomach watching it happen. The substance surrounded the three of them, until all Aradia saw was blackness. The substance did not feel thick like smoke, but was cold, as if they were encased in shadow. Aradia could only hear the rapid beating of her own heart.

After several minutes the dark substance faded away. Aradia looked up. The witches with their searchlights had passed over them, and were nowhere to be seen now. She looked back at Erzeben. His eyes were red again, and he looked even more exhausted than before, his chest rising and falling.

"Thanks, Erz," Wanda said. "We've got to be more careful. The Lanterns will have witches everywhere looking for us now."

"Why did you do that?" Aradia asked. "You could've let them take me."

"Bad Witches wear black, and Bad Witches have your back," Erzeben said through labored breaths, "and Bad Witches have your back. I do not like it, but we are in this together now."

Aradia looked at him inquisitively. What was going on inside of his head? He certainly would be an interesting character study. Maybe she could trust him. Maybe.

"We need to find a place to stay the rest of the night, and come back here tomorrow night to meet Cal. I can probably get the motorcycle running again but we probably shouldn't go too far," Wanda said.

"I've been messaging Cal. Maybe he knows someone close by. I'll witchboard him again," Erzeben said, reaching into his pocket.

"It's pretty late. How is he even still awake?" Aradia asked, stifling a yawn.

"He's even more nocturnal than I am, I would not be surprised if he had some empusa in him," Erzeben said, not looking up from his witchboard.

"I bet you'd like that," Wanda said with a cheeky grin. Erzeben's pale cheeks turned a slight pink as he continued to move his finger around the board. His eyes shifted from wide with excitement to scrunched with disapproval.

"What's wrong?" Wanda said.

"Nothing's wrong," Erzeben said, continuing to move his finger around the board. "He said his ex-girlfriend lives close by and that we might be able to stay with her."

"Ah," Wanda said, as if that explained everything.

"Who is she?" Aradia said.

"Baroness Brigitte. They broke up some time ago. She's . . . interesting," Erzeben said, judgment laced through his voice.

"We've only met her a couple times. I always thought she was cool. She's into that Voodoo stuff," Wanda said. Aradia's memory flashbacked to school, to her teacher mentioning that Tituba taught Voodoo to the village girls. She wondered if there was any truth to it. Maybe while they stayed with Baroness Brigitte she could teach her about Tituba and what her magic really was. Her heart leapt at the idea.

"Apparently Baroness is not happy with the idea, but she will allow it this once," Erzeben said, looking up from the board. "She lives on Crescent Street."

Wanda cracked her knuckles.

"Alright, that's not too far from here," the witch said and turned to Aradia. "You ready for another motorcycle ride?"

Aradia thought of holding Wanda close again as they rode through the night. Her cheeks warmed.

"Absolutely."

CHAPTER
Twenty-One

Wanda parked the motorcycle sloppily in front of a small, rustic cottage, which stuck out against the large, concrete buildings near it. A glowing red-orange light emanated from the windows, giving the house a look of a fairytale witch's cottage. Sitting at its doorstep were a couple jack-o'-lanterns with intricate symbols of crosses, hearts, and diamonds carved into them. Wanda approached the cottage door first and gave three hard knocks.

Aradia glanced at Wanda. What would Baroness be like? If she really did practice Voodoo, it would be different from the Triple Goddess-inspired witchcraft she had seen so far. Voodoo was just as maligned as witchcraft was by her mother; it was all the Devil's work as far as Tana was concerned. But her mother had been wrong about witchcraft, so perhaps she was wrong about Voodoo as well.

The door opened, framing a tall figure standing in the threshold against the red-orange light. She was a young woman, slightly older than Aradia, with dark skin that glowed like the night sky. Her arms were crossed over a regal purple dress, which matched her dark purple braids piled high on her head. She looked over her purple, round glasses in disapproval, lips painted a deep purple pursed in judgment.

"Hi. Thanks for letting us stay here tonight," Wanda said, stepping forward.

"Not so fast," Baroness said in a smooth, husky voice. She raised a hand against Wanda's shoulder. "I'm not taking in a fugitive and her friends without something in return. Last thing I need is the Lantern Coven to come swooping down on me with a holy vengeance because I helped an accused Witch Hunter."

"What do you want?" Aradia asked.

"What do you got?" Baroness said.

Aradia, Wanda and Erzeben looked at each other. Erzeben's food was all gone, and they had lost track of their lanterns some time ago. Aradia did not have much, but she did have a little bit. She pulled her bag off of her shoulder and sifted through it, pulling out Goody Poppet. She held it out to Baroness, who looked at her with curiosity.

"Will this work?" Aradia said. Baroness took the doll from Aradia's hand, and examined it.

"Where did you get this from?" Baroness asked, her brows drawing together.

"I got it from a lady named Candy in Boston."

Baroness looked up at Aradia with something like surprise on her hauntingly beautiful face.

"This will do," she finally said. "Come in."

The three of them followed Baroness into her cottage. Trails of smoke wafted in the air, carrying with them the smell of sage. They stepped on hardwood floor decorated with beautiful purple rugs. Flowery wallpaper and portraits framed with elaborate borders covered the walls.

"Take off your shoes," Baroness ordered. "I don't need you dragging in your dirt and mess into my sacred home. And all of you need to take a shower before you touch anything. Y'all smell like corpses and look like grave-dirt. It's not cute."

ARADIA LIED AWAKE ON THE FOLDED-OUT COT IN BARONESS'S PARLOR ROOM, Wanda sleeping next to her. Erzeben slept on a purple couch across from them. Wanda's skin almost glowed in the moonlight creeping in through the cracks of the curtains, and Aradia felt a strange pull, like her fingertips itched to reach out and stroke that skin. She wanted to run her fingers through Wanda's hair, which was sleek and soft from her shower. Aradia forced herself to look away from Wanda. She wished things could be simple for once, there was too much going on, and way too much to figure out.

A door creaked, and Aradia sat up and scanned the darkness for the noise. It seemed to be coming from the hall. Slowly, she slid off the cot without disturbing Wanda, and walked as gently as she could to avoid making the floor creak too much. Aradia crept into the hallway to investigate, and discovered that a door was left slightly ajar, a glowing light pouring out from behind it. The girl approached it slowly, feeling her blood pumping through her body. She cringed and froze every time the floor gave under her, but as nothing came out to stop her, she risked making another step. Eventually she reached the door, and holding her breath, peered through the crack.

Baroness was kneeling in front of an elaborate altar covered with pillar candles. In the center was a large illustration of a beautiful, soft-featured woman with her hair in a white wrap. She seemed to be staring right at Aradia, the uncomfortable feeling of being watched tingling her skin. Next to the illustration were smaller images of what looked like saints, although it was hard to make them out exactly. Baroness was holding out the doll Aradia had given her and was sprinkling something on it. She was whispering something, but Aradia could not quite make out what it was.

The door opened further with a loud groan, Aradia realized with a start that she was leaning on it. Baroness spun around. Her face was painted white like a skull, but that wasn't what made Aradia jump back. The young woman's eyes were milky all the way through, just as ghostly. Aradia tripped as she stumbled back, a gasp pulled from her lips. Baroness raised her hand, her palm out. The door slammed in Aradia's face, nearly hitting her nose. Without another second passing, the girl ran back to the parlor and climbed into bed. She hoped she had not made another enemy in Witch City.

CHAPTER

Twenty-Two

Salem Village, February 1692

Tituba tried to calm the girls, but nothing seemed to work. She tried laying warm, damp cloths over their foreheads, but the girls screamed as if they were being burned and threw the cloths away. She tried feeding them some hot broth, but they knocked the bowls onto the floor, spilling the broth into steaming puddles. Tituba even attempted saying some prayers that she had learned from the Reverend's sermons over them to calm them down, but it only made the girls scream louder. The woman watched with hopelessness as Abigail and Betty thrashed in their beds, screaming out as if they were being stabbed. There was no doubt in Tituba's mind that the evil hand was upon them.

"Tituba," the Reverend said, entering the room, "leave the girls be. Dr. Griggs is here to see what ails them."

Tituba looked to the Reverend. He was a tall, sallow-faced man with white hair, his pale face a permanent frown. He was accompanied by another grim-faced man, the *both of them dressed in dark, gloomy clothing. Tituba nodded and left the room, eager to get out of there. She cared for the children, but there was only so much she could take. The woman left the house in a hurry, gasping for fresh air.*

John, her husband, was outside, chopping wood. She ran to him, tears in her eyes. He dropped his axe and held her close.

"John, it was terrible. The girls seem possessed by evil spirits. I think the Devil is here in Salem," Tituba said.

"I hope not," John responded, his deep voice comforting. "But if there is evil, better them than us."

Tituba looked up at him. John was a handsome Arawak man, his brown eyes normally kind, but now they had something else. There was a firmness in them that worried Tituba.

"But they are only girls. Even they do not deserve to be tortured so," Tituba said.

"That may be so, but one day those Puritan girls will grow to be Puritan women, and just as wicked as the rest of them," John said, gently stroking Tituba's face.

The man had said what Tituba had been thinking, even if she would not admit it to herself. The Puritans were callous and cruel, not only to those they enslaved but to each other as well. She had already seen some of that cruelty in Abigail. She worried about what kind of woman that girl would become.

"Still, I worry," Tituba whispered. "What if whatever evil is upon them gets our Violet? She is younger than both the other girls, and whatever Devil or witch hath bewitched them is aiming for this house. Violet could be next!"

Tituba gave in, crying into John's chest. He rubbed her back.

"I do not wish to intrude, but did you mention something about bewitchment?" a sharp voice cut in.

Tituba broke free from John, knowing how well the Puritans treated any displays of affection. Mary Sibley, ever the nosy neighbor, stood just outside the fence of the parsonage, a basket in her hands.

"I hath heard the poor girls were feeling unwell, so I brought some herbs that might help them feel better. But they shalt not do a thing against bewitchment. Are the girls bewitched?" Mary Sibley asked, her eyes narrowing in something between curiosity and outright glee.

Tituba and John glanced at each other, then looked to their neighbor.

"We do not know, Goody Sibley. The doctor is here to examine them," Tituba said, biting her lip. "But I do fear that they be bewitched."

Mary clucked her tongue and shook her head.

"Such a shame. If the Devil aims to set up his kingdom it only makes sense he would start with the house of a reverend. Let us pray it does not come to that," Mary looked up in silent prayer. "Is it known who bewitches them?"

Tituba and John shook their heads. Mary glanced around them, making sure no one else was near, and gestured for the couple to come closer. Tituba and John exchanged looks at each other, and reluctantly. moved closer to the woman.

"You know," Mary hissed, "there is a way to find out a witch. There is a recipe I learned sometime ago. It is called a witch-cake. You take some of the urine of the afflicted, mix it with rye meal, and bake it with the hot ashes of the hearth and feed it to a dog. The dog will sniff out the witch, and the witch will be compelled to the dog. I have heard it works every time."

"Is it wise to use such methods to find a witch? It is almost witchcraft itself," John said. Guilt formed in Tituba's stomach. Her attempt at fortune-telling ended in disaster. She worried that they would be inviting more evil in if they were to do such a thing.

"The Reverend would be displeased about it," Tituba agreed.

"It is not witchcraft, it is against witchcraft," Mary said firmly, "and the Reverend would not have to know. Once the witch is discovered, I am sure he would be pleased then."

Tituba and John stared at the woman as if she had declared herself a witch. Counter-magic was still magic.

"You do not have to heed my advice; I am not your master. But I strongly implore that you do. If there is a witch in Salem, they must be found so we can burn them. We must not suffer a witch to live," Mary said.

The last few words Mary spoke sent a chill down Tituba's spine. Something about its certainty was particularly ominous.

"I shall bid ye farewell now. Do tell me what happens if you make the cake," Mary nodded tersely and walked away, leaving Tituba and John alone. Tituba grasped her husband's hand, watching the woman disappear down the path.

"Should we make the witch-cake?" Tituba asked, her voice barely a whisper. "Sounds a dangerous idea."

Tituba looked at John. A mischievous grin appeared on his face.

"Remember when we would get dangerous?" John said.

"I am serious, John. I want those days back more than you know. But now we must deal with what is yet to come. Something bad has begun, and I worry there will be more."

John sighed. "If we find the witch before the witch finds our Violet, then perhaps we should make the witch's cake."

Tituba nodded and squeezed John's hand. She heard the girls' screams coming from the house, her resolve growing as firm as stone. It was time to hunt a witch.

CHAPTER
Twenty-Three

Crone's Cross, November 2

They ate breakfast quietly, Aradia avoiding eye contact with Baroness as much as possible. Their host had not mentioned or even hinted that Aradia had seen her do her ritual, but instead had a much more cheerful demeanor than the night before. She had prepared for them a delicious meal of pumpkin-flavored waffles topped with cinnamon, with some sweet potato biscuits to the side. Aradia devoured the food quickly, her body reminding her how hungry she was.

"Thanks so much for the food," Wanda said as she reached for yet another biscuit.

"It's really appreciated," Erzeben said with forced politeness.

"You're welcome, but now I have a request. I need some chicken feet and some chicken bones. They sell them at the corner store a couple blocks away. I'd like the two of you to go get some for me," Baroness said, nodding towards Wanda and Erzeben.

"What about Dia?" Wanda asked, freezing with the last bite of her biscuit halfway to her lips. Baroness levelled her gaze on Aradia, forcing the girl to look back.

"Aradia can stay and help me clean up. It's best not to be out and about and catching attention as she's a wanted woman," she said. Aradia wanted to shrink into her seat. This was it; this was when Baroness was going to confront her. When they were alone.

"But we don't have any money with us," Wanda said. "At least I don't."

"I'm happy to help, but this isn't a charity house, I'm not giving out free favors. It's either that or dig up some grave-dirt for me. You choose," Baroness said, pointing a spoon at her. Wanda looked like she was about to give her a piece of her mind, until Erzeben interjected.

"It is fine. I have a number my parents gave me to access their account; I already did it yesterday when we got lunch," Erzeben said, standing up. "Come on Wanda."

Wanda continued giving Baroness the stink-eye until she turned to Aradia and pulled out her witchboard.

"Here, take this. Write out Erz's name and contact us if you need anything. Erz has his board with him," Wanda said, handing her the witchboard.

"Thank you," Aradia said, warmed by the softness in Wanda's eyes.

Wanda and Erzeben left Baroness's kitchen, Wanda back to glaring on her way out. Aradia heard the front door slam, leaving her alone with Baroness.

"Come, pass me your plate," Baroness said. Aradia obliged, and Baroness took it to the sink, greenish light pouring in from the window above. For a moment she stood half a pace behind her, just staring.

"You can help by passing me the plates, cups and cutlery," Baroness told her. In awkward silence, Aradia picked up the rest of the plates, and handed them one at a time to Baroness. Baroness scrubbed them with a greenish potion that smelled strongly of lime.

"So who are you, really?" she asked, not looking up from the sink.

"I'm Aradia the Holy Strega. I've come to save Witch City," Aradia said, trying to sound more confident than she felt.

"Mhmm, and what are you saving Witch City from exactly?"

"Well, there's the Lord of Samhain, and the evil spirits, and of course I'm helping Wanda and Erzeben save Vivivine from the Monster Coven."

Baroness's lips twitched. "And what's your plan to defeat the Lord of Samhain, oh Holy Strega?"

Aradia went quiet as she handed Baroness another plate. That was one question she could not answer.

"You see, that's what I thought. I don't believe in any of this Holy Strega witch savior, daughter of the Moon Goddess hocus pocus."

"Then what do you believe in?" Aradia asked, crossing her arms. "If you don't believe in Aradia or the Moon Goddess, do you have a religion?"

"My religion is Voodoo, of the New Orleans tradition. I believe there is a greater power, and that there are very powerful spirits called the Loa that are connected to it, but above all that I believe in the power of my ancestors. They're the ones that guide me, to allow me to save myself. I don't need a Holy Strega."

"My ancestors have caused me nothing but trouble," Aradia muttered, then scrunched her lips, realizing what she had admitted to.

"So you admit you're not the Holy Strega then," Baroness said with a triumphant smile.

"Fine, you're right; I'm not," Aradia said, a little relieved to say it out loud. "All I wanted was to find the truth about Tituba, but all it's done is led me down an endless rabbit-hole."

"What do you know about Tituba?" Baroness asked, accidentally dropping a plate into the sink.

"She's my ancestor, or at least I think she might be. I was kicked out of the house for trying to contact her, and it's how I ended up Witch City."

Sadness clouded Baroness's face, her luminous features darkening, "I know what that feels like. Come, let me show you something."

Baroness left the kitchen, gesturing for Aradia to follow. Aradia's pulse quickened. Was Baroness going to show her something about Tituba? Was she finally going to find what she had been looking for?

Baroness took her to the room that she had performed her ritual in and flipped on the overhead light by batting at a switch on the wall. Now that the room was easier to see it was much less foreboding. It was a small room with shelves lining the walls. Dolls, jars of herbs and animal parts, candles, small boxes, miniature coffins and small bags lined the shelves, a faint herbal smell floating in the air. Baroness knelt in front of the altar, gesturing for Aradia to sit next to her. Aradia knelt down and stared at the altar in awe. It had three levels, each decorated with photos and illustrations of various people, candles, flowers, cigars, and liquor bottles interspersed throughout.

"This is my personal altar; I don't show it to many people. Even Calaveran only saw it once."

"It's beautiful," Aradia whispered, her voice hushed with emotion.

"Thank you. On the bottom level are my ancestors, both blood and chosen. When I left home, I had to cut ties with some of them unfortunately. The ones that remain I still honor daily, they are the closest to me and help me the most. Especially Aunt Marsha, a chosen ancestor. I never met her when she was alive, but as a spirit she has guided me through some of my darkest times. She fought for freedom until the day she died."

Baroness indicated a photograph of a smiling woman with angular features wearing bright makeup and a flower crown. She seemed to have so much joy and life in her. There was something so kind and inviting about the woman, Aradia almost felt some of her warmth.

"Why did you leave home?" Aradia asked, curiosity pulling the words from her. Baroness sighed darkly.

"They didn't agree with who I was. With who I am. Despite the gender-fluidity of some of the Loas, my family just could not accept that I was a woman, so I had to leave."

"What are you saying?" Aradia said. "Did you used to be a guy?"

Baroness turned her head sharply to Aradia, her eyes pointed.

"No. I never used to be anyone else. That's what they had decided I was at birth, but I always knew my truth. Despite what they said, I always knew I was a woman. When I finally told them, they said I was confused, and kept praying that I would come to my senses, said I was being too influenced by Erzulie. You know, our own damn culture. One day I left and never came back, and I've been happier ever since."

Aradia reached for her hand. She could not relate to everything Baroness had gone through, but she understood her pain. Baroness took Aradia's hand and focused her gaze back on the altar.

"These are the Loa, very powerful spirits that are intermediaries to the Supreme Creator. I generally petition them when I am of need of help, especially with my conjure work," Baroness said, pointing to the second level of the altar. Pictures of saints and beautiful African deities were spread across it, little plates before each one.

"And that," Baroness said, pointing to the portrait sitting on top of the altar, "is Madame Marie Laveau, the Voodoo Queen of New Orleans."

Aradia was able to get a better look at the portrait. A mesmerizing woman with golden brown skin stared from it, her eyes holding a mystery, her lips pursed as if holding a secret. Around her neck was a large snake, which even in the still painting almost seemed to move.

"Marie Laveau, the Widow Paris, is the ancestor to my craft. She secretly helped many Black witches find their way to Witch City while choosing to stay in New Orleans, at least that's what the stories say," Baroness said in a tone of reverence. "Either way, my family can trace its traditions and practice back to her. Madame Laveau ran New Orleans and didn't let anyone intimidate her. Everyone knew to respect her, for they all knew her power. Now she is an elevated ancestor, and commands respect from beyond the grave."

Aradia stared at the portrait in awe. To have an entire city under your persuasion, to truly be a queen and not have to take crap from anyone . . . Aradia craved that. Maybe that was why she agreed when Wanda said she was the Holy Strega; she wanted to belong to something greater than herself.

"Aradia," Baroness said in a commanding tone. Aradia looked over to her. Baroness stared intensely at her, her vulnerability gone.

"Please do not ever forget what your ancestors have done for you. They have paved the way for you in ways you don't even realize. Tituba was forced to use her wits to survive a terrible situation, and she made it. She shook that Puritan village to its core, giving them exactly what they were afraid of most. For the first time, the Puritans listened to the words of an enslaved woman. Whether she realized it or not, Tituba developed an influential power over all those small-minded fools."

Baroness held Aradia's glance, nodded gently, and stood up, sifting through the contents of her shelves. "Most witches in this city can trace their craft and lineage to the Salem Witch Trials, in one way or another.

What they don't realize is that it all began with Tituba; unwittingly or not she is the mother of American witchcraft. And you may be her only descendant."

Baroness turned to face Aradia, holding the doll that she gave her.

"I'm giving this back to you. This doll was made by another powerful Salem Witch, Candy, another enslaved woman that used the Puritans' fear against them, and it only seems right that you have it. I have sewn in some gris-gris to help protect you."

She handed the doll to Aradia. Aradia clenched the doll tight. Now that she understood the significance of it, she did not want to let it go again. Candy was no ordinary cashier or shopkeeper; she was one of the original Salem Witches, and was still alive after all these centuries. Now it made sense why she gave her the doll.

"Why don't you come with us?" Aradia asked, "We could definitely use your help finding Vivivine."

"I'm sorry, I truly am, but if the Monster Coven has her then I will not get involved. I'm not about to risk my life for a rich lady I've never met. You know," Baroness said, sitting next to Aradia, "I could teach you my craft, my conjure. You could let your friends go find Mrs. Frankenstein, and I could teach you the ways of my ancestors. Our ancestors."

Aradia looked at Baroness's altar, focusing on the portrait of Marie Laveau. It would be a dream to learn magic from Baroness, especially if Tituba had practiced something similar. Vivivine was nice, and Aradia did not want anything bad to happen to her, but fighting a coven that had flying monkeys while trying to hide from a coven that thought she was a Witch Hunter was all a little too intense.

She opened her mouth to take Baroness's offer, but then she thought of Wanda. Wanda was determined to find Vivivine, and to protect Aradia herself. Wanda had such fire and passion, and the largest heart Aradia had ever seen. She did not want to let the witch down. And part of her couldn't imagine leaving her side.

"I would love to, I really would, but I've got to do this," she said instead.

Baroness nodded again, her dark eyes inscrutable.

"You don't need to be the Holy Strega anymore."

"I know, it's not because of that, it's because of . . ." Aradia said, looking back at the door.

"The green girl, Wanda, I figured," Baroness said gently, with a bit of sadness. "I just hope that you don't get hurt because of it."

"Me too," Aradia said quietly.

"Well, once you have found Vivivine, you are welcome to come back here," Baroness said. Aradia looked back at her.

"And remember, you are the heir to the Queen of Salem. Go get your crown."

CHAPTER
Twenty-Four

The trio spent the day trying to come up with plans to save Vivivine in Baroness's parlor. Calaveran would meet them in the evening, and they wanted to be as prepared as possible. They bounced back several ideas between the three of them, Baroness casually suggesting something here and there, but no ideas seemed to stick. The odds seemed insurmountable.

"What if we tried to summon my mother, Hecate," Aradia said. Baroness raised an eyebrow but said nothing. Aradia looked down. She had thought about telling Wanda and Erzeben the truth about who she was, but could not bring herself to do it.

"Do you think you could do that?" Wanda said, her eyes wide in excitement.

"I mean it's worth a try," Aradia said, choosing her words carefully, "I mean, I don't have special contact with her, but maybe she'll listen."

"There is a crossroads near the WITCH CITY sign where Cal said he'd meet us, we could leave an offering for her there when it gets dark," Erzeben said, Aradia surprised he was agreeing with her. "At this point we might need divine intervention to help save Vivivine."

The trio looked over at Baroness. She sighed and raised her hands.

"I'll make some honey biscuits but that's all I'm doing."

THE TRIO LEFT BARONESS'S HOUSE AS THE GREEN SKY FADED TO BLACK AND waited by the WITCH CITY sign for Calaveran. Talking with Baroness left Aradia feeling empowered, that perhaps she could take on the city and survive. Eventually she would go back to Baroness and the learn secrets of her ancestors, but now she needed to fight.

"So, did Baroness show you any Voodoo?" Wanda asked as they wound down the paths, the cottage disappearing into shadows.

"No, not really. She told me about her ancestors and stuff, which I think Voodoo's kind of about anyway," Aradia said.

"Too bad," Wanda said.

"I'm just glad she decided not to come with us. The last thing we need is for her to have drama with Cal," Erzeben said, rolling his eyes.

"I would've liked her to come along," Aradia said.

"Why?" Wanda said.

"She does not even believe in the Triple Goddess," Erzeben said.

"Look, there's different kinds of magic, and as the Holy Strega I respect that," Aradia said, getting irritated. "And besides, we need all the help we can get."

"Yes, but Cal . . ." The empusa trailed off and looked to the sky.

Aradia and Wanda looked over. A dark figure on a broomstick flew towards them and landed a short distance away. He stepped into the glow of the streetlights, revealing broad shoulders and the arcs of muscles, visible under a black satin jacket. Moving closer, it was easier to see the rest of his appearance. He wore a mask decorated like a sugar-skull, beautiful flower designs framing gold eyes. His jacket had rose designs sewn into it, and the words *Bad Brujo* were written across a torn black t-shirt, spread tight against his wide chest. Across his shoulder was a black strap attached to a glowing skull. He was striking, almost intimidating to look at. Removing his mask, he smiled brightly when his eyes alighted on Erzeben, his skin tanned and tattooed like a sugar-skull almost identical to his mask.

"Hey Cal," Wanda said.

"Hey!" Cal said, removing skull-shaped headphones, then turned to Erzeben. "Hey, buddy."

"Hello," Erzeben said a little quietly. "How was your family's Day of the Dead celebration?"

Calaveran's handsome face stretched in a smile. "It was okay. It's still going on, but I left early. I can only handle so much family time. But yeah, we already did the important stuff, like making the trip to the cemetery and leaving offerings for the dead. Especially because my abuela passed earlier this year it was nice to speak to her again, if only for a little bit."

"Still so jealous that your family can do that," Wanda said. "By the way, this is Aradia the Holy Strega."

Calaveran looked over to Aradia. He stared at her at first in fascination, then reached for Aradia's hand. She offered hers to shake, but he bent it gently at the wrist and placed a light kiss on the back of her hand.

"I didn't realize the Holy Strega would be so attractive. My name is Calaveran," he said. Aradia wasn't sure how to react.

"I'm Aradia," she said, then retracted her hand and crossed her arms over her stomach. She did not care if some boy thought she was attractive. The girl glanced at Wanda, who rolled her eyes.

"What?" Calaveran said.

"Stop flirting. We have important stuff to do," Wanda said.

"What? She's a beautiful girl. Am I not allowed to say that? From what Ben told me she sounded like a frightful hag, but I'm glad she isn't," Calaveran said with a wink to Aradia. Aradia suppressed a groan. Calaveran was handsome, sure, but her attention lied elsewhere.

"You sure she is not a frightful hag?" Erzeben asked, his voice acidic.

"Can we focus please?" Aradia asked.

"Yeah, we have a fancy lady to save. Every second we wait is another second the Monster Coven could be doing despicable things to her. Did you bring an extra broomstick?" Wanda asked.

"Yup," Calaveran said. The male witch took what looked like a wand from his back pocket. He closed his eyes and held it out. The wand grew long until it was the size of a broomstick, with one end forking into branches. He smiled and opened his eyes when it was finished. Wanda reached for it, but Calaveran held it back.

"Careful, it's a little temperamental. It was my abuela's old broomstick. It's called Catemaco," Calaveran said with a grin. Wanda took the broomstick.

"Got it," Wanda said curtly. "So, Cal, we're going to summon Hecate so she can help us find Vivivine."

Calaveran's eyes widened.

"Hecate? Goddess of Witchcraft, Guardian of the Underworld Hecate? Seriously? Like actually summon her?" Calaveran said. The trio nodded. "She is not a goddess to be messed around with. I am more dedicated to Santa Muerte, and she can be a jealous spirit. Not sure it would be a good idea."

"Who is Santa Muerte?" Aradia asked.

"Nuestra Señora de la Santa Muerte, Our Lady of the Holy Death. She is a powerful saint of death and protection, as well as many other things," Calaveran said, pulling a necklace out from the collar of his shirt, flashing the image of a woman with a skeleton face dressed in robes. "My family always favored her."

"Let me get this right. You're saying you're scared that your family's goddess is going to get mad at you if you try to summon Hecate?" Wanda asked.

"No! It's not that I'm scared, I'm just not sure that it's a good idea. There has to be a better way," Calaveran said.

"Big tough Cal is afraid of a scary skeleton lady. Ooo," Wanda said, wiggling her fingers.

"Hey, don't talk about Santa Muerte like that! That's disrespect!" Calaveran said.

"Will you two stop? We are running out of time and options to save Vivivine. I do not particularly like the idea either, but summoning Hecate may be our only choice," Erzeben said.

"I still don't know," Calaveran said.

"Come on, spells are best performed with three witches. I don't know if this spell will even work, but at least I'm not a coward and am willing to do it," Wanda said.

"Are you calling me a coward?" Calaveran asked, stepping closer to Wanda.

"Wanda, Cal," Erzeben said, placing his hands in between them, "please. Vivivine needs us."

Still Wanda and Calaveran stared at each other, neither backing down.

"Okay. Let's do it," Calaveran finally said, relaxing half a step back. "But I don't understand why Aradia can't be your third witch to cast the spell. Isn't Hecate her mama?"

The Bad Witches looked over to Aradia. Anxiety rushed into her. How was she going to explain that she could not summon a goddess because she was not even a real witch?

"I'm, uh, well," Aradia said. "I am forbidden to summon her directly. It would be an abuse of my power."

"We need someone to keep watch anyway. And it's better if we cast the spell because we've been taught magic the same way," Wanda said.

Aradia sighed in relief. Casting that little spell on Halloween would be nothing compared to actually summoning a mythical witch goddess. If she survived Samhain she would have so much to write about. Aradia placed the honey biscuits Baroness had given them at the base of the WITCH CITY sign where the crossroads met.

"Let's get this over with," Wanda said. "I guess we can use the traditional *Hymn to Hecate*."

"We will each do three lines, including the last part," Erzeben said.

"If you say so," Calaveran said. The Bad Witches faced the neon sign. Aradia stood watch close by. She was not going to miss a summoning of a powerful witch goddess. The three witches closed their eyes and held each other's hands.

"*We call the goddess of the crossroads, mother of hounds, snakes, and toads,*" Wanda chanted.

"*Dark-cloaked goddess of graves and ghosts, come to us as we need it most,*" Erzeben continued.

"*Queen of night, of witches, and the moon, fly to us, fly to us, fly to us soon,*" Calaveran sang out.

"Torch-bearing maiden, and key-bearing crone, we summon you now from your chthonic home."

"Three-faced goddess, who lights the way, come to us this night, this we pray."

"We pray you, Dark Mother, to attend this rite, bring us your magic on this darkest night."

"Hecate, Great Queen, we summon thee."

"Hecate, Great Queen, we summon thee."

"Hecate, Great Queen, we summon thee, so mote it be."

Aradia held her breath. The Bad Witches' eyes scrunched in concentration. For a few minutes nothing happened. And then came a breath of cold air, as all the hair on the back of Aradia's neck stood on end.

"Hello, children."

CHAPTER

Twenty-Five

Aradia and the Bad Witches spun around. Floating off the ground behind them was a figure shrouded in dark robes, a hood concealing their face. Only slender, pale green hands were visible. Aradia's heart beat hard and fast in her chest. Could they possibly be in the presence of Hecate, the Goddess of Witchcraft?

"Are you Hecate?" Wanda asked in awe.

"No, but I am someone who can help," the figure said, lowering their hood. She had a porcelain-like face that practically glowed, her eyes tired and red. Wispy, silvery hair floated around her as if on its own.

"Careful, she is a banshee," Erzeben loudly whispered. "A faerie spirit."

"Hey, don't be racist. I'm part faerie," Wanda said.

"Who are you then?" Aradia asked.

The banshee leveled her gaze at Aradia. "My name is Badb. I mean you no harm; I only scream when someone is meant to die. You are looking for your lost friend, yes?"

"How do you know that?" Erzeben said.

"Eastwitch is my domain, as I was killed here many years ago and can't cross the border to Westwitch. I return here every Samhain Night looking for someone to help me," Badb said.

"And you think we can help you?" Aradia said.

"I know you can," Badb gestured at her, arms wide and welcoming. "You're Aradia, aren't you?"

Aradia felt the gaze of the banshee and the Bad Witches all on her, and again she felt herself shrinking within her skin. The moment she feared had arrived, when someone would expect her to be the Holy Strega and save them.

"What do you need?" Aradia said slowly.

"My spirit will never rest until those who murdered me are brought to justice."

"Who murdered you?" Calaveran asked.

"The Lantern Coven. I dared to speak against them and so they crushed me to death, like the witches of old. And now I must return here every Samhain Night. Will you help me?"

"Are you seriously asking us to bring vengeance down upon the most powerful coven in the city?" Erzeben asked, raising an eyebrow.

"No, of course not. They are much too powerful, even for the Holy Strega. But there is someone who hates the Lantern Coven even more than I, and she hates the Monster Coven just as much, so she would be able to help us both," the banshee said, looking beyond them wistfully. "She is the only one alive other than the Monster Coven themselves who knows where they are."

"Then who is she? I wanna meet this spiteful witch," Wanda said with something like interest in her voice.

"The guardian of the HagHollow Woods," Badb said.

"You can't mean . . ." Calaveran said.

"I do mean," Badb said quickly. "Find her, and she will be able to help all of us."

"But isn't she dangerous? Doesn't she eat people?" Erzeben asked, and Aradia suppressed a shudder.

"Yes, when crossed. That is why you must be careful with her. She can make a valuable ally or ferocious enemy, so make sure to follow her rules. She hates all of the major covens. If you respect her rules, she will help all of us."

"Could you give us a minute?" Wanda asked.

The banshee nodded. Wanda, Aradia, Erzeben, and Calaveran huddled together.

"So what do you think, should we trust her?" Wanda whispered.

"I am not sure; it sounds as if we are being sent on one dangerous quest after another. But if she knows where Vivivine is . . ." Erzeben whispered back.

"Then she's worth the risk?" Aradia asked. Erzeben paused.

"Yes, I suppose she is," the empusa said.

"Right, then let's do it," Wanda said. They broke free from the huddle and faced the banshee.

"We'll do it," Wanda asked.

"Hexcellent," Badb cooed. "As you should know, the HagHollow Woods is to the south of the city. When you arrive there, chant the word 'Izbushka' three times and say, 'turn your back to the woods and your front to me.' Then she will find you."

"But wait, what if she does get angry with us and tries to eat us?" Calaveran asked, and for once the boy looked scared, his broad smile cracking.

"That is a good point," Erzeben said.

Badb only smiled. "You seem like capable young witches. I believe you can figure something out."

"And you will be waiting here?" Erzeben said.

"Until the last Samhain Night," Badb said. "Four nights from now."

"I guess we better be on our way then," Aradia said.

"Merry meet, and merry part, and merry meet again!" Badb said, vanishing into the darkness.

"Who is the—" Aradia was interrupted by the barking of dogs. They looked around. There did not seem to be any dogs anywhere. The last time Aradia saw a dog was with the woman who drove her to the Witch

City on her motorcycle—Trivia. Who was also possibly Hecate. Had they summoned her after all?

A shrill screech interrupted her thoughts. Aradia and the Bad Witches looked over to where the sound came from. Not too far off from them, floating towards them, were figures dressed in shrouded, dirty white robes. Instead of faces, they had ripped holes corresponding to their eyes and mouths, an eerie glow coming from them, as if they were horrific versions of cartoon ghosts. Each of them was holding a glowing, carved turnip. Aradia stared in dark fascination as the phantom creatures advanced on them. They emerged out of the shadows of the streets, creating a nightmarish fog.

Calaveran got on his broomstick and flew upwards, and Erzeben transformed into a bat, flying into the air. While running, Wanda struggled to mount Catemaco, her new broomstick. The second she was successfully perched on it, she looked at Aradia.

"Come on, get on!" Wanda said.

Aradia ran and lifted a leg over the back of the broomstick, straddling it while holding onto the witch.

"Catemaco, fly for me!" Wanda cried.

With a jolt the broomstick lurched into the air. Catemaco wavered for a bit, but soon they were all flying, the wind rushing at them. The screeching of the spirits did not stop. Aradia looked back. The spirits had flown upwards behind them, their ghostly hands reaching up. The Bad Witches flew higher and higher, but there seemed to be no escaping them.

A phantom grabbed the broom, and the broomstick wavered violently. Aradia screamed. Wanda jolted the broom to the side, flinging the spirit off the way a horse might flick a fly off with its tail. The phantom screeched horribly, tumbling down through the air. Without a moment to breathe, Aradia felt a hand on her arm, the boney fingers biting her flesh. Aradia screamed again and reflex took over, punching the creature in the face with her other arm. The spirit fell away, disappearing into the city lights. The Bad Witches zoomed through the city, almost scraping along a skyscraper, twirling around an apartment building. It had several balconies, and on them were sharp posts with glowing jack-o'-lanterns on them, to presumably protect the tenants from the spirits. This gave Aradia an idea.

"Fly closer to the balconies!" Aradia shouted over the wind.

"What?" Wanda called back.

"FLY CLOSER TO THE BALCONIES!"

The broom wavered as Wanda moved closer to the apartment building, almost like it was shaking. With an unsteady hand, Aradia reached out at the pumpkins. She tried grabbing one but missed as the broomstick faltered.

"STEADY THE BROOM!" Aradia shouted.

"I'M TRYING!"

Aradia reached out at another pumpkin. She grabbed it and pulled it off its post, the lantern still glowing. With a jolt, the broom flew to the side, nearly knocking Aradia off. Wanda glanced back at Aradia to check if she was still holding on. She noticed the jack-o'-lantern in Aradia's hand. Her eyes widened, and quickly she looked back forward.

But Aradia smiled as Wanda's tense shoulders relaxed a little. Aradia heard her chanting something, but it was hard to hear what from the howling of the wind. Various jack-o'-lanterns flew up into the air, from porches, from windows, from the roofs of buildings, and levitated around them. Calaveran looked over and nodded, also chanting. Jack-o'-lanterns floated up in the air around him and Erzeben. The spirits flew around the jack-o'-lanterns, screaming in confusion. The glowing pumpkins around Calaveran transformed into glowing skulls, screeching and chattering back at the spirits. The ghosts hissed and disappeared into the darkness. A smile of relief came to Aradia's face. They lost them.

"We did it!" she cheered, hugging Wanda tight. The other girl whooped in joy. They continued to fly over the glowing lights of the city, Calaveran in the lead. The buildings seemed to go on forever. Aradia's legs were sore from clutching onto the broomstick, and she found herself wishing they would land soon. Hopefully it would not be too hard to find the Monster Coven once the guardian helped them. They would find Vivivinc, hide out for the rest of Samhain, and then Aradia would go find Baroness and learn everything she could about Tituba and her magic. She just kept on having to tell herself everything would be fine.

Eventually the city thinned, until they were flying over a barren landscape. Calaveran flew downwards as a large, dark forest unfurled under them. Wanda angled the broomstick downwards as well, following

Calaveran's lead, slightly churning Aradia's stomach. Erzeben also flew downwards, closely following the witch boy.

They landed with some roughness in the barren field. The forest stretched out ahead of them, gnarled, claw-like trees reaching as if for them. A cold breeze blew out some of their jack-o'-lanterns, plunging them into darkness. Aradia looked back. In the distance was the industrial cityscape, dotted with green and orange lights. She put her arms close to her, the wind blowing her curly hair into her face.

"So where are we exactly? Who is supposed to be helping us?" Aradia asked.

"Well, these are the HagHollow Woods, and if legend is correct, she will find us," Calaveran said.

"I do not like the way you said that," Erzeben said.

They all looked out at the forest, as an eerie whistle echoed through the trees.

"Well, here goes nothing! Izbushka!" Wanda called out, and looked to the others.

"Izbushka!" Calaveran called out next. He glanced at Erzeben.

"Izbushka!" Erzeben said.

"Turn your back to the woods and your front to me!" Aradia said as loud as her lungs would let her. A loud, metallic creaking echoed in the night air. The wind picked up and started to howl. Aradia grabbed Wanda's arm.

The creaking grew louder, followed by a loud crunch of tree branches. The wind picked up, Aradia having to hold onto her hat. Leaves blew up into the air, brushing past her, the wind howling in her ears. Aradia vaguely made out something moving towards them in the trees. Machine-like grinding and crashing, echoed from the trees growing even louder. Everything in Aradia's body was telling her to run, but she was unable to. She was almost in a trance, and her curiosity of what was coming outweighed her fears.

Crashing through the trees of the forest and into the open field was a monstrous house. It was large, crooked, and dark in color. Green and black smoke swirled out of several chimneys. A few windows were shaped like glowing, green eyes, and sharp teeth-like posts decorated the porch. The porch was lit by torches shaped like glowing skulls along the edges.

Twisted vines and rusted iron pipes covered the house, more glowing skulls intertwined with them, tree branches sticking out from various odds and ends of the building. The house bounded towards them on large, practically skeletal chicken legs.

A screeching crash erupted. The house no longer pursued them, but sat on the ground on its chicken legs. Aradia stood awestruck. She knew whose house this was from fairytales she had read as a child. The front door of the house creaked open. Slowly, a hunched over figure emerged. Wanda kept on pulling on Aradia's arm, but the girl was still, entranced. The figure stepped into the light of the torches, revealing the terrifying form of the Baba Yaga.

CHAPTER
Twenty-Six

The Baba Yaga was hunched, yet cut an imposing figure. Layers upon layers of dark fabrics billowed out in the wind. Her hands, reaching forward, were long and crooked, practically skeletal. Long, curled, yellowish nails came from the tips of them. Long, wispy gray hair blew around in the wind, partially covered by a bandana. She was ghastly pale, a slightly bluish tinge to her skin, which was lined with wrinkles so deep that they looked like cracks. Her nose and chin were long and sharp, with several warts on them. One eye was stitched up, the other was large and glowing yellow. Her large mouth made a grimace, revealing sharp, iron teeth.

"Did you come here by your own free will, or were you sent here?" the Baba Yaga said with a Russian accent, her elderly voice powerful.

Aradia stood transfixed. If she wanted to run, she could not. She was certain there was a spell keeping them there. Still, despite the frightening circumstance, Aradia stared wide-eyed in excitement. A fairytale was unfolding right in front of her eyes.

"We came by our own free will," Calaveran said, trying to stand his ground.

"Such brave, such foolish children. Coming so close to the woods. I see all that comes here. The covens may fight over the city, but the woods have always been mine," the Baba Yaga said, taking a step forward. The witch sniffed the air, and her glowing eye zeroed in on Aradia. The girl clenched her hands, her feet shifting, but she stared back.

"Ah, a girl from the outside realm. How delicious," the Baba Yaga said. "What is your purpose for summoning me?"

"A banshee told us to come find you. She said that you could help us find someone that has gone missing," Aradia said quietly. The Baba Yaga snorted.

"And why would I help a ragtag group of miscreants, on this night of all nights? I should broil you all alive for your impudence!"

"Because our friend was abducted by the Monster Coven," Wanda said. "You know, *the* Monster Coven."

The Baba Yaga's eye went large, her frown tightening. "So? They are a bunch of wretches; all the covens of this city are. Why would I ever do anything to get involved with their messes?"

"Because I'm Aradia, the Holy Strega," Aradia said, hoping that it would help. The Baba Yaga smiled, amused.

"I see. Well, that is simply fascinating, to have the Holy Strega in our midst. Fine. I shall only speak to one of you. The rest of you must wait, and I choose to speak to her," the Baba Yaga said, pointing at Aradia.

Wanda clutched Aradia's arm. "You don't have to do this."

"The choice is yours to make, Holy Strega. I ask again, did *you* come here of your own free will? Or were you sent here?" The Baba Yaga asked.

Aradia thought about this. She was not sure. So far in Witch City she had been taken along for the ride. She wanted that to change. All her life she had to do everything while keeping her mother in mind. She did not have to worry about that anymore. The thought of being alone with a terrifying witch who ate children unsettled her nerves, but right now Vivivine was at the mercy of much more terrifying witches. Aradia thought of Tituba facing the trials. She needed to be brave like her.

"I'll go," Aradia said.

"Dia, don't be stupid. She'll eat you alive," Wanda said.

"For once I will have to agree with Wanda," Erzeben said.

"Do not test my patience or I will eat all of you! Are you coming or not, girl?" The Baba Yaga called.

"I am!" Aradia said, then turned to the other Bad Witches. "Please, since I've arrived here all I've done is watch all of you. Let me do something useful for once. I'm the Holy Strega. I will be okay."

Wanda nodded and slowly released Aradia's arm. Aradia smiled at her, although she felt her lips quivering, and tried to seem brave as she faced the Baba Yaga. The old witch smiled, making her face seem all the more disturbing. Aradia swallowed hard and told herself she was doing this to help others, to help Vivivine, to help the Bad Witches, and mostly, to help herself be brave. She wanted to be Aradia, so it was about time she started acting like it. She walked forward to the witch's house, silently praying to Tituba for strength, and slowly stepped up onto the rickety porch. It groaned almost like a human under her feet. The girl took one last glance at the Bad Witches—who stared back at her with wide eyes and seemed to strain against the spell immobilizing them—and let the Baba Yaga lead her into the monstrous house.

Aradia followed the witch down a dark hallway, illuminated by glowing skulls fixed on the walls. She ducked a stream of steam from a rusted pipe scrawling along the walls. It seemed so industrial, so factory-like, nothing like what Aradia expected to see inside a witch's hut, especially of a witch that was supposed to be a guardian of the woods. Aradia's eyes were wide with curiosity, but something gnawed at her gut as she was led down the hallway. Was this just a trick, and the Baba Yaga would eat her? Or would she show her magical secrets? Aradia dared not hope.

The hallway led into a small, cramped room. In the center stood a large cauldron, engraved with an image of a triple spiral, a glowing green potion bubbling in it. The walls were lined with shelves with bottles and jars. Aradia swept her eyes over the jars and shelves and jumped back as hands appeared, reaching for ingredients like bat wings and hellebore in dusty jars and corked vials. An unsettling, tangy scent came from the concoction bubbling in the cauldron. Baba Yaga moved to the other side of the cauldron, sniffing it, and looked Aradia straight on. Aradia squirmed. That eye seemed to see more than just the scared girl standing there, and Aradia didn't care to show anymore. She folded in on herself, unsure of what to do or say.

"The first thing to know is that things in Crone's Cross, this 'Witch City,' are not what they seem," the Baba Yaga said, finally breaking the uncomfortable silence.

"In what way?" Aradia asked.

"Do not ask questions; it bothers me," the Baba Yaga said sternly.

"I'm sorry," Aradia said.

The old witch's gaze softened slightly. "Do your little friends know that you are not truly the Holy Strega?"

Aradia's heart dropped. "No, but, I . . ."

"Do not worry about that, I believe that is hardly relevant. You do have magic in your blood, Salem Witch, and that is what will allow you to thrive here."

Aradia was stunned. "What—"

The Baba Yaga glared. Aradia quickly cut off her question.

"You are trying to save your friend from the Monster Coven, while on the run from the Lantern Coven, yes?"

"Yes," Aradia said, wondering what the Baba Yaga was getting at.

"Tell me, what have you been told of these covens?" Baba Yaga said.

"Well, the Lantern Coven is led by the Queen of Lanterns, but cowen disappear when they arrive at the Queen's castle. Most likely because they sacrifice the cowen to the Lord of Samhain," Aradia said. She paused, looking at the witch. The Baba Yaga was taking the various ingredients the floating hands passed to her and throwing them into the cauldron, stirring with a long bone as she did it.

"Go on," the witch said, not looking up from her potion.

"Well, the Monster Coven are Wicked Witches who terrorize Witch City on Samhain Nights, with flying monkeys apparently," Aradia said, trying not to flinch as a pair of hands flew by her hair.

"So, Salem Witch," Baba Yaga said after a moment of silence, the potion bubbling, "as you are clearly not here to hunt witches, why did you come here?"

"Well," Aradia said, caught off guard, "I was originally planning on going to Salem, to find out more about Tituba, to find out if she really was a witch, to understand if maybe I could be a witch. And it was the only place I could think of when, when . . ."

"Get on with it."

"When my mama kicked me out for casting a spell," Aradia said, an unexpected tightness closing her throat. She swallowed down the sob.

"Get yourself together, child. What you do not understand is that you have been given a great gift, an opportunity if you will. Tituba is here!"

Aradia felt her mouth drop open, not sure if she understood the witch properly. "She's in your house?"

"Stop being a jabberwocking fool!" the Baba Yaga clicked her tongue against her iron teeth. "She is in this city! Tituba escaped here after those wretched trials were over."

Still Aradia stared, open-mouthed. "Tituba's alive?"

"If you ask one more question I will broil you alive!" The Baba Yaga said, nearly screeching.

"I'm sorry," Aradia said quietly. "But that changes everything. I really am here for a reason after all."

Aradia's heart soared at the possibility. To be united with Tituba, that would be incredible. Tituba could tell her stories, teach her magic, and be her new family. Tituba would not abandon her for being a witch; she would embrace her. Aradia felt her eyes sting, and swallowed thickly again as the Baba Yaga shot her another narrowed glance, apparently as allergic to emotion as she was to questions.

"Perhaps," the old witch allowed. "However, I'm not telling you all this from the kindness of the empty cavity where my heart once was. There is another reason you are here."

Aradia looked at her curiously, wanting to ask the witch a question. Instead, she settled on holding her face open and her mouth shut.

"Something great and terrible happened here many years ago," the Baba Yaga thankfully continued. "It changed this world forever, and has been ever so slowly killing it. If left unchecked, Crone's Cross will crumble onto itself, and all life here, including mine, will be destroyed. We have had to use more magic than ever to keep this world in one piece, and only the wise know why."

"It . . . it seems like the city is doing fine to me," Aradia stuttered, fighting not to pitch her voice up like a question.

"Pay attention, girl. The amount of magic used to create and sustain this city isn't natural. All the witches here have ever known is an endless autumn, but that has not always been the case. All that green smoke you see in the city? That's the excess magic being burned through to keep this land alive. It won't last forever."

"Is it . . . it's because of the Lord of Samhain," instead of a question, the conclusion escaped Aradia's lips, surprising her.

Baba Yaga nodded grimly, her lips flattening in a suppressed grimace. "It is because those in power are not willing to do what is necessary to protect their people, so afraid they are of losing their power. I don't care about most people either, but their irresponsibility to do the right thing will cost everyone's lives, even their own."

"That's terrible, but I don't understand why you're telling me this," Aradia said. "That isn't something I can fix."

"But you are Aradia, the Holy Strega. You came here to save the witches of this city," the Baba Yaga cocked her head to one side, staring mockingly at Aradia. Heat rose to her cheeks, the already cramped room feeling smaller.

"But I already told you, I'm not the Holy Strega! That just isn't fair!"

The Baba Yaga cackled loudly, throwing her back.

"Oh boo-hoo. I'm not here to mollycoddle you on a whimsical adventure. You want me to help your friends find Vivivine, you're going to have to do something for me. You chose to be Aradia, so now it is time to live up to that. You can't go telling people you're the Holy Strega if you have no intention of being one. There are consequences to such carelessness."

"But I'm just trying to survive!"

The Baba Yaga leered forward, her face dangerously close. Aradia stepped back, her heart thundering in her ears. The witch's face was all the more fearsome up close; the Baba Yaga looked ready to eat her, her lips pulled back.

"We are all trying to survive!" The Baba Yaga barked. "If you don't like the responsibility, then you never should have lied! Fools will not survive this city."

"So I'll tell them the truth," Aradia said quietly. The Baba Yaga leaned back, her grimace tightening to a frown.

"It is much too late for that, little girl," the Baba Yaga said, pointing a gnarled finger at her. "Don't look so glum. I would not expect you to do this if I didn't think you were capable. I wouldn't waste my time. You have a unique gift for storytelling, like your ancestor. When used wisely, you can conjure worlds. Or destroy them."

Aradia stared into the bubbling cauldron. She had not thought of her storytelling as a gift. After all, it had gotten her into this mess in the first place. She was still not sure if her story on her birthday had summoned the Lord of Samhain, or had created something else entirely. And wasn't Tituba's storytelling what had caused the Salem Witch Trials?

"So, I guess you want me to defeat the Lord of Samhain," Aradia said sullenly.

"No," the Baba Yaga said. "I want you to make a sacrifice to him."

CHAPTER
Twenty-Seven

Aradia's neck snapped up, not believing what she had heard.

"What?"

"I won't repeat myself," the Baba Yaga said with a glare.

"Why do you want me to do that?"

"I won't abide questions!"

The Baba Yaga's eye glittered dangerously. Aradia's gaze wandered to the various skulls in the room. They all had to come from someone. If she was not smart about this, she would never make it out of the Baba Yaga's house alive.

"I'm sorry. But I thought the whole point was to stop him," Aradia said quietly.

Again the ancient witch pursed her lips. "Was it now? I'm sure as the Holy Strega you must know best."

A flare of frustration rose in Aradia. Why couldn't anything in Witch City be straightforward for once?

"I'm really struggling to understand what you want from me," Aradia forced out.

"Fine, then let me make it easier for your little mind to comprehend. All of this began with a sacrifice to the Lord of Samhain, the Salem Pact if you will. So it needs to end with one. You need to finish what has begun."

The Baba Yaga paused and stared at Aradia grimly. "There are three things that are a sufficient sacrifice to the Lord of Samhain, and it is up to you to choose. The life of the one who made the first sacrifice, the tool with which it was made, or the witch accused of wickedness fed to the flames."

Aradia pressed her hand to her stomach to still a wave of nausea. An actual human sacrifice? She did not think she ever would have the stomach for it. It was the type of thing her mother always warned her about when talking about the evils of witchcraft. Would it turn her into a truly evil Wicked Witch?

"I'll even make it a tad easier for you by telling you what the first two things are. The first is Abigail Williams, the wretched brat that accused your ancestor and started the Salem Witch Trials. Yes, she is still alive too. She sold her soul to control this world, and it was she who created what it has become. She . . . disappeared when the Lantern Coven rose to power, which brings me to the next suitable sacrifice: The Crown of Nicnevin, which was stolen by Abigail, and now rests on the head of Gourdina, Dread Queen of the Lantern Coven. The last thing you will have to figure out on your own, Salem Witch, if that is the path you so choose to tread. It would be the easiest to find, but the hardest to destroy. The choice is yours."

Aradia glared at her, scuffing a foot angrily against the dusty ground. "So I would have to essentially sacrifice Abigail Williams or the Queen of Lanterns then. There is no way I could accuse a witch and sacrifice them."

"That will be your decision to make," the Baba Yaga replied calmly, stroking her chin. "Either way it will need to be done in Morrigan's Grove, where the first sacrifice took place."

"But how? I mean they both probably deserve it, but that's something for somebody actually powerful to do, like you! You're this great guardian of the woods, you could do it," Aradia said.

"Life is not fair, Salem Witch. I have lived countless lives to learn that," the Baba Yaga said. "However, there is a benefit to this other than saving your Frankenstein friend. With the sacrifice you will be granted the knowledge of which you seek. The truth about your ancestry, the truth of your power. And you will become the Holy Strega that you hope to be. But a sacrifice is the price. After all, the true meaning of Samhain is sacrifice."

Aradia felt her mind spinning. It seemed simple but it wasn't. Sacrifice a person, an enemy, and she would get what she had been looking for, and save Witch City and Vivivine in the process. But unless she could somehow separate the Queen from her crown, which already seemed impossible, there would be blood on her hands. Maybe she could leave Witch City and start over in Salem, and she would not have to worry about evil spirits or dangerous covens. Except she would be just as lost as she was before. Finding Abigail Williams, or stealing the Queen's crown and possibly killing her, seemed impossible. But she had already come this far. Her thoughts turned to Wanda, and she felt a tug at her heart. If Wanda needed her to be the Holy Strega, then maybe she could try to be her.

"Fine, I'll make a sacrifice, but only if you tell me where Tituba is."

"I don't do bargains," Baba Yaga said gruffly. She held Aradia in a single-eye staring contest, one that Aradia didn't dare break. Finally, the old witch sighed. "But I will tell you this. The solution to my request and yours lie in the same place. Solve one problem and you will solve the other. But if you continue to test my patience, I will see to it that you will never see your friends again."

"Alright, I promise to make the sacrifice," Aradia said.

"Good. You made the right choice. This will all turn out right in the end, you'll see," the Baba Yaga said, an unsettling smile spreading across her crooked face. "I will show you where the 'Monster' Coven is. But you and your little Bad Witches or whatever they call themselves will have to go there on your own. Now, gaze into the cauldron."

Aradia peered over the edge of the cauldron, staring at the bubbling green concoction, the tangy scent burning into her nostrils until it was all she could smell.

"Now, relax your mind and focus on finding your lost little friend," the Baba Yaga commanded.

Aradia tried to focus on finding Vivivine, on rescuing her from the evil clutches of the Monster Coven. But her mind wandered to finding Tituba, to the possibility of finally being connected with her. She wanted to save Vivivine, she did, but she could not deny to herself that she wanted to find Tituba more so, as guilty as she felt about it. A blurry image slowly materialized on the surface of the potion, but it kept fading in and out, as if it couldn't quite settle on one thing. She saw glimpses of what looked like a pumpkin patch, interspersed with images of a brown, church-like building.

"Focus your mind girl! You're not going to find anything if your energy is scattered!" the Baba Yaga said.

Aradia tried clearing her mind of intrusive thoughts. Find Vivivine first. Vivivine was in danger, Tituba could wait. Vivivine, then Tituba.

Where is the Monster Coven? Where is the Monster Coven? Where is the Monster Coven?

The pumpkin patch faded away, and the other building slowly came into focus. It was a worn-down cathedral, brownish in color, and had two brick turrets out in front. In between the turrets was a cracked, red, stain-glass window, framed with intricate black iron. Barren trees stood at either side of it, and it was covered with twisted vines. A spiked iron fence stood in front of the building, a gate locked with chains. A battered sign was posted above arched black doors.

Aradia had to squint to make out the words.

"Witch Trial Museum," she whispered. "Where's the Witch Trial Museum?"

Aradia looked up at Baba Yaga, who glared at her with a frown.

"Right, no questions," Aradia said, and looked back down at the cauldron. "Let me get a better look."

Witch Trial Museum. The Monster Coven was keeping Vivivine at a Witch Trial Museum somewhere. Surely one of the Bad Witches knew where it was. But where was Tituba?

Tituba, Tituba, help me find Tituba.

The museum faded, and the pumpkin patch materialized again. Pumpkins seemed to go on forever, and she could faintly make out a tree that had pumpkins growing from its branches. Where was this place? Aradia reached out.

"No touching!" The Baba Yaga yelled.

Aradia pulled her hand back. The image suddenly shifted to a monstrous jack-o'-lantern, its carved features bursting with flames. Aradia let out a startled cry.

"That's enough of that," the Baba Yaga said.

Aradia looked up from the cauldron. The old witch stared at her with disapproval.

"I think it is time you leave my house," the witch said, her tone dangerous.

"Yes, of course, thank you Baba Yaga," Aradia said, turning to leave.

"Wait, before you go, I believe there is one more thing left for me to show you."

Aradia faced Baba Yaga. The old witch stroked her long chin with her gnarled nails, as if contemplating something.

"It would be foolish of me to send you out into the world without preparing you in some way. Irresponsible even, and old Bucca wouldn't like it after all he's done for me," the Baba Yaga said, though she mostly seemed like she was talking to herself. "Fine. I'll let you do it. But do not expect this ever again, do you understand? If you seek me out, I shall not come, even if you're bleeding out from your eyes. The only way you'll see me again is if you don't do what I've asked of you by the last Samhain Night, before the Lord of Samhain returns to the Underworld. And trust me, Salem Witch, if you do see me again, I shall be the last thing you ever see. Do you comprehend?"

Aradia nodded, though she felt she was digging deeper and deeper into grave-dirt, as Wanda would say.

"Good, good," the Baba Yaga said tiredly. "Now, dip that little dolly of yours into the potion. I want you to see what the Salem Witches were really capable of."

Aradia had stopped questioning how the Baba Yaga knew everything. With a little hesitation she unzipped her bag and pulled out the cloth doll. She held it in her hand, feeling the rough fabric between her fingers. Should she do it?

"Well get on with it, girl! I haven't got all night, and neither do you!"

Her curiosity winning out, Aradia dipped the doll into the potion, careful to not get any of it on her fingers.

"That's enough now!" the gruff bark came quickly, "No use in wasting it!"

Aradia lifted the doll out of the cauldron. She stared at it, watching Goody Poppet absorb the potion. The doll dried quickly, and Aradia looked to the Baba Yaga expectantly.

"Wait," the Baba Yaga said.

She was staring expectantly at the Baba Yaga when the doll caught on fire. Aradia screamed and tried to drop it, but the doll was stuck to her hand. Aradia looked up at the Baba Yaga, but she was no longer there. Instead she was in a meeting room, a stern-faced judge staring at her with contempt. Screams and cries rang out from behind her. Aradia looked back. It was a group of young Puritan girls, some of them clawing at their own faces.

"I'm burning! I'm burning! She is burning me!" they shrieked.

Despite the chaos, Aradia was satisfied at seeing these ridiculous girls suffer. She knew in her heart that they deserved it after everything they had done. The heat in her hand did not bother her, like the flame was nothing more than a warm cup of tea, and the scent of smoke strong in her nose. It was acrid on her tongue. It tasted like power.

"Put that fire out, you wretched witch!" the judge sternly shouted.

A man approached her with a bucket of water, holding it out in front of her. Aradia, with one last smile at the girls' screams, dunked the doll into the water. Like a switch, the meeting room disappeared. Aradia was outside, standing in front of the woods, the doll dripping in her hand, wind chilling her. The Baba Yaga and her house were nowhere to be seen.

Aradia sat down, staring at the doll. She had been given a vision, a real clear vision of one of the Salem Witch Trials. Was it Tituba's? Baroness had said the doll had belonged to another Salem Witch. Candy, who had been hiding in Boston this whole time. Surely she must have known what happened to Tituba. Why didn't she say anything?

Aradia placed the doll in her jacket pocket for protection and lied back down, her thoughts stormy as the skies before a hurricane. Tituba was somewhere in Witch City. After the trials she had somehow escaped to this world. Aradia needed to find her, but first she had to make a sacrifice to the Lord of Samhain. Aradia slowly stood up and gazed around her. None of the Bad Witches were in sight. Where could they have gone?

The nasty voice in her head uncoiled and purred. *They abandoned you. They had finally grown tired of you and left. They know you are a fraud.*

Aradia's heart sank. She would be stranded in Witch City on a Samhain Night, with vicious spirits wandering about, and on top of that she had to sacrifice someone. It was all too much to handle. Tears pooled in her eyes, her anxiety threatening to consume her.

"Trick," a voice said from behind her. Aradia flinched and tried to turn around, but before she could move, a hard blow hit the back of her head, and everything went dark.

CHAPTER
Twenty-Eight

Salem Village, February 1692

The witch-cake had only made things worse. The Reverend caught Tituba attempting to feed it to Mary Sibley's dog, and threatened to beat her within an inch of her life. He had screamed and screamed, saying they were inviting the Devil in with witchcraft. Tituba had attempted to explain it was Mary Sibley's idea, but he would not listen. In his eyes she was no better than a witch.

Tituba bitterly stirred her cauldron, warm steam rising to meet her face. It was supper for the Reverend's family, that is if the children were feeling up to it. She had tried everything to make them feel better, but now she was treated as if she had been the one to curse them.

Screams pierced down from upstairs, the girls' fits having grown worse since the witch-cake. There was a fear in Tituba's mind that perhaps she had invited the Devil in by making that cake. But she reminded herself that the Devil was already in Salem, it was not her fault that she tried to root him out. Tituba eyed the stew. A cloudy shape *formed on the surface. She leaned down to get a better glimpse. It appeared like a thin line, twisting around itself. A noose. Tituba straightened her back. That was a bad sign, a very bad sign indeed.*

"Tell us, children, who is it that afflicts you?" the Reverend's voice shouted from above. The screaming only got louder.

"She aims to burn me! She aims to burn me dead!" Abigail shrieked.

"Who is it, who is it that bewitches you, Abigail?" the Reverend's voice shouted again.

Tituba paused her stirring. There was a moment of eerie silence, dread looming over her.

"Tituba!" Abigail yelled back, so sharp Tituba felt it like a knife between the ribs. "It is Tituba! Oh, Tituba, why do you torment us so?"

"Tituba! Tituba!" Betty's voice moaned.

Tituba dropped the ladle.

"Fetch the slave!" the Reverend yelled.

Heavy footsteps trampled down the stairs. A man in dark clothes stormed into the room, fear and fury in his face. Without a word he roughly grabbed Tituba's arm and dragged her out of the room and up the stairs. Young Betty moaned and thrashed in a bed; Reverend Parris held Abigail as she attempted to throw herself into the fireplace. The room smelled of sweat and fear, and Tituba felt the chaos settle in her own lungs, strangling her heart as it fluttered.

"Are the children well?" Tituba asked meekly.

Upon hearing her voice, both of the girls began screaming.

"Look at what you have done! Foul witch, why do you torment them?" Reverend Parris shouted at her.

"No, I don't hurt them! I love Betty!" Tituba said.

"Lying wretch!" the man holding her said, pushing her to the ground. "The girls hath confessed it was you!"

Tituba looked up at the girls with hurt and betrayal. She could hardly bear it.

"No! No! Betty, Abby, why? Why?" Tituba asked, her eyes burning with tears.

"She witched us! She witched us!" Abigail screamed louder.

"No, no Abby! Tituba not witch you! Tituba love you!" Tituba said, her voice pleading.

"She witches us, she witches us! Tituba's a witch!" Abigail yelled in one terrible, unbroken cry. "And Goody Osburn, and Sarah Good! The three of them are witches!"

"Witch, witch, witch," Betty echoed.

Abigail, her entire face contorted with malice, pointed a finger at Tituba.

"WITCH!"

CHAPTER
Twenty-Nine

A radia opened her eyes, rubbing at the blurriness. A stabbing pain shot through her ears, the worst she had ever had. She used her hands to steady herself, digging into rough and scratchy ground. Aradia sat up as her sight gradually came back to her. She was in a clearing of a cornfield, the stalks dried and yellowing.

Standing in the center of the clearing was a scarecrow tied to a large stake. It was dressed in dark shrouds, its head a burlap bag, the semblance of a skull face painted on it. Gnarled hands made of tree branches thrust out of its sleeves. Several unlit lanterns and sharp-looking farm tools surrounded the stake, as if within arm's reach. Aradia felt all the hairs on her arms stand on end. It was like a childhood nightmare.

The girl heard a groaning noise and looked. Not too far from her was something big and bulky lying on the ground. It made another groaning sound and it moved. Squinting in the darkness, Aradia discovered that it was Wanda, Erzeben, and Calaveran lying on the ground in a heap. Relief washed over her. They had not abandoned her and they were alive. She ran over to them, trying to ignore the throbbing in her head, and knelt down next to them. At least they were all together. Wanda slowly sat up. Erzeben's head was resting on Calaveran's chest, the skull-faced witch trying to sit up.

"Uh, Ben?" Calaveran said, nudging at his head gently.

"What?" Erzeben asked, opening his eyes. After a couple seconds realizing where he was, the empusa sat up quickly in embarrassment, looking away from Calaveran.

"I'm sorry," Erzeben said, turning slightly pink.

"Don't worry about it, bud, just glad you're okay," Calaveran said with a smile.

"Where are we? What happened?" Wanda asked groggily. "What happened to our masks?"

"I do not know. The last thing I remember is Aradia going into the Baba Yaga's house and . . ." Erzeben trailed off when he noticed the scarecrow, his eyes widening in terror. "Is that what I think it is?"

"A scarecrow?" Aradia asked. She had meant to sound sarcastic, but her voice trembled.

"Not just any scarecrow. That looks to me like a Samhain corn spirit," Erzeben said.

"What is that?" Aradia asked, her voice frayed even more.

"Scarecrows used to be built all the time to appease the spirits. It was believed that in turn for creating one, spirits would in turn protect the crops, and keep the maker from harm. They are forbidden to be made nowadays, because they violently attack intruders to the cornfields, but some still make them anyway," Erzeben said.

"How do you know all this?" Wanda asked.

"I hate school as much as you do Wanda, but at least I pay attention," Erzeben said.

"Well, you know what—" Wanda was cut short by a howling wind that blew around them, kicking dead husks and dirt into small dust devils. The young witches huddled close together. Like candles being lit, green light flickered on in each of the lanterns surrounding the stake, and then finally in the scarecrow's eyes. The scarecrow turned its head, until it faced the three of them.

It was alive.

For a moment, the bound scarecrow twitched all over and struggled to free itself from its restraints. As the wind died down, Aradia, Wanda, Erzeben, and Calaveran stood up warily. Their broomsticks, masks, Calaveran's skeleton pail, and Aradia's bag were all gone. Wanda conjured a fireball in her hand, aiming to throw it at the scarecrow. Erzeben put his hand on her arm.

"We cannot destroy the scarecrow, or the spirit will be freed, and do all the more damage to us," Erzeben said. "And besides, if you miss, you will set this whole cornfield on fire, and then we are definitely dead."

Wanda extinguished her fireball, clearly not too happy about it. Aradia surveyed the clearing for some way of escape; if there was a way in the cornfield there had to be a way out. Squinting, she vaguely made out a large enough space in the cornstalks that could possibly be a path. It was behind the scarecrow, but it seemed like it was their only way out. Aradia nudged Wanda and pointed to it.

"What? Where?" Wanda said.

"I see it!" Erzeben said. "Let's go before—"

The scarecrow released itself from its restraints and toppled to the ground. Aradia and the Bad Witches took that as an opportunity and ran. Aradia heard the clinking of metal. The scarecrow must have been sifting through the farm tools, deciding which one to use as a weapon. Aradia risked one terrified glance back and then darted after her friends. It was a narrow path, with only the greenish moonlight showing their way. Her mother had never taken her to a cornfield maze before, and now Aradia would be fine if she never went in one again. They ran and ran, Aradia trying her best to ignore her stabbing headache. She faintly heard heavy footsteps crunching down on straw behind them, faster and faster. It only made Aradia run faster, her ragged breath punctuating the air as crisply as the husks underfoot.

They reached a crossroads in the path. This time they had no time to try and summon Hecate; they needed to make a decision, and they needed to make it fast. Aradia looked over at the Bad Witches, hoping that with their witchcraft they could give an answer. The footsteps grew louder; the scarecrow was close.

"Witch's intuition says that way," Wanda said, pointing to the left path. Without another second passing, the four of them bolted to the left. They came to another fork in the path. They continued again on the left path, Aradia hoping dearly that they had made the right choice.

In a movement so fast she barely saw it, the stalks on the side of the path rippled and with a flash of burlap and dark cloth, the scarecrow appeared, flinging itself into their path. Four screams rang out, Aradia feeling hers clawing along her throat, sharp as the pitchfork in the creature's hand.

"Dia!" Wanda shrieked, reaching for her hand to tug her back down the path, away from the scarecrow, who watched them silently, burlap face unreadable.

"So that way didn't work," Calaveran said jovially, but even his perfect façade was cracked with fear. They headed down the other path, and now Aradia heard nothing but their breathing, her pounding heart ringing in her ears and so hard in her temples she could almost taste it.

Again, a flutter of cloth was the only warning as the scarecrow leapt into their path. This one held a sickle, not a pitchfork, a horrifying realization dawning on Aradia. This maze held more than one scarecrow. Nervous sweat streaked down her forehead, burning her eyes.

"Do you trust me?" Wanda whispered, clutching her hand tighter. "I may do something drastic."

"Do what you need to do," Erzeben barked, cutting in before Aradia could respond. "Things are already drastic."

The witch dropped to her knees and, releasing Aradia's hold, put her hands on the ground. She closed her eyes and chanted.

"Powers of Earth,

I harken thee.

Please shield us

from dangers that be.

Please I beg, protect us from harm,

I honor your greatness as I cast this charm."

Several cornstalks grew out from the ground, springing up right in front of Aradia, so dense they blocked Aradia's view of everyone, separating her from them in a small prison of corn.

"Wanda! Erzeben!" Aradia called out. "Calaveran!"

A scythe cut through the corn stalks, startling a scream out of Aradia. In her panic she turned and tried to push her way through the cornstalks. She needed to escape. The dried leaves pressed and pulled against her, scraping her skin. Her curly hair got snagged by the stalks, pulling her back, slowing her down even further. Untangling herself, her breathing grew shorter and more strained. The further she went the more desperate she became, her head pounding to the point of near-dizziness. Tearing through the cornstalks recklessly, she fell forward, sprawling onto the ground. Aradia quickly pushed herself up and stood. There were no more cornstalks ahead of her. She looked back, seeing a wall of them behind her. She had escaped the cornfield maze.

Aradia turned back around, and held her hand to heart in shock. Standing close to her was the biker woman they encountered before. Large, black sunglasses concealed nearly half of her face. But now that she could see the lower half of her face, Aradia noticed it was greenish and slightly scaly, her mouth drawn into a sneer. Instead of hair she had hissing snakes, snapping in Aradia's direction. Now Aradia knew why the woman, the gorgon, kept her face concealed. One look into her eyes and she would turn to stone, like Medusa. The woman grabbed Aradia's shoulder, and held it firmly.

"You thought you could get rid of me easily, did you, bunny? Send me out on a little noose chase, having me drive around the city looking for you? I am so much smarter than that, you stupid girl. But, I was so certain that you would die in there, a succulent sacrifice to the spirits of Samhain. But it would appear not. Now it seems as if I am going to have to take matters into my own hands. I didn't want to have to do this myself, but it seems that I must. I have been offered a great reward for your disposal."

"Who is offering you a reward?" Aradia squeaked out.

"None of your concern! Phobos, Deimos, glasses please," the gorgon said. Two snakes from her head grabbed the sides of her sunglasses, lifting them up. Aradia shut her eyes, as tight as they would go, and tried to struggle out of the gorgon's grasp, but she was too strong.

"Open your eyes, girl!" the monstrous woman cried. "This does not have to hurt, but it will if you make it difficult for me. Open—"

A loud, drawn-out scream, as if someone was slowly dying, rang in Aradia's ears, throbbing her already sore skull. The gorgon's grasp slackened, then her hands fell off Aradia's shoulders completely. The screaming stopped, abruptly, like it had been snatched from the air. An unpleasant throbbing pounded around Aradia's ears, and she massaged them as best as she could. Slowly, Aradia opened her eyes, keeping them on the ground, in case the gorgon was still around.

The woman lay face down on the ground, her body sprawled. Aradia took a step back, holding her mouth in revulsion. The gorgon's head was now a mess of dead snakes, shattered bone, and green goop. The woman's head had exploded. Aradia had never seen a real dead body in person before, and she felt her stomach churn. Who was she? She doubted it was actually Medusa, although she had to remind herself that she had also met the Bride of Frankenstein, the Baba Yaga, and had a terrifying encounter with flying monkeys. She looked up. Floating not too far off from Aradia was none other than Badb, the banshee from the crossroads.

"What, what are you doing here?" Aradia said.

"This is Giles's Farm; it is on the outskirts of Eastwitch. I knew a death was meant to happen here, and as a banshee I was compelled to be here," Badb said.

"So your scream killed her?"

"No. Not exactly. Someone had cursed her. My scream simply sped up the process."

"Who was she?" Aradia said, looking down at the body.

"Stheno, one of the three Gorgon Sisters. Medusa has been dead for a very long time, and Euryale, the other sibling, she keeps a relatively low profile. Stheno, however, was the cruelest of the three, though perhaps out of desperation. But it was time for her to join her sister Medusa," Badb said. "Did you see the guardian of the HagHollow Woods?"

"Yes, she showed me where to find Vivivine," Aradia said. "But I don't know how we're going to get there. The broomsticks are gone."

"I think they're in there," the banshee said, pointing behind the girl. Aradia looked back. A large black bag rested against the gorgon's motorcycle, which was propped up against a gravel road. Aradia surveyed her surroundings. The cornfield was in the midst of a barren field, and everywhere she looked she only saw grass and gently rolling hills, with two electrical towers and an old barn piercing the landscape.

"I'm still not sure how I'm supposed to help you. Baba Yaga wouldn't let me ask any questions," Aradia said, guilt creeping into her. "All she told me was that I needed to make a sacrifice to the Lord of Samhain. It had to be Abigail Williams, the Queen's crown, or something else."

"Very curious," Badb said solemnly. "But don't worry. When you have done what the Baba Yaga has asked of you, you will be able to help me, especially if you choose the Dread Queen's crown. Merry meet, and merry part, and merry meet again!"

The banshee vanished. Aradia was slightly confused by her comments, but did not have time to dwell on them. The Bad Witches were still trapped in the cornfield maze and she needed to get them out of there. She ran over to the motorcycle, and pulled out the broomsticks from the large bag. Aradia would give the brooms to Wanda and Calaveran, then they could fly their way out. Taking a deep breath, Aradia ran back into the cornfield, shouldering her way between the stalks.

"Wanda! Erzeben! Calaveran!" Aradia called out. The girl knew she was likely drawing attention from the scarecrows, but that did not matter to her as much as finding her, dare she call them, friends. They at least proved that they could be, and it was time that she at least tried looking out for them. Cornstalks rustled around her. Her heart thumped loudly in her ears. Aradia took a deep breath, trying to get her heart to quiet down as she strained to hear her friends over her headache. Her heart slowed, and then she heard faint calling. But that was soon cut out by the slick slice of blades cutting corn-stalks, much, much closer. She bolted, running as fast as she could in the dense cornfield. Aradia needed to find the others, she needed them to be okay.

An arm shot out from the cornstalks and yanked her in a tight chokehold. Burlap scratched her neck, and she saw the glint of something sharp in her peripheral vision. She thrashed and choked, her vision going blurry as her lungs screamed for air. She pulled hard on the arm holding her, snapping the branch. The scarecrow let out a guttural, inhuman sound. Free from its grasp, she raced forward unevenly, fighting to steady herself.

Eventually the cornstalks thinned, and she was back in the clearing where they started, where the first scarecrow came to life. Aradia sighed with relief. Erzeben and Calaveran were standing close to the stake, Erzeben holding a pitchfork, and Calaveran a scythe, both of them looking terrified, but unharmed. But where was Wanda?

Aradia ran over to them. Calaveran held his scythe raised but Erzeben grabbed his arm. "Wait, it's Aradia."

"Where's Wanda?" Aradia asked, as Calaveran lowered his weapon.

"She's still out there somewhere, and, wait, you have our brooms? How?" Calaveran asked.

"I've got to find Wanda. Here," Aradia said, throwing the broomsticks at Calaveran, who dropped the scythe to catch them.

"Aradia, you can't go back in there," Erzeben said.

"I have to," Aradia said simply. She picked up the scythe that Calaveran dropped and dashed back into the cornfield, slicing at the cornstalks ahead of her. She had to find Wanda. After all that the young witch had done for her, she simply had to. A scarecrow lunged forward at her, and without thinking she sliced the scarecrow's head clean off, the straw-filled body crumpling to the ground. She could not stop to think of the consequences of possibly freeing the spirits, not until she found Wanda.

"Wanda! Wanda, where are you?" Aradia called out, her swipes quicker and messier, frantically felling the corn. She felt a hand on her shoulder and spun around, almost decapitating Wanda. Relief washed over her.

"Easy there, you coulda almost killed me," Wanda said. "Have you seen Erz and Cal?"

"Yeah, they're in that clearing, let's go, your brooms are with them," Aradia said.

"Hold the board, what? How?"

"Let's just get out of this cornfield," Aradia said. With a somewhat of a confused look, Wanda grabbed Aradia's hand, and the two of them ran back through the stalks. When the corn tried to tear them apart, they only clung to each other tighter. When Aradia thought her legs couldn't take another step and her lungs couldn't gasp in another breath, they reached the clearing once more. Erzeben and Calaveran stared at them in bewilderment. Wanda ran over to them with Aradia.

"Oh my Gods, I was so worried that you were all dead," Wanda said, then noticed the broomsticks. "You really do have the brooms! Dia, what's going on?"

"We don't have time; let's just get out of here," Calaveran interrupted.

An axe flew towards them from the stalks. Nearly hitting Wanda, it became lodged in the stake. They looked out. Several scarecrows emerged from the cornfields, their arms outstretched, sharp farm tools in their hands. Another one threw a pitchfork at them, Aradia's arm stinging as it grazed her, but it landed firmly in the ground behind her.

"Alright, that's it," Wanda said, conjuring a fireball.

"Wanda, no! Remember what I said!" Erzeben said.

"Yeah, yeah I remember," Wanda said with a slight pause. "Too bad I don't care."

The witch threw the fireball at a scarecrow. The creature took an unsteady step backwards, then another, stumbling backwards into the cornstalks. Aradia heard the lick of the flames, smelled the sweetness of burning corn. The fire spread rapidly, until the four teenagers were surrounded by a blazing inferno. Calaveran tossed a broom over to Wanda, who swung it under her legs, and grabbed Aradia. Aradia dropped the scythe and jumped on the back of the broomstick. The flames seemed to sharpen, and Aradia squinted against the brightness and the smoke as a burning scarecrow lunged at them, shrouded in flames so hot the air seemed to bend and ripple. Just narrowly missing the scarecrow's long finger, the broom flew into the air. Calaveran followed suit, Erzeben on the back of his broomstick. They flew up high above the ground, and watched the cornfield go up in flames, the smell of burning straw wafting through the air.

CHAPTER

Thirty

They sat by the gorgon's motorcycle, watching the burning cornfield. Heat reached them from the blaze, warming their faces against the chilly night. Despite the destruction, it was beautiful. Witches were always supposed to have danced around bonfires, Aradia wondered if there was any truth to that. For a moment she could forget her troubles, and just listen to the crackling of the flames, and watch as the cornfield became the largest bonfire she had ever seen. It brought her back to her birthday, when the Lord of Samhain appeared in the fire. If she could go back to that night and change what happened, would she? Aradia and the Bad Witches ate some treats from Calaveran's pail. There were sugary cakes. If Aradia had much else to eat she would have thought them too sweet, but at that moment they were the most delicious food she could ask for.

"So," Wanda said in between bites, "it seemed you two boys were getting a little cozy in the maze there."

Erzeben and Calaveran stared at Wanda. Erzeben shot her a death glare, and Calveran at first was stunned, and then tried to laugh it off. Aradia smirked. Something felt familiar in that moment, to the way Gale had talk about boys. Aradia had never understood it—never felt that way for anyone. But as she glanced over to Wanda, her heart quickened slightly.

Yes, distraction is exactly what I need.

"I don't really know what you mean," Calaveran said.

"Sure ya don't," Wanda said mischievously. "Erz might, though."

"Why doesn't Aradia tell us what happened in the Baba Yaga's house?" Erzeben said, blushing, quickly changing the subject.

Wanda smiled impishly, but relented, and looked over to Aradia. Aradia flushed.

"Well, Baba Yaga showed me in her cauldron where the Monster Coven is hiding, but she said I had to make a sacrifice to the Lord of Samhain or she would come for me," Aradia said.

"Sacrifice? What kind of sacrifice?" Wanda asked.

Aradia hesitated. No matter how she spun it, the Baba Yaga wanted her to sacrifice a witch. Even if it was a Wicked Witch, that did not look well for someone accused of being a Witch Hunter.

"She said that the true meaning of Samhain is sacrifice," Aradia said. "That the Lord of Samhain was brought into this world because someone made a sacrifice to him. It was Abigail Williams, who also started the Salem Witch Trials. I have to sacrifice her, which no matter how evil she is I don't think I could ever do, or the Queen's crown which was somehow used to make the sacrifice."

Aradia intentionally left out the part about "the witch accused of wickedness."

"The Queen's crown? Surely she cannot be serious," Erzeben said.

"Did she say why?" Calaveran asked.

"Because that's the only way to stop the Lord of Samhain from destroying Witch City. Because I'm the Holy Strega I gotta do it," Aradia said.

"That's totally wicked. I don't know much about Abigail Williams, but I am so down for stopping the Samhain Lord. And if the Dread Queen is the one that needs to be taken down, so be it," Wanda said.

"How in the name of Hecate do you expect to steal the most powerful witch's crown in all of Crone's Cross? She is the head of the Lantern Coven; she controls this city. And she already thinks you're a Witch Hunter," Erzeben said.

"I'm sure she can think of something. She is the Holy Strega after all, right, Dia?" Wanda said, smiling at Aradia.

Aradia could not bear to look at her anymore, the heaviness of guilt pressing down on her. She did not want to let the witch down. "I don't know anymore. I . . . I just don't think I'm powerful enough."

"What do you mean? Why not?" Wanda asked, scooting closer along the dirt.

"Well," Aradia said, pulling her knees to her face, "I have never used my powers before, at least not intentionally. I don't know what I'm even capable of."

"Wait, hold on, never used your powers before? How is that even possible?" Calaveran asked, his face wrinkling in confusion.

"Are you even a witch?" Erzeben said. The two boys shared a look. Then they all stared at Aradia. Erzeben with suspicion, Calaveran with confusion, and Wanda with hope. How could she let her down? But how could she keep on lying to her?

"I . . . I honestly don't know," Aradia said, her voice small. For a moment, she hoped it would be swallowed up in the crackle of flames, but the bright stares and wide eyes told her otherwise. "I'm not the Holy Strega. I mean, my ancestor was a Salem Witch, but I am definitely not the daughter of a Moon Goddess."

"I knew you weren't the Holy Strega," Erzeben said bitterly, chucking a piece of candy into the flames. Wanda's face fell in disappointment, and Aradia felt it sharp under her collarbone. But the disappointment quickly shifted into determination, lighting up her green face.

"Well, if you don't know you're a witch, then there's one way to test it," Wanda said. She stood up and grabbed Catemaco, forcing the broomstick into Aradia's hands.

"Here. Only a witch can make a broom fly," Wanda said.

"You want me to fly?" Aradia asked, her fingers tracing the bumpy wood of the broomstick.

"Every witch worth their warts can fly. Some use brooms, others turn into bats or other animals, but every witch can. A witch needs to be connected with all the elements, and flying is how a witch connects with the air. So get up off your hearse and fly," Wanda said.

Aradia looked up at Wanda. The young witch stared at her with expectation, hands on her hips. And so, even though she felt her nerves starting up, she slowly stood up, holding the broomstick. She had no idea how she could possibly make a broom fly. Did Wanda honestly believe that she could do it?

It will never work. You are not powerful; you are not magical. Stop trying to convince yourself otherwise.

Aradia knew the voice inside her was right, but she needed to at least make an effort. She straddled the broomstick and held it tightly, closing her eyes. She focused her intention on making the broom fly.

"Catemaco, fly for me!" Aradia said.

The broom did not move. It did not even twitch.

"Catemaco, fly!" Aradia said, desperation making her voice break. Again the broomstick did not move. Aradia deflated. She had allowed herself to fantasize about being a witch, but now the cold reality of it sank in, her stomach unsettled. She was no witch. And now the Bad Witches knew.

"See, I did not think she was actually a witch," Erzeben said.

Humiliated, Aradia dropped the broomstick. Her heart thundered in her chest, and she swallowed hard. One look up at Wanda's broken face, and she ran.

"Dia, wait!" Wanda called. But Aradia kept on going, wind stinging her eyes. How could she face them after that? They believed she was something she was not, and now that they knew, they would never trust her. She needed to find a way, someway out of Witch City, to where the Lord of Samhain, the Baba Yaga, or even the Lantern Coven would never find her, even if it meant losing Tituba. She did not have the power to face them on her own.

Aradia ran to the barren fields that surrounded the cornfield. It got colder the further she went, the smell of burning corn fading away.

Exhausted, she fell to her knees and looked up at the sky, gazing at the triple moon.

"Why? Why is this all happening to me?" Aradia asked. "I never asked for any of this!"

But of course you asked for this. Wasn't this what you wanted?

Aradia was not so sure anymore. Her character of Aradia in her writing was a brave warrior witch, able to fight off monsters of all kinds. But now that she herself had faced real monsters, Aradia was not sure if she could ever be as strong. Maybe fantasy was just that. Fantasy. There was no clicking her heels to get out of this mess.

Did you not help get the Bad Witches out of the cornfield maze? Wasn't it your idea to try and summon Hecate, your decision to meet with the Baba Yaga? Listen to that old witch. You have to take responsibility for your choices.

Aradia heard someone running towards her. She stood up and turned around. She squinted from the darkness into the brightness and there, silhouetted by the flames, Wanda was running in her direction.

"You . . . aren't going anywhere. You will die if you go out into Witch City alone, with all the things out to get you now," Wanda said between gasps for air. She reached for Aradia, clutching her shoulders. Aradia pulled Wanda's hands off of her.

"Why not let them get me? You already know I'm not really the Holy Strega, let alone a witch," Aradia said, and to her shame she felt hot tears burn down her cheeks. "Why would you even trust me? I lied to you! I'm just dragging you from problem to problem! And you heard the Lantern Coven. For all you know I could really be a Witch Hunter."

Wanda shook her gently, fingers firm and close around her.

"Shut up. You obviously aren't a Witch Hunter or you would've tried to kill us by now. Instead you came back to save us in that nightmare of a cornfield. And true. You're a cowan. But that's okay. Was I hoping you would be this boss witch with powers beyond my comprehension? Yes. Am I disappointed that you aren't? A little. But it doesn't mean that I've stopped caring about you. You may be a fluffy bunny, but you're *my* fluffy bunny, and I'm not going to let you die on this night, okay?" Wanda whispered, her eyes wide and glistening under the tripled moonlight. "Whatever real reason you have for coming here, I'll support you. Unless, yeah, you are really a Witch Hunter, then we might have a problem."

Wanda's face was close enough that Aradia could breathe her in, her scent somehow still fresh, like an apple orchard. Her electric green skin was close to Aradia's, the girl almost able to feel the sweat on the witch's skin. Aradia's legs trembled, her heart threatening to break out of her chest. Maybe Wanda was stupid for trusting her like this. But she had the biggest heart of anyone that Aradia had ever met in her life. What had she done to deserve meeting her? She hiccupped, pressing a hand to her mouth like she could stem the tears.

"But what about Erzeben and Calaveran? I doubt Erzeben wants to protect me as much as you do," Aradia sniffled. Wanda looked back, and Aradia followed her gaze. Erzeben and Calaveran were standing a short distance away. Erzeben was staring at her, his blood red eyes squinted in judgement. Calaveran seemed confused, and as they watched he muttered something to Erzeben.

"Well," Wanda said, and Aradia looked up at her. "He'll come around. I know Erz can be a bit icy sometimes, but he's not as bad as he seems. We're all going to get through Samhain together."

"Thank you," Aradia said quietly, letting a small smile form on her lips.

"Come on, let's go talk to them," Wanda said, offering her arm. Aradia took it. They walked to Erzeben and Calaveran, arm-in-arm, even as Aradia stared at the ground, barely able to meet their eyes.

"Hi, I'm sorry for not telling the truth. I . . . I panicked and didn't know if it was safe at first, and then it was too late," Aradia said.

"Honestly, I am not very surprised," Erzeben said, frowning again. "But why would you hide that from us? That is suspicious. People already think you're a Witch Hunter."

"Well, you were the one that said that bunnies were dangerous. How was I supposed to know how you would react?" Aradia asked, drawing in a shaky breath. She thought of Tituba, of her own life. "I know we've done terrible things. But we're not all like that. I was kicked out of my mama's house because I was trying to cast a spell. She hates anything related to witches, because I'm descended from a woman that was accused during the Salem Witch Trials. That's why I took a train to Wonderland, that's why I ended up here. I thought I was going to a very different Witch City, but here I am."

Aradia barely dared to look up, and what she saw in their faces was the same sadness that pushed another tear down her face. She batted it away in frustration. "I wanted to go to Salem to find Tituba, my ancestor. But according to Baba Yaga, she is actually in this city after all."

The Bad Witches stared at her in stunned silence. And then Wanda smiled.

"See, she really is one of us! Fluffy bunny or not, she's a Bad Witch to me," Wanda said.

"But, but . . ." Erzeben said. "But she still has to make a sacrifice to the Lord of Samhain. Why would Baba Yaga want *Aradia* to do that? She is just a bunny. Besides, is there no way to reason with the Baba Yaga? Perhaps offer her something else?"

"I'm sorry, bud, but I don't think there's any reasoning with Baba Yaga. She's not gained her fearsome reputation by being *agreeable*. We're lucky she did not eat us on the spot," Calaveran said. He broke off to laugh. "You know, I was expecting excitement when you told me about looking for Vivivine with the Holy Strega, but I wasn't exactly expecting all of this."

"Are you scared?" Wanda challenged.

"It's not that I'm scared," Calaveran said, sobering. "I'm more worried about all of you getting hurt. I'm pretty hard to kill, trust me on that."

"And what makes you say that?" Wanda said.

"I'm protected by the Saint of Death, but I can't say the same for all of you. I don't really care what trouble we get into. It's all a ride to me," he looked around, his eyes scanning the flames and settling on Erzeben, "but I just want to make sure you all don't get killed."

"Because you've been doing a great job of that so far," Wanda said.

"Hey now, I've saved your tailbones tons of times," Calaveran argued. "Samhain Nights are just on a whole other level."

Aradia's thoughts drifted. She had to somehow make a sacrifice to the Lord of Samhain, or be eaten by the Baba Yaga. And that is if they were able to save Vivivine from the Monster Coven. Vivivine. Aradia had almost forgotten about her.

"I think we're forgetting something important. Vivivine is still being held captive by the Monster Coven. I think we should focus on finding her first, and then try to make a sacrifice to the Lord of Samhain," Aradia said.

"But what if we run out of time and Baba Yaga comes and eats you?" Calaveran asked.

"Vivivine may be running out of time," Aradia said. In truth, she was terrified of the idea of making a sacrifice, and wanted to delay it as much as possible.

"Yeah, we'll take on the old hag ourselves if we have to," Wanda said. The others stared at her in disbelief. But she laughed boldly, brashly, a noise that echoed into the night. "What? I'm not being stupid here. Even Baba Yaga has her weaknesses. She may be this powerful witch with goddess-like powers, but she is only one witch. Plus, she's the Guardian of the Woods, isn't she? She's got to be weaker in the city. Aren't her powers tied to nature or something? Besides, I think she's bluffing. She must be onto something else."

"I suppose," Calaveran said. "But what about your Salem Witch ancestor, Aradia? Don't you want to find her, too?"

"I do. But Vivivine's life is the one that's in danger. Tituba can wait until this nightmare is over," Aradia said. "When we find Vivivine, we can make a plan. I can pretend to turn myself in to the Lantern Coven or something and steal the crown when she gets close. I don't know. There's still four more Samhain Nights left, right? I'm sure we can come up with a plan before then."

"Atta girl," Wanda said with a smile.

"Then where is the Monster Coven?" Erzeben asked.

"Apparently they're at an abandoned Witch Trial Museum. It kinda looks like a church. Does that ring a bell to anyone?"

"There's an old Witch Trial Museum that I must have walked by three hundred times. They shut down some time ago, and a long time ago I think it was a temple to some old god, Macha or something. The Monster Coven is hiding in there?" Calaveran asked.

"Well, that kinda makes sense then—meet in an abandoned building nobody's used for years, who would figure?" Wanda said.

"Hiding in plain sight," Erzeben said, nodding.

"So, you know where it is then?" Aradia asked Calaveran.

"Yeah, it's in Westwitch, close to where I live," Calaveran said.

"Then we'll head out first thing tomorrow. I don't know about all of you, but I'm getting tired. We can sleep in that abandoned barn over there," Wanda said, pointing to a dilapidated wooden building a short distance away from the cornfield.

"Is that such a good idea? What if there is something in it?" Erzeben asked.

"Don't worry, bud, I'll protect you from anything that goes bump in the night," Calaveran said with a cheeky grin. "If you get too scared, I'll even let you cuddle."

Erzeben's eyes went large as if he was internally screaming. Wanda barely suppressed an amused snort, hiding it as a cough. Aradia hid a smirk behind her hand like a yawn. But unease dampened her amusement. Tomorrow they would face the Monster Coven. These were not ordinary witches they would be dealing with, but something truly, terribly wicked.

CHAPTER

Thirty-One

November 3

Aradia tossed and turned for most of the night, her thoughts refusing to settle. It did not help that she was lying on stale bales of rough hay, and the wind whistling through the barn was loud and eerie. Wanda seemed unbothered; her loud snores only added to Aradia's sleep-deprived aggravation. Erzeben and Calaveran seemed fine as well, Erzeben cuddled close to Calaveran with a smile on his face. Aradia felt like she had just finally fallen asleep when Wanda woke her up to tell her they needed to go. Grumbling sourly, Aradia ate what was left of Calaveran's treats and followed Wanda out of the barn.

"I'll lead the way," Calaveran offered. Wanda and Calaveran picked up their broomsticks and mounted them, ready to go. Aradia swung her bag over her shoulder and got on the back of Wanda's broomstick. Despite her grogginess, she was comforted by this, being so close to the witch. Erzeben got on the back of Calaveran's broomstick again. He looked particularly exhausted—maybe because he couldn't eat much of the sweets and needed blood—although Aradia suspected that was an excuse for him to get closer to Calaveran again. She noticed Wanda smirk mischievously at Erzeben, who looked away.

They took off, Wanda and Aradia trailing close behind Calaveran and Erzeben. They flew over the gravel road until industrial structures sprang up around them, the green and orange lights blurring by. The air was cold but invigorating. They were finally going to save Vivivine. The Baba Yaga's threat still loomed in Aradia's mind, but if the witch had never helped her, they would have never been able to find Vivivine, and she would not have known that Tituba was in Crone's Cross. Aradia had to tell herself that they would find some way, somehow to get her out of this mess, otherwise anxiety would consume her whole.

They flew up over highways, and flew around the skyscrapers so fast that Aradia felt her stomach protesting, the world whirring around her too quickly. She realized just how big and expansive Witch City was, crossing from east to west. The further they went west into the city, the less congested it was. Occasionally they would pass another witch flying on a broomstick, but, for the most part, the skies were empty.

"We've just passed the Hecate Trivia Statue, which means we should be entering Westwitch now!" Wanda shouted back at Aradia after what felt like hours.

Hecate again. Of course. The Goddess of Witches that this world seemed devoted to, or mostly devoted to. Aradia wondered if it really was Hecate that she had met at Wonderland Station on that motorcycle. Perhaps the Goddess really was the one that led her into the city. If that was the case, then perhaps she had been sent there for a reason after all, but doubt still clouded her mind. If they did somehow find Vivivine, make a sacrifice, and survive Samhain Night, what would Aradia's life be like in Witch City? Ideally she would find Tituba, and figure out who she really was. But until that happened, perhaps she could live with Wanda, and seek out Baroness to guide her. Was that a joy too much to hope for?

The buildings in Westwitch were smaller and spread further apart. The further they went, the more dilapidated and run-down the city became. Before they had flown over what Aradia thought looked like a living factory, but now all she could see was industrial wasteland, with not much life in sight. They flew downwards under a high bridge that connected two tower-like buildings. Aradia's gut churned, until they were close to the roads on the ground. Just when her stomach was settling, she saw a dark cloud. Then the cloud separated into black specks, each screaming in a high-pitched voice.

"Winged monkeys!" Erzeben shrieked. As they came closer, Aradia could see they were large and covered in dark fur, their skin a bluish-green color. Their eyes glowed brightly, and they had large bat-like wings. The monkeys gnashed their sharp fangs viciously as they shrieked, their arms outstretched. Aradia's pulse raced, and she wanted to scream; these creatures were more terrifying than the ghouls and spirits just from their pure ferocity.

"Hold on!" Wanda yelled, releasing the broom so she could form a fireball. Aradia lurched forward, wrapping her arms around Wanda so she could wrap her hands around the broom, and Wanda fired off her spell. But there were too many of them. Calaveran summoned fiery skulls and shot them at the creatures, stunning a couple of them, but still the monkeys relentlessly came at them.

"Wanda!" Aradia screamed, but it was too late. A monkey, terrifyingly close, so much so that Aradia could smell the bloodlust, ripped Wanda from the broom. The witch screamed. And then Aradia was falling—she clutched onto the broomstick for dear life, closing her eyes while screaming. Rough, strong hands grabbed her by the arms and lifted her up. She opened her eyes. The winged monkeys had caught her, and they were now flying full speed to the museum.

Aradia twisted under the claws, looking for Wanda and the boys. And sure enough, they flew in a pack, each one of them looking as powerless and ridiculous as she felt with a couple of monkeys carrying them. They flew up over the museum, then rapidly shot down a large hole in the roof, into a dark, cavernous room. They approached a glowing red-orange circular design illuminated the ground, the number 1692 in its center. The glowing circle slid to the side, revealing a hole underneath. They descended into it, bringing Aradia and the Bad Witches into darkness.

CHAPTER
Thirty-Two

own, down, down they went, the only light the glowing eyes of the monkeys. Aradia felt a wave of icy terror. Where would they end up? At least they would be able to find Vivivine, but would they be able to escape alive?

Eventually the monkeys slowed their descent, and pulled Aradia and the Bad Witches down a curved, stone tunnel lit by green lanterns. Aradia heard murmurs of voices ahead as the tunnel opened up into a room. The room was filled with witches dressed all in black. They wore identical green hag masks and black, pointed witch hats. And they all stood stock-still, facing the tunnel, as if they were waiting for something to happen. Flying monkeys crawled up the walls and lurked on the sides of a platform, chattering to themselves like grating giggling. The monkeys carrying Aradia and the Bad Witches dropped them violently in a clearing before the platform, landing hard on the stone ground. Aradia clutched her elbows in pain. She looked up, many of the masked faces turning to them. Some whispered "bunny" under their breath.

Aradia crawled backwards until she found Wanda, Erzeben, and Calaveran. They stood up together and huddled close, Wanda stepping in front of Aradia. What was the Monster Coven planning on doing to them? Why did they bring them here? And where was Vivivine? The noise surged, and Wanda defensively conjured a fireball in her hand. Some of the witches laughed, while others conjured fireballs themselves.

A black trail of smoke weaved its way through the crowd, accompanied by the cawing of crows, and swerved around Aradia and the Bad Witches up onto the platform. Aradia, Wanda, Erzeben, and Calaveran turned around to face the platform. The black smoke became a large cloud as the witches fell silent. The cloud expanded until it covered almost the entire platform, and a tall figure slowly emerged from it, a murder of crows flying out from behind them. At first the figure was difficult to see, but as they stepped into the light of the torches, Aradia stared in awe.

Standing in the center of the stage was a tall woman, who seemed taller as a result of the incredibly large, pointed black witch's hat on her head, shiny as PVC fabric and calfskin leather. She wore a tattered black dress and cape of a similar material, and stepped forward in buckled black boots. With each step, the sharp end of a black umbrella made a loud click on the ground. A PVC balaclava framed the woman's bright green face, her nose and chin jutting out sharply like a crow's beak. The rest of her face was concealed by a pair of spiked, black sunglasses. She stopped at the edge of the platform as the crows settled into the rafters, the black smoke dissipating behind her, and looked out at the crowd, her expression unreadable.

"My beautiful friends," the witch said in a high-pitched voice, not appearing to notice Aradia or the Bad Witches, "it is a Samhain Night once again, and the Lantern Coven is still in power. Why is this? Why does this group of degenerate hags still have power over the witches of this city? Why have we not been able to take them down?"

The Monster Coven watched the witch, rapt, as some quiet murmurs broke out and undulated throughout the crowd. They seemed to have forgotten that Aradia and the Bad Witches were there. Even the Bad

Witches stared, transfixed by the witch on the platform. This had to be the Wicked Witch that led the coven. Grim Old Mombi.

"Why is it that we have been forced to live in the shadows of Witch City, while Gourdina and her comrades control everyone and everything that sets foot in Crone's Cross through terror? Are we not just as powerful? Are we not strong enough to destroy them once and for all?" Mombi called out, her voice strong and passionate, as her leather-clad frame remained still, imposing, and just as sharp.

More mutters cascaded, as some of those assembled began to nod. The monkeys, along the periphery, picked up on the energy, muttering and shifting. This wasn't a coven, Aradia realized. This was a mob.

"It is because of this night!" Mombi continued, her voice echoing now. "This horrid, wretched night! The Lanterns have taken what was once a passionate celebration of the changing of seasons, and honoring those that have passed, and have turned it into a night of horror! Why is it that since the Lantern Coven have been in power, green-faced witches, the witches descended from the fey, have been disproportionately the ones that have disappeared on this night?"

Green-skinned witches were descended from the fey? From fairies? Aradia looked at Wanda. Did she know that? She remembered Wanda mentioning something about it before.

"Why are we the ones that have been taken by the so-called Lord of Samhain and the ghouls that wander this night?" Mombi continued. "That whenever someone attempts to take a stand against the Lanterns, or even attempts to bring to light the injustices that the green witches, the poor witches, or the witches otherwise disenfranchised by the Coven's rulings, they are the ones that supposedly get devoured by ghouls on this night?"

The murmurings of the crowd got louder, the monkeys doubling the noise. Aradia felt a stirring in her own gut, excitement or nerves.

"It's the Lanterns! It has always been the Lanterns! Who amongst us has not lost someone dear on this night? Who amongst us has not been afraid for their very lives simply by walking down the streets, or flying on their broomstick when Samhain Night hits?"

Aradia looked back to Wanda, remembering that the witch said she lost someone on this night. The young witch was drawn in by the woman's words, her violet eyes scrunched, her mouth tight with anger. Aradia could only imagine what she must be going through.

"The Lantern Coven killed my sister!" Mombi exploded, and yet she still held herself rigid and queen-like on the front of the stage. "She led the Morrigan Coven with all the fury of a vengeful god, taking down the Walpurgis Coven, our former malevolent oppressors, only to be destroyed by new ones! The Lanterns have always been our enemies, our largest nemesis, and we've waited too long in fear of them, but tonight this all ends! This Samhain we will see their mighty reign come crashing down!"

The crowd erupted into a roar of excited cheering. Wanda joined in, Erzeben looking on in horror, Calaveran's skull face unreadable. Aradia felt a knot in her stomach. The amount of energy in the room was getting overwhelming and her hands began to shake. Mombi held up a hand for silence.

"But how shall we do this? How shall we take down these great and mighty fiends? What do we have on this Samhain Night that we did not have before? We have what the Lantern Coven have been desperately trying to get their nasty little claws on since Samhain began, something that has just been out of reach of their dying grasp," the witch cried, finally turning on the huddled group of Bad Witches. "Aradia!"

The witch pointed a sharp, black-nailed finger. Aradia felt like her heart stopped. All eyes in the room were zeroed in on her, and all she wanted to do was shrink away and disappear. The witch on stage beckoned with her slender fingers for Aradia to come up onto the platform. The girl held still, petrified, the only movement her quaking hands.

"Do not worry my dear, pretty girl. You have nothing to fear from me or my friends. We shall not harm you or your companions," Mombi purred.

"What about Vivivine?" Wanda shouted out, snapping out whatever trance she had been held under.

"Vivivine?" Mombi asked, her voice bored. "Oh yes, the corpse woman. She is alive and safe. I'm afraid the only reason why she was captured was because Aradia dearest was with her. I was aiming for the girl, but alas my dear monkeys got her instead. Accidents happen."

Aradia felt Erzeben's icy look, guilt rising from her gut. He was right; it was really all her fault that Vivivine was abducted, that they had this wild and dangerous journey in the first place. They could have been safe in Vivivine's apartment by now if it had not been for her.

"Come up, my dear girl. I shall explain everything," the Wicked Witch said, a smile on the visible half off her face.

Aradia looked to the Bad Witches. Erzeben shook his head, Wanda whispered "go" and Calaveran just stared. Aradia looked around at the expectant crowd, the monkeys mulling around with tails twitching, the crows flapping wings, and the terrifying, faceless witches watching her as if with baited breath. What would the Monster Coven do if they did not cooperate? With slow steps, Aradia walked to the platform and up the steps. She stood awkwardly at the side, but the Wicked Witch gestured for her to come closer. With reluctance, Aradia walked forward, and stood next to her. Grim Old Mombi placed a sharp-nailed hand on the girl's shoulder and Aradia fought every instinct that screamed at her to run, to shrink away, to hide. She stood as straight and tall as she could, shoving shaking hands behind her back.

"You see, my dear little girl," Mombi cooed, "the Lantern Coven fears you, more so than they fear us. The Lantern Coven feels threatened when an outsider arrives in their city, especially when they claim to be the Holy Strega."

"But I'm not the Holy Strega. I just made that up to protect myself," Aradia said, holding her head as high as she dared.

Mombi cackled. "That hardly matters. What does matter is that the Lantern Coven believes, or fears you are. Lord of Samhain or no, *the Lanterns* are the ones that want you dead, which is why they immediately called you a Witch Hunter. I do not know how involved the Lanterns are with the dark spirits that roam this night, but they most certainly use the witches' fear of them to control the city. There is a reason why the witch-hunts of your land are taught so heavily in our schools, why witches call cowen bunnies, not because they do not have any power, but the fear that they might. We belittle them so we can convince ourselves that they are harmless, ineffectual creatures, when we know that in the deepest darkest parts of our hearts that they pose a real threat to us.

"However, I choose to see your people as a symbol of hope. The cowen of your land hunted us, tried to exterminate our very existence, and yet we still live on. If witches as a whole can survive and thrive after being hunted down by cowen, then we can survive being targeted by the Lanterns!"

For a moment Aradia had forgotten she didn't stand alone with Mombi, until the cheers surged even louder than before.

"But what do you want me to do?" Aradia asked, her voice barely a whisper. "Baba Yaga already wants—"

"Don't speak her name here," Mombi cut in fiercely. "She could have helped us when we first fought the Lantern Coven, but she turned her back on us. That traitorous, haggish—"

"But she told me I had to make a sacrifice to the Lord of Samhain, that it had to be Abigail Williams, Gourdina's crown, or—" Aradia cut herself off. The witch turned her gaze on her, her eyes unreadable behind the dark sunglasses.

"Or what?"

The third option was a witch accused of wickedness. It dawned on Aradia that it could have meant Grim Old Mombi. It would be impossible. And if the Wicked Witch had the slightest inclination that Aradia had any intention of sacrificing her, the girl would not have the slightest chance of making it out of that room alive.

"Or a sacrifice by flame," she said quickly, the lie twisting her tongue. The room turned to a tense silence. The Wicked Witch's grasp on her shoulder tightened. Aradia looked out to Wanda, Erzeben, and Calaveran, a range of concern and fear on their faces. Finally the witch relaxed her grip on Aradia's shoulder.

"Well, this is fascinating. Is the enemy of my enemy my friend, or are they still my foe? I suppose only time will tell. But what is certain is that the Lantern Coven must fall this Samhain!" the Wicked Witch said, lifting her umbrella into the air, her hand clenched like a fist around it. "We cannot lose any more innocent lives on Samhain Night. We have failed the witches of this city for far too long! It is time to snuff out the Lanterns' flame!"

On her cry, the umbrella transformed into a black broomstick. Another cheer erupted from the crowd, the coven members lifting up their broomsticks in similar fashion.

"*Morrigan Gu Bràth! Morrigan Gu Bràth!*" the witches chanted.

"Tonight we shall fly! Fly high unafraid of Gourdina and her ghouls! And you," the Wicked Witch turned to face Aradia, "my dear pretty one, the Dread Queen's crown you shall certainly have. By the time we are through with that mock monarch, it will be the only thing left of her. But we need time to prepare. As my covenmates and I decide on the next course of action, you shall be kept somewhere safe until the time is right."

"But what about Vivivine? I'm not going anywhere with anyone until I know for sure that she is safe," Aradia said.

The witch frowned, a small twitch of anger on her lips. "Your friend is being held in a different part of the city. We shall release her once Samhain is over, and the Lanterns have fallen. If you do not help us, none of you shall see her again."

Aradia did not like this at all. Although Aradia hoped that Vivivine was being kept alive, part of her, a part in her gut that twisted uncomfortably, wasn't sure she could trust Mombi. This Wicked Witch, this leader of the Monster Coven, or the Morrigan Coven as they called themselves, was certainly powerful, if not for her own magic then certainly for the powers of persuasion she had. Wanda ran forward as Erzeben reached for her, and she jumped onto the platform, startling Aradia. Many of the witches in the crowd conjured fireballs, but the Wicked Witch on the platform held out her palm to stop them from throwing them.

"You aren't taking her anywhere! You aren't taking her away from me! I can't lose somebody else!" Wanda cried, conjuring a fireball.

The Wicked Witch let out another high-pitched cackle, many of the other witches of the Morrigan Coven joining in laughter.

"How very sweet! Do not worry, you, as well as your pretty little friends," the Wicked Witch said, pointing to Erzeben and Calaveran, "shall be going with her. I can't have you scampering along telling people what you have seen tonight. Again, you all shall be released when the time is right. I will not murder innocent children; I am not like the Lanterns."

Wanda stood in front of Aradia defensively, her fireball still held high. Aradia felt the same fire in her chest kindling as Wanda gave her a reassuring glance. That was all Aradia needed to know that she trusted Wanda—and that wherever she went, they would be together.

"Too much time has already been wasted," the Wicked Witch said. "My winged children, take them away!"

The winged monkeys jumped off from the walls and screeched, flying at them. Even as Wanda screamed and released her fireball, they breathed out a green vapor in Aradia and Wanda's faces. As Aradia's vision went dark again, she heard the Wicked Witch's voice one last time.

"Welcome to Witch City, my pretty."

CHAPTER

Thirty-Three

Salem Village, March 1692

Tituba stood in a drafty meetinghouse, wringing her hands. Chatter filled the room, almost noiseless in her ears but for the sharp punctuation of the word "witch." The room quieted for a moment, the sound of footsteps echoing through the meeting house. Tituba glanced back. The coven of girls marched into the meeting house with their heads down, all the more like a sinister murder of crows. They took their seats at the front of the meeting house, and when they did look up, their accusatory glares burned into her.

Tituba turned away as the room grew noisy again. Why had they done this to her? Days ago she had felt betrayed and hurt, but slowly that had been replaced with pure terror—terror for her life. The judge, John Hathorne, stared at her with fierce contempt from behind his table. He was a cruel and unkind man from what she had heard. Tituba wanted to spit in his face, but she knew better. If he found her guilty, what would happen to her? The visions of nooses and hanging bodies returned to her mind. If she was not careful, she could lose her life.

"Tituba," John Hathorne said, silencing the room, "what evil spirit have you familiarity with?"

"None," Tituba said quietly.

"Why do you hurt these poor children?" The judge persisted.

"I do not hurt them."

"Why have you done it?"

"I have done nothing!" Tituba cried out, pleading with him. There were some murmurs behind her. Tituba glanced back. She received icy stares from the girls. Especially Abigail. Why was she doing this?

"Tell the truth. Who is it that hurts them?" Hathorne said, his voice sharpening.

"The Devil for aught I know."

"Did you ever see the Devil?"

Tituba paused. She had to be careful about how she answered this question. If she was persistent in her innocence, they still might think she was a witch and hang her anyway. However, if she confessed, if she proved useful to the Salem villagers, they might let her live. Images flashed in her mind of the Reverend beating her, threatening her to confess. She was not going to let that happen again. And her life was not the only one at stake. If she died, what would become of her daughter? She was so young, younger than the rest of the girls. Born into slavery. Violet, her precious flower. The Reverend and his family could easily abandon her. Tituba had to do what was right. If a witch was what they wanted, a witch she would become.

After all, it was just another story to tell. A story that could save her life.

"The Devil came to me and bid me to serve him. Last night he said 'kill the children,'" Tituba said with exaggerated malice. An astonished gasp spread among the villagers.

"What have you seen of the Devil?" the judge choked out.

"He goes in black clothes," Tituba said, thinking of Reverend Parris, the most devilish man she knew. "A tall man with white hair. He show me a book. He said write and set my name to it."

"Did you write?"

"Yes. Once I made a mark in the book and made it red like blood."

A few cries erupted from the villagers. Hathorne banged the gavel loudly, silencing them.

"Have you seen any other witches with him?" Hathorne asked, his eyes boring into Tituba with something like hunger. Or excitement.

"Yes," Tituba said, slowly, the bile of the lie rising from her throat.

"Who were they?"

Tituba paused again. How could she damn others with her words? But, if the girls had already accused them like herself, then she was not doing them further harm. She tried telling herself this at least. She had to survive.

"Goody Osburn and Sarah Good," Tituba said, swallowing hard as she remembered the other names the girls had called out. "They would have me hurt the children, but I would not."

The judge leaned forward, that glint of steel back in his eyes, teeth flashing. "What did they say to you?"

"They said to hurt the children. They tell me if I will not hurt the children they will hurt me."

"But did you not hurt them?"

"Yes, but I was sorry, I will hurt them no more."

A small, satisfied smile appeared on Hathorne's thin lips. Tituba hoped it was enough.

"When did you see them last?"

"Last night, at Boston."

Hathorne gave her an inquisitive stare. "How did you go?"

Tituba wracked her brain. How should witches fly? "We ride upon sticks."

Another astonished gasp spread throughout the crowd. They were believing every word of this wicked tale. Tituba was not going to hold anything back now.

"What attendants hath Sarah Good?" Hathorne asked.

"A yellow bird, it did suck her between her fingers."

"What hath Sarah Osburn?"

"She had a hairy thing with a head like a woman with two legs and wings," Tituba said, thinking of the monkeys in Barbados, how nightmarish they would be if they could fly.

"How doth the women go?"

"In black silk hoods with topknots."

"Did you practice witchcraft in your own country?"

"No. Never before now."

Tituba began to realize how true that statement was. Back in Barbados she was as ordinary as anyone else. In Salem Village, through the words of the girls, through her own stories, she had become a witch. She turned to face the girls. They immediately went into fits, screaming and convulsing violently. Where she had once felt care and sympathy, now felt nothing but cold scorn. They may have made her a witch, but she knew who the true wicked ones were.

"Do you see who it is that torments the girls now?" Hathorne said, leering forward, his face the very image of the Devil. Tituba looked back to the Judge, her gaze growing firm and resolute, her rage growing stronger as the girls grew louder.

"There is four women and one man!"

"Who are they?" Hathorne spat out.

Tituba decided she had had enough. She wanted no more part in this witch hunt that was sure to come. Now she understood what those visions had all been about, but she did not care anymore. Let the Puritans hang and burn each other trying to find these other witches. Let all of Salem become a Witch City. It was what they deserved. But she would not be the one to light the pyres.

"I am blind now, I cannot see!"

CHAPTER
Thirty-Four

Aradia awoke screaming covered in sweat. After taking a few breaths in, she sat up and looked around. She was sitting on a concrete floor in a dark room. A large window covered with iron bars let in the moonlight, the only light in the room.

"Dia? Is that you—are you okay?" Wanda whispered.

Aradia looked behind her. Coming towards her, ghostlike in the moonlight, was Wanda.

"Yes, I'm fine, just a bad dream," Aradia said.

"Like a good bad dream or a bad bad dream?" Wanda said, sitting down next to her. Aradia smirked.

"A bad bad dream," Aradia said.

"Do you want to talk about it? Is that what cowen do, talk about it?" Wanda asked.

Aradia stared at her for a moment, at her green skin in the moonlight. She looked too beautiful to be real. Finally, she whispered the words that had been swirling around her brain: "Wanda, what makes a person a witch?"

"What do you mean?"

"Never mind, it's stupid," Aradia said, feeling her cheeks burning. She looked down at the unforgiving concrete floor, feeling it bite under her nails as she nervously tapped her fingers against it.

"It's not stupid. I've been a witch all my life, and I don't know what it *really* means."

Aradia looked over to Wanda and the concerned smile on her face. Aradia just wanted to be held by her, to disappear into her embrace. Wanda was the only thing she could count on, the one thing in her life that still made sense; looking at her made Aradia feel safe.

"Witches are people that have some sort of magical power. With the use of rituals, spells, chants, and potions, witches can direct that power to make something happen. That's my understanding of it at least," Wanda said.

"Do you have to be born with that power? Or can you learn it?" Aradia asked. Wanda looked up, contemplating.

"I don't know. I mean, it is called witch*craft* after all, so I guess being a witch is like learning another creative skill. Like singing, painting, writing, you're making something that wasn't there before. Some people just have a more natural skill at it I guess."

A spark lit in Aradia's thoughts. Wanda's words reminded her of some of the things the Baba Yaga had said, about creating worlds and destroying them. That she had a unique gift as a storyteller.

"Wanda, you're a genius!"

"I am?"

"Yes!" Aradia said, getting more excited as she spoke. "I think I know how to get Gourdina's crown, at least I have an idea. I think I might just be—"

"YOU!" Erzeben shrieked. Glowing red eyes appeared in the darkness. Erzeben ran into the moonlight, his eyes fierce and angry, fangs bared and hands outstretched like claws. He pounced into the air, about to jump on Aradia. She sat still, too startled to react. Erzeben froze in the air just as he was about to land on her. He looked confused and angry, and hissed and snarled. Calaveran stepped in from the darkness, his palms facing forward, his gaze focused on Erzeben while the empusa levitated.

"Ben, this isn't you," Calaveran said calmly.

"This is all her fault! All of this! I was right the whole time!" Erzeben screamed.

Aradia stepped back, guilt twisting her stomach. She knew the empusa was right. If Vivivine had not been at the wrong place at the wrong time, none of this would have happened to them. Aradia would have been the only one that this would have all happened to. They might not have even tried to rescue her.

"Erz, shut up! Dia never asked for this! None of us ever asked for this!" Wanda screamed back at the empusa.

Erzeben hissed, his blood-red eyes still focused angrily on Aradia. Aradia had to look away. The last time she saw someone this angry at her was when her mother had caught her trying a spell. When she had been kicked out of her home. The memory rekindled in her mind, alighting her pain. She thought that she and Erzeben were finally starting to trust each other. Now Aradia knew she was wrong.

"Sorry to do this to you Erz, but I don't really have another choice," Wanda said. She lifted her hands up and swung them to the side. Erzeben flew to the side and hit hard against a wall, then fell over, slumped to the ground. Calaveran looked at Wanda in horror. He was about to run to Erzeben's side, but Wanda held up a hand.

"Cal, don't. When an empusa hasn't had blood in a while they become less witchlike and more, well, like that," Wanda said, gesturing to where Erzeben was a moment before. "You wouldn't have been able to hold him up like that for long. We've just got to get some blood into him before he wakes up again and tries to attack Dia."

"You say that like it's an easy thing to do," Aradia said, grateful that Erzeben was knocked out. Bloodlust or no, his anger was certainly real. He blamed her for everything. Maybe she deserved his anger, but not like this.

You should not be so surprised. It was bound to happen eventually.

"It can be. Cal you're better at transforming stuff than I am. We need a syringe," Wanda said.

"I'm good but not that good. I would need something similar in shape," Calaveran said. The brujo put his hand to his neck, his fingers clasped around his necklace.

"Maybe Santa Muerte can help," Calaveran said. Wanda rolled her eyes.

"How?" Aradia asked, intrigued.

"Just give me a second," Calaveran said, taking off his necklace. He held it up out in front of him, the Santa Muerte figure facing him. He stared at it, his gold eyes softening. Wanda loudly sighed.

"Shhh," Calaveran said without looking away from the necklace. Wanda rolled her eyes again.

"La Santísma Muerte, La Flaca, La Madrina, La Niña Blanca, La Señora Negra, I have no offering but my eternal devotion. I need a miracle. Show me a way to heal my friend, my buddy Erzeben. Ben needs blood, and I have blood to give. Show me a way so he can live. Please, La Dama Poderosa, give me a way," Calaveran said, emotion cracking his voice.

"Is that even a spell?" Wanda whispered. Calaveran ignored her, and continued staring at his necklace. He whispered some unintelligible prayers, his body rocking back and forth. Aradia was fascinated. This form of spellcraft was a little different than what she had experienced so far. She hoped it would work, not just for Erzeben's sake, but because she wanted to see something happen. And then something did.

Droplets of blood dripped off the necklace. First it was a few, but soon it was streaming down like a tap. Aradia's mouth hung open; Wanda grimaced with slight revulsion. Calaveran smiled widely, the skeletal designs of his face stretching. He put his other hand beneath the necklace to catch the blood, and speedily walked over to where Erzeben was slumped on the wall. Aradia was excited to see something both miraculous and disturbing. Was it Calaveran or Santa Muerte that caused it? Was it both? Aradia never knew what she believed in before. Even now she was unsure of just how much was real.

"Do you need any help or anything?" Aradia said.

"No, I'm good!" Calaveran said, back to his cheerful self. Aradia looked away as Erzeben began to feed, and went close to the window. Wanda came up next to her. A cool breeze blew through the iron bars, oddly comforting Aradia as she watched the glowing lights of the city. It all seemed so quiet, so peaceful. So much had happened—and so much more was going to happen, she was sure—but the city seemed so still at the moment. Aradia could almost get herself to believe that she was just looking at a nice view of the city from an ordinary apartment, that she was not locked up in some mysterious building by some Wicked Witches, that an undead woman wasn't being held hostage in her place, and that the Baba Yaga was not out there waiting for her. Wanda put her hand gently on Aradia's shoulder.

"It almost does look pretty from here. Too bad we're in this creepy place, thanks to the Monster Coven, or Morrigan Coven I guess they're really called," Wanda said.

"Who's the witch that's leading them? Is she like the Wicked Witch of the West or something?" Aradia asked, looking at Wanda.

"I guess you could call her that. She's the Wicked Witch of Westwitch. Her name is Brimombi, although most people call her Grim Old Mombi. Her sister, Emerald something or other, used to be the leader of the Coven, until I guess the Lantern Coven killed her. We were always told that Old Mombi is worse than her sister was. Now I'm not really sure what to believe," Wanda said.

Aradia searched her face, as Wanda stared out the window, her eyes faraway.

"Wanda," she said gently, "you said that you've lost someone on Samhain Night, I don't want to pry, but . . ."

"It's alright I guess. My mom, I lost my mom on a Samhain Night last year. That's why I was out in the cemetery. It's always been said that on Samhain Night those that have died in the past year return as animals. I was hoping that she might appear, or at least her spirit. She was out later than he should have been, and then we got the news that the Lord of Samhain got her. It was bad enough to learn she died, but if Mombi is right, and that it was a targeted attack from the Lanterns . . ." Wanda said, trailing off.

Her face crumpled, though no tears came out from her eyes. Aradia put her hand gently on Wanda's shoulder. She would never know what kind of pain Wanda was going through. Aradia's mother was the one that chose to let her go. Her pain was of a different sort. But she understood nonetheless.

"She was just such a good mom, you know?" Wanda said, forcing the words out. Araida could tell they hurt to say, in a way that would only get better through it. "Such a good witch. She didn't get mad at me if I got in trouble; she'd always try to understand where I was coming from. Like when I got in a fight at school one time because some jerks were calling me frog-face, she said she was proud of me for standing up for myself, but to try and not hurt others, even if you've been hurt, because that just turns you wicked, that the cycle of pain and anger just won't stop. She was just so accepting, so non-judgmental.

"That's really why I decided to protect you, because I know that's what she would've done. She was always looking out for me, even when I was being a brat. I'm a total Bad Witch, but sometimes I wish I was half as good as she was."

Wanda breathed out a shaky sigh, and her eyes darted over to Aradia. With no warning, she lunged and hugged Aradia tightly. Aradia sniffled into Wanda's hair, feeling her own eyes filling. She never had someone open up to her like this before, not even Gale. And the fact that it was Wanda, the toughest witch she knew, meant that she really meant something to her, that Aradia was not just a new toy to play with. Aradia felt Wanda's heartbeat against her own. She had never felt this close with someone. For a brief moment, it was like they shared one heart, one hurt.

"Wanda, I'm so sorry. I wish I had someone like that, but my mom—"

A faint noise came from outside the window. Wanda gently let go of her, and they both looked out. A streak of bright green smoke spread across the sky. Aradia vaguely made out that the noise was cackling laughter. The green smoke formed into letters, and then into words. Aradia put her hand to her mouth in shock.

WE

HAVE

ARADIA

CHAPTER
Thirty-Five

The Morrigan Coven was sending a message to the Lanterns.

"They're going to come find me, aren't they? The Lanterns?" Aradia asked, her voice barely a whisper. "And then they're going to sacrifice me to the Samhain Lord, or they're gonna kill me themselves. What are those witches doing?"

"I don't know," Wanda replied, her voice grim. "I wouldn't be so sure. I mean, the Lantern Coven has been trying to snuff out the Morrigan Coven for years. If they knew where to find them, they would have done something by now. They would've killed Old Mombi if they knew where to find her. What makes you think they would be any more likely to find where the Morrigan Coven has hidden us?"

Aradia continued to gaze at the city, now overshadowed by the threatening message. She sighed. All this running, all this hiding, it was taking a toll on her. She had half a mind to give in. What was a life that was always on the run?

The Lantern Coven, Lord of Samhain, and soon Baba Yaga. They are all after you. The Morrigan Coven already has you. Why continue to fight? You know you can't win.

"Wanda, I . . ."

Tituba. She had to remember Tituba. Tituba gave in and confessed after being treated so horribly, but she survived. She was imprisoned and bided her time in terrible conditions, until she was eventually released. Should she do the same? With the dreams she was having, she wondered if Tituba herself was trying to show her something.

"What is it, Dia? You have that weird hexed-out look on your face again," Wanda said.

"My ancestor, Tituba, was a storyteller, and I'm one, too. Sort of. At least I want to be. Something I've always been good at is coming up with stories. Tituba used her stories to save herself from being killed by Witch Hunters," Aradia said. "I just need to figure out a way to tell a story that will save us, and get Gourdina's crown. I just wish there was some way she could give me an idea of what I should do. Baroness was right. I need to trust my ancestors. But I need to figure out how."

"Tell me a story," Wanda said. Warmth and excitement grew in Aradia's chest.

"Here? Now?" she squeaked out.

"Yeah." There was something lazy in Wanda's smile. Something lazy and a little mischievous. "I mean we're stuck in this place, might as well pass the time."

Aradia coughed. "Uh . . . what about?"

"I don't know, something exciting that won't be depressing. All of this is already depressing enough."

Aradia gazed up at the triple moon, letting the moonlight bathe her skin. Creative energy seemed to flow into her through its rays, filling her with a light she had not felt in a long time.

"Once there was a witch who was betrayed by her coven, and was banished to a dark and cold forest. She was left there all alone, with not even a lantern to guide her."

Wanda smacked her lightly on the arm. "I said something not depressing."

"Hold on, it gets better. One night, when she had been wandering for hours trying to find shelter, she came across a lonely cottage. In it lived another witch, who, seeing the wretched state the banished witch was in, felt sympathy towards her, and let her stay with her in the cottage. The cottage witch healed the banished witch with her magic, and she showed the witch around the forest, telling her how to avoid the monsters, and where to find useful ingredients for potions.

"One day the banished witch asked the cottage witch if she had been banished to the woods, too. The cottage witch shook her head and said that no, she was not banished. She chose to live in the woods because it was the only place she felt truly free. At first, the banished witch did not understand, but as the days turned to months which turned to years of living with the cottage witch, she gradually understood. She had never been happy with her coven—they were judgmental and restricting—but with the cottage witch in the woods, she had found freedom she never had before."

Aradia shyly looked into Wanda's eyes, drawn in by their rich purple color. Aradia's chest felt tight as she rushed to get the next part of the story out.

"One day, the banished witch realized that of all the adventures the cottage witch had taken her on, the greatest one had been meeting her in the first place."

Wanda's face was open and vulnerable, her eyes large. Aradia had an instinct to lean in, but as she was about to, the green witch's face fell into its usual smirk.

"That is really candy-corny," Wanda said. "But it's also really sweet. You know sometimes I wish I could just run away and live in the woods. Fly away from all of this."

Aradia tried not to look disappointed. "Why don't you?"

"I dunno, I guess I'd get bored by myself. And I know Erz would never come with me. That boy likes his creature comforts."

Aradia wondered what it would be like to run away with Wanda and never look back. Her heart lifted at the idea. To be alone with Wanda without any of the problems of Boston or Witch City, that would be freedom.

"Wanda, maybe . . ." Aradia said, but then she realized something.

"What?" Wanda said.

"My bag! Where's my bag?" Aradia said, glancing around.

"Isn't that your bag there?" Wanda said, pointing behind her. Aradia looked back. Sitting in the corner, nearly concealed by the shadows of their cell, was her shoulder bag. She rushed over to it, picking it up and holding it close to her.

"Now I'm kinda wondering why they didn't take it. Makes me kinda suspicious," Aradia said.

"I dunno," Wanda said. "Maybe they felt they didn't need to. I mean, in their minds this isn't a prison. And to them you're just a fluffy bunny."

"Well it sure feels like a prison," Aradia said, opening her bag. She took out the doll, Goody Poppet, feeling the roughness of it in her hands. Candy had used it in the Salem Witch Trials, and Baroness had sewn some gris-gris in it to protect her. This doll was very powerful, and if Aradia was descended from a Salem Witch, perhaps she could find a way to use it.

"I thought you gave that to Baroness," Wanda said.

"I did, but she gave it back," Aradia said, looking at the doll's blank features. "It belonged to Candy, who was a Salem Witch like Tituba. I'm just trying to figure out if it can help."

"I'm not so good with poppet magic, but I know they can be used to either curse or heal people," Wanda said.

Curse or heal.

Aradia was reminded of the vision the Baba Yaga had shown her. The doll on fire, the girls screaming out. It was possible the girls were just acting up as they usually did, but what if the doll had actually cursed them in that one moment? What if they really did feel like they were burning?

"Wanda, I have an idea. We're going to use this doll to burn ourselves out of here," Aradia said, grinning.

"Sorry, I'm not following," Wanda said, eyes squinted.

"I'm gonna get you to set this doll on fire while I think of the Monster Coven. They will feel like they're on fire until I tell the doll to let us out of here. They will then feel like they have to and then we'll be free to get the hell out of here."

Wanda's eyes went wide, her head nodding in approval.

"This is why I hex with you," Wanda said, grinning. "Let's do it. But let's first see how Erz and Cal are doing so we're all ready to get outta here as soon as possible."

The thought of Erzeben waking up made Aradia slightly unsettled. What would happen when he did? Would he still be angry? And if not, could she forgive him?

"Cal," Wanda called, turning away, "how's Erz doing?"

Aradia looked over, unsure of what she wanted the answer to be. Erzeben seemed to be sleeping peacefully. Calaveran had his headphones on, holding the empusa in his lap, looking down at him.

"Calaveran!" Wanda shouted. Calaveran startled, taking off his headphones.

"He's doing good. The blood worked fine, thank Santa Muerte. He should be fine when he wakes up."

"Good, good. I don't know if you heard us talking, but we're going to break out of this place," Wanda said. Calaveran froze and stared.

"What? Why? We're safer in here than we are out there," Calaveran said.

"What makes you so sure of that?" Aradia said.

"Well, I mean think about it. The Lantern Coven is out to get you, there are spirits wandering everywhere, yeah I mean the Monster Coven locked us up in here, but at least we're safe," Calaveran said.

"Look, I don't know if it's going to work, but I have a plan on how to get out of here, and find Vivivine. The whole reason we went looking for the Monster Coven was to find her, right?" Aradia said.

"She's probably locked up in this same building, wherever this is. Erz would want us to rescue her," Wanda said.

Calaveran looked down at Erzeben.

"I guess," he said. "But I mean how are we even going to get out of here? The Monster Coven is incredibly powerful. There's probably a huge amount of enchantments keeping us in here."

"I'm gonna burn Dia's doll and then she's gonna curse the Morrigan Coven," Wanda said with a grin. Calaveran looked between the two of them, his eyes wide.

"You're going to do what now?"

"What, what's going on?" Erzeben asked sleepily.

Aradia and Wanda looked over. Erzeben opened his eyes, and realized Calaveran was holding him, his pale face pink. He instantly sat up and got to his feet.

"What happened?" Erzeben asked.

"Well, the Morrigan Coven captured us, locked us in this cell, and then you tried to kill Aradia, but then Cal gave you some creepy skeleton lady blood," Wanda said nonchalantly. Erzeben looked even more embarrassed than before. He glanced back and forth at Aradia and Calaveran.

"I am so sorry, Aradia, I do not know what came over me. I guess I just needed blood. Thanks Cal," Erzeben said, not looking anyone directly in the eyes.

"Not a problem," Calaveran said with a smile. Aradia simply nodded at the empusa, not wanting to say anything. She was still processing that he nearly killed her.

"Anyway," Wanda said after an awkward silence, "now we have a plan to get out of here."

"Good. I did not trust Brimombi for one second. A lot of propaganda is what it sounded like to me," Erzeben said.

"Well, they did have some valid points though," Wanda said. "I mean, my mom . . ."

She trailed off into another awkward silence. Aradia was uncomfortable, a tension growing in the room. If the Lantern Coven was in fact responsible for Wanda's mother's death, she could imagine how Wanda would side with the Morrigan Coven. On the other hand, Aradia did not trust them, especially after the night she was having—trustworthy people didn't kidnap other people, for starters.

"Anyway, Wanda," Aradia said, holding out Goody Poppet, "set her on fire."

"With pleasure," Wanda said, conjuring a fireball in her hand.

"Wait, you're doing what now?" Erzeben said.

Screams cut through the thick metal door. Aradia and the Bad Witches looked over and watched the door carefully. What was going on outside? Had the Lantern Coven found them already? The door thudded, shaking like someone huge had crashed into it. Wanda aimed her fireball, Calaveran conjured a flaming skull, ready to throw, while Erzeben's fangs and nails grew larger and sharper. Aradia held the doll close to Wanda's fire, ready to set it ablaze if need be. She did not have the powers or strength of her friends, but she was not the same scared little Alicia that first arrived in Witch City. Not anymore.

With another loud bang, the door swung open, and a large figure fell into the room. Wanda and Calaveran lunge forward, poised to throw their fire. Aradia put the doll in her jacket pocket and placed her hands on their arms. She had an intuitive feeling about who it was. When the figure stood up and got their bearings, Aradia was right, but could hardly believe it. Standing in front of them, disheveled yet determined, her eyes wide and teeth clenched, was Vivivine.

CHAPTER
Thirty-Six

Vivivine's familiar large smile spread across her face as she recognized them. She ran over, arms outstretched. She hugged Erzeben first, then the others. A wave of relief washed over Aradia.

"I am so happy to have found you all again! I was so worried!" Vivivine said.

"We were worried about *you*!" Erzeben said.

"Yeah, we've been looking for you all Samhain," Wanda said.

"How did you find us?" Aradia asked.

"That's so very sweet of you! I'm afraid we don't have too much time, but to say in short, some of those Wicked Witches let it slip that you were all locked in here, and I would not have that. I mean, you're children for Hecate's sake! And like I've said before, Vivivine can find her way out of anything. But let's get out of here before it's too late," Vivivine said.

"Wait, are you witches sure that this is such a good idea? I mean, if we leave this room now, we will have made enemies of the Monster Coven *and* the Lantern Coven," Calaveran said.

"That may be the case, but children should not be held hostage in an adults' war. I will not allow it. You may all feel very grown up, but the fact of the matter is that you are just kids. I'm taking you out of here, and I swear I will do my best to keep you all safe," Vivivine said. "Properly this time."

The thought of making enemies of both of the most powerful covens in Crone's Cross did not sound appealing to Aradia, but deep down she knew as long as she was labelled a Witch Hunter, she would never be safe. The group exchanged a few tense nods, and then Aradia and the Bad Witches followed Vivivine out of the room, Calaveran reluctantly trailing behind. They were led into a hallway, dimly lit with green, flickering, fluorescent lighting, Aradia's eyes straining. A few bodies lay slumped on the floor. Aradia looked at Vivivine. As nice as she was, the Frankenstein woman was a little terrifying.

"They're not dead. Just unconscious," Vivivine said lightly, tilting her head with another broad smile. Aradia did her best to return the smile, although she was certain hers was more of an awkward grimace.

They walked around the bodies, Aradia careful not to step on any of them. Vivivine picked up the pace, her heels clicking loudly. Aradia trailed behind her with the Bad Witches, her breathing heavy as she tried to match the Frankenstein woman's pace. Their footsteps echoing down the hall. A thrill pumped in Aradia's heart, the threat of being caught pushing her forward. They turned right down the hall, and Aradia's eyes caught on the glowing green EXIT sign above a door at the end of it.

"What's that noise?" Wanda asked.

"What—" Aradia cut herself off. That's when she heard it: hollering and screeching that sent her blood running cold, and the flapping of bats' wings.

"Monkeys!" Calaveran yelled, rushing them forwards, and as Aradia turned, she saw them. The monkeys barreled into the hallway. Vivivine, Aradia, and the Bad Witches ran faster. Vivivine reached the door and swung it open, but stopped in her tracks. Aradia and the Bad Witches ran up behind her, almost knocking her forward. The exit led outside, but they were several stories off the ground. Aradia clung to the doorframe, a wave of dizziness making her sway. A cool breeze blew in, blowing Aradia's curly hair into her face. And behind them, the monkeys jeered, louder and louder.

"I don't think I can smoke us anywhere close this time, seeing as I have no idea where we are," Wanda said. "Erz, use your echolocation or whatever it's called!"

"That only works with bats!" Erzeben said.

"They're part bat—just try it!" Wanda said. Erzeben nervously turned around. The monkeys were nearly upon them. He opened his mouth large, extending his jaw. A high-pitched noise cut the night air. The monkeys stopped and screeched in confusion, flying and crawling around each other.

"Is it working?" Aradia said. The monkeys continued to move around in confusion. Then, as if a switch was pulled, they broke free and flew at them. Aradia clutched Wanda's arm. The witch conjured a fireball, and threw it at the monkeys, lighting them aflame. The acrid smell of burning hair wafted into Aradia's nostrils. The monkeys screamed louder, piercing Aradia's ears, but continued to fly at them. Aradia, Vivivine and the Bad Witches jumped.

Aradia screamed as they fell. The wind blew fiercely up against her, and the ground came up quickly to meet them. With all their magic, this was it. She closed her eyes. At least they found Vivivine.

A force lifted Aradia up by her shoulders. At first she thought it was a winged monkey, but looking up saw that it was several bats. The others also had bats holding them up. More bats flew around them, creating a cloud around them. It seemed that Erzeben's communication worked, just not in the way they expected. She could see the monkeys in the distance, still on fire. They were screaming and flying around frantically in the air, trying to smother the flames. Aradia cringed to see them in pain like that, but she knew it was what they needed to do to escape.

As the bats pulled them into the fresh night air, Wanda whooped. Aradia looked back at where they were held captive. It was a nondescript concrete tower, blending in easily with the dilapidated skyscrapers that surrounded it. The Monster Coven was again hiding in plain sight, where the Lanterns would never think to look.

The bats flew over several of the factory-like buildings of the city. Green and orange smoke curled up around them from smokestacks, and though it tasted foul, Aradia felt a calmness steal through her from being hidden from view, at least for a bit. The bats chattered amongst themselves, high-pitched chirps, and suddenly the group pulled to the side.

Aradia glanced over at Wanda, itching to reach out for her hand. But the bats again tugged them, veering to a new course over a less dense part of the city. It was darker, seemingly less inhabited. The mountains grew the further they went, the air colder. More chattering, and Aradia felt herself pulled up higher and higher, and shivered hard. The mountains were rocky and barren, a crumbling castle almost blending in with it. Monstrous gargoyles leered from Gothic towers, thorns covering the castle like vines. The bats dropped them in front of its large, foreboding doors. For a moment, they danced around just overhead, wings fluttering and interweaving, and then they flew out into the night sky. Erzeben looked up at them, and made another high-pitched noise, smiling.

"So, you can control bats?" Aradia asked.

"I suppose, but control is not really the right word, more like influence," Erzeben said. "I told the monkeys to bring us to a safe place, a place far enough that neither coven would think to look. It seems as if the bats did instead."

"Of course now the Monster Coven will be after us again, and more angry this time," Calaveran said, looking at the bats as they left. "And the Lanterns . . ."

"A little thank you would suffice," Erzeben said.

"I'm sorry, Ben, thank you. You did save all of our lives. But I'm worried about the Monsters now. I mean, one coven out to get us was bad enough," Calaveran said.

"Fair enough, I suppose," Erzeben said icily.

"Whatever, I thought that was total Bad Witch material right there," Wanda cut in, nudging Erzeben fondly. "We found Vivivine and we escaped, I'm not afraid of Grim Old Mombi and her 'pretty little friends.'"

"Thank you, Erzeben," Aradia said as well. "But where are we? I mean clearly nowhere is really safe tonight, but we need a place where we can at least hide and plan what to do now. I still have Baba Yaga's threat looming over my head."

"If I am not mistaken, I do believe we are on Mount Nemain, and that is Castle Tartarus, where the Walpurgis Coven used to rule," Vivivine said cheerfully. "Thank you, Erzeben for your quick work, but are you sure this is a safe place? I mean, I can take you all back to my house until Samhain ends, I am sure you will all be much safer there."

"Thanks for the offer, Viv, but if the Morrigan Coven knows you're missing, your place will be the first place they look. Like Cal said, they probably won't be too happy that we escaped. But of course, they've got bigger toads to boil; they've practically declared war on the Lantern Coven now," Wanda said, and grabbed Aradia's hand. "Come on Dia, let's check out this creepy castle."

Aradia's gut was telling her to stay away from this castle, that something evil lurked within. But again she found herself melting from Wanda's smile, willing to go wherever the witch would take her.

"The Monster Coven won't find us here, right?" Aradia said, looking into the witch's violet eyes.

"This place has long been rumored to be haunted by evil spirits," Erzeben interjected. "But that is what makes it a perfect place to hide. No one is going to come looking for us here."

"And you're not worried about the evil spirits?" Aradia asked, turning towards him.

"Honestly, I am much more worried about the Lord of Samhain and all the witches that are after us, well, more you than us, but us by proxy, than I am about some ill-tempered ghosts," Erzeben said.

"Hiding in a haunted castle after we have escaped being captive by Wicked Witches. Alright," Calaveran said. Erzeben gave him a look.

"Well, if you have a better suggestion other than turning ourselves in to the Monster Coven, I am all ears," Erzeben snapped.

"Looks like the bat's claws are out," Wanda whispered to Aradia.

Calaveran sighed. "I'm sorry buddy. You're right. Let's stay here, at least for now."

Erzeben continued to glare at him, then turned around and walked into the cavernous entrance of the castle, the doors half rotted away. Wanda smirked at Calaveran, and walked hand-in-hand with Aradia into the castle. As they stepped into the darkness, Aradia wondered if perhaps Calaveran was right about staying in the castle. She had a very bad feeling about this place. As she stepped into the dark threshold, she had the sensation that the building was swallowing them whole.

Wanda and Calaveran lit the way with fireballs and glowing skulls. They walked down a narrow dark hallway, an oppressive, almost suffocating feeling weighing down on Aradia, as if the castle itself did not want them there. This was a dark place, in more ways than one. Great evil had been done here. Even though the Walpurgis Coven no longer lingered there, their actions still did. Aradia shivered and clutched her bag tighter. But what other choice did they have? Nowhere in the city was safe.

"What is the Walpurgis Coven, anyway?" Aradia asked, looking warily around her. Goat skulls mounted the walls, spiders crawling into them as the group passed by, making Aradia shiver.

"The Walpurgis Coven used to rule Crone's Cross a long time ago. There was this war between them and the other two covens, and the Lanterns won when the Walpurgis Coven's leader, Walpurga Lucifera, was destroyed. The rest of them were practically obliterated. They were a really evil coven, a coven of warlocks, so it was for the best," Erzeben said, brushing cobwebs out of the way.

"Aren't warlocks just male witches?" Aradia said.

"No, not exactly. Warlocks do tend to be men, as their system of magic is very male-centric; it was very unusual for a woman to be in charge, like in the case of the Walpurgis Coven," Erzeben said. "Warlocks are witches that were once cowen, but made pacts with Lucifer to gain powers."

"Lucifer? The Devil? He's actually real?" Aradia asked, nearly stopping in her tracks. A cold, icy feeling formed in the girl's chest. She had grown up to believe that the Devil was responsible for the corruption in the world, the one that was responsible for witchcraft. If the Devil was real, it scared her more than anything else.

"Well, I am not sure about 'the Devil.' But according to the *Vangelo*, the Gospel of the Witches, Hecate-Luna-Diana created light out of her darkness and called him Lucifer. He was the father of Aradia, as the Moon Goddess was her mother. But he descended to Earth, to teach his own form of witchcraft."

They approached a large set of iron doors, images of grotesque demons molded into it. With fangs, forked tongues, and claws, it was as if they were inviting them in through the gates of Hell. Aradia's stomach clenched.

"Lucifer is the real Aradia's father? What the hell? Why didn't anyone tell me that before?" Aradia asked. Erzeben shrugged.

"We thought you knew," Wanda said, gently letting go of Aradia's hand. The witch extinguished her fireball, and she and Erzeben pushed open the doors, a loud, high-pitched squeak echoing through the castle. Aradia reached for Wanda's hand, and the group passed through the doorway.

The doors led to a cavernous great hall, a dead, stale energy to it. Everything was gray and bleak. A staircase, covered with cobwebs, led to a large platform at the back of the room, which in turn branched off to two other staircases. Standing in the center of the platform was a tall stone altar, Aradia shivering at the idea of what it might have been used for. Behind the altar stood a large stain-glass image of a figure wearing flowing white robes, the face shattered. Leaves fell from a large hole in the city, small piles of them scattered everywhere.

"Look at the floor," Erzeben murmured.

The group looked down. Lit by the moonlight was an image of a white, engraved goat's head, its horns forming a W, an inverted pentagram behind it. It was encased in a circle, various names written around the image. Aradia crossed her arms against yet another chill that shook her body. Witchcraft was one thing, but actual demonic rituals was quite another.

"This place is so drafty, so dark, and I'm getting the heebie-jeebies all over. This does not seem like a good place to hide. I really should be taking you children somewhere else," Vivivine said.

"Will you stop calling us children?" Wanda retorted.

"I do not particularly like it either, Vivivine, but the bats took us here for a reason. If we try to go back to one of our homes, we will be putting our loved ones in danger—and that's if we can even find our homes. I still have difficulty turning into a bat, and none of us have any more broomsticks," Erzeben said.

"I suppose. But this castle . . .?" Vivivine said, disgusted by their surroundings.

"Bad Witches do what's necessary," Wanda said.

"Bad Witches?" Vivivine said.

"It is what we call our little group," Erzeben said.

"Oh, I see," Vivivine said.

"Let's make camp in here," Wanda said. "Cal, let's start a fire, it's colder than a witch's ti—"

"Ahem, language," Vivivine said.

"Let's just make the damn fire," Wanda said.

Wanda and Calaveran levitated the fallen leaves into a large pile, and flung in any piece of broken furniture they could find. Wanda shot several fireballs from her hands at the mound, until a large bonfire sparked. The smoke wafted up into the air through the hole in the ceiling. The group huddled around the fire, tired and hungry, rationing what was left of Calaveran's treats. Aradia and Erzeben sat on either side of Wanda. Vivivine sat a little farther away from the bonfire, claiming that she just "had some issues" with being too close to fire. Calaveran sat on his own across the flames, a guilty expression on his skull-like face. Erzeben still glared at him.

"Maybe you should talk to him," Wanda whispered to Erzeben.

"I have nothing to say," Erzeben said.

"We all know you like him. We don't need your angst about it on top of everything else that's been going on," Wanda said. Erzeben looked down, his cheeks flushed.

"It is really none of your business how I might feel about Cal, and I do not really see how it would matter anyway. I'm just a friend to him, his 'buddy,' and that is all I will ever be. I do not even know if he is into guys. He's had ex-girlfriends, but no ex-boyfriends. And he's made eyes at Aradia a couple times at least," Erzeben said. Aradia glanced at Calaveran. She never noticed it. Was it true? Not that it mattered.

"Maybe," Aradia said, "but if you just gave him a chance—"

"I am fine, thank you," Erzeben said. Wanda sighed.

"Whatever, man, just don't come complaining to me about it later," she said.

They sat there in silence. Aradia replayed their long day in her head, how Erzeben had lunged at her, and found her eyes drifting over him in distrust. Despite the warmth of the fire, she still found herself shivering.

CHAPTER

Thirty-Seven

Salem Town, July 1692

Tituba sat in her cramped cell, the summer's heat boring through the bars. Sweat dripped from her brow. The other women they had brought in as accused witches avoided her mostly, seeming to believe that she truly was a witch. Tituba let them think that, not wanting to be bothered by any of the so-called Puritan goodwives. There was a small amount of satisfaction knowing where once these women had viewed her as a slave, as something lesser, they were now prisoners just like her. According to the outside world they were all Salem Witches, all deplorable, all wicked. Although the conditions of the prison were horrid, it somehow felt safer inside of it than out.

The jailers brought in a new prisoner. She was a young African woman, with beautiful brown skin and voluminous hair unrestrained by Puritan bonnets. She reminded Tituba of a younger version of herself, before the world had eaten her up. Tituba hoped it was not too late for her.

The woman was forced into Tituba's cell, her eyes large and warily taking in her surroundings. She looked at Tituba with some fear, but Tituba saw there was some hope there too, that perhaps she was not alone.

"What is your name?" Tituba asked.

"Candy," the woman said, sitting across from her, looking Tituba up and down. "You are Tituba."

"You know me then."

"Yes, everyone knows Tituba the Salem Witch."

Tituba nodded. "And what do they say of Tituba out there in Salem?"

"They say you made pact with the Devil, that Good and Osburn forced you to become a witch. You fly on sticks and see many strange things, but don't want to be a witch no more," Candy said, then added hesitantly. "Is it true?"

Tituba looked Candy in the eyes. Now there was no fear, no revulsion—only curiosity. It was not the same devious curiosity she saw in Abigail, but something brighter, purer, an inspired wonder.

"I made no pact with the Devil, but if I be a witch or not I do not know," Tituba said honestly, sighing. "Are you a witch?"

Candy shrugged her shoulders. "I can make poppets like Mistress showed me, but Candy only be a witch because the girls say Candy be a witch."

Tituba nodded sadly, fighting a wave of tears. Those girls, Abigail and her little coven, were making witches of them all. For what reason? For what purpose?

"How many witches be hanged?" Tituba asked instead.

"One, Bridget Bishop. More soon."

A sickly feeling rose in Tituba's stomach, but she suppressed it. It was not her fault that Bridget Bishop had died. She had not tied her noose, or pointed an accusing finger at her. She did not even know who the woman was. But something still gnawed at her.

"Have you heard any word of a John Indian, or a little girl Violet?"

"Heard nothing of any Violet."

Tituba rested her head back against the wall in relief. Those awful girls had at least let her precious flower be.

"John Indian," Candy said quietly, "he bewitched like the girls. Fits and screams like the rest of them."

Tituba's head shot forward, her eyes wide in surprise. At first she was disgusted by the idea, but realized John must have known that with his wife in prison that he was an easy target. Better to beat the wicked Puritans at their own game than to become a losing victim of it. And that way it deflected all attention away from Violet.

"Smart John," Tituba whispered.

The cell went quiet, and the stuffy heat forced a wave of exhaustion over Tituba. It reminded her of those summer days in Barbados, although there were no refreshing fruits to quench her thirst, no swimming in the bright blue oceans to cool her down.

"Candy, you know Barbados?" Tituba asked, her voice sounding as tired as she felt. Candy's face lit up, a beautiful smile forming on her face.

"Yes. Barbados is my country."

Tituba smiled back. It would be wonderful to talk to someone who knew Barbados the way she did. They could both escape the Salem Jail for a while.

"Candy, tell me of Barbados."

Candy shifted uncomfortably.

"It is very pretty, very warm, but I'm no good at telling stories."

Tituba nodded gently.

"That is fine. Let me tell you a story about Barbados," she said instead. "Let me take you back to our country."

CHAPTER
Thirty-Eight

Crone's Cross, November 4

Morning dawned through the hole in the ceiling, the extinguished bonfire of leaves and furniture now a smoldering heap of ash that burned Aradia's eyes and made her nose run. Around her, the other Bad Witches also pressed themselves awake, Wanda rubbing her eyes like she could push the sleep away. Apparently no one had slept well.

"So, we've found Vivivine," Aradia said, her voice too loud so early in the morning. She cleared her throat. "Now we should figure out a way to steal the Queen's crown."

"Do we really have to?" Erzeben asked. "We are safer in here."

"You may not seem to care, but my life is still at stake, Erzeben. If I don't manage to steal Gourdina's crown or sacrifice Abigail Williams, Baba Yaga will come for me!" Aradia said. Her harsh words echoed through the chamber; she imagined them following the last curls of smoke up into the mountain sky. Wanda scrunched her eyebrows in concern, as if she was about to say something.

"Okay, I get it, sheesh!" Erzeben said, raising hands in defeat. "I was just saying it might be better if—"

"If I was better off dead? Is that what you were saying?" Aradia asked, her anger bubbling up to the surface.

"No, I—"

"Are you sure? Because you did nearly try to kill me back there, or did you forget?" Aradia said, standing up and pushing herself away from the group. She had to get away from them—something surged inside of her, white-hot, angry, and vulnerable all at once. Calaveran and Vivivine looked over, concerned.

"Aradia, I am sorry!" Erzeben said.

"Sorry for being a bloodthirsty vampire?" Aradia asked, and felt her face pull in a snarl.

"Dia," Wanda said, standing up, "leave it alone! What he did was bad, but he couldn't help it. He didn't even hurt you!"

"No but he tried to! I can't believe you're defending him, after all that!" Aradia said.

"Aradia, what the hex has gotten into you? This isn't like you," Wanda said, gently placing her hand on Aradia's arm.

"And what would you know what I'm like? We barely know each other!" Aradia said, shaking off Wanda's arm.

"So that's how it is," Wanda said, her face falling.

"What? You would have never helped me if you didn't think I was the Holy Strega, and now the only reason you're doing it is because you feel sorry for me! The only reason why I'm here is to find Tituba! I don't really care what happens to Witch City or Lord Stingy whatever, I just want that Baba Yaga hag off my back! Let's not pretend any different!" Aradia said, looking away to wipe away her tears.

"I see," Wanda said. "I thought you had what it takes to be a Bad Witch, but it looks like I was wrong."

Aradia felt dry leaves hit her back and she turned around, picking them out from her hair. Wanda stood with legs apart, burnt leaves in her hands. Her green face was pulled taut, a flash of anger Aradia had never seen. "I thought we could trust you! But it turns out you're just a selfish cowan no better than a Witch Hunter!"

"Girls, please, there's no need to fight," Vivivine said, coming towards them.

"No, Wanda's right. I don't belong here. I'm going to go find Wonderland Station and get the first train out of this nightmare, and I mean it this time. Tituba isn't worth all this," Aradia waved her hands around, indicating the horrifying hall, the Bad Witches and all. She swung her bag over shoulder, stomping to the entrance of the hall.

"Aradia, dear, wait!" Vivivine said, her heels clacking loudly as she ran after her. But Aradia was already gone. She ran down the dark hallway. Tears of anger and hurt burned her cheeks. Aradia did not belong in Witch City; she was not a Bad Witch. She was betrayed by those she trusted. Again.

Aradia's legs slowed down as if they had weights on them. Her whole body grew heavy, nausea churning her stomach. Suddenly the whole room seemed to spin around her. She placed her hand on a nearby wall and closed her eyes, breathing slow and deep.

"What do you want from me, Tituba?" Aradia whispered through tears. "All you've done is ruin my life!"

"You're not the only one."

Aradia stood up, startled. She was alone in a small dark room. Had she imagined that voice? But she had a deep, unsettling feeling that she was not alone, the sort that made the hairs on the back of her neck prickle. Maybe the castle was haunted after all.

"Who's there? I've had a really long-ass week and I'm not into playing any more games," Aradia said.

"Look behind the curtain."

Aradia squinted and looked around her. Vaguely she made out a dark fabric hanging on the wall. She looked at it with nervous uncertainty. Who was in the room with her? And why were they hiding? The girl slowly stood up, not taking her gaze off of the curtain.

"Show yourself," Aradia said.

"I can't."

Aradia frowned, unsure if that was a realistic excuse in a place like Witch City. "Why not?"

"See for yourself."

Aradia hesitantly walked towards the curtain, her palms sweaty, chills running down her back every step she took closer. But her curiosity would not let her be. Aradia pulled the fabric to the side quickly as if ripping off a bandage. She let out a cry of surprise to see a figure there. But after a moment, as her thudding heart quieted, she realized it was her own reflection. The drape had covered a large, round mirror.

She stared at herself in wonder, hardly able to recognize herself. Had she really changed so much in Witch City? She saw a girl with tangled dark hair, leaves sticking out from it, wearing a torn and dirty leather jacket. The girl seemed fierce, perhaps even a little dangerous. Could this person really be her? She looked so different than how she remembered herself.

The reflection faded, and a new one formed. A beautiful, pale-faced young woman with long, white-blonde hair appeared. She had sparkling blue eyes, plump red lips, and wore a silvery dress decorated with jewels. The woman looked hopeful, her eyebrows lifted, a small smile on her face. Aradia stared, entranced by the reflection that was not her own.

"Please, help me," the reflection said, and Aradia flinched in surprise.

"Who are you?" Aradia asked, taking a step back.

"Aradia, dear child," the reflection said. "I'm the *real* Aradia."

"The real Aradia?" Aradia said, trying to remember what Wanda had said about her. "So that means—"

The woman smiled calmly, her blue eyes fluttering shut. "Yes, daughter of Tituba, I am the first witch, daughter of the Moon Goddess, Hecate-Luna-Diana."

CHAPTER
Thirty-Nine

Aradia stared at the reflection, trying to grasp what the woman had said. Was it really possible that she was talking to the real Aradia? She did not know much about her, but she suddenly felt very small. "How—how is that possible?"

The beautiful woman in the mirror smiled patiently. "I was there when the Salem Pact was made. It happened at the beginning of the Great Witch War, when the three most powerful covens battled for sovereignty. My mother sent me to stop it, but I was too late."

"The war? The one that put the Lanterns in power?"

"Yes. Abigail Williams started it. She summoned the Lord of Samhain and sacrificed the first witch she had ever accused."

"Tituba? But Baba Yaga said she was still in the city!" Aradia said, not wanting to believe that her whole quest had been for nothing.

"She is. Just not in physical form. As part of the ritual, her spirit was trapped in Morrigan's Grove."

Solve one problem and you will solve the other.

"So that's where she's been, all this time," Aradia said with a quiet excitement. The other Aradia nodded. Her excitement fell as a realization came to her.

"So either way I have to go there, to be sacrificed or to make a sacrifice to save Tituba."

"Perhaps you do not have to. You have been thrust into this world and have dealt with hardship after hardship. I believe it is time for you to rest."

Aradia's body was sore and tired, everything aching at least slightly. She had not taken time to notice before because she had to keep going, keep running, never paying too much attention to her own physical needs. A break would be a godsend, and if the real Aradia was offering to fight her battles for her, who was she to refuse?

"I want to rest," Aradia said to the face in the mirror. "I could probably sleep for a hundred years after all of this. But I need to find my ancestor."

"Understandable. Let me at least help you."

"So you can bring me to her?"

"Yes, of course dear girl. And I can help you make the sacrifice. I can even do it for you. It was what I was meant to do as the Holy Strega. But there is something I need you to do for me, to set me free from this prison."

"What do I need to do?"

The mirror Aradia smiled.

"It is very simple," the reflection said, placing her hands on her side of the mirror. "Place your hands upon mine, and chant—"

"Dia, no!"

Aradia turned around and saw Wanda standing in the open doorway, catching her breath as if she had just run hard. Erzeben stood slightly behind her.

"How did you find me?" Aradia asked, still braced against the mirror as the reflection had requested.

"I can explain, but you need to step away from that mirror, it's dangerous!" Wanda said, rushing to Aradia's side.

"Why?" Aradia said, stepping away from her. "Why do you care?"

"Erz and I talked, and he feels really really bad. You were right. Blood-deficient or no, he shouldn't have taken it out on you. Like obviously you'd be upset. And we could not just let you go out into Witch City and probably die. As upset as I might be, you're still important to me. Bad Witches wear black, and Bad Witches have your back. I'm not letting you go," Wanda said.

Aradia felt the hardness of her heart crack a bit, but she could not forget the anger still simmering in her veins. And who were they to stop her from summoning the real Aradia from the mirror? Wouldn't they want that anyway? It was about time that Aradia did something all for herself, with no expectations from anyone else. She would save herself, just like Tituba did.

"Thank you, but I need to do this. This is the real Aradia. She can stop Lord Samhain, and she can help me find Tituba," Aradia said. "I'm sorry."

Wanda was flung out of the room by an invisible force, and the door slammed, shutting her out of the room. Aradia jumped, startled.

"Did you do that?" Aradia asked the reflection.

"No, Aradia. You did."

Aradia turned and faced the mirror, trying to ignore Wanda's shouts and slams from the other side of the door. The mirror Aradia had a satisfied smile on her face.

"See, you are more powerful than you thought. Just imagine the other powers you can unleash if you realize your potential."

"But I didn't mean to hurt her," Aradia said, unable to tear her eyes away from the mirror.

"After they hurt you? She will recover," the reflection said, an edge to her voice. She smiled again, all softness. "Now, I think it is time to unleash your true power, and free me from this glass."

Aradia stepped forward, plagued with doubt. What were the real Aradia's true intentions? If she really was the real Aradia, and not some Wicked Witch trying to trick her. Was the possibility of finding Tituba worth the risk of possibly unleashing a great evil upon the world? But when the world was already against her, what did it matter?

"I honestly don't know what to believe anymore," Aradia said.

The mirror Aradia looked at her with sympathy. "I can understand that. Every witch has a story. But one thing you can believe in is yourself. You have power, my dear. Don't waste it."

Aradia nodded. The other Aradia was right. She was not going to accomplish anything by doubt. She placed her hands on the mirror.

"I'm ready."

The other Aradia smiled.

"Wonderful. Chant this spell three times," the reflection said. "*Through the looking-glass thou shalt pass.* And after the last time you chant it, chant: *This Samhain Spell is bound and cast.*"

"That's it?" Aradia said.

"That's it. But make sure to say it with true intention."

"Okay." Aradia closed her eyes and took a deep breath in. This was it; she was really going to do it. She focused her mind on freeing the real Aradia, but, more importantly, she also focused on using this spell to unleash her own power. But as she pulled her thoughts together, she froze.

"Wait," she said, "something doesn't make sense to me."

"What is it?" the reflection spoke with thinly veiled impatience.

"How did Tituba ruin your life? And how did you get in this mirror?"

The woman sighed. "Tituba being sacrificed to the Lord of Samhain was what caused all this chaos. It wasn't her fault, but if it was not for her meddling it never would've happened. Abigail knew I was here to stop the war so she had me captured as chaos was taking over the city, and trapped me in this mirror."

"Then why would you help me find her? Unless . . ."

"Look child, I want what is best for witches, *all* witches. That includes your Tituba. But I cannot do a thing from within this mirror!"

Aradia flinched at the sharpness in the reflection's voice, lifting her fingers from the glass.

"I am sorry," the other Aradia said, pouting prettily. Her voice was soft as silk again. "When this is all over, Tituba can tell us all stories by the fire like she used to, but you need to free me from this."

"Tell us stories?" Aradia said. "When did she ever tell you . . ."

Who was the one that Tituba told stories to?

"Abigail Williams," Aradia breathed, stepping backwards. Of course.

"What?" the reflection asked, her voice growing harsh.

"You're Abigail Williams, you're the one who accused Tituba and started the Salem Witch Trials!"

What had been a beautiful face in the mirror twisted into sharp edges and bared teeth.

"And you are a fool!" Abigail shrieked. "You are an unloved mistake! That is what you are! You should have never come to Witch City!"

The words were sharp as a dagger driven into Aradia's stomach. It was like Abigail had looked into Aradia's deepest fears. And what did Witch City really have to offer her other than danger? The woman in the mirror's eyes turned black, her beautiful face distorted into an expression of pure malice, all the kindness gone. Aradia wanted to say something, the words were caught in her throat.

"That's right, Aradia, or should I say Alicia?" Abigail bit out, each word like venom. "I know all about you. I know what you really are; I can see straight into your damaged little soul. You are pathetic and weak, but not only that, you only truly care about yourself. You deserve every atrocity that you have experienced. Your mother did not want you, your friends don't really want you, and the world certainly doesn't want you. You are worth nothing to this world, or any other, and life is wasted on you. You are not even worth being sacrificed."

Aradia felt a cold, sick feeling in her stomach. As much as she wanted to argue, the words felt true, true in a way that shook to her core. The mirror shimmered, and Abigail's demonic face was replaced by Aradia's own: just a scared little girl. She had come so far and still that's who she was. Nothing could change that.

The door slammed open as Wanda and Erzeben burst into the room.

"Don't you believe a single shred of the minotaur-dung that comes from that hag's mouth. You are worth it to me," Wanda bit out.

"Oh, would you look at that," Abigail cooed, rippling back into view. "The frog girl has come to the rescue. You remind me of a witch I used to know, and just like her you are a pathetic wretch that failed to save those they cared for. You will fail to save this filthy little bunny just as you failed to save your mother. Mark my words, wicked little witch, you will visit her grave knowing you failed her, if your own foolishness does not kill you first.

"Tituba was pathetic, as is she! The only way to power is to take it, something a slave like her was too stupid to understand."

"That is enough!" Aradia said, standing up.

Tearing into her was bad enough, but going after Wanda and Tituba, that was going too far. Aradia stared into Abigail's cold, soulless eyes. The warlock looked at her contemptuously.

"And who are you to stop me, slave girl?" Abigail spat.

"Once upon a time there was a queen that everyone loved. She was beautiful and kind, and always said the right thing," Aradia said, her voice shaking.

"Oh we're getting a fairytale now?" Abigail rolled her crystalline eyes. "How dull."

"But," Aradia continued, clenching her hands into firsts for strength, "she had dark, dark secrets. For every life she destroyed, the more powerful she became, and eventually she had many kingdoms under her command. The people continued to love her, for all they saw was her beauty and kindness. But a rot started to settle in her, from all the evil she had done. Bit by bit, she was starting to become undone."

The words filled her up with strength, heady and surging through her. A click startled her, drawing her eyes to the glass. A small crack had appeared on the mirror.

"This story is idiotic. Stop it at once," Abigail said nervously, eyeing the fracture.

"It got so bad that she could not look herself in the mirror, for fear of what would look back at her," Aradia continued, her voice strong and sure. "Soon she became worried that her subjects were suspicious of her, that they had found out all the people she had sacrificed along the way, so she sacrificed more and more people to retain her power. But it only made it worse."

Another crack rang out, spreading and spider-webbing across the glass.

"Stop it, stop it right now!" Abigail shrieked.

"Eventually," Aradia said, her voice rising over Abigail's screams, "she became haunted by all those she had destroyed. She saw their faces everywhere, heard their voices late at night and eventually even her most loyal subjects saw that something was wrong with their beloved queen, that something had broken in her."

Aradia brushed at the sweat collecting on her forehead, straining as the story pushed out of her like she was giving birth.

"I am sorry! I did not mean those nasty things. I am willing to teach you powerful magic!" Abigail said desperately as the crack jumped and spread, tearing along the mirror. Aradia paused, only for a second.

"However," she said through gritted teeth, "one day she accidentally glimpsed into a mirror as she walked by. She did not see her reflection, or even a distorted version of it."

Aradia's knees shook, her words straining to be spoken. "She saw the burned face of the first person she had destroyed, the one that had loved her the most. The one that had forgiven her even as she had set them ablaze. It was only then that the queen truly cracked."

Abigail's expression turned to one of horror, and she let out an agonizing scream. Aradia stuck her fingers in her ears while Wanda and Erzeben covered theirs. The mirror shattered like a spider's web, exploding into the air. Glass flew everywhere, and Aradia, Wanda, and Erzeben ducked as shards glided over them. When the scream was over, they slowly stood up. All that was left of the mirror was broken glass in mounds on the floor. Aradia sighed and felt the energy leave her body as her knees folded under her. Wanda and Erzeben ran to her side and Wanda quickly propped her up.

"How did you find me in here?" Aradia asked again, barely a whisper.

"Empusae can see very well in the dark, so with that and with some of Wanda's intuition, we found you," Erzeben said. "Again, I am so sorry for how I acted. You have every right to hate me."

"I don't hate you," Aradia said quietly, leaning against Wanda. "I've been betrayed before and it hurts like hell. But I'm sorry too. It was my fault Vivivine got abducted, why the Monster Coven and Lantern Coven are after us."

"No, it's not," Wanda protested, helping Aradia to her feet.

"Yes, it is," Aradia said.

"No, it's not. We could have left you for dead at any point, but we chose not to. All of us, including Vivivine. We chose to stand by you," Wanda said.

"She is right," Erzeben said. "And this is coming from someone who did want to leave you for dead at first."

Aradia felt a warmth spread through her chest. Wanda might have been physically holding her up, but Erzeben was supporting her, too.

"Still, I am sorry," she said, her throat tight. "Thank you both. For everything. Thank you for being there for me, even when I don't think I deserved it."

Wanda pulled Aradia in for a hug, holding her tight. Aradia let herself be held by the witch. She now remembered how she had survived Witch City so far. Erzeben's hand tentatively patted her shoulder, and she laughed a little bit. She was not alone. And she had already destroyed Abigail Williams. Who knew what else they could do together?

CHAPTER
Forty

Aradia, Wanda, and Erzeben returned to the great hall. Even as Wanda pulled her in with a warm arm over her shoulders, Aradia couldn't help but shudder. Abigail's words wouldn't be that easily pushed from her mind. Maybe the warlock was right. At least Aradia had the satisfaction of finally destroying her. Tituba got her vengeance. And Aradia understood her power. But she was not satisfied, something felt incomplete.

"So, do you think that counted as a sacrifice?" Aradia asked, joining the other Bad Witches by a new fire they had built from broken picture frames and furniture.

"Most likely not, I would say. There was no invocation to the Lord of Samhain," Erzeben said.

"Dammit. I mean, I figured, but I was hoping. Kinda feels like I did that for nothing now," Aradia said.

"Nah, I think that showed that despite what you say, you're a boss witch not to be messed with. I mean all you did was tell a story and boom that hag shattered to pieces," Wanda said, adding a warm cackle for good measure.

Aradia looked over to Wanda, the grin on the witch's face filling her with warmth. How lucky she was to have the green girl in her life. To think she almost had let her go. The moment was cut short as Calaveran ran towards them. Vivivine stood a short distance behind him, tapping her fingers nervously.

"The Monster Coven, they found us!" Calaveran called.

"What, how do you know?" Erzeben said. A loud shatter crashed from behind them, releasing a rush of screeching. They turned around. The winged monkeys had broken through what was left of the stained-glass window, and flew towards them, their teeth viciously gnashing, their eyes glowing with fury.

"Let's go!" Wanda yelled, grabbing for Aradia's hand, and the group raced away, ducking claws and wings. Wanda and Calaveran attempted throwing fireballs and flaming skulls at them, but the monkeys had learned, and dodged with ease. Aradia felt a jolt of adrenaline but her whole body felt so heavy each step was like wading through mud. They ran through the open doors into the hallway. It was dark, and Aradia felt cramped on all sides, but they kept on going forward.

Glowing eyes and high-pitched screeches flew at them from the dark, Aradia's heart nearly stopping.

"Monkeys!" Vivivine shrieked. They were forced to run back into the great hall, cornered by the winged monkeys. How many of them were there? Aradia wondered how the Monster Coven was not able to take down the Lanterns if they had so many of these simian creatures at their disposal

One of the monkeys flew directly at Aradia, claws outstretched. Vivivine jumped in front of her, and grabbed the monkey. She struggled with it for a few seconds, but she threw the monkey off her and into the open chasm where the stain-glass window was. Wanda and Calaveran shot lightning bolts at the monkeys, knocking down a few of them. Erzeben transformed into his bat form, and aggressively dove at a couple monkeys. He had changed so much since Aradia had first met him. She had changed so much herself.

Aradia tried to tell another story, of the winged monsters being finally defeated and flying away, but it was too difficult to concentrate in the chaos, and their screeching drowned out any words. The winged monkeys fought harder and fiercer than before. There were just too many monkeys, and the Bad Witches and Vivivine were just becoming too overwhelmed.

"Perhaps, children, we should consider our other options!" Vivivine shouted over the commotion as she punched a monkey in the face.

Wanda stopped in place and closed her eyes. Her face scrunched up in concentration. A purple fog materialized in the air, clouding Aradia's vision. Soon everything was purple. The screeches of the monkeys got more frantic, but fainter. Aradia called out to Wanda and the others but heard no response. She wandered, looking for any sign of the Bad Witches or Vivivine.

The purple fog faded, revealing her surroundings. Before her was a familiar, witchy cottage in the midst of the metropolis. Vivivine stood close to her, looking confused but relieved. Erzeben and Calaveran stood near as well, looking around. Where was Wanda? Aradia's eyes frantically darted around. Finally, she spotted her. The young witch was nearby, her hands on her knees, dry-heaving, practically collapsed onto the ground. Aradia and the male witches ran to her side, making sure she was okay.

"Yeah, yeah I'm fine. I've never smoke-travelled that far," Wanda said, having to stop herself from gagging. "I just focused on getting us to the last safe place we had this Samhain."

"Oh hell no," someone muttered.

Aradia looked up as they helped Wanda to her feet. Baroness stood in front of her cottage, a large basket of herbs in her hands.

"Hi, Nessie," Calaveran said sheepishly.

"No, no, no, I'm not getting involved with this again. This," Baroness said, gesturing to all of them, "is way too much."

"Please, Nessie, we have nowhere else—" Calaveran

"No, you don't get to 'please Nessie' me," she interrupted. "You lost your Nessie privileges a long time ago, sweetheart. Give me one good reason why I should help any of you."

"The true meaning of Samhain is sacrifice," Aradia said.

"Yes? And?" Baroness said, raising an eyebrow.

"We're on our way to make a sacrifice to the Lord of Samhain, to stop this city from dying," Aradia said.

"So?" Baroness put a hand to her hip, the basket jutting out. "Go along and do that then. I don't want any part of it. Like I said before, I don't want any coven coming here and getting up in my business. Y'all better get out of here before I witchboard the WCPD myself."

Baroness pointed a sage bundle at them threateningly.

"Why you—" Wanda started.

"No," Aradia said quickly, "she's right. I know what she's gone through. She doesn't deserve to be thrown into all of this. Nobody does."

Aradia looked Baroness in the eyes. An unspoken understanding passed between the two of them. They alone knew the pain of being rejected by their families, of having to forge a new life on their own. Baroness at least seemed to have a peaceful life, while Aradia's was filled with chaos, a life she would not wish on anyone.

"How about then we head to my house. I really do insist that it will be the safest place for you all, away from all the hustle and bustle," Vivivine said.

"Vivivine, I am not sure—" Erzeben tried.

"Hey!" a voice barked "What's going on over here?"

The group looked. Standing not too far off from them were a couple of male witches in black and orange uniforms, jack-o'-lantern insignias on their coats. Aradia felt a surge of panic. The Lantern Coven had found them.

CHAPTER
Forty-One

Vivivine stepped forward, poised and calm.

"Oh, hello Vivivine Frankenstein, what exactly is going on here?" one of the officers asked.

"It's pronounced Frankenst*een*," Vivivine said, her smile never faltering. "Something you and the Lantern Coven would like to know is that I was abducted by the Monster Coven where I was held captive until just last night. My friends here found me and rescued me, and I must say, as grateful as I am, I was rather surprised that the Lantern Coven had not come to my aid earlier. Nor have I heard of even an attempt at a rescue. An embarrassing oversight, don't you agree?"

"Many apologies, Mrs. *Frankensteen*," one of the uniformed witches said with false sincerity. "We are glad however you have such resourceful friends. But if you were captured by the Monster Coven, surely you can tell us their whereabouts? So that of course, we can prevent any such repeated unpleasantries."

"The Witch Trial Museum in Westwitch. They attacked all of us there," Erzeben said.

The Lantern Coven witches surveyed them with suspicion in their eyes. Aradia kept her head low, her heart thumping loudly in her ears. She wanted the witch guards to lose interest and leave them alone to go find the Monster Coven for all she cared. She just wanted them gone.

"Who is she?" one of the Lantern Coven witches asked, pointing at Aradia with a broom. Aradia looked up. Her forehead dampened, her mouth dried up, and all words flew out of her brain all at once.

"This is my cousin, Alice," Baroness said, gently placing her hands on Aradia's shoulders. "After they rescued Mrs. Frankenstein, she came and found me."

Aradia looked at Baroness, who betrayed no hint of what her true intentions were. Why had she changed her mind and decided to help?

The Lantern Coven witches harrumphed, sharing glances. "Still, if you had all encountered the Monster Coven, the Lantern Coven would be very interested in speaking to all of you. I am sure the High Priestess in particular would be very keen to talk to you, 'Alice.'"

The witch hadn't lowered his broom, and his eyes were sharp on Aradia. In less than a second, Baroness moved forward and threw small bags in both of the Lantern witches' faces. The bags exploded into dark, thick clouds. The uniformed witches to cough and cry out in pain.

"You little hag!" one of them choked out.

"Baroness?" Calaveran said in surprise.

"Let's go!" Baroness said, grabbing Aradia's arm. The group turned and ran, nonstop questions running through Aradia's mind. They moved down the winding streets, other witches staring at them and moving out of the way as they rushed forward. So much for being inconspicuous.

A violent force pulled Aradia back, nearly twisting her neck and arm. She was flung to the ground, the uniformed witches standing over her, their faces distorted and covered with soot.

"Prepare to burn, Witch Hunter," one of them growled.

"You first," Aradia said shakily. The words were barely out of her mouth as a blast of green fire and black smoke shot down from overhead and hit one of the guards, instantly igniting him into a blazing green inferno, unlike anything she had seen before. Before the second guard had a chance to react, another blast hit him, and he too went up in flames. Aradia crawled backwards, the heat burning her face. Within moments, the flames dissipated, leaving charred skeletons. Aradia screamed, barely able to breathe. Wanda, Baroness, and Vivivine rushed to her side, Erzeben and Calaveran trailing after.

"Dia, Dia are you okay?" Wanda said, gently grabbing Aradia's face, looking her in the eyes. "Dia, talk to me!"

Aradia could not stop crying, burying her head into the witch's collarbone.

"Shh, shh, we got you Strega," Baroness said, rubbing her back. A wicked cackle pierced through the streets. Tears still streaming out of her eyes, Aradia looked up in its direction. Standing on the roof of a factory close to the neon WITCH CITY sign was Brimombi, pointing her broom in their direction like a rifle, black smoke rising up from the black straw of her broom. The Wicked Witch grinned as if she had won a twisted game. She lifted the broomstick above her head, standing up tall, focused on the horizon.

"*Morrigan Gu Bràth! Morrigan Gu Bràth!*" she cried.

An ominous whirring erupted from buildings in the far distance, which grew into the loud flapping of wings. An army of flying monkeys rose into the air, their dark shapes a storm-cloud against the green sky. Wanda and Baroness helped Aradia to her feet as the winged monkeys flew over them, missing them entirely. The monkeys were not after them. Aradia looked back up at Brimombi. The Wicked Witch smirked knowingly, and disappeared in a cloud of black smoke.

"I think . . . I think she wanted us to escape," Aradia said, each word a labored breath.

"That does not make any sense," Erzeben said.

"No, listen to me," Aradia said, gasping in another breath. "She made such an effort to capture us, sent monkeys after us when we tried to hide, and now when she finds us in the city, she doesn't even try to kidnap us."

"Then why go through all that trouble in the first place?" Calaveran asked.

"To test her. To see if she can fight and escape and be worthy enough to be used as a tool. To see if she can truly be 'The Holy Strega,'" Baroness said, giving Aradia a meaningful look. "And to get her into the city to cause chaos."

Aradia nodded. She could not claim to know she understood why, or what Brimombi's true intentions were, but the Wicked Witch had a bigger plan for Aradia. A plan that the girl wanted no part of.

An explosion shook the ground, bits of debris flying overhead. A large chunk of the WITCH CITY sign ahead was obliterated, only a few letters were left remaining. Green smoke rose from it as parts of it still sparked. A few witches flew overhead, wearing the green masks and pointed hats of the Monster Coven, cackling as they went. Another explosion erupted in the distance, thick green and black smoke rising in the air.

"A storm has arrived to Witch City. It's not safe here," Vivivine said.

"The storm has always been here. If you've never felt it, you are more privileged than most," Baroness said. "I really did not want to get involved, but Marsha and Marie reminded me that it's not all about me."

"That may be so, but you are all children. I don't care who or what is out there, you can't be expected to stop it. It just isn't right," Vivivine said, her smile falling. "I am taking you all to my place. It's outside of the downtown area and is well protected. I have seen enough riots in my lifetime to know when one is about to happen."

"Aradia should stay with me. She needs to be taught the ways of her ancestors to protect herself," Baroness said. "The rest of you can go with Mrs. Frankenstein."

"No, there is no way I'm leaving her behind," Wanda said, holding Aradia tighter. Aradia felt a rush of euphoria being held so close to her, like she could explode.

"This isn't all about me, or all about you, right now it's what's best for her," Baroness retorted.

"She's going to be a sacrificial goat if she stays downtown. We need to get her out!" Wanda said.

"Wanda, everyone, please," Aradia said, struggling to get out the words. "I am tired of running, of hiding. The Lantern Coven is going to find me if Baba Yaga doesn't first. Let me at least try to be the Holy Strega.

We need to get the Queen's crown and the only way to do that is to bring her out in the open. We need to get to the Hecate Trivia statue."

"Are you sure?" Wanda asked, her violet eyes glistening. "What if that's what Grim Old Mombi wants?"

"I don't care what she wants," Aradia bit back, her blood boiling. "I want to do what Tituba did. Fight and survive, even if I have to sacrifice everything else in the process. There were three women first accused during the Salem Witch Trials, and she was the only one that survived. All the odds were against her, but she survived. This is something I need to do."

Aradia didn't break her gaze with Wanda, as if no one else was with them.

"Do you even have a plan?" Erzeben said.

"I do," Aradia said, not leaving Wanda's gaze, wanting to be held in it forever. The witch's eyes were focused and steady, and they told the girl one thing.

I've got you.

"Alright," Wanda said, the usual mischief returning to her eyes. "Let's burn some witches!"

CHAPTER
Forty-Two

They briefly went back to Baroness's house, where Baroness treated Aradia's burns. Baroness gave a bag of gris-gris to each person to protect them, but then told them to be on their way. She could do no more for them.

Aradia, the Bad Witches and Vivivine left Baroness's house. Wanda held tightly to Aradia's hand, not letting her go for a moment. Aradia's heart soared as they ran down the city's streets. The cold rush of air, the metallic scent of the city, the bright green and orange lights flying by. Everything reminded her that this was real, and that she was still alive.

Vivivine, Erzeben, and Calaveran kept a short distance behind them, in case Vivivine drew any attention from onlookers or authorities. The Frankenstein woman had been right; the city was devolving into chaos. Witches ran in the streets screaming. Monster Coven witches and winged monkeys flew overhead. Every so often a scream rent the air as the monkeys found a hapless victim and dragged them off into the sky. Soon the smell of burning singed their nostrils, as the Monster Coven witches threw fireballs at buildings. A wave of heat pressed against Aradia's face as a nearby building exploded into flames. Nowhere in the city was safe.

Wanda led Aradia through the back-alleys as much as possible, avoiding major streets and intersections. They reached a tight crossroads between four tall metallic buildings, glowing jack-o'-lanterns nearly filling up the walking space. Aradia and Wanda made it across, kicking over the jack-o'-lanterns that stood in the way. As the others were about to follow them, a small group of panicked witches ran by, tripping over the jack-o'-lanterns. The knocked over candles ignited the pumpkins, a small fire blocking Vivivine, Erzeben and Calaveran from reaching them. Aradia stopped, and Wanda stopped with her, and looked back. The fire spread, and more witches ran by screaming, making it impossible for Aradia and Wanda to communicate with the others. They were cut off from the group.

"Let's go!" Wanda said. "We need to keep moving! We'll either meet them at the statue later, or we'll regroup at Viv's! We need to go!"

Aradia nodded, and let Wanda pull her forward. They wove through the city, each step harder and harder as adrenaline faded and the exhaustion of the day hit them. The glow of the jack-o'-lanterns lining the streets melted into an indistinct blur and the screams and explosions in the near distance became vague noise. The city seemed like it was a never-ending labyrinth of industrial buildings. Aradia felt herself slowly pulling away from her surroundings, as if she was slowly melting.

"Come on Dia, we're almost there!" Wanda encouraged.

The Hecate Trivia statue came into view, standing tall over the buildings of the city, as if it was watching over them. As they got closer, the statue seemed to blur. In snapshots, fuzzy and indistinct, Aradia saw Trivia, the woman that drove Aradia to Witch City, superimposed over the statue. She rubbed at her eyes, which burned from smoke. When they stopped a short distance away, Aradia gasped for air, breathing until the world solidified around her. The statue loomed over them, as if expecting something from them. Aradia was sure now that it was the Goddess who had sent her here, and this was what she was supposed to do.

"We need to get as high up on the statue as we can," Aradia said, her thoughts slowly coming back together.

"How?" Wanda asked. Aradia gave her a look.

"Oh, right." The witch closed her eyes and clutched Aradia's hand harder, digging her nails into the girl's skin. Purple smoke materialized around them, swirling rapidly. Aradia felt a lightheadedness, as if her body was rising from the ground. In a few seconds the smoke dissipated, the air suddenly much colder, the wind fiercer and louder. They stood on the edge of one of the torches, the glowing green light eclipsing everything else. Half of the entire city stretched out below them, endless green sky above. Aradia was once again struck by how magical the city looked, the green and orange lights illuminating a metropolitan Wonderland. She smiled and looked at Wanda. For a moment she could forget what was happening out there, and just think of the potential the city had.

Wanda returned her smile, the witch's long black-and-purple hair blowing over her face. Wanda was so enchanting, her emerald complexion illuminating her beauty. So high, it felt like the gravity of the earth was weak, and all Aradia felt was the pull towards Wanda. As she was about to give in, her neck prickled with the feeling of strange eyes on her. Aradia looked back. The face of the Crone aspect of the Hecate Trivia statue seemed focused on her, scrutinizing her. Up close it seemed even larger and more intimidating, its eyebrows lowered and lips pursed. Aradia saw each wrinkle lining the statue's angular and otherworldly face, its nose and chin jutting out like a hawk's beak. The statue's eyes seemed to be demanding something.

Finish what you began.

Refocused, Aradia turned to face the city once more. She let go of Wanda's hand, closed her eyes, and breathed in deeply, summoning the strength within her to say what she needed to.

"WITCH CITY!" Aradia cried, projecting her voice as loud as she could over the wind. "IT'S ME, ARADIA! IF ANYONE CAN HEAR ME, PLEASE LISTEN!"

"Y'KNOW I DON'T THINK ANYONE CAN HEAR YOU FROM UP HERE!" Wanda yelled back over the wind. "BUT THIS MIGHT HELP!"

Wanda gently placed her hand over Aradia's neck and chanted as loud as she could.

"POWERS OF AIR, MAKE HER WORDS LOUD.
POWERS OF AIR, MAY THEY REACH THE CROWD.
POWERS OF AIR, STRENGTHEN HER VOICE.
POWERS OF AIR, MAY IT CUT THROUGH THE NOISE!
SO MOTE IT BE!"

Aradia felt a warm, tingling sensation in her neck, as if a ball of fire was slowly growing, reaching up into her mouth.

"THERE!" Wanda said, letting go of Aradia's neck. "NOW TRY!"

"Witch City!" Aradia's voice boomed easily, echoing across the city. "This is Aradia! Please listen to me! I am not a Witch Hunter! I am the descendant of a Salem Witch, the original Salem Witch Tituba! I came here to look for her! But now I want to help free this city from the Lord of Samhain, and I'm prepared to make a sacrifice to him! I just need—"

Suddenly everything around her swayed and blurred, dizziness spreading throughout her body. She glanced down to see her sleeve alit and some witch—Morrigan Coven or Lantern Coven, she couldn't tell—speeding off into the dark green sky. She had been hit with a fireball. With time for only one startled glance at Wanda, Aradia stumbled and slipped off the edge of the torch, barely making out Wanda's screams.

CHAPTER

Forty-Three

Salem Town, April 1693

Tituba sat in a dark prison cell, the air damp and sickly. Day in and day out she wondered when her time would finally come to an end. The trials were over, but she had been left in jail to rot. She had been betrayed time and time again, and now she would never see her husband or child ever again. Even Candy, who had been her only light in the prison, was gone—eventually released. Nineteen had been hanged, another man crushed to death with rocks, and she had seen others die in that very prison, but everyone had moved on so quickly. Everyone was so willing to forget that the trials had ever happened, so willing to forget her. She was but a relic of a gruesome past, so easily swept under the rug. What was to become of her now?

Tituba rested her head against the wall. She had told many stories of witches and demons and spirits now, she found it hard to work out where the fantasy started and where reality ended. Perhaps she had been a witch after all. Perhaps this whole trial has been her doing, her secret desire to escape bondage to Samuel Parris and to watch the

Salem Village burn itself to the ground manifesting before her eyes. Her horrible vision had come true, the Devil had come and wreaked havoc in Salem. All those things she had learned in Barbados, how to ward off evil, how to divine the future, none of it helped her in Salem. It was difficult to ward off evil when you lived amongst it every day.

"If the Devil be real, I pray he release me from this life!" Tituba said, raising her hands.

If the Devil really did come to her and offer her freedom, to let her fly away from Salem and go wherever she pleased, she would take whatever deal he offered. She had already sacrificed so much, what difference did a soul make?

The cell door slammed open. A prison guard stood in the doorway, a look of contempt on his face.

"Tituba, you have been sold," he barked. "Get up. Your new master is waiting."

Tituba slowly stood up, not fully grasping what had happened. Should she be elated? Or apprehensive? Sold or not sold, she still would not be free.

"Sold? Sold to who?" she asked, her voice trembling.

"Not my business to know. Now get out!"

Tituba left the dank cell, her legs wobbling. She had barely used them in over a year. She was led outside, taking a moment to close her eyes and breathe in the fresh night air. Tears rolled down from her eyes, and she almost let out a cry. If nothing else, she was out of the cramped filth of the jail.

Tituba opened her eyes. A man wearing a tall, wide-brimmed hat, his face cast in shadow, stood nearby holding a lantern, wind whistling around him. Tituba was a little frightened. Who was this person? Who in this Puritan Hell would purchase a witch?

"Here is Tituba. She caused quite the stir in Salem Village, confessed to being a witch. Be careful with her," the guard said.

The man simply nodded and beckoned for Tituba to approach. Tituba walked slowly to them, as if compelled to do so. She had half a mind to run away into the night, but she would have been caught soon and all the worse for it. The man gently grasped her hand, and led her to a black carriage parked on a nearby road. He opened the door for her, and helped her inside. Tituba was not sure she could trust him. A Puritan had never treated her with such care before. It made her wary.

The man joined Tituba in the carriage, sitting across from her. The door closed on its own, startling the former Salem Witch. With a slight jolt, the carriage moved forward. Tituba listened to the sound of the horses trotting, her mind at unease. She had not recalled seeing a driver.

"I suppose you have many questions, Tituba," the man said, removing his hat.

Tituba nearly gasped. The man was very beautiful, his skin nearly aglow. He had a close-cropped dark beard, accentuating his angular cheekbones and full lips. But his eyes. His eyes were a shining gold. They stared at the woman intensely with a determination that both intrigued and frightened her.

"Are you the Devil?" Tituba said. The man smiled.

"I hath been called many names over the years, that one seems to hath stuck the most," the man said, his voice deep and smooth.

Tituba shivered, not sure if she was in danger. The Devil was the Wicked One, the Prince of Darkness, the King of Hell. He was everything evil in the Puritan world. And yet she did not feel as afraid as she felt she should. The woman had already lived through hell.

"Why did you purchase me?" she asked instead.

"I have not bought you, Tituba, but I hath purchased your freedom. A person cannot be purchased, bought, or sold. There is a place I aim to take you to live out your life in peace. Will you allow me to?"

Tituba stared, too stunned to reply. Freedom? Was that possible? The Reverend always warned that the Devil was a liar. But she was not bound to the Reverend's word anymore.

"I sense you must be wary," the man said with a deep sigh. "Understandably so. But you were the one that called me to release you, and I only come when called."

Tituba put a hand to her chest. She had invoked the Devil after all.

"Will you take me to Barbados?" Tituba asked, barely daring to hope.

"I can. But I am not sure that is what you want."

"Not what I want? I want Barbados more than anything!" Tituba said, bristling with indignation.

The man shook his head slowly. "You want freedom more than anything, not Barbados. You remember Barbados fondly because there was more life there than in this wretched Puritan country, but you were enslaved there as you were here. If you were to go back there it would not be long before you would be snatched back into your old life."

Tituba did not want the man to be right, but she knew he was. She had been in Salem for so long she had nearly forgotten how brutal the hardships were in Barbados. She had been stolen from her parents at a young age, and was forced to work laboriously for all her life there. The moments of joy, the ones she remembered so fondly, were few and fleeting. The stories of Barbados that sustained her in Salem were all created from a fantasy of her past. The stories allowed her to survive the trauma.

"Where you taking me?" she asked, as darkness passed the small carriage windows.

"It is your choice, Tituba. But there is a land that has become a haven for witches, and you were the most famous witch of Salem. It is only there that you will be truly free."

Tituba breathed in a sharp gasp of air. "But I am no witch."

"Perhaps not, but I believe you are more witch than you know. Ultimately, it is your choice if you want to embrace that path. Witchcraft is the path that allows you to create your own future."

Tituba stared out the carriage window, watching as they passed the crooked trees and grim buildings of the town. If she were to become a witch, to truly become a witch, what would that mean for her? Would it make her a wicked abomination, as the Puritans said? There was a cost to freedom.

"If I go to the witch place, I would not see John or Violet, even Candy again. They would still be slaves here," Tituba said, her eyes wet.

The man stroked his beard, contemplating. "Yes, that would be true. How about I propose an offer. If you choose to embrace being a witch and start a new life, in this, what should I call it, Witch City if you will, I will ensure your loved ones find their freedom. They will live long, fulfilling lives, and it will be all because of you."

A small smile formed on Tituba's lips. That was what she wanted most, for her precious flower to be free. It broke her heart to know she would never see it happen, or spend another night with her handsome John, but as long as they were free, she would be at peace.

"I will go to the Witch City. I will be a witch," Tituba said. "But what do you want from me?"

The carriage rocked gently, as the stranger fixed his eyes on Tituba, gold and burning as the sun.

"There may come a time in the future when I will be of need of you," he said finally, his voice low. Like a threat. "All I ask is that you are available to me then."

Tituba looked into the man's eyes. They really were glowing now, like embers from a fire. It frightened Tituba; she had no doubt he truly was the Devil. Even from her own stories she knew that deals with the Devil were dangerous. Yet she had already lost everything she had, and she did not have much to begin with. Freedom was all she needed now.

"Yes. I will."

The Devil smiled kindly at her. From under his chair he pulled out a large black book, and a bottle of ink. He opened the book and held it out to Tituba.

"Make your mark in the book, then you shall become a witch," he said, and shivers broke out on her arms. Just like she had described in her story. "Then you shall be free."

Tituba looked at the book with apprehension. Once she made her mark there would be no going back. There would be no going back to Salem, no seeing her family again. She would, undoubtedly, become a witch, and live in a city of witches forever more. She would become what everyone feared her to be.

Tituba dipped her finger in the ink bottle, the ink coming out as red as blood. Before any doubts could linger, she pressed her finger hard against the page.

"I am Tituba, Witch of Salem."

CHAPTER
Forty-Four

A green fuzzy blur slowly came into view. Aradia reached out to it, as if it could somehow help her. Something gently grabbed her hand, and with another blink the world sharpened around her. Wanda was leaning over her, her eyes wet, her lips trembling, her face ready to break.

"Dia?" Wanda asked.

"Wanda," Aradia said, smiling.

Wanda smiled back, impatiently rubbing at her eyes. She let out a watery laugh.

"Hey witches, get over here! Dia's awake!"

Aradia breathed in deep, sinking into the luxurious pillows propping her up, the silky comforter under her. A fruity perfume permeated the room. As she glanced around, her eyes fell on purple, purple, more purple. Posters of Vivivine posing in high fashion lined the walls, her large eyes

236

seemingly watching Aradia through them. The real Vivivine rushed to the edge of the bed, all tidied up and wearing a fresh button-down purple dress.

"Aradia, dear I'm so glad you're awake! Are you alright?" Vivivine asked.

"What happened?" Aradia barely croaked out.

"You were hit by a fireball and fell off the Hecate statue, but luckily Erz saw you and turned into a bat and caught you right before you hit the ground. I'm just glad you're okay," Wanda said, holding Aradia's hand tighter. Aradia lifted her hand and touched Wanda's face; it warm and damp to the touch. "You are okay, right? You didn't really wake up all day. You just kept muttering things about the Devil and . . ."

Aradia nodded stiffly.

"Erzeben and his boyfriend are just downstairs. I took you all back to my place once you fell. Enough was enough," Vivivine said.

"Cal isn't Erz's boyfriend," Wanda said.

"He isn't? I was so certain that they had something going on," Vivivine said, her eyebrows scrunched in confusion. "Anyway, it doesn't matter. I'm keeping you all safe here until Samhain ends. And that is not up for debate. This house is spell-locked—nothing can come in or out without my permission."

Aradia didn't feel like fighting, for once. She was in no state to go running off to make a sacrifice, no matter what the Baba Yaga threatened. The Lantern Coven would not be able to find her either as long as she was in Vivivine's house. She would stay in her sanctuary for as long as she was able, and with Wanda at her side it could almost feel like home. Aradia looked into the witch's violet eyes, making her feel warm with comfort. But she sensed something new in her stare, or maybe just something that had always been there but she was only now just noticing. Pain, and a deep, deep rage.

Now that Aradia had seen it, she wondered how she had not noticed it before. Wanda's mother was taken from her by the Lord of Samhain and his ghouls, and the Lantern Coven did absolutely nothing about it. They did not do anything to protect Witch City from the Samhain terrors, and for all Aradia knew, they could very well be in league with them. She blinked, her mind spinning and clicking into place. No, Aradia could not sit and hide and wait for Samhain Night to be over. Not anymore. The Lord of Samhain needed to be stopped, and the Lantern Coven needed to be punished.

Aradia sat up. Vivivine was not going to let them leave for the rest of Samhaintide, but Aradia could no longer be cooped up while the world burned around her. She had seen too much in such a short period of time to let herself be shielded from it any longer. But how could she convince Vivivine that the best thing was for her to leave, and finish what she was supposed to do?

"You know, I think I'm feeling a little better," Aradia said, raising her eyebrows at Wanda and desperately hoping telepathy was somehow part of her powers. The witch squinted as if she understood that Aradia was giving her a message, but couldn't quite figure out what it was.

"I'm glad to hear it," Wanda said slowly. "Maybe we should go talk to Erz and Cal. They will be glad to know you're alright."

"What a splendid idea. I'll go get them," Vivivine said.

"No, I want to go down to see them," Aradia said quickly.

Vivivine lingered by the door, her beautiful and stitched face pursed in confusion. "Are you sure? I don't want you to strain yourself."

"Yes," Aradia said firmly. "I need to get up and stretch my legs."

"Very well," Vivivine nodded, relaxing a bit. "I shall have Georgie make us all some dinner."

Wanda helped Aradia out of the bed, the girl's legs wobbling. Being held by the witch still gave Aradia butterflies, her hands warm to the touch. Wanda made her feel safe, but more than that, she made her feel worthy of being wanted. They left Vivivine's room and followed the hall to a smaller staircase that took them to the main spiral staircase. Looking down, they could see that the staircase resembled a mechanical spider-web, smaller staircases branching off to each door. Vivivine led them up to another small staircase that led to a different room.

"The boys are in there; I'll just head down to the kitchen to get George to start preparing dinner. Normally we'd have our chef do it, but we always give Samhain off to our workers," Vivivine said cheerfully.

The Frankenstein woman sauntered down the stairs, her heels clicking loudly. Aradia and Wanda looked at each other and headed to the door.

Wanda was about to push it open, but stopped. Aradia leaned in and also heard Erzeben and Calaveran inside.

"Look," Erzeben was saying, his voice low but insistent, "you did not have to come with us on this messed up journey if you did not want to. I mean I did not even want to, but Wanda is my best friend, and I could not let her die."

"It's not that Ben," Calaveran's voice answered. "I'm just really worried about you. You're a really sensitive guy, and I worry that all of this is too much for you."

"I'm sensitive?" Erzeben snorted. "Cal, I literally almost killed Aradia! If anything, you should be worried about yourself and everyone else. If I am pushed just a step too far I become a monster!"

Aradia frowned. It hurt to hear him saying it, but she remembered how terrifying Erzeben was, how angry and bloodthirsty he looked. He was the only one of the Bad Witches that had directly threatened her life. There was still a part of her that was nervous around him.

"All the more reason I'm worried about you!" Calaveran retorted. "I know you're a good guy, Ben. I know you don't really want to hurt anyone. You were also the one that saved Aradia when she fell."

"Because I felt guilty that I almost killed her!" Erzeben's voice rose, and Aradia took a step back from the door, her face warming with the shame of eavesdropping. "And we do not even know if she is still alive! I messed up and it put her in danger, and then I put everyone in danger by bringing us to that castle! I just keep on messing up. Of the Bad Witches I am the only one who is actually bad."

Aradia looked at Wanda, who shared a surprised look with her. She did not expect to hear Erzeben open up about this, to truly admit he was wrong. It made her think of him a little differently. She doubted he would have said it to her face, but knowing how he felt about it helped understand him more. Aradia's shoulders dropped slightly. They were both just scared kids.

"Ben, you're not bad." Calaveran's voice was quieter, more vulnerable. The two girls shared another look, eyes wide, and then leaned in close to hear the rest. "Trust me, I've seen true evil and you don't even come close. What you need is someone to help guide you. Someone that really sees you for who you are and isn't scared of you. And someone that will be there for you when you're scared."

"Oh my Gods, is it finally going to happen?" Wanda whispered excitedly.

"What are you saying Cal?" Erzeben said, that same naked emotion in his voice.

There was a moment of silence, as if Calaveran was thinking of what to say next. And then the door opened, spilling Wanda and Aradia forward into the room. Calaveran was at first confused, but a grin spread across his skull-like face when he saw them.

"Aradia, you're okay!" he said. "See, Ben, you did save her buddy!"

Erzeben, standing a short distance behind him, forced a smile, although there was some disappointment in his eyes. He was still looking at the brujo, his red eyes pleading.

"I'm glad you are okay," Erzeben said after a pause, his gaze shifting to Aradia.

"Thank you for saving me," Aradia said awkwardly.

"I think I owed you that much," Erzeben said. Aradia nodded, an unspoken agreement settled between the two of them. She walked into a small lounge room decorated with more glamorous posters of Vivivine. Wanda shut the door behind them.

"So, what were you guys talking about?" Wanda asked smugly, flopping onto a black suede couch, pulling Aradia down with her. Erzeben's eyes focused sharply on Calaveran. The brujo rubbed his neck, smiling awkwardly.

"I was just saying that I'm worried about everyone. Aradia almost died, there have been riots going in downtown over the past two days, and the Lantern Coven has been doing raids because of it. Baroness is still downtown and I'm worried she could be targeted after helping us. She's tough, but she isn't invincible," Calaveran said. Erzeben's eyes tightened in concern.

"Do you think we should have stayed with her?" Erzeben asked, grimacing like he was trying to swallow the hurt. Calaveran looked at him with tenderness, his eyes soft.

"No," the brujo said after a pause. "I mean, I do still care about her, but one of the reasons it didn't work out was because, well, I could tell she needed space. She made it very clear she doesn't need me looking out for her."

Erzeben looked away. It was obvious to Aradia that the boys had feelings for each other, but neither of them seemed able to admit it. It was as if an invisible force-field was keeping them apart, from truly embracing their feelings for each other. Aradia side-eyed Wanda, her hand still in hers. Not that she would know anything about what that felt like.

"And speaking of protecting," Aradia said, cutting through the tension, "we can't stay here, or at least I can't. I need to sacrifice the Dread Queen's crown to the Lord of Samhain before Samhain is over."

"Not this again," Calaveran said, rolling his eyes. "We finally find an actual safe place and you want to run headfirst into danger again."

"I don't want to, Cal, but I have to," Aradia said, her throat tightening as she realized the words were true. "If I don't, Baba Yaga will come to get me. I don't think whatever spells Vivivine has on this house would stop her. And besides, aren't you all tired of Samhain Night? Of evil spirits killing people, of all the riots the Morrigan Coven is doing to protest it? This all needs to stop."

"But what if this is exactly what the Monster Coven wants you to do? Become the Holy Strega, kill the Dread Queen, destroy the Lantern Coven," Calaveran said. Erzeben nodded in agreement, even though his eyes still drifted, unfocused, along the floor.

"So what?" Aradia retorted. "I still have to do it. I don't have a choice anymore. Whether it's Trivia, Tituba, Baba Yaga, Brimombi, it doesn't matter who sent me to do this. It's just what needs to be done. It's not right, it's not fair, but nothing has been fair since my mom kicked me out of the house. You all have families to go to when this is all over. I don't."

Her voice broke on the last words, the bottled hurt she had been carrying spilling out.

"That's not true," Wanda said, the same rawness in her voice as she squeezed Aradia's hand, warm palm against warm palm. "You've got us. We might not be your family, but we're your coven, Dia. Bad Witches wear black, and Bad Witches have your back. You don't have to do anything, but we'll support you no matter what. Well, at least *I* will."

Aradia looked at Wanda and smiled, blinking against the sudden tears collecting in her eyes. What would have happened to her if she had never met the witch? She'd be dead, probably, or at least hopelessly lost. Wanda smiled back, giving Aradia a warm, safe feeling in her chest. Wanda was wrong. They were her family.

"If you're really planning on doing this, then I won't let you go out and kill yourselves. I'll do whatever I can to help," Calaveran said. At that moment, the door swung open on a smiling Vivivine.

"Dinner is ready!"

THEY SAT AT A LONG TABLE, VIVIVINE AND GEORGE AT THE HEADS. ARADIA and Wanda sat next to each other across from Erzeben and Calaveran. Greenish moonlight bathed the dining room from a wall-length window, pulsing with the glow of the city in the near distance. George made them a meal of roast goat, which despite having not eaten since the day before, was hard for Aradia to get through, and it was not just its gaminess. Her shoulders were hunched with tension, her hands slightly shaking. Having dinner in Vivivine's nice house as if nothing was wrong while another Samhain Night brought its chaos to the city bothered Aradia, but no amount of arguing could change Vivivine's mind. She did not know how to bring up that she needed to sacrifice the Dread Queen's crown to the Lord of Samhain without upsetting Vivivine.

"Vivivine?" Aradia asked nervously. Wanda shot her a look, but Aradia just cleared her throat as delicately as she could.

"Yes, dear?" Vivivine glanced up with a smile, still cutting into her dinner.

"I'm a little worried about the Lord of Samhain, and his ghouls. Are you sure we will be safe here?" Aradia asked.

"Of course, there is nothing to worry about. I have many jack-o'-lanterns out front that will scare away all those horrible nasties," Vivivine said, smiling as she popped a bite of goat neatly into her mouth.

"But what about Baba Yaga?" Wanda cut in, nodding at Aradia. "Or the Lantern Coven? Like, no offense Viv, but whatever magic protection you have isn't going to work on them if they find out Dia's here."

"It will be fine!" Vivivine said a bit too forcefully, her smile faltering. "I was the one captured by the Monster Coven; don't you think I know what you're up against? Before coming to this city, George and I were chased and hunted by mob after mob. When Elizabeth and Vlad, Erzeben's lovely parents, brought us here all those years ago, I made very sure that what we went through would never happen to us again. I've survived in this city for more than a century. I think I can manage to keep a few teenagers safe during Samhain Night."

The musical ring of a doorbell reverberated through the room. Vivivine dropped her cutlery in surprise.

"Now who in the name of Hecate could that be?" she asked, a tightness in her voice that Aradia knew meant she was fighting to keep it even. "Georgie, honey, would you mind getting the door? Whoever it is, do not let them in. Tell them that I am quite tired from the Samhain festivities and I am not seeing any guests."

George nodded and left the room, shutting the door behind him.

"What's the deal with you and George anyway?" Wanda asked.

"I beg your pardon?" Vivivine replied, a bit sharply.

"Why is he, you know, like that? Like a zombie or something," Wanda said.

"Wanda!" Erzeben said indignantly.

"Although I cannot imagine what you are referring to, what I can tell you is this. George and I have been through a lot over the past two hundred years. Sometimes, we lose parts of ourselves along the way. But it's all worth it. We all make sacrifices for those we love the most," Vivivine said, taking a sip from her wineglass. "Some sacrifice more than others."

A pit formed in Aradia's stomach. Her own mother sacrificed her relationship with her, forcing her to sacrifice everything she had known— her friends, her home, her old life. She had not thought about it for a while, the cold guilt returning to her chest. How much more sacrifice would there be? Would it even be worth it?

"Are you okay?" Wanda asked. Aradia realized her eyes were burning and blinked quickly, looking up at the chandelier to hold in the tears.

"I'm fine," Aradia said quickly.

"Are you sure?" Wanda asked. "With all we've been through you know you can talk to me."

Aradia sighed, poking at her roast goat with the tines of her fork. "I just wish sacrifices weren't so difficult."

Wanda held her other hand, and Aradia looked up into her soft purple eyes.

"I know what you mean," Wanda said.

"I wonder what is taking my George so long," Vivivine said casually, cutting into a piece of meat.

"Should we check on him?" Aradia asked.

"No, he should be fine. Whoever's at the door is likely giving him a hard time, poor dear. Perhaps in another couple minutes," Vivivine said.

"Vivivine?" Erzeben said, his gaze fixed on the window.

"What is it Erzeben?" Vivivine said, focused on her food.

"The jack-o'-lanterns outside are not lit anymore."

CHAPTER
Forty-Five

Vivivine froze. Everyone around the table shared a horrified look, barely daring to breathe. And then the moment shattered. Vivivine bolted up from her seat and rushed to the door, flinging it open. She ran out of the room, Aradia and the Bad Witches on her heels. They hurried down the spiral staircase that connected each of the rooms, Aradia feeling her stomach churn. The stairs blurred under them as they raced forward until they finally reached the bottom. The hall was hauntingly empty compared to how Aradia had last seen it. Party streamers and various cutlery dotted the ground. The food table was still there, still piled with some treats, now looking cold and uninviting, flies buzzing over it.

"So sorry for the mess," Vivivine said under her breath without pausing. Still she rushed onwards, not breaking stride in her heels. George stood motionless in the open doorway, staring out into the night.

"George, George honey, what is it? Who was out there?" Vivivine asked as she reached his side.

"No one," George said slowly. "Just the wind."

"That's okay pumpkin, let's just close the door. It looks like our jack-o'-lanterns have blown out so let's get some new candles inside, okay?" Vivivine suggested softly.

George nodded and shut the door. Aradia's unease did not go away. Something was out there, toying with them. Aradia stepped closer to Wanda, for whose protection she was not sure.

"Bothersome trick-or-treaters, always playing pranks," Vivivine said, forcing her voice light as she moved away from the door, guiding her husband with a steady arm, even though Aradia heard the edge of a tremble in her voice. "Now, I'm going to go to the kitchen to get some matches. Those jack-o'-lanterns need to be relit."

"I can just do it," Wanda said, conjuring a fireball in her hand.

"Nice try, dear, but you need to be kept safe inside, all of you," Vivivine said. "I will just quickly light the jack-o'-lanterns and hurry back inside."

"Vivivine, something is out there, stalking this house. I don't think any of us should go outside," Aradia said. "It could be the Lord of Samhain."

"The Lord of Samhain?" Vivivine asked, and then she laughed. It sounded fake, forced. "My dear, I know you're new to town. But no one has ever seen such a man, monster, whatever he is. No, it is probably children playing pranks, perhaps those dreadful monkeys at work. But the Lord of Samhain? I'm sorry but that's ridiculous!"

"My mom was killed by the Lord of Samhain last year!" Wanda shouted, her fireball extinguishing. Vivivine stopped herself, pressing a hand to her chest.

"I am so sorry to hear that," she finally said. "Have no black cats crossed your—"

The lights of the room violently flickered. Creaking, groaning noises echoed throughout the room, as if the walls themselves were haunted.

Oh no, Aradia thought, *not again.*

The front door blasted open. Aradia whirled around. Several children wearing crudely made masks and ragged clothing pressed against the threshold, holding out large bags, slowly lurching into the entryway.

"Trick-or-treaters!" Vivivine shrieked.

"Cal, do you have any treats left?" Wanda asked. Calaveran shrugged his shoulders.

"Hecate's hags," Wanda hissed.

"What is it?" Aradia whispered, unsure why trick-or-treaters were causing such panic. After a moment of holding their bags out, the trick-or-treaters cocked their heads at an unsettling angle. Aradia and the rest of the group took a few steps back. The treaters' lower parts of their masks vanished, revealing grotesquely large mouths filled with sharp fangs. A hiss issued forth, as if from one mouth, and then, all at once, they dropped to the ground, scuttling towards them on all fours.

"Quick, everyone into the fireplace!" Vivivine cried out.

"The fireplace? Seriously?" Wanda yelled back. But Aradia pulled her as the group surged towards the fireplace. More and more treaters crawled in like a swarm of insects. The ground shook, as if there was an earthquake. Aradia stumbled forward, knocking into Wanda as the girls held each other up so they could run. Vivivine, George in tow, headed inside of the fireplace.

"Quickly!" she called, waving them forward. Wanda surged forward, tugging Aradia. She looked up at the ceiling, at the lanterns dancing violently as the house shook. And then a dark spot blurred as it dropped—a large, cast-iron lantern.

"Wanda!" Aradia screamed, but as she tugged, Wanda was pulled forward directly into the path of the plummeting lantern. In a moment, she was on the ground, the lantern having hit her head. Aradia threw herself beside her, landing hard on her knees, grabbing at Wanda's hand. The witch was knocked out cold.

"Wake up! Wanda wake up!" Aradia cried out desperately. A treater jumped on Wanda's leg and Aradia glanced back. The wave of creatures had reached them like an incoming tide, and with their claw-like hands they pulled at Wanda, dragging her back into the depths.

"No!" Aradia cried. She took the lantern that had fallen on Wanda and, straining her muscles, hurled it hard at the treater. The lantern smacked the creature in the stomach, catapulting it off the witch. More of the treaters crawled towards them, hissing angrily.

"We have no time. Help me pick her up!" Erzeben said, having come next to her. She nodded, and the two of them lifted the witch up with some struggle. They hobbled forward as fast as they could.

"Wait, where is Cal?" Erzeben said, stopping. Aradia glanced back. The skull-faced witch was standing very still, facing the treaters as they crawled towards him.

"What is he doing?" Aradia said.

"Casting a spell I think," Erzeben said, then shouted, "Cal, what the hex are you doing? Come on!"

"No, you go ahead!" Calaveran shouted back.

"No, we cannot leave you! *I* cannot leave you!" Erzeben cried, his voice breaking.

Calaveran's eyes fixed on Erzeben, something burning and molten in their depths. "I'm doing this for you Ben! I need you to be safe—just go!"

A treater lunged for Erzeben's leg, but he kicked it away, his eyes never straying from Calaveran.

"Let's get Wanda into the fireplace!" Aradia shouted. Erzeben glanced back at Calaveran, but started forward again, stumbling under Wanda's weight. Aradia barely noticed the strain of carrying the other girl as she and Erzeben reached the fireplace.

"You all in?" Vivivine asked.

"No, Cal is still out there!" Erzeben said. Aradia lowered Wanda to the ground, kneeling by her side, and looked out of the fireplace.

Misty images of skulls circled around Calaveran. The treaters were surrounding him, distracted and thankfully no longer approaching the fireplace. They didn't seem able to get too close, hissing at the skulls. As Aradia watched, the glowing skulls formed into skeletons, and they fought off the treaters. Some of the treaters backed off and seemed to remember their other prey—they started bounding towards the fireplace.

"No time," George said and lowered a large lever, just as a trick-or-treater's hand reached in.

The fireplace floor lifted up into the air at a tremendous speed. Aradia held onto Wanda's hand. Like a possessed elevator, they shot up the chimney, going faster and faster, but Aradia remained calm. As long as she was with Wanda, she would be okay.

With a puff of ash, they rocketed out the top of the chimney, the view of the glittering city unfolding below them. When they were up a considerable distance above the tower, Aradia felt the pressure under her weaken, and her stomach flip-flopped. They were falling, and falling fast. Erzeben sat next to Aradia, taking her other hand, worry in his eyes. The floor of the fireplace landed with a sudden jolt in the middle of the cobblestone road a few blocks away from Vivivine's house, bricks flying. Aradia clenched Wanda's and Erzeben's hands tighter and looked down at Wanda. A massive, dark bruise was visible on the witch's green forehead, and she did not seem to be breathing.

"Please Wanda, please," Aradia said through tears. "I won't survive without you."

"Come on Wanda, you are tougher than this. You can make it—I know you can," Erzeben whispered. "Maybe I can give her some of my blood."

"What?" Aradia said, looking at the empusa.

"Empusa blood, when given in small amounts, has healing properties. It can bring someone back to life if they're on the brink of death," Erzeben said, his red eyes large with worry. "But it's dangerous. Even the smallest amount of blood loss could weaken me considerably, and if Wanda is given too much blood it could kill her. Or worse."

Aradia looked back at Wanda, clenching her hand tighter.

"I have a better idea," Aradia said, remembering the first spell Wanda had cast on her. "*Hecate, Hecate, Hecate, power flow through me. I heal this girl from her pain, rid her of any ache or strain, may she be healed so she can walk free, as I do will it, so shall it be.*"

Aradia rested her head against the witch's chest, listening for a heartbeat. She could not hear anything. Then suddenly Aradia felt Wanda's hand clench back. A sob burst out of her. Wanda looked up at her, a smile on her black-painted lips.

"Oh my God, Wanda!" Aradia said, helping to lift her up, and hugging her tightly. She could not imagine what she would do if she lost the witch. Aradia would be lost in so many ways without her. Her whole body trembled with relief; Wanda was alive.

"I was so worried, oh my God," Aradia said.

"Now you know how I always feel," Wanda said, her voice softening. "Thank you."

"Oh sweet Hecate no," Erzeben said. Aradia looked at Erzeben, confused. He was no longer looking at Wanda but at something in the near distance. Aradia followed his gaze. As it continued to shake, Vivivine's tower was crumbling to the ground, as if collapsing in on itself. Bricks tumbled downwards, creating large clouds of dust, until there was nothing left of the tower but rubble. Vivivine's home was gone.

And so was Calaveran.

CHAPTER
Forty-Six

radia stood next to Wanda on the broken road as she watched the ruins of the tower, guilt crawling back into her. It was likely her that those trick-or-treaters were after. Everything in this city was coming after her.

Erzeben cried, his sobs breaking Aradia's heart. Calaveran was still in there. He stayed behind to delay the treaters, and there was a good chance he had been killed. All because Aradia came from the Old Country and was an accused Witch Hunter.

"Erzeben," Aradia said, reaching out.

"Don't, just don't," Erzeben said, more sad than angry. Aradia looked on sadly and turned to Vivivine. The Frankenstein woman stared at the ruins of the tower rather calmly.

"Vivivine, I am so sorry," Aradia said.

"What for my dear?" Vivivine asked.

"For your tower, I feel if I hadn't—"

"Aradia, it is not your fault," Vivivine interrupted, her voice serene as she patted her husband's arm. "Do not think that for a moment. Unless you personally summoned the little demons and caused the tower to collapse, which I doubt very much, you're not to blame."

Vivivine sighed. "Well, it looks like we are going to have to move into our apartment downtown; I knew it was a good idea. And I'm going to have to get a whole new wardrobe. Oh well, I suppose that is what spell insurance is for."

"But still," Aradia said, "I still—"

"That is enough. Is a house that gets sucked into a cyclone responsible for it? No. I will not hear any more self-guilt from you. It is not healthy for any of us," Vivivine said.

"But—" Aradia tried again, but a cry cut her off.

"Cal! Cal!" Erzeben ran down the road to the ruins of the tower, crying.

"Erz, stop!" Wanda said. "The treaters could still be in there!"

Erzeben did not listen. He ran until he stood at the edge of the rubble. He collapsed onto his knees, sobbing uncontrollably. Wanda ran to his side, and let him fall into her arms, as he cried. Aradia tentatively followed Wanda, but stood a short distance away. The grief was too much to for her to process. It did not seem like her place to reach out to him.

Orange smoke materialized close to the group. Perhaps it was Calaveran, maybe he escaped. Hope tightened Aradia's throat. The smoke cleared. Lady Katherine, the High Priestess of the Lantern Coven, stood in front of them, and several guards clothed in black-and-orange uniforms closed in on them at all sides. There was no doubt about it now, the Lantern Coven had them.

"Ah, Vivivine and George Frankenstein. I was not aware that you were involved with the Witch Hunter. You do realize that hiding her from us is considered a treasonous act?" Lady Katherine said. She snapped her fingers and in one smooth motion, the guards grabbed them.

"I was just doing my best to protect her. She is, after all, only a child," Vivivine said coolly. Lady Katherine snorted.

"What she *is* is a threat to Witch City's safety," the High Priestess snapped. "You would endanger the lives of *witch* children to protect an outsider? I would have expected better from you, Vivivine."

Vivivine stared defiantly at the Priestess. Aradia wondered why it was so important for the Frankenstein woman to protect her, meanwhile endangering herself, and committing treason against the most powerful coven in Witch City. What did Vivivine really have to gain?

"You are all under arrest, and the Queen of Lanterns requires your presence immediately," Lady Katherine said.

Orange smoke materialized in the air. It blew around them rapidly, the smell sulfurous, making Aradia cough. All this running, it really was coming to an end now. Aradia was almost relieved, an unexpected calm stealing through her body. Whatever happened next, she was ready.

The smoke cleared, revealing an elegant throne room, heavily decorated with glowing jack-o'-lanterns. Large pillars made from thick, twisted vines, reached up to an impossibly high ceiling, disappearing into darkness. Chandeliers hung down from the darkness, jack-o'-lanterns lighting them. Aradia stood directly in the center, staring dizzily down at her reflection in the shiny black marble. When she dared raise her head, the room seemed to spin around her. More vines artfully decorated the walls, as if they were purposely put there as opposed to a result of neglect. At the back of the room were thirteen thrones, the largest, most ornate one standing in the center. Above the thrones was a large flag with a jack-o'-lantern face surrounded by black and orange stripes on it.

Many of the thrones were vacant, but those that sat in them held glowing jack-o'-lanterns in their hands. None of the witches had Wanda's bright green skin. A tall, dark figure sat in the largest throne, sitting very still.

"Bring her to me," the figure said, power in every word.

Two guards prodded Aradia forward. Every bit of her wanted to resist, but she knew there was no point now. She let the guards lead her close to the thrones, until she was close enough to see what the figure looked like. She wore a long, black Victorian gown that trailed onto the ground. Large, puffed sleeves decorated her shoulders, and her waist was cinched tight by a corset. A large crown rested on curly black, heart-shaped hair. On her face she wore an ornate mask of a smiling jack-o'-lantern, two glowing orange orbs staring out from the eye-holes. Her black gloves with long, pointed fingers, curled and uncurled around a pumpkin-tipped scepter as she held her other hand out in a gesture to stop. This was Gourdina, the Queen of Lanterns.

"Aradia. You have been quite difficult to get hold of, haven't you?" Gourdina said slowly and coolly, without passion. "How did you arrive in Crone's Cross? This city has been protected from Witch Hunters since its inception, and yet one has snuck her wicked way in."

"I am not a Witch Hunter," Aradia said.

"Then why are you here? To be the Holy Strega and start a rebellion?" Gourdina asked again, as if it was a joke. Aradia's cheeks burned.

"As if she could ever be the Holy Strega," the High Priestess said.

"Silence, Katherine," Gourdina said, something like a smile in her voice. "Let the cowan speak."

Aradia focused on the Queen of Lanterns, on her pumpkin mask. What was lying behind that frozen smile? There was no way to tell if Gourdina would even listen to anything the girl had to say. The Queen had already decided that Aradia was a Witch Hunter, or at the very least a political threat. What story could the descendant of Tituba weave so that her interrogator would listen?

"I came to the city after casting a spell, to connect with Tituba, the first Salem Witch," Aradia said, fighting to keep her voice level. "You see, she is my ancestor, and I wanted to find the source of my power."

"Your power?" Gourdina repeated.

"I have a very special ability," Aradia said, lifting her head proudly. "When I tell stories, I can make them real. I can conjure worlds with my words. I can also destroy them. I destroyed what was left of Abigail Williams in Castle Tartarus by only using my words."

"Abigail Williams?" the Queen echoed.

"Walpurga Lucifera," Aradia spat the name and for a moment it seemed to soak up all the words in the room, leaving them in a tense silence.

"She lies your Imperial Highness," the High Priestess cut in. "No witch could do that, and Walpurga Lucifera has been dead for over a century."

"It's true—we saw her do it!" Wanda said.

"Silence!" the Queen said, anger seeping into her cool voice. "Aradia, if that be your name, do you have any proof?"

"Shall I tell you a story then?" Aradia suggested.

The Queen of Lanterns seemed to tense, if ever so slightly. Nervousness spread across the other seated witches as they whispered amongst themselves. Aradia suppressed a smile. She did not know what she was doing exactly, but she knew something was getting to them.

"We have no time for parlor tricks," Gourdina said instead. "Tell me the truth, Aradia. Was coming to Crone's Cross to find your Salem Witch ancestor your only motivation? Or did you have other goals, perhaps a more insidious intention? You go by the name of the Holy Strega, but I have not ruled out that you have chosen that name to either gain the trust of unsuspecting witches, or to inspire revolt. If you are found guilty of being a Witch Hunter or attempting a coup on the Lantern Coven, you will be executed immediately."

Aradia took in the weight of the Dread Queen's words. Even with two of the Bad Witches and the Frankensteins, they were in the Lanterns' domain. They were no match for them.

"You're right, I do have another reason why I'm here," she said finally.

"Dia, don't," Wanda said.

"I must tell them, Wanda," Aradia said, looking back at her. She gave her another look to tell her she had a plan. Wanda squinted in confusion, but nodded slightly.

"Tell us what?" Gourdina said.

"It's Baba Yaga, the witch of the woods," Aradia said, and at the name a wave of nervous whispers drew through the room. "I went to her for advice and she told me that I needed to be the Holy Strega, to defeat the evil in Witch City. That's the only way I could come into my power."

"And what, do tell, is this 'evil' in Witch City?" the Queen scoffed.

"The Lord of Samhain, what else could it be?" Aradia asked, trying to sound as innocent as she could.

The room went silent. Aradia felt everyone looking at her, the Queen of Lanterns unnaturally still. The desire to shrink and disappear crept into her, but she pushed it down. She needed the Lantern Coven's undivided attention.

"How in the name of Hecate would that hag expect you to do that?" the High Priestess barked out, turning to face Aradia, her gaze cold and skeptical.

"Well, she said I needed to make a sacrifice to him," Aradia said.

"What kind of sacrifice?" Gourdina asked. Aradia took a moment to consider how she was going to answer the next question. How she responded could potentially decide if she was to be executed by the Lantern Coven. What could she say that would both terrify the Lantern Coven, but also to get them to do what she wanted?

"Baba Yaga said I was the heir to the Queen of Salem," Aradia said, thinking of Baroness's words, "and she said I needed to get my crown."

The Queen reached up to her crown, her gaze never leaving the girl.

"What right does the Guardian of the HagHollow Woods have to my crown? That meddlesome hag should leave her business to that wretched forest. If she is attempting to overreach her authority, I will see to it that the HagHollow Woods is burned to the ground."

"She knew you might say something like that, but she isn't afraid of you," Aradia said. She felt the thread of the story, and tugged on it, letting her words spin from her lips.

"You see, what matters most to her is that Witch City is saved from the Lord of Samhain. The crown needs to be sacrificed to him in order to save the city. If it isn't, the Lord of Samhain will destroy everything, and the Baba Yaga will come for you," Aradia continued, glancing at each member of the coven. "All of you."

The Lantern Coven members' eyes were wide with fear. Even the High Priestess seemed unnerved, glancing back at the Dread Queen. Gourdina, her face hidden behind her mask, was unreadable, but Aradia could guess that the pumpkin ruler was trembling herself. Aradia secretly delighted in seeing the coven like this, even if it was only power she would have over them. Even the Lantern Coven conceded to the Baba Yaga's fearsome reputation.

"We cannot risk the Baba Yaga emerging from the woods with Goddess-knows-what in there," the witch seated closest to Gourdina said.

"Do not tell me we are to meet the terrorist's demands," the High Priestess bit back. The Queen raised a hand to silence her covenmates. Her stare never lifted from Aradia, the girl feeling the heat of her glowing orange gaze.

"If the Baba Yaga demands a sacrifice to the Lord of Samhain, then that will be exactly what she will get," Gourdina said. Aradia wanted to smile, but something in the Dread Queen's tone promised danger. The descendant of Tituba had not won yet.

"I must do the right thing for the good of my people," Gourdina said, pointing her scepter at Aradia, her voice raising to ring out through the room, "and send Aradia, Queen of Salem, to the Morrigan's Grove to be sacrificed to the Lord of Samhain. That should appease him well enough."

Aradia's stomach dropped. This was not what she wanted at all. She had made things much worse.

"You cannot do that; she is just a child!" Vivivine said, straining against the witches holding her.

"Yeah, that just isn't fair!" Wanda said.

"Do not speak out of turn!" the Queen said severely. "I had almost forgotten the rest of you were here. Your little, and not so little it would seem, accomplices. I would ask how you all got involved with this Salem Witch, but there are more urgent matters at hand. It is a Samhain Night, and even I am aware that this night causes desperate people to do desperate things. All too aware in fact. But I cannot have the lot of you causing more trouble tonight. No, my dear esteemed covenmates shall take you, and you shall be placed under house arrest until Samhain Night is over, and then it will be decided what to do with you."

It was eerie how much Gourdina's words echoed Brimombi's. Would the Monster Coven be any better than the Lantern Coven if they got control of Witch City? Would they be any worse?

"I shall let you all say your farewells, and then you must all be on your way," Gourdina said. "Remember, this may all seem very harsh to you, but it is the right thing to do. Lanterns light the way."

"This is all a bunch of minotaur-dung and you know it! You can't do this!" Wanda cried, the sparks of a fireball forming in her hand.

"Wanda, don't," Aradia said, giving her a pleading look. If Wanda threatened the Lantern Coven, they would kill her on the spot, and that was far more than Aradia could take. Wanda looked at Aradia, tears collecting in her eyes, her lips trembling.

"I promised I was never going to leave you. I-I can't let you do this," Wanda said.

"Wanda, please," Aradia said, reaching for her as much as she could, held by the Lantern guards. "You've done everything you could. Let me go."

"But they're going to kill you," Wanda said, her voice breaking.

"We all make sacrifices for those we love the most," Aradia said. As one tear traced down Wanda's cheek, Aradia reached out and gently wiped it away. Her hand burned from the warmth. Wanda pulled Aradia in for a tight hug, and the witches holding them muttered but let them embrace. Neither of them wanted to let go. She had only known the witch for just a few days, but she already felt that she did not know what her life would be like without her. It seemed they were stuck at a dead-end; they had no chance of defeating the Lantern Coven. Aradia's last plan had failed, and in doing so she had failed her friends, too. She tried holding back her tears. When they broke apart, Wanda looked away.

Aradia turned to Erzeben. She would miss him, despite everything. Her feelings toward him were complicated and conflicted, but at the end of it all she was grateful for his help. They hugged, although briefly.

"I am sorry I doubted you," Erzeben said. "And for everything else."

"Thank you," Aradia said as they let go of each other. "For that, and for everything else."

Aradia at last turned to Vivivine. The Frankenstein woman spread her arms out, a sad smile on her face. Aradia went in for the hug. For the brief times that Aradia was with her, Vivivine acted like how the girl thought a mother should. A kind of person that Aradia never had in her previous life.

"Vivivine, why did you protect me?" Aradia asked.

"Because it was the right thing to do," Vivivine said, letting go of her. "Stay brave."

"Thank you," Aradia said, wiping away tears. The guards, led by the High Priestess, escorted Vivivine, her husband, and the Bad Witches to the front door of the throne room. Wanda looked back one final time, and then they left the room, the door shutting behind them.

Aradia let the tears flow from her eyes. She never thought it would hurt so much to miss someone. The girl was always so used to not having to care so much for anybody and now she was being ripped away from the people that had almost become her family. It was the cruelest thing she could imagine, even crueler than her mother abandoning her.

"They must have been very good friends," Gourdina said.

Aradia wiped her tears and turned around. The Queen of Lanterns stood over her, almost leering, her mask disguising her expression. Aradia took a small step back.

"I think Aradia, it is time you should be on your way as well," the Queen said. "Come with me."

"And why should I go with you? I have nothing to lose," Aradia spat.

"We both know that is not true," the Queen of Lanterns said. "I would absolutely hate to discover that famous socialite Vivivine and her husband George, as well as two underage witches, got into a tragic accident on Samhain Night, wouldn't you?"

Aradia went silent.

"As I said, Aradia, come with me."

CHAPTER
Forty-Seven

They stood in a cobblestone courtyard, Aradia flanked by two guards. The courtyard was surrounded by spiked walls covered in thorns, black and orange roses, and glowing orange lanterns. A large, dark shed stood forlornly in a corner, seemingly neglected.

"Wait here," Gourdina said and headed towards the shed.

Aradia gazed around the courtyard, looking to see if there was any possibility of escape. There was no way she could fight the Dread Queen on her own, so her only hope would be to run. But there was nothing. There were no exits, and the walls were too tall to climb. If only she could fly. Aradia heard a loud click, a pair of doors on the shed swinging open.

"Bucca! Bucca Dhu! Mother needs your help," the Queen called out. A loud grumbling rumbled from inside the darkness.

"Come on, my precious," Gourdina sang. Aradia strained to hear more grumbling. The Queen stepped out of the way of the door. A huge, monstrous black goat almost the size of a pony waddled slowly out of the shed, a strong farmyard stench emanating from it. Its mouth was drawn into a frown, its eyes squinted in judgment. Upon noticing Aradia it snorted derisively.

"This is Bucca Dhu. He is a very special goat," the Queen said, sweetness coming into her cold voice. "He will take you to Morrigan's Grove where the Hierophant shall sacrifice you to the Lord of Samhain. Bucca has been a familiar little friend of mine for a very long time; I am sure he is thrilled at this opportunity to save Crone's Cross once and for all."

The sour, unimpressed expression on the goat's face said otherwise.

"Get on him, child. And do not dare to think of jumping off or running away from him. He is a very grumpy goat and will get quite aggressive when bothered."

Aradia slowly approached the goat, who glared at her intensely. She reached out to touch its forehead and jerked back quickly when he snapped his flat teeth at her fingers. With another lost glance around—and no help from Gourdina or her associates—Aradia awkwardly climbed onto the back of Bucca Dhu, clutching his rough long hair and trying to avoid being impaled by his large horns. The goat let out a loud grumble in protest.

"You know," Aradia said as she got a firm grip, "I'm going to survive, and stop the Lord of Samhain."

"Are you now?" Gourdina asked, cocking her head as she surveyed the girl.

"And when I'm done, I'm going to come for your crown," Aradia said, and she meant it. The Queen of Lanterns stared at her with her glowing eyes, no expression readable.

"Merry part my child," Gourdina said after a pause. "I pray that the Lord of Samhain is merciful. Bucca Dhu, take Aradia to Morrigan's Grove, and do not let her leave under any circumstances. Now go!"

The goat bleated and raised his head. A light flickered between his horns, until a ball of fire formed. He trotted a couple of steps and took off into the air. Aradia clutched his back for dear life. She buried her head in Bucca Dhu's long hair, trying to ignore his strong smell. Soon they were flying, but this wasn't like Wanda's broom. They surged forward as the goat galloped through the air.

The wind blew relentlessly against them, but the goat continued on. Any moment Aradia feared she would lose her grip and fall to her death. Eventually Bucca Dhu changed direction, and levelled in pace, the wind blowing them forward instead of against them. Aradia slowly opened her eyes and lifted her head. The triple moon ahead of them seemed larger than it had been before, taking up a great portion of the sky. It illuminated their journey to Morrigan's Grove, a comforting beacon in the night.

Below them the green and orange veins of the city glowed. Aradia's thoughts turned to her friends. Would they be okay? Calaveran was probably already dead. If Wanda was killed, Aradia would burn down the Lantern Coven, the entire city, and then herself.

"The two witches that lived in the forest were separated by the evil Sam Hain, for he feared their power. The cottage witch was taken far, far away, too far for the other witch to find her. The other witch was taken away to be sacrificed," Aradia said aloud, telling herself a story to keep calm. "But the witches were very strong, brave, and clever. They found ways to escape their captors, and teamed up to destroy Sam Hain once and for all. But they needed to make a sacrifice first. They sacrificed . . . they sacrificed . . ."

Aradia had trouble coming up with the rest of the story, her mind going blank. What more could she sacrifice to the Lord of Samhain? How could she possibly save herself from the Hierophant sacrificing her to him? The ending of the story was what always troubled her the most.

"Hecate, Tituba, what am I supposed to do now?" Aradia asked, looking out to the triple moon. If Hecate brought her to Witch City, she must have had some sort of plan for her, and Tituba was the reason she went looking for a Witch City in the first place. For the first time since she had arrived in Crone's Cross she was completely alone, with only an unfriendly goat taking her to her doom. She grasped the goat's hair harder, and once again buried her face in it, the goat grumbling loudly in protest.

Bucca Dhu gradually stopped moving, pausing in midair. Aradia lifted her head and gasped. The triple moon was larger than ever, as if it was close enough to touch. Although she was not sure, Aradia thought she could make out the face of a severe elderly woman in its craters. The wind had stopped blowing, and the goat was not even twitching.

Everything was still.

The ball of fire between Bucca Dhu's horns grew brighter and took on a greenish tinge. Aradia was drawn in by it until everything in her vision was consumed by light.

CHAPTER
Forty-Eight

Crone's Cross, October 31, 1792

Tituba picked some herbs from her garden, humming a half-forgotten song of Barbados. She held her shawl close to her, the autumn wind chilling her bones. Soon it would be winter, the woman shivering at the thought. Winters in this city were as cold as death. How many had she gone through now? Eighty? Ninety? Had it been a century already? She had lost track some time ago.

"Tituba?" a familiar voice called. "Tituba of Salem?"

Tituba slowly turned around, her bones not quite what they used to be. An older woman with earth-brown skin stood nearby, her eyes wide and hopeful. At first Tituba did not recognize her, but after studying the woman's eyes discovered who it was. It was Candy, many, many years older.

"Candy," Tituba said with a smile, arms reaching for a hug. The older woman embraced her, the two women holding each other close. Tituba had never thought to see Candy again; she suspected that the woman had died long ago.

"Candy, how did you get here?" Tituba said, releasing the woman. "Did the Devil find you too?"

"No, Tituba," Candy said with a smile. "Someone else brought me here. She says she's been looking for you for a long time, that you were an old friend. She told me to find you."

Tituba pondered who that could be. Was it perhaps Violet, her daughter, coming to find her after all these years? Tituba's heart rose at the idea, but she quickly dismissed it. She had known long ago not to keep her hopes up about such things.

A hooded figure swooped down next to them on a broom, their face in shadow. Tituba took a step back, startled. The figure lifted their hood, and Tituba's eyes went wide with surprise. It was a young, beautiful woman with icy blue eyes, cream-white skin, and soft blonde hair. It was Abigail Williams, and she had only aged about ten years, despite nearly a century having passed since Tituba had last seen her.

"Hello, Tituba," Abigail said, her mouth a malicious grin. "I've missed you so much."

"Abby," Tituba said, taking another step back. "What are you doing here?"

"Do not call me that," Abigail said, her eyebrows furling. "You may address me as Walpurga Lucifera."

Tituba grabbed her nearest garden tool, a rake, and held it pointing at the woman.

"What be the matter, Tituba," Candy said, gently touching Tituba's shoulder. "Walpurga said she was your friend."

"No friend of mine, the wicked she-devil. She accused me of being a witch, after years of taking care of her," Tituba spat. "That wench started the witch trials in Salem. I want nothing to do with her."

Walpurga's mouth turned to a frown. "It pains me to see you hold such a grudge after all these years, Tituba. Can't you let the past be past?"

"Because of you I suffered for over a year," Tituba said, hot anger boiling to the surface. "Because of you I never saw my John or Violet again!"

Candy looked between the two, eyes wide with surprise. "I am so sorry Tituba, I did not know this! I should have remembered who this was."

"Well, it's too late anyway," Walpurga said, her face smug. "I have a task of you, Tituba, and you daren't refuse."

"Over my rotting corpse," Tituba said, flinging the rake at the woman. Walpurga snapped her fingers, and the rake instantly incinerated. Tituba turned and ran, but found herself dragged back by an invisible force, an icy hand squeezing her neck. Her body was *spun around, so she was forced to face Walpurga. The young woman's eyes were cold with malice, her hand outstretched like a claw.*

"That is precisely how I intend for it to happen. You see, if you don't help me," Walpurga said and made another clawlike motion, lifting Candy into the air as well. "Your helpful little friend will die."

TITUBA FOLLOWED WALPURGA LUCIFERA WITH HER HEAD DOWN, HER WRISTS BOUND, the rest of the coven around her. Candy had been released under the condition that Tituba would willingly come with them. They trod through the pumpkin patch, Walpurga kicking over whatever gourds stood in her way. The wind howled as if nature itself knew the wickedness that was to come. They approached a great tree, hundreds of pumpkins hanging off its branches. An old woman wearing a dark gray mantle kneeled before it, lighting jack-o'-lanterns and chanting under her breath.

"Hello, Nicnevin. Happy All Hallows' Eve," Walpurga said. The old woman jolted as if startled and stood up to face them. At her full height she was nearly as tall as the tree. Her electric green face was sharp and pointed, her fierce purple eyes staring with anger. Underneath her gray mantle was a regal orange dress, and a tall spiked crown rested on long gray hair.

"What are you doing here? This is a sacred place; I command you to leave at once!" Nicnevin spoke, her voice booming with power. The woman raised her hand into a claw, as if trying to summon something. When nothing happened, she looked at her fingers in confusion.

"We have bound your little sanctuary with iron, faerie queen. Your magic shall not work here, unfortunately," Walpurga said.

Nicnevin looked at her with utter disdain. "I should have never let Hecate bring her witches here. I made it very clear to her that if the witches were to live here, they would have to respect the rules of the sídhe or they would suffer the consequences."

"Yes, but we are not Hecate's witches," Walpurga said. "We are the light-bringers, the Covenant of Lucifer. We are here to enlighten this realm, and free it from bondage of the old, primitive ways. And that includes you, Queen of Elfhame."

The other members of the coven advanced. Nicnevin's eyes darted at them in a nervous rage. Even as she was forced to step forward, Tituba felt bad for the poor woman. If it had not been for her, she would have never found a safe place to live once she had arrived in the city. Tituba had lived peacefully there for nearly a century, but that peace was coming to an end. She now understood what the Devil meant when he said he would require something of her later. There always was a sacrifice.

"You do not know what you are doing, foolish girl, and on Samhain of all nights," Nicnevin said, her voice breathy with fear. "I am of the direct bloodline of the Cailleach Beira, Queen of Winter and creatrix of this world! I am the daughter of Badb Nemain of the Morrigan, the Triple Goddess of Death, Sovereignty, and War and Goddess of Samhain! If you destroy me, you will destroy this world and everything in it, including yourself!"

Walpurga laughed mirthlessly. "I already knew that, you old fool. I have no intention of destroying you. I just need you out of the way. Your daughters, on the other hand, will have to be eliminated."

"My daughters are named for the Morrigan and have her warrior spirit within them. They will be the ones to destroy you," Nicnevin said with venom in her voice, dangerous as any viper. And yet still Walpurga's witches pressed in and two coven members restrained her.

"And they will fail tremendously in trying to doing so. I know Macha's weaknesses in particular," Walpurga said wickedly. "No matter, as this is a sacred part of your fairyland, you shall be bound here until the end of time! Prepare the sacrifice!"

Two coven members grabbed Tituba's arms. Her eyes widened. Once again Abigail had betrayed her. She was to be the sacrifice.

"Abby why?" Tituba began. "After everything—"

"Do not call me that name!" Walpurga interrupted, turning to face her, her blue eyes burning. "I am finishing what I began a long time ago. The world will finally be rid of you."

"What did I ever do to receive your hatred, Abigail?" Tituba asked, even as the hands of the coven held her tighter. "All I did was tell you stories!"

Walpurga paused, her eyes cold.

"You were in my way. Through destroying you I found my power in that cruel village. And I will do it again," Walpurga said.

"You will never destroy me, Abigail. You may destroy my body, but my spirit and blood will live on, and I shall return to undo everything you've ever done," Tituba said, hot fiery rage pulsing through her body. "I have lived a lifetime of freedom in this city, and it shall not end with you."

"We shall see, won't we?" Walpurga said with a frown. She turned back to face Nicnevin and walked towards the woman, who stared defiantly back at her.

"One who sacrifices in bad faith will bring a greater cost to themselves. Your holy crusade will bring you nothing but ruination," Nicnevin said coldly.

Walpurga yanked Nicnevin's crown off her head, and Nicnevin's agonized scream rent the air. Walpurga turned again to face Tituba, her blue eyes burning with hatred. Tituba was brought down to her knees as the woman she had once known as little Abby approached her. The last shards of Tituba's heart broke. Walpurga raised the crown over the woman's head.

"I sacrifice the old to bring in the new,
my resolve is firm and my intention is true.
I bind Nicnevin, Queen of Elfhame,
to be buried here in endless pain.
Nicnevin will be one with the hallowed tree,
rotting away and never set free.
I sacrifice my past to bring forth a new light,
to create a new world on this Samhain Night.
Tituba will die, a life for a life,
killed by the crown sharp as a knife.
By Tituba's blood and Nicnevin's blade,
their fate is bound as their lives start to fade.
To change the future by killing the past,
thus now I seal the Salem Pact!"

Walpurga Lucifera brought down the crown upon her, forcing it upon her head. Tituba screamed from the searing pain, as if it was burning her, and everything in Tituba's vision was consumed by fire.

CHAPTER
Forty-Nine

Crone's Cross, November 6, 2022

Aradia came to, gasping loudly. She clutched Bucca Dhu tightly, tears streaming from her eyes. The goat was moving forward again, the night fading slowly into the greenish day. Everything about the vision felt all too real, as if she herself had just lived it.

Abigail Williams had killed Tituba with what was now the Dread Queen's crown. But it was not to summon the Lord of Samhain, it was to trap the true queen of Witch City. At least, the world that had become Witch City. If Abigail Williams didn't summon the Lord of Samhain, it was possible that the sacrifice accidentally summoned him, but something in Aradia's gut told her otherwise. There was only one explanation that made sense now.

"There is no Lord of Samhain, is there?" Aradia asked the goat. Bucca Dhu gave her a side glance, and nodded with a bleat.

It was as if Aradia had been hit with a stone. Everything about Samhain had been a lie, which meant that anyone who had ever been killed by the Lord of Samhain was actually murdered by the Lanterns. Like Wanda's mother. What could she have possibly done to incur the wrath of Gourdina and her covenmates? Suddenly Brimombi's perspective made more sense. But there was another thing Aradia was trying to figure out. If the Lord of Samhain was not real, then why had the Baba Yaga demanded she make a sacrifice to him? The old witch must have known the truth. Why did she make her go on this dangerous quest for nothing?

The rage and pain spread red-hot throughout Aradia's body, culminating in a loud, drawn-out scream. She screamed at Baba Yaga for making her go through all of this. She screamed to curse everyone and everything that perpetrated this lie. Tituba deserved better than this. *She* deserved better than this. Aradia had wanted to know the truth about what had happened to Tituba, and now that she knew she did not know how to handle it. She had destroyed Abigail at Castle Tartarus, but that did not make her feel better at all. The injustice remained. Bucca Dhu bleated and shook his body, nearly knocking Aradia off.

"What are you so grumpy about? You're not the one that's been sent away to be secretly murdered," Aradia said as she regained her grip. "Why do you help that pumpkin monster anyway? What makes her so powerful that she can control an entire city of witches?"

Bucca Dhu gave her another side glance and looked away quickly.

"You know something, don't you?" Aradia said. The goat snorted in response.

"You aren't taking me to be killed, are you?" Aradia said, realization coming to her like an unpleasant chill. "Baba Yaga wants me to make a sacrifice, but it isn't to stop the Lord of Samhain. It's to bring back Nicnevin."

Aradia grasped the goat tighter, another realization coming to her. "She mentioned something about you when I talked to her, that 'old Bucca wouldn't like it' if I was unprepared. You work with the Baba Yaga. You all want Nicnevin back."

Bucca Dhu bleated and nodded as if in agreement.

"But what if I don't want to? I'm technically not bound to any deal with Baba Yaga anymore if there is no Lord of Samhain. I don't have to do anything anymore. I'm free to escape when we land and go find Wanda," Aradia said, her heart lifting at the thought. Then she and Wanda could run away together, far away where the Lantern Coven would never find them.

Bucca Dhu bleated in annoyance, shaking his head, nearly hitting Aradia with his horns. A gloomier thought came to her, as she was reminded of something Baroness had said. As much as she wanted to run away from everything she could not, not that she finally knew the truth. Bringing back Nicnevin was the only way to set things right in Witch City, and the only way to truly get vengeance against the Lantern Coven for all they had done. If not because it was the right thing to do, then for Wanda. Her mother was dead because the Lantern Coven had killed her. The witch deserved retribution.

"Not everything's about me, I know," Aradia said with a defeated tone. "Fine. But how am I supposed to get Gourdina's crown now? Unless . . ."

There was one other thing she could sacrifice to bring back Nicnevin, and defeat the Lantern Coven, at least according to the Baba Yaga.

The witch accused of wickedness fed to the flames.

Aradia finally understood what that really meant. Tituba, the first accused Salem Witch, was sacrificed the first time. There was only one person left that could finish what was started, to undo everything Abigail had ever done. If she was unable to sacrifice the Dread Queen and her crown, she would have to sacrifice the only person left alive with Tituba's blood. Herself.

CHAPTER
Fifty

After several long hours, a pumpkin patch appeared in the distance. It expanded along the horizon, seeming to have no end. Aradia breathed in deeply. This was it. This is where it all began. And this is where it would all end.

Bucca Dhu descended as they approached it, Aradia clutching his hair tight. They landed just a short distance away by the large iron gates guarding the entrance. Aradia slid off the goat. Her legs were grateful for the relief, having spent the entire day clutching Bucca Dhu for dear life. Already the green sky was fading to black. The last Samhain Night was beginning. Aradia looked at the goat, her eyes tired and body weary.

"Look's like this is it, Mr. Grumbles," she said. Bucca Dhu looked back at her with his usual grumpy expression, unimpressed with the nickname, but did not make a sound. Aradia approached the gates of the pumpkin patch, summoning her resolve. She closed her eyes and breathed in deep to calm her heart. Although she had not realized it then, everything she had experienced since arriving in Witch City had led to this moment. Her shoulders trembled from the weight of the thought. She opened her eyes and pushed open the gates, the sound echoing through the quietness. Clenching her fists to her sides, Aradia crossed the threshold.

All around her were pumpkins, of various shapes and sizes. Some were even large as houses, the pumpkin patch a village. Aradia held her arms close to herself, looking around. The Hierophant was supposed to be there, or be there very soon. Under the Dread Queen's orders he would kill her, sacrifice her to the "Lord of Samhain." Doubt crawled back into Aradia. She had no idea what she would do. Would she let herself be sacrificed to bring back Nicnevin? She did not want to die, but she was not even sure what she was living for anymore.

After wandering amongst the endless rows of pumpkins, Aradia found the tree from her vision, illuminated by the triple moon as it rose in the sky. She tilted her head up.

"Well?" she called into the encroaching darkness. "What are you waiting for? Come and sacrifice me!"

For a moment she stayed frozen, until her resolve cracked and she sighed. Aradia sat under the tree and pulled her knees to her chest. No one seemed to be coming. She was not even sure if Mr. Grumbles was still out there. Was it too late to run away from it all, to try and find Wanda on her own? There was only one thing left Aradia felt she could do.

"The witch was about to sacrifice herself to save her people from the evil Sam Hain, but before she could, the witch she met in the woods found her. Together, they burned Sam Hain alive, ending the evil for good. Then they flew off together to somewhere far away, where no one would ever hurt them again," Aradia said, trying to stop herself from crying. She placed her head against her knees, and tried to disappear from the world. The wind picked up around her, the scent of autumn filling her nose. For a moment she could pretend that everything was okay, that she was far away from all her problems.

"Aradia! Dia are you here?" Wanda's voice said faintly. She must have been imagining things, wishful thinking. Wanda was trapped somewhere by the Lantern Coven.

"Aradia! Where are you?" the voice called, getting louder.

Aradia tried to ignore it. It was just voices, right?

"Aradia!" Louder, this time. Closer.

Aradia felt a hand on her knee, shaking her. She was not imagining it. She looked up. Wanda stood in front of her. Aradia could not believe her eyes. Where had the witch come from? She stood up and embraced her in the tightest hug she had ever given, as if letting go of Wanda would destroy them both. Aradia had thought she had no more tears left, but she cried enough tears to melt everything away.

"Wait, where is Erzeben?" Aradia asked, after eventually releasing the witch.

"He went to Vivivine's tower to see if he could find any trace of Cal. I think there's still a part of him that's hoping he's alive," Wanda said.

Aradia nodded. She hoped so, too. Calaveran may have died because Gourdina had sent spirits to find her. The Dread Queen needed to pay for what she had done.

"And what happened to Vivivine and George?" Aradia asked.

"Well, you see, what happened was that we were all forced to go into this big sketchy van, 'cuz we were apparently being driven to the 'safe place.' But Vivivine was having none of that. While we were being driven, Vivivine, with George's help, forced open the door of the car and screamed at us to get out and go. We ran, and it turns out they bought us just enough time, because as soon as we were a safe distance away, more Witch City officials showed up, and took her and George away. I swear though, she was smiling at us as we looked back at her," Wanda said. "She's an honorary Bad Witch if I ever saw one."

Aradia's stomach dropped. Vivivine and George had sacrificed themselves to save the Bad Witches, just like Calaveran did. Vivivine had to be the most selfless and courageous woman that Aradia had ever met. Now she was worried about what the Lantern Coven would do to the couple.

"Don't worry too much about them, Dia," Wanda said, nudging her. "If there's anything I learned about Vivivine, it's that she's a powerful force not to be messed with. She never needed to be saved. Like she said, she can find her way out of anything. I truly believe that now."

"But wait, how did you find me here?" Aradia said.

"I broke into a broom shop and stole a broom," Wanda said, picking up a broomstick off the ground. Aradia stared in disbelief.

"What? We're already wanted witches anyway. I knew the Lantern Coven was taking you to Morrigan's Grove, and boom-tada here I am. I wasn't going to give up looking for you. Bad Witches wear black, and Bad Witches have your back," Wanda said, moving a strand of hair out of Aradia's face. "I would have searched until next Samhain to find you."

Aradia was filled with warmth. Even when they argued, Wanda did not abandon her. The witch was with her from the beginning and would stay until the end. Aradia could not believe how lucky she was.

"I thought I'd never see you again," Aradia said.

"I knew I was going to see you again, in some way or another," Wanda said with a reassuring smile. Aradia smiled back.

"So what happened to you?" Wanda said, gently holding Aradia's hand.

"The Queen sent me out on a flying goat named Bucca Dhu, but I call him Mr. Grumbles. He might be still waiting at the gate, I don't know. But when I was on the goat, I had a vision of what really happened."

"What do you mean?" Wanda said. Aradia paused, the traumatic images flashing in her mind. The blood of her ancestor was the seed that created Witch City.

"It wasn't the Lord of Samhain that Walpurga summoned by sacrifice. There never was a Lord of Samhain. Walpurga sacrificed my ancestor to take control of this world, a sacrifice that now keeps the Lantern Coven in control."

A mix of confusion, shock and anger appeared on Wanda's face, her dark eyebrows furled.

"But wait, if the Lord of Samhain isn't real . . ." Wanda said. Aradia's heart broke as she watched the pain on Wanda's face. She gently squeezed the witch's hand.

"That would mean that she's the one that had my mother killed," Wanda said, quiet in anger.

"I'm so sorry," Aradia said.

"No, it's the Dread Queen that should be sorry. My witch's intuition was just bristling when I saw her. She gave me the creeps, and not in a good way at all," Wanda said, her quietness turning to frustration. "Why would she kill my mom?"

Aradia gently put her arms around her, holding her close.

"We'll tell everyone what that fiend has done, start a revolution or something against her. The Morrigan Coven was right—they were right the whole time. The Queen is the real evil, and if Baba Yaga wants her sacrificed, I say let's do it," Wanda said.

"We think not," a voice rang out. They looked over. Standing very close to them were two tall figures with snow-white skin, short dark hair, and blood-red eyes. They wore black-and-orange uniforms, one a woman, the other a man. All of this signified they were empusae from the Lantern Coven.

"They have been sent to kill me," Aradia said, absolutely sure.

"They're gonna have to catch us first," Wanda said, raising her broomstick.

The female empusa opened her mouth and let out a high-pitched screech. In a moment, several bats descended from the dark sky, immediately enveloping them in a hostile swarm. With them distracted, the male empusa pounced towards Aradia, but she dodged him just in time, jumping out of the way, nearly tripping on a pumpkin. The empusa ran at her and pounced again. Aradia jumped, but he got hold of one of her ankles and she toppled forward. Her body throbbing, she reached for the nearest pumpkin, trying to pull herself up. The empusa grabbed her shoulder and flipped her over. He lowered himself onto her, his mouth open, revealing his long fangs. It was as if Erzeben was trying to attack her again, but so much worse.

A sharp stick drove through the empusa's body from behind, sticking out through his heart, black blood dripping off of it. The empusa let out the high-pitched scream of a dying animal. In half a second he burst into flames and became ash, falling everywhere. Aradia looked up, bewildered and horrified. Wanda stood over her, holding up the other half of a snapped broomstick. She reached for Aradia's hand and helped pull her up, pulling her in close for a hug.

"There was no way I was going to let that happen, not again," Wanda said.

The female empusa came running, screaming at them, manicured hands outstretched. Wanda pointed the broken broomstick at her. A blast of bright, yellow light hit the empusa from behind, knocking her over. Aradia watched as the empusa slowly got up onto her knees, her skin sizzling and steaming. The empusa looked at her hands horrified, an expression of anguish on her face. Her skin soon caught fire, and she screamed. A flare went up, consuming her body, then she too was only ashes on the ground. The bats she had summoned flew away at once. Aradia looked over to where the light had come from. Standing not too far off from her, with his staff steaming, was Lord Ra, the Hierophant of the Lantern Coven.

CHAPTER

Fifty-One

Erzeben flew over the glittering greens and oranges of the city, flying against the wind. He heard the sounds of the city with resounding clarity, but tuned them out as best as he could. He had one thought running through his mind over and over.

Find Cal. Find Cal. Find Cal.

Slowly the crumbled remains of the Frankensteins' tower came into view. Erzeben felt a tug at his heart. Calaveran could still be in there. The thought of potentially finding his corpse made his stomach churn. Calaveran meant so much to him. He was brave, handsome, and strong, but more than that he was patient and kind, two qualities the empusa never saw in himself. He made Erzeben want to be a better person for him. The thought of being held in his strong arms while dancing to one of Calaveran's DJ mixes sent a shiver down the empusa's spine. Erzeben was always too afraid to say how he felt. Now he worried he was too late.

Erzeben landed a short distance away from the ruins and began the uncomfortable process of transforming back into his humanoid form. He felt every muscle tighten, every bone shift. No matter how many times he had done this in his life he could never fully get used to it. When he was done he ran to the rubble, frantically searching through it.

"Cal! Cal!" Erzeben called out, barely able to get the words through the tears that threatened to fall. Then slowly, unmistakably, he heard a heartbeat. It was faint, and slow, but it was there. He perked his ears, trying to hear where it came from. Growing more urgent, he navigated around the ruins, not caring when sharp corners tore into his clothes.

"Cal! Cal I'm coming!"

He stopped when he saw a figure standing in the midst of the ruins. They were dressed in a regal black hooded robe, lined with deep red. A golden, halo-like crown rested on their head. Under the hood was a skull, staring impassively at Erzeben.

Santa Muerte.

At her feet lay Calaveran, his heartbeat growing fainter.

"No, I am not letting you take him!" Erzeben ran to Calaveran's side, kneeling over his body. The brujo's normally tanned skin was ashen and gray. He was cut in several places, dried blood mixed with dirt on his skin. He seemed smaller somehow, as if without his big personality he shrunk. Erzeben had never seen Calaveran so vulnerable and weak and he hated it.

"No, no, Cal," Erzeben said, his face wet with tears. The empusa gently brushed the dirt off of Calaveran's face.

"Cal, wake up! It's me, your buddy, Ben! Wake up!" He looked up at Santa Muerte. She continued staring blankly, her cloak blowing gently in the wind.

"Santa Muerte, please, let him live! I need him!" Erzeben said and looked back down at Calaveran. "I would give anything."

A skeletal hand emerged from the cloak holding a small dagger, presenting it to him. Erzeben looked at it with apprehension. Then he realized what Santa Muerte was saying.

Blood. Of course.

Erzeben took the dagger. It was the only way. Calaveran once saved him by giving him blood. Now it was time to repay the favor. Summoning his resolve, his own heart beating rapidly, Erzeben sliced his palm with the dagger. The pain was searing and he cried out. Biting his lips, he dropped the dagger and lifted Calaveran's head up, gently opening his mouth. Black blood dripped out of Erzeben's hand and into the brujo's mouth. Already, the empusa felt a wave of dizziness and gritted his teeth even harder. After a few more drops, he closed Calaveran's mouth, and kept him propped up on a nearby broken chair. Erzeben picked up the dagger and cut off a piece of his own sweater and tied it around his hand to bandage it. It was messy but it would have to work. The wound would heal quickly but he could not risk losing any more blood. Erzeben held Calaveran's hand and stared at his face, waiting.

"Come on, Cal," Erzeben said gently, "stay with me. I need you here, in Witch City. I know the world is a mess right now, but it would not be the same without you. The Underworld is not ready for you yet."

Erzeben clenched the boy's hand tighter.

"If you stay, I promise we will go to whatever electronic dance music show you want, I will be there for every DJ set you play, I will listen to your music every night. Please, Cal, I need you," Erzeben said, choking back a sob that threatened to stop his voice. A grin formed on Calaveran's face and his eyes opened slowly.

"You promise, buddy?" Calaveran said weakly.

"Oh my Goddess, Cal!" Erzeben said, pulling the brujo close. "I thought you were going to die!"

"Santa Muerte's brujos are hard to kill," Calaveran said, rubbing the empusa's back.

"What were you thinking? You nearly died!" Erzeben said, nearly shaking him.

"Somebody needed to buy you guys time to get out of there. And I'm a tough witch. I can handle it."

"Well, do not do anything like that ever again or I might have to kill you," Erzeben said, gently pulling away from the brujo.

Calaveran already seemed brighter and filled with life, his golden eyes shining. Erzeben's heart quickened. He had never been this near to him before, and up close he was unbearably beautiful. The empusa saw every tattooed line on Calaveran's face, each detail of the sugar skull designs. The brujo was a living piece of art.

"Cal, I . . ." Erzeben quickly glanced around to make sure Santa Muerte was no longer there. Luckily, she was nowhere to be seen.

"What is it, Ben?" Calaveran asked, sitting up properly. Erzeben swallowed.

"Cal. There has been something I have been wanting to say to you for a very long time, but I was never sure how to say it. But now, now that you have almost died I feel like I have to, in case there is not another second chance. Calaveran, I really like you, and have wanted to be with you since the beginning. You are incredibly brave and kind, your creative passion is inspiring, and you are the most gorgeous witch boy I have ever seen." Erzeben swallowed thickly, fighting to keep his eyes on Calaveran's. He rushed through the rest, pushing the words out as quickly as he could before he thought better: "I have never mentioned this before because I was worried that you did not feel the same, that I was just a 'buddy' to you."

Calaveran looked at him with his eyes wide, shock on his face.

"And now," Erzeben said, his heart falling in his chest, "I see that I was right and have just made an incredible fool of myself."

"Ben," Calaveran said, shaking his head, "how can I put this? The whole reason why I joined this loco journey during Samhain was because I would get to spend time with you. You make every time we hang out an adventure, and I don't think you even realize it. The whole reason I always called you buddy . . . I didn't think you wanted that from me, and I wasn't brave enough to say it."

Erzeben's eyes went wide, not believing what he was hearing. As much as he wanted this to happen, he never thought it actually could. Calaveran gently touched his hand, sending shivers throughout his body.

"Like what Vivivine said," the brujo said, looking Erzeben in the eyes, "we all make sacrifices for those we love."

Erzeben could not handle it anymore. Calaveran, the guy who he had been crushing on for a year, a guy whose only ex was a girl, was admitting he wanted him. That he loved him. Erzeben pulled Calaveran by the shirt kissed him urgently, as if their time was running out. Calaveran's hand drifted to Erzeben's hips, pulling him even closer. Their need for each other was strong, now that they were free from their self-imposed barriers to each other. Erzeben savored every taste of Calaveran's mouth, his fangs nearly biting into him.

"Wait," Erzeben said, regretfully pulling away from him, "the Lantern Coven has Aradia. Wanda went to go looking for her. We should probably go help her. Help them."

"Yes," Calaveran said, catching his breath, "yes, you're right. They need us."

Erzeben and Calaveran shared a look of longing, the empusa biting his lip.

"But Aradia's pretty tough, and no one's more determined than Wanda. I'm sure a few more minutes won't hurt," Calaveran said, smiling. "And besides, I still need a little bit more time to recover from almost dying. I'm sure they'd understand."

That was all Erzeben needed. "That is true. I will take care of you the best I can."

Erzeben pulled him close, and together they made up for lost time.

CHAPTER
Fifty-Two

Aradia was more confused than ever. The Hierophant was a member of the Lantern Coven. He was the one that told everyone to bring her to Morrigan's Grove. Why wouldn't he let the empusa kill her? The Baba Yaga was once again right. Things in Witch City were not what they seemed.

"What do you want?" Wanda asked.

"I mean you no harm. I am here to protect you," the Hierophant said.

"Then why were you planning on sacrificing me to the Lord of Samhain?" Aradia said.

"I never was. That was a ruse. I hoped that someone would bring you here so I could protect you from the Queen."

"And why do you want to protect her exactly?" Wanda asked, suspicion in her voice.

"Well, I believe that there is one person standing in the way of the Queen's power, someone that could dethrone Gourdina in an instant. Someone who disappeared a long time ago, but if they were to return, the covens would end their futile struggle once and for all."

"Nicnevin," Aradia said.

"Yes," the Hierophant said, nodding slightly, "although that was not who I was referring to. Nicnevin would restore order to Crone's Cross, but what I am referring to is this world's soul, and the only one who can salvage it is the first witch herself: The Holy Strega."

Aradia felt small. "But I'm not really the Holy Strega."

The Hierophant met Aradia's gaze, his gold hawk-like eyes burning into her. "Yes, you are, child. For centuries I have consulted the Goddess in my workings, and she has told me, in her glorious form of Isis-Hecate, that three hundred and thirty years after the end of the Burning Times her daughter would arrive to the Witch City on a Samhain Night. The end of the Salem Witch Trials marked the end of witch persecution in the Old Country, and here you are, the descendant of the first Salem Witch no-less. You harken the end of oppression of *all* witches."

Aradia just stared and shook her head. Bringing back Nicnevin was one thing, but to truly be Witch City's savior?

"See, I hexing knew it!" Wanda said. "I sensed it right from the beginning!"

"Then tell me how in the name of bloody Hecate am I supposed to do that?" Aradia asked Lord Ra. "People keep on telling me to make a sacrifice, save the city, but nobody has even given me the smallest idea on how to do it!"

"You will understand in time," he said calmly. "However, time is what is crucial now. This is the last Samhain Night of this year, and then it will be too late. You do not need to sacrifice yourself to save Witch City's soul, but you do need to—"

Lord Ra cut off in a scream. Aradia and Wanda stepped back in shock, clutching each other, as a blade pierced through his chest, red blood leeching outwards. He toppled forward, and his body rapidly decayed, skin peeling back, dark features turning corpse-like. By the time he reached the ground, all that was left was a skeleton. Standing in his place was Gourdina, the Queen of Lanterns.

"Filthy, traitorous, mummified wretch," the Queen spat, looking down at the corpse. She stepped forward slowly, the red-coated blade at the end of her scepter glittering dangerously. Wanda stepped in front of Aradia, conjuring a fireball in her hand.

"You better not come any closer," the witch said, shaking with anger.

The Dread Queen paused. "How cute. How utterly charming. Your mother thought she could take on the Lanterns . . . and look what happened to her."

"What?" Wanda said, lowering her fireball.

"I recognized you the moment you stepped into my castle; the resemblance was too uncanny. Your mother, Auzma Spelbruhm, was a member of the Monster Coven, those nasty criminals. She needed to be eliminated. What, she never told you?" Gourdina said in an amused tone, sheathing her blade.

"I will kill you!" Wanda said, lunging towards the Dread Queen.

"Enough," the Queen said, pointing the scepter at Wanda, "*Entrap!*"

Two vines grew rapidly out of the ground and tied around the witch's wrists and dragged her down onto the ground. Two more vines grew up from the ground and tied around Wanda's ankles.

"Wanda!" Aradia said, ripping at the thick vines tightening around Wanda's wrists even as more sprang up and held her just as tight.

"Just kill the hag," Wanda spat out. Aradia looked up. The Dread Queen continued to walk slowly towards them, the dagger glinting at her side.

"Why are you doing this? I haven't done anything to you!" Aradia screamed at the Queen.

"You, my dear, have done nothing," the Queen of Lanterns said, pausing again. "It is your species, your awful race that has done great damage. Many years ago, a young man was found in Crone's Cross, in Old Burying Point, the same cemetery you were, claiming to have gotten there by train to Wonderland Station, just like you. An outsider had not been seen in our city for years, so my husband and I thought to have a welcoming party for him, to perhaps promote peace between us. Well, we could not have been more wrong. At midnight of the great celebration, he murdered my husband, claiming that we had murdered his ancestor. Such nonsense. Tituba was murdered by the Walpurgis Coven ages ago. But it reminded me that cowen can never be trusted. I had him executed on the spot, naturally."

Something clicked in Aradia's mind. Her father had disappeared going to search for Tituba. It was what started Tana's hatred for all things witchcraft-related, why she had kicked her only daughter out. Her father had found Witch City. And died there.

"You killed my father, too!" Aradia said, her heart shattering. "That was my dad! I always thought he was just an asshole that abandoned us, but you killed him!"

"Yes, I figured as much," Gourdina simpered. "So many dead parents. Poetic justice it would seem, for leaving my son fatherless."

"You have a son?" Aradia asked.

"Yes, although he is forbidden to leave Castle Lantern, and for good reason. There are traitors within this city that want the Lantern Coven gone, like that horrible Monster Coven. There are enemies everywhere, inside and out of this city, and for some reason they all seem to be rallying around you, the so-called Holy Strega," the Queen said, placing her fingers on the forehead of her mask, as if she could massage a headache from her temples through the pumpkin. "It has been a long week, and, quite frankly, I am tired, having had to send wraiths and whatnot after you each night."

"So you really do control them," Aradia said, hot rage boiling to the surface.

"Yes, of course. The Lord of Samhain is no more than mere legend, but the spirits are real. And they *are* terrified by the light of a jack-o'-lantern," Gourdina said.

The Queen slowly took her mask off. Aradia was open-mouthed in shock. Hiding beneath the smiling jack-o'-lantern mask was another, more horrific pumpkin face. It was gaunt and thin, almost skeletal. The orange of her face was tinged green in some places, as if a rot had set in. She glared at them through triangular empty eye-sockets, an orange glow emanating from them. She smiled cruelly, her mouth forming into a jack-o'-lantern grin, her teeth all sharp and jagged edges.

"I, and I alone, have been able to control them," the Dread Queen said.

"The Morrigan Coven was right about you the whole time—you're the real Wicked Witch!" Wanda shouted.

"I am not wicked!" Gourdina screeched, pointing her scepter at Wanda. More vines sprang up, wrapping around the green witch's face and silencing her. "You are, you loathsome wretches! You are reckless and destructive, the seed of evil is within you. You have already killed one of my covenmates!"

Gourdina broke off, drawing a few steadying breaths. "At any rate, I am through with playing games. The time has come, my dear Aradia, for you to accept your fate. It is time for your suffering to come to an end."

The Dread Queen pointed her scepter downwards, her pumpkin features practically aflame.

"*Rise.*"

CHAPTER
Fifty-Three

Rotting, skeletal hands broke through the ground. Aradia knelt close to Wanda for comfort, hoping to keep her safe somehow. Slowly, several ghouls crawled out from the ground, their features more gruesome in the greenish light of the moon. Aradia was taken back to her first night in Witch City, when she first met Wanda. Aradia was not as afraid of them as she was then. The ghouls looked at Aradia and Wanda hungrily, their claw-like hands outstretched.

"Slaves!" Gourdina shouted. The ghouls faced the Dread Queen, and cowered, moving away from her. Her jack-o'-lantern features glowed brightly now, flames rising out of her face. She was fearsome to behold. Gourdina pointed her scepter at Aradia.

"Kill the Witch Hunter!" she shrieked. The ghouls turned and faced Aradia. The girl stood up. She needed to get them away from Wanda to protect her. She turned and ran. The ghouls screeched and charged towards her. Aradia ran around the many pumpkins in the pumpkin patch, careful not to trip over any vines, her breathing becoming unsteady. A short distance off she noticed an exceptionally large pumpkin, larger than the others. Ghouls were afraid of jack-o'-lanterns, and she was in a field of potential ones. An idea came to her of just how she could defeat the evil spirits. This was the time to test her storytelling power.

Aradia ran to the large pumpkin, her legs burning. The sides were smooth, and her hands kept on slipping trying to climb it. The stench of rot filled her nostrils as the ghouls grew closer. She threw her bag off her shoulder, and dug her fingers into the flesh of the pumpkin, slime under her fingernails. Aradia tried to not look back as the ghouls' screeches got louder.

Finally Aradia reached the top. She stood up and looked behind her. The pumpkin was nearly surrounded by the glowing, rotting faces of the ghouls. The girl closed her eyes and held her arms out. From what she learned about magic in Witch City, she just had to focus on her intention, and will it into reality. Without thinking, she let the words flow out of her mouth.

"It was the last Samhain Night," she called into the night, "and the witch was surrounded by an oppressive darkness. She summoned her inner fire, her inner witch-flame, and with it lit a hundred jack-o'-lanterns. The light of the jack-o'-lanterns chased the darkness away, and the witch herself became a beacon of light!"

Aradia opened her eyes. The monstrous ghouls were close. One of them reached out its boney hand, brushing her face. Aradia cringed and smacked the ghoul's hand away. Was her storytelling not working? As the ghouls clustered around her, she jumped off the pumpkin and continued to run.

Why isn't it working?

Aradia heard the roar of a sudden burst of flame. She glanced back. Wanda was standing up, slightly singed. The witch had burned her way out of the vines. The green girl ran towards the ghouls, fireballs in her hands, her eyes wide and teeth bared in ferocious determination.

"Get the hex away from her!" Wanda screamed, throwing her fireballs at the nearest ghouls. Some of the ghouls instantly ignited, but there were too many of them to get at once. The ghouls formed a hellish mob, Aradia running as fast as her legs could carry her, her breathing heavy. She was relieved that Wanda had escaped, but the witch running into the group of the ghouls was the last thing Aradia wanted.

A loud bleating erupted in the chaos. Aradia looked forward. Bucca Dhu ran headfirst towards her, the flame between his horns growing brighter. The goat had not abandoned her after all. He stopped next to her, giving her just enough time to get on his back. When she had a steady grip, Bucca Dhu rushed forward. The ghouls flew out of his way under his hooves and horns, but trailed close behind them. They headed straight for Wanda, her eyes wide with bewilderment.

"Wanda, grab my hand!" Aradia cried. The witch extinguished her fireballs and took her hand. Aradia pulled her onto the back of the goat, and Wanda held tight to her. Aradia grinned, feeling unstoppable. They were going to escape the ghouls and Gourdina and go somewhere far away.

"What's in your pocket?" Wanda said. Aradia had all but forgotten Goody Poppet, the doll that had belonged to Candy, the doll that Baroness had sewn in some gris-gris to protect her. Instantly she was reminded of the vision the Baba Yaga had shown her in her cauldron.

"Wanda, it's the poppet! Take it out and set it on fire!" Aradia said.

"Okay, whatever you say!" Wanda reached into Aradia's pocket, and with some effort pulled the doll out. The witch conjured a fireball, instantly igniting it. As if a switch was pulled, all the pumpkins in the vast pumpkin patch burst into flames, pumpkin flesh popping out to form terrifying jack-o'-lantern faces, a glowing bright green sea of grins. The pumpkins floated into the air and propelled themselves towards the ghouls. The ghouls screeched and pushed each other out of the way, not getting out of the pumpkin patch fast enough, disappearing into a dark cloud over the horizon.

A large jack-o'-lantern came flying towards them. Bucca Dhu reared up and screamed. Aradia and Wanda fell off, Wanda dropping the doll. The goat, continuing to scream, cantered away from them and flew into the air, trying to get away from the jack-o'-lanterns himself.

"Hecate's hags," Wanda swore, dusting herself off. Aradia looked up. It never occurred to her that Bucca Dhu would be just as affected by jack-o'-lanterns as other spirits. It explained how the Queen had control over him too.

The Queen.

Aradia looked to where Gourdina stood. Smoke rose out of her pumpkin features, almost as if she was ready to explode.

"Warlock! You made a pact with Lucifer and sold your soul to him! With the help of that brat!" the Dread Queen said, pointing an accusing finger at Wanda. "And for that, she shall be burned at the stake, for the crime of dark magic!"

The Queen pointed her scepter at Wanda, and lifted it up in the air, the young witch raising up with it. Tossing and turning with her feet above the ground, Wanda cried out.

"*Pyre!*" Gourdina spat out. Vines grew out of the ground behind Wanda, twisting together to create a large post. With another motion from the Queen, the witch was forced against the post, and more vines grew out of it. Aradia watched helplessly as her beloved friend was tied up, more viscously and tightly than before.

No, no, this can't be happening!

Aradia screamed and ran at the Dread Queen, but stopped just short of her as Gourdina blew a fireball into her hand from her jack-o'-lantern features. She looked at Aradia, disdain in her hollow eyes.

"Your choice, Salem bitch! Either she burns, or you do!"

CHAPTER
Fifty-Four

radia was shaking. Seeing Wanda in pain, her life threatened by the Dread Queen, filled the girl with a cold rage. She wanted to take Gourdina's scepter and stab her with it, to finally end her, but she could not. Aradia was sure if she took another step closer the Queen would burn Wanda alive in less than a second, and she would not let that happen. She would rather die.

"You heard me correctly, Witch Hunter. If you so nobly give yourself up, I shall let this goblin of a girl live," Gourdina called, her voice as ugly as her face. "Her memory will be wiped of the entire week of course and she will never remember having met you. She will go back to her normal life, as if this Samhain never happened, but closely monitored of course. Otherwise, she shall burn, and you shall live. You shall be forced to survive Witch City on your own, desolate and destitute with no one to help you this time around. And you will forever have the memory that you let your friend die, and watched it happen. Your choice, Aradia."

Perhaps that would not be so bad. Aradia did not want to die, she really did not, but if no one even remembered her, no one would have to mourn her. She would have disappeared from both her old world, where her mother chose to forget her, and her new one. It would have been like she never existed. And she could hardly imagine being haunted with the memory of watching the only one she cared about die, and die horribly. That would be eternal damnation.

"Don't do it Aradia! She'll kill me either way!" Wanda shouted.

"Silence cretin! This is her decision to make, not yours! You already chose to damn yourself by befriending her!" Gourdina said, and pointed her scepter at Aradia. "Well, what will it be, girl? Time waits for no one. You need to make your decision now!"

Aradia knew what needed to be done. Her anger turned into a cold clarity. She knew her power now, but she was not nearly as powerful as the Queen of Lanterns.

The true meaning of Samhain is sacrifice. We all make sacrifices for those we love the most.

"I'll do it, I'll let you burn me. But you have to let her go first," Aradia said.

"My, I am quite surprised. Perhaps not all your kind are as selfish as they seem. I was almost certain you would have saved yourself. However, I am afraid I cannot allow that. I cannot have her running to save you, can I?" Gourdina said, her carved mouth smiling wide. The Queen pointed her scepter at Aradia. Vines rose up behind her, creating a stake. More vines grew out, and forcibly tied her to the stake, digging harshly into her skin. Aradia wanted to cry out from the searing pain, but she would not let the Dread Queen see that she had won.

"Any departing words, cowan?" Gourdina said.

Aradia was about to say something, but paused. This was how her story ended. Everything had led to this moment. This was why Hecate brought her to the city, this was the sacrifice that the Baba Yaga had wanted her to make. With her sacrifice she would bring back Nicnevin and restore justice to Witch City. Aradia looked up at the triple moon in the sky, her eyes wet. It was not fair that she was the one that had to do this, but it was the only way. She had chosen to be the Holy Strega, even if it was reluctantly. She had to finish what she began.

"I came to Witch City to find my ancestor, Tituba, to find the truth of her power. Along the way I've met a few witches who've helped me discover my own power," Aradia said, recounting her story. She looked at Wanda, tears streaming from the green witch's eyes. Aradia swallowed, then turned her attention back to the Queen, forcing herself to continue.

"However, you accused me of being a Witch Hunter, and now I'm here, tied to a stake. Soon you will burn me alive, like a Witch Hunter yourself. But I won't die. I will become the Lord of Samhain myself, and I will eat you alive with your own lies!" Aradia said loudly and firmly, her voice echoing through the night.

"Enough! I have heard enough of your fancy," Gourdina said, sneering. "Merry part, and merry never meet again."

The Dread Queen pointed her scepter at the pumpkin tree.

"Crack!"

Some of the tree branches broke off, the tree groaning as if in pain. With another flick of the scepter, the branches flew through the air and surrounded the base of Aradia's stake, creating a pile of kindling. The girl looked down at it, shivering. This was it; this was really happening. She was an accused witch about to be burned at the stake. This was her own Salem Witch Trial.

The pumpkin-headed woman raised her hand and threw her fireball at the kindling. Wanda screamed out loudly and hoarsely, as if in agony. Aradia kept her eyes on her, trying to smile as if everything would be okay. The flames erupted around her, enveloping her in oppressive and dense heat. Her clothes stuck to her skin from the sweat, and she twisted against the makeshift stake. She breathed in the smoke and her throat tightened against it, burning from the inside as much as she burned on the outside.

"Tituba!" Aradia screamed out with the little breath she had left. The Holy Strega's vision grew blurry. As the flames grew higher, a face appeared within them. It was her own, but older. Slowly a whole figure wearing a long, tattered dress formed in the fire. The figure looked at her kindly with sympathy, and moved towards her, arms outstretched. Aradia accepted her embrace calmly, not minding as the flames touched her skin.

The figure melded into her, a strong burning sensation spreading inside of her. Aradia screamed out in pain as memories flooded her senses.

Aradia remembered being taken away from her family by terrible men. She remembered the summer heat and the cool ocean breezes of Barbados. She remembered being taken away from Barbados by the cruel Samuel Parris. She remembered her own husband, John, and their beautiful daughter Violet. She remembered the hardships of the trials after the village girls had turned against her. She remembered all the torturous months in that cramped cell, where she became friends with Candy. She remembered finally escaping and finding Crone's Cross where she had lived peacefully and quietly for many years. She remembered Abigail's arrival to the city, and her final moments alive. She then remembered her spirit following Candy as she left for Boston, through the eyes of Goody Poppet. She remembered sitting in Candy's shop waiting for the right time to return. She remembered all the events of the past week, leading her to this moment. To change the ending of the story. To undo what had been done.

The scream of three centuries of injustice and pain shook her body. Agony clouded her senses, with one intention flowing through her.

"I sacrifice the past to create a better future!" Aradia screamed out, her voice hoarse as the flames enveloped her, covering her face like a hood. A deep moaning came from the earth, the ground vibrating. Leaves fluttered all around in the air, a sudden wind extinguishing the fire. Aradia zeroed in on the Queen of Lanterns. Gourdina looked around in confusion, with slight fear.

The largest jack-o'-lantern in the pumpkin patch grew larger and larger. Gourdina froze in place. The pumpkin's jack-o'-lantern features molded into a grotesque demon of a face as a black pilgrim's hat materialized on it. It rose into the air, supported by a body of black, shadowy robes. Two hands made from twisted vines protruded out of the robes, forming into claws. The creature grew higher and higher, until it was tall as Vivivine's tower. Aradia stared in awe, recognizing it. It was Sam Hain.

"HOW DARE THEE! HOW DARE THEE INSULT MY PRESENCE, THOU MONSTROUS QUEEN! HOW DARE THEE MAKE A MOCKERY OF SAMHAIN! HOW DARE THEE INSULT ME, THE LORD OF SAMHAIN, THE SPIRIT OF HALLOWEEN,

THE SPIRIT OF ALL HALLOW'S, THE SPIRIT OF WITCH CITY!" a low, demonic voice belched forth from the creature.

"You—you're real?" Gourdina exclaimed with nervous astonishment. "I—I am so sorry, b-but this foolish—"

"ARADIA IS NOT THE FOOL! SHE WAS THE ONE THAT CONJURED ME HERE! THOU ART THE FOOL! AND THOU SHALT BE PUNISHED!" the spirit said.

The Queen of Lanterns turned and ran. She barely made it two steps before the shadowy creature's mouth extended, as if unhinged, and flew at the pumpkin-faced ruler. She tripped over a vine, her crown flying off of her head, and she fell, sprawled onto the ground. The Dread Queen looked up in terror. She had time for one terrified scream before the creature consumed her whole.

CHAPTER
Fifty-Five

The Lord of Samhain dissolved into a cloud of black smoke and rose into the air, disappearing into the night. Aradia rested her head back against the stake, smiling in tired relief, the night air cooling her burns. She did it. She had made her Samhain sacrifice, and found what she had been looking for. For the first time in three centuries, Tituba's spirit was free.

Aradia looked at Wanda, who despite being tied to the stake, had a wicked grin across her face. Aradia smiled back. She would have never had the courage to do what needed to be done if it had not been for the witch. Wanda was her glowing torch in a world of darkness.

A familiar grumbling echoed through the air. Aradia looked as far as she could in its direction. Bucca Dhu flew towards her. He chewed the restraints open, and let Aradia climb onto his back.

"Thank you, Mr. Grumbles," Aradia said. The goat snorted in response. He flew over to Wanda and chewed on her restraints, and Aradia helped her onto the back of the goat. Bucca Dhu flew downwards, landing a short distance away from where the Dread Queen had been devoured. Aradia and Wanda slid off the goat, Aradia stroking Bucca Dhu's nose affectionately.

"You are a very special goat," Aradia said. Bucca Dhu snorted and pointed his horns to all that was left of the Queen of Lanterns. Her crown. Aradia nodded. She was not completely finished yet. The Salem Witch picked up the crown and placed it at the base of the large pumpkin tree.

"I sacrifice this bloody, stolen crown,
the one that killed to create this town.
I sacrifice the horrors of the past,
I end injustice with this spell I cast.
I bring back Nicnevin; I set her free.
I end the Salem Pact, so mote it be!"

A strong, healing warmth emanated from her body, as if all the bad things in the world were fading away, that only love remained. Everything felt right. Her hair blew into her face as a wind picked up. She opened her eyes. Leaves danced around the crown. More and more of them piled upward until they created a dense wall. Green light glowed behind the cracks of the leaves until they scattered everywhere in a big gust of wind. Aradia had to step back and close her eyes to protect them.

The wind died down, and Aradia opened her eyes with her mouth agape. Standing in the center of the circle was a green-faced elderly woman with sharp features and pointed ears, limping towards them. She wore an elaborate gown with a gray mantle that looked like it was once beautiful and regal but was now tattered and worn. Wanda conjured a fireball, but Aradia gently grabbed her arm.

"It's okay," Aradia said, all instincts telling her to trust this woman. With reluctance, Wanda extinguished her fireball.

"Thank you, my child," the old woman said, stopping in front of them. She looked worn out and tired, as if it was a strong effort just to get close to them.

"I am Nicnevin, the Faerie Queen of Elfhame, although it is called Hecatesia nowadays," the woman said slowly and deliberately. Wanda reached for Aradia's hand, and squeezed it hard.

"But now that you're back, you'll be able to set things right, right?" Aradia asked. Nicnevin shook her head tiredly.

"Unfortunately, it is too late for me. I have been bound for too long. I am too weak. I'm afraid I do not have much time left," Nicnevin said. "But all is not lost. I am no longer bound, so my spirit will return to this land, and I will restore it back to life. This city will be reborn, and it shall grow and thrive for centuries to come. By saving me you have saved the soul of the city."

Nicnevin smiled, her wrinkles crinkling. But her smile faded, concern growing in her eyes, and she looked at the city lights in the far distance. "As for the conflict growing in this city, as long as there are those that fight in the name of the Morrigan there is hope."

"Who is the Morrigan anyway?" Wanda said. Nicnevin looked over to her, the smile returning to her face.

"Three sisters who are one. Goddesses of war, sovereignty, phantoms, prophecies, and Samhain itself. The great three-headed crow. My mothers. Her warrior strength runs through you, little witch," Nicnevin said, and shifted her gaze to Aradia, "just as the three-faced goddess of the moon brought you here."

Aradia and Wanda looked at each other. When Aradia had decided to go find Witch City, Hecate brought her to who she needed to find.

"Thank you, Aradia, I am forever in your debt, and thank you, Wanda, for fighting by her side. And you, my dear friend," Nicnevin said, stroking Bucca Dhu, "thank you for everything you have done while I was gone. I apologize that I have to leave so soon. Merry meet, and merry part, and merry meet again."

Leaves blew up into the air, and flew around the crone. Aradia held onto Wanda, gazing on. The leaves covered Nicnevin completely, and a green light glowed behind them. They spun around the Queen of Elfhame faster and faster, the wind blowing fiercely against the young witches. In a few seconds the green light faded, and the leaves blew away into the sky. Nicnevin was gone, but her spirit was free to become the new Witch City.

Aradia and Wanda held onto each other tightly, and stared at the sky in wonder.

CHAPTER
Fifty-Six

Aradia and Wanda walked hand in hand in the pumpkin patch, Bucca Dhu following a short distance behind. The air was cool and crisp, carrying the fresh scent of pumpkins. Aradia tried to feel accomplished and at peace, but something was still nagging her.

"Wanda? Do you think this was all set up? Like it was all some secret plan?"

"Honestly, I dunno," Wanda sighed. "But I don't think it matters much. At the end of the night, I chose to protect you, and you chose to sacrifice yourself for me, and I will never forget that. If anything, it just means that no matter what happens, we were meant to find each other."

She smiled, glancing shyly at Aradia. "Like soulmates or something."

Aradia stopped and looked at Wanda, at this beautiful, self-assured witch. Wanda looked back at her, her violet eyes wide. The greenish moonlight always enhanced the witch's prettiness, her green skin nearly glowing. Aradia wanted to stare at her forever. How lucky she was that Wanda had decided to be hers.

"Wanda, I think I might be making another sacrifice by asking you this, but after everything we've been through— and it's been such a short time—but I've never been as close to someone as I have been with you, and I like being close to you and I want to go on more adventures with you, and, and . . ." Aradia's heart interrupted her, beating so loud she couldn't force the words out.

"Just spit it out already," Wanda said.

"Can I kiss you?" Aradia asked, her cheeks suddenly hot. Wanda looked at her with surprise, her face softening.

"Well, you could've just said so," Wanda said, grinning. Aradia and Wanda reached for each other, and their lips met. Aradia felt a different kind of fire, her heart opening to a new warmth. She had never kissed anyone before, but everything felt like it was falling into place. They kissed gently, comfort radiating throughout Aradia's body. With every moment the pain from her past melted away, replaced with soothing waves of euphoria. She was safe and finally home.

"Wanda! Aradia!"

Aradia and Wanda broke apart, Aradia still reeling from the high, unable to stop smiling. They looked over to the voice. Erzeben and Calaveran ran towards them.

"Cal! Cal you're alive!" Wanda cried. The four Bad Witches embraced each other, smiling until their faces hurt. The sky was slowly fading to green. They had all survived Samhain.

"What happened to you?" Aradia asked.

"Well, I felt like I was close to dying—I swear I could hear Santa Muerte calling my name. But Ben here brought me back to life with his blood," Calaveran said, looking at the empusa affectionately. Erzeben looked up at him, his eyes brighter than Aradia had ever seen them, the smile never leaving his face. He was practically glowing.

"Wait, did you guys . . .?" Wanda said, looking back and forth at them.

"Yes," Erzeben said, not looking away from the brujo.

"Thank the hexing Gods! It's about damn time!" Wanda said.

"Wait, did everyone know that Ben was into me but me?" Calaveran said with mock indignation.

"Pretty much," Aradia said.

"What happened here anyway? Did you make a sacrifice to the Lord of Samhain?" Calaveran asked.

"Yeah, about that," Aradia said.

"Basically, the Lord of Samhain wasn't real—it was all really Gourdina all along. But then Dia made the Lord of Samhain real, and he ate the Queen," Wanda said.

"What? The Queen of Lanterns is dead now?" Erzeben asked, his mouth hanging open in shock.

"Yeah, but considering she was the one that had my mom killed, killed Dia's dad, and has been trying to kill Dia all week, I think she deserved it," Wanda said, taking Aradia's hand and smiling at her.

"I am sorry we could not get here earlier. After I gave Cal some of my blood, I was too weak for a while to turn into a bat," Erzeben said.

"Yeah I'm sure that was the only reason why," Wanda said with a wink. Erzeben turned slightly pink. He cleared his throat awkwardly.

"I just cannot believe the Queen is dead. And Aradia, why is your hair silver?" Erzeben said.

"What?" Aradia said, feeling for her hair. She examined it. It was now indeed silver, shining like moonlight.

"Oh yeah, when it looked like you were burning at the stake, your hair did that," Wanda said. "I like it, though—makes you look like a moon goddess."

Aradia smiled. Witch City had changed her so much in such a short time. The girl understood the true meaning of her sacrifice now. She had sacrificed her old life as Alicia, everything she was before and all the guilt that came with it to create a new one. She was Aradia, the Holy Strega, and she had reclaimed her power as the blood of the first Salem Witch. Erzeben took his witchboard out of his pocket.

"You still have that after all this time?" Wanda asked, dumbfounded.

"Yes, and apparently Vivivine still has hers," Erzeben said, looking down at it.

"What? What is she saying?" Aradia said.

"'Hope you're alright. We escaped. The Lantern Coven was attacked by flying monkeys. I don't know what's going to happen now. We're going to go into hiding. Hope to see you soon. Hugs and hexes, Vivivine,'" Erzeben read from the board.

"Well, that's good news, I guess," Calaveran said.

"I guess Vivivine really can find her way out of anything. Huh," Wanda said.

"What are we going to do now?" Aradia said.

"Uh, well—" Wanda started.

A loud meowing came from behind them. They turned around. Sitting on a pumpkin was a black cat, with bright purple eyes, staring inquisitively at them. Aradia and Wanda looked at each other.

"Do you think it could be her?" Wanda said.

The witch went over to the cat, and gently picked it up in her arms. The cat nestled itself in her arms and purred contentedly. A huge smile spread across Wanda's face, and she looked at Aradia, then Erzeben and Calaveran with her violet eyes.

"It's her, I just know it," Wanda said, her voice breaking. Her mother's soul, returning to her in a new form. Seeing Wanda so happy filled Aradia with a new warmth, which only grew inside her. It seemed to her that each of the Bad Witches had each gotten what they wanted that Samhain, even herself. But now, she was tired, and just wanted to go home—wherever that was.

"What now?" Calaveran said.

"Well, like they say, there's no place like home," Wanda said, scratching the cat's ears. Aradia surprised herself with a laugh.

"Well, I guess I don't really have one of those."

"You know that's not true anymore," Wanda said with a smile. Aradia glanced over to the lights of Witch City in the distance. Her own Wonderland. She thought back to the train station. That mysterious woman, the woman she thought could be Hecate. Maybe the Goddess of Witchcraft really had shown her the way home, with the help of Tituba's spirit along the way.

"I guess you're right," Aradia said. "Let's go home."

Aradia, Wanda and her new cat got on the back of the grumbly Bucca Dhu, who bleated begrudgingly. Erzeben turned into his bat form, and

Calaveran held him tight. They flew to the Samhain sky, and headed for Witch City.

Brimombi, watching from a distance, cackled.

CHAPTER

Fifty-Seven

Massachusetts, April 30, 1693

Tituba stood at the edge of a cliff, overlooking a great forest and a village in the distance. The Devil had dropped her off there, saying that was as far as he could take her. He had transformed her ratty clothes, insisting on a new start for a new witch. Instead of a dress of rags she now wore a beautiful black gown, the type she had seen wealthy women wear. A black cloak rested on her shoulders, and instead of worn-out shoes she now wore shiny black pointed ones with buckles. Her dirty bonnet was replaced with a tall, pointed black hat with a wide brim, with a buckle that matched the shoes. In her hands she held a long broomstick, made with smooth dark wood. The Devil told her it was the tool to her freedom if she were to choose to take it.

Tituba looked up at the moon. It was large and full and inviting, as if it was offering to show her the way. She breathed in the night air. The witch had long left Salem behind her, there was only going forward now. Summoning her courage, she placed the broomstick between her legs and jumped off the edge.

There would be few that would claim they had seen a witch flying across the moon that night, but they would be quickly shushed. Everyone knew the time of witch-hunts was over.

END

AUTHOR'S NOTE

Tituba Indian was a real-life Bajan woman who was born sometime in the mid to late 1600's. She was the first woman accused of witchcraft during the Salem Witch Trials although she ultimately escaped execution. Although there are fantastical elements woven into her life in *WITCH CITY*, I tried to approach her story with authenticity and respect, making sure I did my due diligence in researching her and the Salem Witch Trials. The dialogue from her trial was taken directly from the trial manuscripts with some minor editing for pacing and flow. Of her life after the Salem Witch Trials, all that is known for sure is that an unknown person paid her jail fees in April 1693 and she was released from prison, never to be seen in the official record again.

There have been debates on Tituba's origins. The two most credible theories being that she was either from an Arawak tribe in South America, or of the Yoruba people in West Africa. I left this open to interpretation by the reader to avoid putting a label on her racial background as none can be conclusively made. I thought it was important when writing a story inspired by the events of the Salem Witch Trials to focus on the person who can be considered to be the catalyst of the events. Tituba is often only mentioned briefly and even then often in caricature, which belies her significant role as an imperative figure in the history of witchcraft.

I first heard of Tituba when I went to Salem with my family in 2007 and paid a visit to the Salem Witch Museum. Right from the beginning I was curious about who she was and wanted to know more about her story. I hope I did her story justice and that readers will enjoy getting to know her as much as I did. Although in my version of the story she meets her tragic demise at the hands of Abigail Williams, it is by no means meant to be the end of her story. In *WITCH CITY* she lives on through her descendant, Aradia. Through her descendant she is able to rectify the injustices of the past.

If you are interested in learning more about Tituba and the Salem Witch Trials I hope this book has served as a starting point for more to discover. Some titles I would recommend are: *Tituba, Reluctant Witch of Salem* by Elaine G. Breslaw, *A Delusion of Satan* by Frances Hill, *The Devil's Disciples* by Peter Charles Hoffer, *The Salem Witch Trials* and *Six Women of Salem* by Marilynne K. Roach, and *The Witches* by Stacy Schiff. For a brief but very informative and accessible read I would recommend *WITCHES!* by Rosalyn Schanzer.

If you are looking for more fictional stories inspired by Tituba's life, I would recommend: *Tituba of Salem Village* by Ann Petry for young readers and *I, Tituba, Black Witch of Salem* by Maryse Condé for adult readers; the latter in particular is a large inspiration for *WITCH CITY*. Another title of note is *The Crucible* by Arthur Miller. Although not the most historically accurate, it is a fascinating dramatization of the Salem Witch Trials.

Best witches,
Salem Styles

ACKNOWLEDGMENTS

WITCH CITY HAS BEEN A STORY THAT HAS BEEN WITH ME FOR OVER A DE-cade, and I am so incredibly glad to be able finally to share it with the world. I have had so many wonderful people support this journey over the years, and I am so incredibly grateful for each and every one of them.

I would like to thank my mother Cindy for her endless support and love. I could not have written this without her constant encouragement. I feel incredibly lucky to have such a loving, kind, and generous person to look up to and be such an important part of my life. I want to thank her for all she has done to help me get this book out, and all she has done to support me on my life journey. Thank you mom, I love you so much!

I want to thank Nanny, my grandmother, for always telling me to follow my dreams, and bringing joy wherever she goes. I always enjoy our checkers games and the fun Halloween things she finds for me. And I want to thank my siblings, Griffen and Paige, for cheering me on. I love you all!

I would like to thank Tituba for inspiring this story. She was such a brave and incredible woman that experienced so much hardship, and I hope that after the trials she truly found her peace. I also want to thank Hecate, the Witchmother, for guiding me on this magical journey. I want to thank her for being my guiding light through dark difficult times, and

I want to thank the Horned Witchfather for being a guiding strength. Blessed Be.

I want to thank my father Dennis for helping with very early versions of this story when I was younger, and for helping contribute to make this book happen. I also want to thank Aunt Paula for her guidance and support, for helping me get through terrible writer's block, and for introducing me to Fiverr. It's really been a lifesaver! Thanks so much to the both of you, I love you.

I want to thank my incredibly handsome partner Emil for listening to me ramble on about various ideas over the years, helping me edit sometimes, and overall just being a wonderful, loving guy. He's inspired some of my favorite ideas. I love you, Emil.

I want to thank Alejandro (alejandrob on Fiverr) for designing the beautiful covers! He knew exactly what kind of vibe I wanted, and was patient to my suggestions. The cover designs are gorgeous! I also want to thank my editor, Sara Schonfeld, for helping me elevate this book, and trimming away at wasn't needed, it is really appreciated! I also want to thank my beta and sensitivity reader Alexia (bookishends on Fiverr) for giving me your feedback on this novel. I really appreciated her perspective. I also want to thank Brady (bradymoller) for formatting the interior of the book. I had a great team of people to take this book to where it is now, so big thanks to all of them!

I want to thank Maryse Condé for allowing me to use the name "Grandma Yaya" as a reference to her novel *I, Tituba, Black Witch of Salem*, and for being a major inspiration for Tituba's portrayal in *WITCH CITY*. I also want to thank Gregory Maguire for not only inspiring this work with his novel *Wicked*, but for his encouraging words about my book when we met at the Salem Witch Museum. I am grateful to have wonderful writers to look up to. Storytelling is incredible magic.

There are other writers whose classic works have inspired this book, in particular L. Frank Baum, Ray Bradbury, Lewis Carroll, Charles G. Leland, and Mary Shelley. A huge thanks to all of them for inspiring me with their fantastic worlds and intriguing characters. I also want to thank Lady Gaga for inspiring me with her music, message, and art, Kim Petras for creating the perfect spooky album to listen to while I edit with *TURN*

OFF THE LIGHT, and Tim Burton for his dark, otherworldly visions. I am forever grateful.

I want to thank Rachel Christ-Doane, Director of Education at the Salem Witch Museum, for looking over the book and giving me feedback on an earlier draft, and for her book recommendations and enthusiasm. The Salem Witch Museum is where this journey began.

I also want to thank Alex, Breanne, Jennifer, Joey, Nicki, and Nicole for being nearly as hexcited about this book as I am, and of course Candace and the Viral Ventures Vancouver team for their undying enthusiasm for this book's release. I hope you all enjoy it!

And last, but certainly not least, I thank you, dear reader, for reading this book! I hope you enjoyed the story of *WITCH CITY* as much as I enjoyed writing it. I would love to read your reviews. Welcome to the Bad Witch coven!

With many hugs & hexes,
Salem Styles

Salem Styles

is a devoted witch, writer, and actor. His favorite role so far has been the Queen of Hearts at an *Alice in Wonderland*-inspired pop-up bar show, and is probably already planning his next Halloween costume. He studied screenwriting and Shakespeare at Harvard's summer school program, creative writing at Simon Fraser University, and acting at Vancouver Film School. Although he resides in the west coast, his favorite place is Salem, Massachusetts, the real Witch City. He can be reached by email at salemstyleswriter@gmail.com, and on Instagram @ thesalemwitchwriter.